'Please, Mommy! Over here!'

The voice was coming from behind the curtains that led out onto the patio. A shock of electricity shot through her body and she felt herself swing her legs over the side of the bed. She felt her feet touch the carpeted floor.

'Mommy! Mommy!'

She ran to the heavy curtains and tried to push them back but they wouldn't budge. Then she fumbled for the pulls that she knew must be at the edge of the drapes. She grabbed the rope and yanked hard. The curtains quickly opened and the room was filled with early evening light.

And there was Tony. There was her son.

Also by David St. Clair

CHILD POSSESSED
MINE TO KILL
THE DEVIL ROCKED HER CRADLE

and published by Corgi Books

BLOODLINE

David St Clair

CORGI BOOKS

BLOODLINE

A CORGI BOOK   0 552 13323 X

First publication in Great Britain

PRINTING HISTORY
Corgi edition published 1989

Copyright © David St Clair 1989

This book is set in 9/10pt Mallard
by Busby Typesetting, Exeter.

Corgi Books are published by Transworld Publishers Ltd.,
61-63 Uxbridge Road, Ealing, London W5 5SA, in Australia by
Transworld Publishers (Australia) Pty. Ltd., 15-23 Helles
Avenue, Moorebank, NSW 2170, and in New Zealand by
Transworld Publishers (N.Z.) Ltd., Cnr. Moselle and
Waipareira Avenues, Henderson, Auckland.

Reproduced, printed and bound in Great Britain by
BPCC Hazell Books Ltd
Member of BPCC Ltd
Aylesbury, Bucks, England

*For Oliver Johnson
and Little S.K.
in deepest gratitude . . .*

CHAPTER ONE

'Is that the kid?'

'Yeah. The one in the blue pants. Carrying the tin lunchbox.'

'I thought he'd be bigger,' the first man said.

'He's only six years old,' the other man in the front seat of the black car said. 'What do you want for six?'

The first man shrugged. 'Just thought he'd be bigger, that's all.'

'How do you know that's the right kid?' the first man asked. 'You met him before or what?'

'I told you, they gave me a picture of him and all the necessary info. Look, I showed you this before.' He took a now creased snapshot out of his shirt pocket and passed it to his accomplice. 'See? That's the same kid. The one in this picture and that kid going into the school building. Same kid. Same height and hair colouring, everything. Now we know he's inside, we just come back when school lets out and we grab him.' He took back the photo and stuffed it in his pocket.

'We grab him when he gets onto the sidewalk. Right?'

'Jesus Christ, Don! I told you all that before. At least three times! I wonder about you, I really do.'

He turned the key in the ignition and the rented black sedan pulled smoothly away from the kerb and into the street. He didn't know Don all that well. Don had been suggested to him by a friend after he accepted the job. The man with the accent – he couldn't place the accent but he knew it wasn't Italian or French – had come up to him in the Starlite Bar and Grill and called him by name: Steve. The man was a foreigner yet he knew all about Steve. Even told him about his prison terms and when he had been released from his last sentence.

'We have been looking for you,' the man had said. He ordered a drink for himself, not offering to buy Steve a refill, so as he talked Steve listened and turned his empty glass in

7

his hands. 'You come highly recommended,' the man had said. 'We need somebody who knows this business.'

'Oh?' Steve had said. 'Who told you about me?'

The man had only smiled and offered no information. 'This is the lad we want.' He had taken the photograph out of his wallet at that point and laid it on the bar. Steve had looked quickly around the room but nobody was paying the slightest attention. 'His name is Tony Bruno. He's six years old. He's got red hair. He's in the first grade at St Andrews School on East 73rd Street. He arrives there at about nine fifteen every morning and leaves at three. His folks bring him and pick him up afterwards. Sometimes it's his mother and sometimes it's his father.'

'How do you expect me to get past *them*?'

The man ignored the question. 'After school would be the best time because often he stands and waits for several minutes on the pavement by the street when his folks are a wee bit late. They are never exactly on time. I mean that they are never there to meet him exactly when he and the other children leave the school. I clocked every day last week and his mother was late on the average of four and a half minutes.'

'Only his mother showed up last week? Where was his father?'

The man shrugged. 'You have four and a half minutes to take him and get away with him. From what they've told me about you, it should be no problem.'

'If you know all about him,' asked Steve, 'why don't you grab him yourself?'

'Stealing lads is not my business. I probably couldn't do it as well as you.' This was the first time he had smiled.

Steve motioned to the bartender and he was given another cold beer. 'I guess I'm not supposed to know too much about this, am I?'

'Only what's vital,' the man said, unsmilingly now. 'The least you know the better for yourself. And the better for us.'

'Us?' Steve raised an eyebrow. 'There's more of you involved in this?'

'I repeat: The least you know, the better for yourself.' He took a sip of his neat-no-ice Scotch whisky. 'Now, let's discuss your payment.'

'Wait a minute.' Steve put up one of his large hands as if to block the man's words. 'How do you know I'll go for this?

I haven't said I'll do it. Kidnapping is a serious offence in this country, mister.'

The man took Steve's hand by the wrist and laid it quickly on the bar. 'Of course you'll do it. There was never any doubt in my mind. Or yours either, I'm sure.' Steve looked for another smile. There was none.

'I'm not going to hurt the kid!' Steve said rather louder than he should have. He lowered his voice. 'And I'm not going to do this if you guys are going to hurt him either.'

The smile came back. 'Be assured. No harm will come to the lad. He will be returned to his parents just as soon as they see our point of view. In the interval, he shall be very well treated. The best shall be accorded him, actually.'

Steve still couldn't place the accent. Maybe it was English. In prison there was a fellow in there from Liverpool – they told Steve that was in England – but this guy didn't sound the way that guy did. 'I'll need to get somebody to help me,' Steve said. 'I can't do it alone.'

'Whatever your *modus operandi* is,' the stranger said, 'employ it to the fullest. Oh, by the way, I promise you this will not reach the newspapers. There will be no publicity. The police will not come inquiring to you.'

'How can you promise that?'

'We have ways.'

Steve sighed and hitched up his belt. Since getting out of prison his daily beer consumption had begun to settle around his hips and his trousers didn't fit just right.

'Okay. Let's talk payment.'

'I have in here – ' The man reached into his coat pocket and took out a thin brown envelope. 'Five thousand dollars.' He passed it along the bar toward Steve. 'When you deliver the boy safely to me . . .'

'Five grand? That's all? For grabbing a kid?'

'When you deliver the boy safely to me,' the man continued, 'there will be another envelope. This time with forty-five thousand dollars in it.'

Steve calculated, arrived at the total amount, blinked, opened his mouth, then closed it again. He stared at the stranger, reached out, picked up the envelope, folded it and put it in his pants pocket.

'Good,' the man said. 'Now I'm only going to tell you once. We want the boy next week. You only have one attempt. Any unsuccessful attempt will alert the authorities. One try is all the chance we are willing to take. Deliver him safely to me next week. The rest of the money will then be yours.'

'Deliver him where?' Steve almost whispered.

'I'll only give you the address once, so remember it. Don't write it down.' The stranger lowered his voice and gave a street and number that Steve knew was in the Bronx. 'Next week. Any afternoon after school.' He reached out and shook Steve's hand. 'Until then,' he said and started walking briskly toward the door.

'See you!' Steve called but the man had turned up the collar of his tweed overcoat, had set a tweed cap on his head and had walked out into the unusually crisp for a September-in-New York-afternoon.

*   *   *

Lois Bruno walked around the table lamp for the umpteenth time, looking at it from every angle. Again. She sighed. It had been perfect in her mind. It had looked very good in her final drawing but now – as usual – now that it had been created and had become three dimensional, she wasn't so sure. Her design had lost something. And, as usual, she wasn't sure what that 'something' was. It was always this way. From great idea to fantastic drawing to disappointing product. Never mind that others in the studio liked the lamp, that the hotel chain that had commissioned them were very pleased with the first prototype. Never mind all that. Lois wasn't pleased. She sighed, switched off the lamp and walked away from the small table it sat on in the middle of the room. She leaned against the wall, crossed her arms and stared at the lighting fixture again. 'Maybe the base could taper a bit more,' she said aloud.

'And maybe you could paint them red and green and they'd only put them in the rooms at Christmas time.' The large lady stood in the doorway to Lois' office. 'I don't see a damned thing wrong with it, dear. It looks fine from here.'

'Well, it doesn't from here,' Lois said moodily. 'Maybe if I . . .'

'And maybe if you had them made from brie and Ritz crackers the hotels could put them in their cocktail lounges.'

Midge was grinning now. 'Speaking of cocktails. Shall we? After five?'

'No, I can't. I have to pick up Tony.'

'You did all last week,' Midge said. 'I thought this week was Bob's turn.'

Lois shrugged. 'He's got some tables and chairs coming in from Italy and they've all got to be inspected and tagged and God knows what. He didn't get home until almost nine last night. They've got to be shipped to Iowa. Some restaurant out there ordered them. Why people in the middle of nowhere need Italian tables to eat their Iowa-made pizza on, I don't know.'

'It helps pay the bills,' Midge laughed.

Lois smiled. 'Now *that* it does!' She came back and circled the table and lamp once more. 'What do you think, Midge? I mean, what do you *really* think? Is it okay? I mean really okay?' She shook her head. 'Maybe I've lost my perspective. Maybe my mind and my eye aren't really as coordinated as they used to be.'

'I know one thing that's not coordinated,' Midge said, 'and that's you and your son. It's five to three. School lets out in five minutes. Remember?'

Lois looked at her watch, then walked quickly to her desk. She opened drawers and pushed papers and pens and erasers into them. She hurried to her coat hanging on a hook on the back of the door. 'At least it's not raining,' she said as she started buttoning up. 'Tony doesn't have an umbrella.'

'He's smart enough to come in out of the rain.'

Lois laughed. 'Not if he takes after his mother, he isn't. God Midge, I just can't figure out what's wrong with this electrified turkey.' She walked back to the lamp, studying it intently.

'Well – ' Midge lifted the lamp and both women stared at it from another angle. 'You've been here longer than I have,' she said to Lois, 'and you've been at this business longer than I have. But, of course, you're younger than I am, by almost four years, so that gives me the seniority to criticize.'

Lois stared at her. 'Well? Get on with it. What do you see that I can change?'

'Suppose you made the shade less circular. Suppose you made it more oval. Not completely oval, but less circular. Know what I mean?'

'I think so,' Lois muttered. She went to her desk, opened a jumbled drawer and took out a pad and a felt tipped pen.

11

'More like this? This what you're talking about?' Her practised hand moved swiftly and easily over the blank paper. 'Like this?'

'Cut it sharper here,' Midge took the pen from her and made a line over Lois' drawing. 'More angled, more off-balance.'

'Yes!' Excitement shone in Lois' eyes as she grabbed the pen back. 'I see what you're talking about. Sharper here. Then it will juxtapose with the sharpness here, at the base. And the shaft, then – ' She made a few quick strokes. 'The shaft will widen here instead of narrowing the way I had it and it all falls right into . . .' She looked up at Midge and grinned. 'Of course! Midge you are so right! Look at it *now*!' She put the drawing beside the lamp. 'That's all it needed. I'll buy you a drink,' she promised.

'Yeah,' said Midge urging her toward the door, 'but first go get your kid. It's already after three.'

Halfway out the door Lois turned back to the plump slightly older woman. 'Midge, call the Graham Studio and tell them to come by tomorrow before noon and I'll have the revisions for the lamp waiting for them. Tell them that I need to see the – '

Midge walked over and swung the office door shut. 'Goodbye, Lois,' she said firmly. 'Go pick up Tony!'

* * *

The teacher was surprised.

'No, Mrs Bruno. I thought you had come for him.'

Lois was breathing hard. She had pulled up in front of the school and Tony wasn't on the sidewalk to meet her. She had found a parking place (difficult on that street and at that time of day) and had come back to the school yard. Still no sign of him. She walked through the playground. There were a few children on the swings and sliding board but none of them was Tony. That's when she panicked and ran into the building shouting her son's name. The first grade classroom was halfway down the hall.

'What do you mean you thought I had come for him?' Lois demanded.

'Well, he went out with the other children and when I looked a few minutes later they were all gone. So was Tony. I assumed, naturally, that . . .'

12

'You have no right to assume!' Lois raised her voice. 'You don't get paid to assume!'

The teacher rose to her feet behind the desk. 'Please, Mrs Bruno. I don't see the necessity for you . . .'

Lois interrupted her again. 'For me to be upset? For me to be upset because my son is missing?'

'*Missing* is an unnecessarily strong word. I'm sure he's somewhere on the grounds,' the teacher tried to soothe. 'Maybe when you were late he wandered back into the building. Kids do that sometimes.'

'Tony wouldn't! He had been told to wait right there. Right there on the sidewalk. He would have waited for me. He knows what to do!' She was shouting now and she glanced quickly around the classroom as if she expected to see Tony hanging on the walls or strung from the ceiling light fixture. 'We have to find him!'

The teacher sighed deeply. This was something she had gone through many times before. A child waits. His ride doesn't come. He wanders off, usually back into the building. 'Maybe he had to go to the toilet,' she suggested. 'Let's go and look in there.' She left the room and Lois followed her closely, wishing the woman would walk faster. Her eyes scanned the empty hallway in front of her. The boys' toilet was empty.

'Now where?' Lois had started shouting again.

'Let's try the gym. Little boys like to go in there and watch the bigger boys practise. We've started choosing our basketball team, you know.'

Lois wanted to say that she didn't know and furthermore she didn't care but her nervousness kept her from replying. She kept telling herself that she had to calm down, that everything would be all right, that Tony would be all right.

There were only older boys in the gym. The teacher marched sharply across the varnished wood floor and spoke briefly with the physical education teacher. She came back to Lois. 'No. He hasn't seen him.'

'He doesn't even know him! How can he say he hasn't seen him when he doesn't know what Tony even looks like?'

'He told me no first-graders have been in here. He keeps an eye out for things like that. It's too dangerous for little kids in here, especially with the big kids running around and throwing balls. Come on. We'll try in the playground.'

Lois looked at the 'big' kids. They were nine and ten years

13

old. They were big, bigger than her Tony. Her little Tony. Suddenly her frustration, her anger and her tiredness all came together and she began to cry. She sat down on a wooden bench and groped in her purse for a Kleenex. The teacher patted her shoulder and said some words but Lois didn't respond. Then the teacher marched back across the floor and came back with the basketball coach. Together they managed to get Lois to her feet and they moved her toward the rear door of the gym, the door that led to the playground.

Outside, the cool air revived Lois somewhat and she stopped crying and shook off the hands that had been clutching her. 'I'm sorry,' she managed to say, 'it's just that . . .'

'We understand,' the coach said.

They went outside and the teacher called to one of the small girls who was just about to start down the sliding board. 'Dorothy, can you come here for a minute?'

The girl raised her arms, nudged her behind forward and then slid smoothly down the metal ramp. The sides and the steps up to the board were rusty but the board itself, smooth with the constant polishing of hundreds of small rear ends, gleamed like new in the crisp afternoon light. The girl adjusted her jacket, pulled up her socks and came running to her teacher.

'Dorothy is in your son's class,' the teacher explained. 'Dorothy, this is Tony Bruno's mother.'

'Hello,' Dorothy mumbled.

'Dorothy,' the teacher continued, 'I want to know if you saw Tony this afternoon.'

'He was in school today,' the little girl replied solemnly. 'We painted that picture of the bird together. Don't you remember?'

The teacher smiled. 'Yes. The bird. Of course I do. And very prettily painted it was too. No, Dorothy, I mean after school. After the bell rang and all the boys and girls went home until tomorrow.'

'I was on the sliding board,' she said. 'I was waiting for my sister. She's in fourth grade. We walk home together. I'm allowed to stay and play on the swings and stuff because I go home with my sister. The Principal said I was allowed.'

'No. That's not what I mean,' said the teacher. 'Of course

14

you're allowed to wait for your sister. What I want to know is did you see where Tony went when his mother didn't come to pick him up?'

Something sharp turned in Lois' stomach. It was true. She *hadn't* been there to pick up her son.

'The men did,' the girl said simply.

'The *men* did?' Lois grabbed the girl and knelt down, holding the child's face close to her own. '*What* men?'

Dorothy tried to pull away. Tony's mother was hurting her. 'The two men in the car.'

'Car? *What* car?' Lois was screaming in the little girl's face now.

'It was a *car*,' the girl insisted. 'A black car.'

Lois turned to stare at the teacher. 'Did you hear that? Did you *hear* that? Two men took my Tony! Two men took my baby! You let two men take my baby!'

Dorothy began to sniffle. 'You're hurting me,' she whimpered. 'My arms. You're hurting my arms!'

Lois released her grip, got unsteadily to her feet and Dorothy scurried into the protective folds of her teacher's skirt.

'Oh my God,' the teacher whispered. 'Oh my God . . . did you see what the men looked like?' she asked Dorothy.

The girl shook her head. 'Like men,' she said.

Lois knelt down beside the child again, but this time didn't touch her, didn't frighten her. 'Please, Dorothy, try to remember. Did they hurt Tony in any way? Was he crying when they took him?' She tried to keep her voice calm. 'Was he all right?'

'He waved at me,' the girl said simply.

'Waved at you?' Lois controlled her voice. 'What do you mean he waved at you?'

'From the back seat of the car. He and one of the men got into the back seat and Tony waved at me as the car started. I was on top of the slide.'

'What did you do?' Lois asked. 'Did you run and tell a teacher?'

'No,' Dorothy said. 'I just waved back.'

CHAPTER TWO

Bob Bruno watched the needle plunge into his wife's arm. It was his last resort, calling in a doctor to give Lois a sedative. It had been four days and four long nights since Tony had been taken and both he and his wife needed some rest. He, rather guiltily, had managed to fall asleep every night but Lois had remained awake, pacing the floor, looking out of the living room windows and staring at the phone, waiting for it to ring with news of her son. It didn't ring. Not with news, at least. Her parents had phoned from West Virginia. They were both in shock. Was there anything they could do? Would it help if they came to New York? They could be there in a matter of hours. No, Bob told them, thanks but no thanks. He and Lois would rather be alone at the moment. Yes, he'd let them know as soon as he heard anything. No, his own parents weren't coming either. They were going to stay in Miami. There was nothing they could do in Manhattan. Besides, the weather had turned unusually cool up north and his father's blood had thinned during his retirement years in Florida.

Midge had phoned daily, asking if she could help, was there any news? Lois would talk with her. Lois liked Midge. The woman hadn't been working at her design office all that long, but during the short time she and Midge had become close friends. Midge made her laugh and it helped ease the pressure of the job. Now, with this awful Tony thing, there wasn't much Midge could say that was humorous. Lois could only manage a wan smile when the woman told her of something funny that had happened at work. Midge wanted to know what Lois was going to do about the lamp. Lois had to focus her mind to even remember what lamp Midge was talking about.

'Tell them to make it the original way,' she said dully. 'They liked it that way. I don't want to fuss with it.' And the phone had rung several times for Bob. Always from his warehouse in Brooklyn. What should his secretary do about his appointment with the Japanese cutlery manufacturer? The restaurant booths he had ordered for the place in Wisconsin could only be topped in blue not red. What did he want done? Mr Schimerowski's steam table had sprung a leak and he was demanding they replace it. A new firm in Korea had sent their catalogue of copper-bottomed cooking pots. Did Bob want to have the catalogue sent to his apartment?

Four days and four nights of this. The nights were the worst. Every night was as bad as all the others because with the setting of the sun Lois' maternal anxieties worsened.

'If he got away from them,' she would say, 'then he's out there in the dark. All by himself. Tony doesn't like the dark. You know how he wants that small light left on in his room.'

'Where is he sleeping?' she would wonder aloud. 'Do they have a bed for him? Are they making him spend the night alone in the back seat of that car? Is he sleeping in his clothes? Bob, he's had those clothes on now for *days*. They must be in a terrible state! Do you think they've bought him some new clothes? Thank God he had that fall jacket on. At least he won't freeze. Bob do you think it's warm where he is? Surely they wouldn't keep him somewhere where there was no heat. He catches cold so easily. Bob, you know how easily he gets a chill. His little body is so frail. Surely they would keep him warm, wouldn't they Bob? Wouldn't they keep him warm enough? Couldn't they see he was just a little boy? Oh Bob, he's just a little boy!' And the tears would start again.

Then Bob would come to her, put his arms around her and stand there until her racking sobs became muffled gasps. He would lead her over to the bed, lay her gently down and cover her with a blanket. Two minutes later she would be up and out of bed, pacing the floor, walking hurriedly to the living room and staring out into the silent, dark street below. More than once he had stopped her as she was putting on her coat. 'You can't go searching around New York for him,' he told her. 'Not at night. It won't do any good. It's too dangerous for a woman alone. Besides,' he reminded her, 'the police are searching for him. They're keeping a lookout for him. They'll call us. They promised. They'll call us as soon as they find him.'

Lois had reported Tony missing to the police just as soon as

17

she could get from the school yard to the station house. The police had telephoned Bob and he had come directly from his warehouse in Brooklyn. He found Lois sitting calmly in a small, clean room on the third floor of the precinct building. He had expected to find the place like in *Cagney and Lacey* or *Hill Street Blues*, but the room was quiet and comfortably furnished. She had been crying, he could see that from the puffiness around her eyes, but she sat waiting for him as if she was waiting for the maitre d' to announce their table was ready.

She rose and hugged Bob when he came into the room. She started to say something but her voice broke. All he got – the first news he had about what had happened was – 'Tony, Bob. He's been . . .'

The police officer in charge was a woman. A woman with a very slight accent and just a touch of brown mixed into her creamy complexion. Bob guessed she was Puerto Rican and about thirty years old. The woman got right to the point. 'Mr Bruno, your son has been kidnapped.'

Bob sat down heavily on the sofa beside Lois. She slid her hand over his and he grasped it, holding on to reality, not believing what he had just heard.

It was all too true, the officer assured him. She gave a *Reader's Digest* version of what Lois had poured out onto her. Mrs Bruno had gone, as usual, to the St Andrews School on East 73rd Street to pick up her son, Tony Bruno, who was a first grade student at the aforementioned school. The child, who always waited for his ride home by the sidewalk near the street, was not there. Mrs Bruno, after parking her automobile, had searched the school yard then entered the building and spoken with the boy's teacher, a Miss Wallasin, who informed Mrs Bruno that her son had left the school building at 3.00 p.m., the normal time, and had last been seen by another student, a six year old girl named Dorothy Lynchack, as two unidentified men took the boy into the back seat of their black automobile and drove away. 'Is there anything you can add to that, Mr Bruno?'

'*Add* to that?' Bob's voice croaked. 'This is all news to me. Terrible news!'

'Has your son tried to contact you at your work?' she asked, ready to write down his answer.

'No. Of course not. I don't think he even has the number.

Look, I don't understand. You say two men took my son?' The officer nodded. 'And drove off? With my son?' Another nod. '*What* two men?'

'Can you tell us anything about these two men?' she asked Bob. 'Possibly you know them or know why they would want to take your son.'

'I *know* these men?' Bob said, startled. 'Why should I know them? What the hell do you mean by that?'

'Enemies?' The officer threw the word lightly into the air, like a balloon. 'Someone who wanted to get back at you. An angry business partner or associate? Someone like that?'

'I don't have any enemies,' Bob said.

'We all have enemies,' the woman stated flatly. 'There's always somebody out there ready to do us harm.'

'Maybe for you, there is. Because you're a cop and you deal with trash all day, but not for me! I don't know anyone who could hate me enough to do this. Do this to my son.'

'And you, Mrs Bruno? Is there anyone you know who would do this to *you*?' The officer's pencil was poised to write down the answer. Lois shook her head. It was difficult for her to speak without bursting into tears. 'Someone at work, perhaps? A disgruntled client? An ex-employee of your company?'

'She doesn't own the design company,' Bob said. 'She only works there. She's a senior graphic design artist.'

'How long have you been there, Mrs Bruno?' The woman was writing now.

'Five years,' Bob answered for his wife. 'She went to work there about a year after Tony . . .' He paused . . . 'After our little boy was born.'

'And in those five years, Mrs Bruno, there's never been anyone you can recall who would have taken your son to spite you? Or frighten you?'

Again Lois shook her head.

'And you, Mr Bruno, you own the "Salerno Restaurant Supply" located in Brooklyn?' She read the address and phone number from a paper in front of her. Bob supposed Lois had given the information.

'Yes,' he said. 'I own it along with my father. He started the business and when he retired three years ago, I took over. He's in Florida,' Bob added, 'just outside Miami. He and my mother.'

'Salerno? The officer raised one eyebrow. 'Italian?'

19

'Italian,' Bob said. 'It's the name of the town my grandfather emigrated from. My father was born in New York City. He's an American.' Bob glared at the Puerto Rican woman. 'And so am I,' he added. 'I'm an American too.'

'Nobody is questioning your patriotism, Mr Bruno, but I am curious about the name "Salerno" and your Italian background. Are you connected in any way with The Family? Could someone in The Family have taken your son as a reprisal? To get back at you?'

'You mean the Mafia? Is that the "family" you're talking about?' Bob rose to his feet and confronted the woman. 'Listen, lady. My son has been kidnapped and I'm here to get him back. I'm not here to listen to insinuations and insults about myself and my parents. You want to write something down? Then write this: I am not a member of the Mafia. Neither my father nor my grandfather were members of the Mafia. I do not deal with the Mafia and I don't know anybody that does. If, and I repeat *if*, the Mafia took Tony, then they took the wrong kid and they'll soon figure it out and bring him back in a hurry!'

The officer took it all down, word for word. 'Mrs Bruno, are you also Italian? I mean of Italian parentage?'

Lois opened her mouth, surprising herself that she could form words again. 'No,' she said softly. 'My grandparents came from Scotland. All four of them. On both sides. They settled in West Virginia. To work the coalfields.'

'That's where she grew up,' Bob said. 'There's no Mafia in a West Virginia coal mine.'

'How long have you been in New York City, Mrs Bruno?'

'About nine years. I went to design school in Cincinnati and came here when I graduated.'

'You found employment right away? As soon as you arrived here?' For some reason the officer wanted to write this down as well.

'Yes,' Lois replied. 'I only spent a couple of weeks looking for a job and then I got one with a small company in the garment district. I quit there when I was pregnant with Tony. Then after he was about a year old, I started to work where I do now.'

'Yes, I already have that,' the officer said. 'And you met your present husband when?'

'I don't like that word *present*,' Bob said, hardly moving his lips.

The officer ignored him. 'How long have you been married, Mrs Bruno?'

'Eight years. It'll be eight in March.'

'This is a first marriage for both of you?'

'Yes, it is,' said Bob, 'but I don't understand what this has to do with getting Tony back.'

'Another angle,' the officer said. 'A jealous ex-wife. A vindictive ex-husband. That sort of thing.'

'Then you've got the wrong angle,' Bob replied. 'Put that right up there with your Mafia angle.'

'What about money? Personal wealth. Are you a wealthy man, Mr Bruno?'

'I own half my company. Lois gets a pretty good salary. We're not rich.' He shrugged. 'But we're not on Welfare either. I can tell you where our bank accounts are if you want to check us out, but I can't see that money is a motive for taking our son. We don't have a kidnappers' ransom. It would be tough for me to arrange the kind of money they usually want. No.' He shrugged again. 'Money is not the reason. They want something else. Either that or else – ' Here he brightened a little – 'it's as I said. Maybe they've made a mistake and will let Tony go when they realize it.' Lois gripped his hand tightly at this. 'It is a possibility,' he said as he tried to smile at his wife. 'It is a hope.'

'Yes,' said the officer, 'it is a possibility. For your sake I hope it comes true.' She got up and walked toward the door. 'We're going to question the little girl in the playground and also some of the teachers who should have been more vigilant.'

'There should have been someone with Tony until I got there,' Lois said rather loudly.

'I don't think you can blame the school,' the policewoman said. 'You made your own arrangements with your son. One of you should have been there to meet him when his class was dismissed. You, Mrs Bruno, were late.'

'I was on my way,' Lois felt the tears starting up again.

'But you weren't there,' the woman insisted. 'You were late. You gave the kidnappers enough time to steal your son. Don't blame the school. Your son is your responsibility.

21

You were late. If you had been on time, this probably would not have happened.'

* * *

The sedative had worn off about noon of the fifth day since Tony had been missing. Bob was in the kitchen, standing against the counter munching a peanut butter sandwich and washing it down with instant coffee. He looked up to see Lois standing in the doorway. Her red hair was jumbled in every direction, her large blue eyes were wide open and she kept kneading her fingers as if trying to pull them out of their sockets.

'I saw Tony,' she said in a frightened voice.

'You what?' Bob almost choked on the bread. 'Where?'

'In a vision . . . He was there in this large room and he was sitting at a table and he was colouring in a book.'

'Oh,' was all Bob could say.

'He looked fine,' she continued. 'He was wearing other clothes. They must have given him some new ones because they weren't the clothes he went to school in that day. He didn't seem to be hurt. I'm sure of that. There were no bruises on him and he looked calm. I didn't see the two men,' she rattled on. 'I looked for them but they weren't there. There was someone – I'm not sure, but I think there was a woman sitting in a chair. On the other side of this large room. She was reading a magazine. Bob, Tony looked healthy. He didn't look as if he had been abused. Isn't that wonderful?' She smiled for the first time in days.

'Lois,' he said softly, 'it was only a dream. You didn't really see him. I don't want to shatter your bubble, but – '

'No!' Her voice rose. 'I *saw* him! It was more than a dream! I actually went to where they are keeping him and I *saw* him!'

'Darling, the doctor told me that the sedative he gave you might have some minor side effects. I guess vivid dreams are one of them.'

'No!' She whirled around, her night dress billowing out around her feet. 'I saw him! I know what I saw!' She walked quickly into the living room and looked out of the window. He came up behind her and put his hands on her shoulders. They seemed thinner suddenly, he thought. All this anxiety was eating away at her physically. She kept staring out onto the street below. 'You don't believe me,' she said. 'You don't believe I saw him.'

'I want to believe,' he replied, 'but . . .'

'Every time before when I have had an experience like this, you've made fun of me. Each and every time.'

He tried being very calm with her. 'It's just me. I simply don't believe these things are possible. You know that. I find it all very improbable.'

'Even the other times when I've *seen* things and they turned out to have come true, you never believed them. Not really.' Her shoulders started shaking slightly. 'I told you about this stuff before we were married. I told you how these things happen to me and how I believe in them. Didn't I?'

He bent closer to her ear and whispered, 'Yes and I said then that I didn't believe in any of this psychic nonsense. I said that until someone proved it, I wasn't going to change my mind.'

'What about the time I warned you about hiring that Jergens guy? I was right, wasn't I?'

Peter Jergens had been hired at Bob's warehouse. As soon as Lois had met him she told Bob to get rid of him. Bob had kept him on but had to fire him six months later when he found all the doctored invoices and discovered the kick-backs Jergens had been receiving. Yes, she had warned him and he hadn't listened. 'You did,' he said, 'and you were right, but that didn't make a believer out of me.'

'And the time I said we weren't going to get that house in New Canaan?' She still wasn't looking at him. He shrugged. They had found a wonderful small house outside the Connecticut town and both of them had fallen in love with it immediately. After the papers were drawn up, and even after the bank loan had been approved, Lois started 'seeing' that they would never move into it. Bob had laughed, then scoffed and then finally told her to stop talking so negatively about the place. It was in the bag. It was theirs. On the day they were to sign the papers, the bank informed them that the seller of the property had no right to make the final agreement. The house was part of a large entangled estate that was going through complicated litigation with dozens of heirs. So Lois had been right then, too.

She turned to him, her face almost touching his. 'I *saw* Tony, Bob. He is all right. They will be getting in touch with

23

us soon. Believe me on this one. Trust me, Bob. Don't take this away from me. Leave me one small shred of hope to cling to. Please!'

He kissed her and they stood like that, in the window, for several minutes. Bob sighed. He would go along with it. If she wanted to believe that she had seen Tony, then let her. If these visions calmed her, all the better. It would be cruel of him to destroy whatever small speck of hope she still retained. 'What do you say,' he said, grinning at her, 'that you get dressed and we go out for some lunch? That little Indonesian place serves great shrimp curry with their Sunday brunch. What do you say?'

She managed another smile. 'Sure. Why not? Fresh air and curry. That's not a bad combination. We both could use some of it. But,' she laughed, 'I have to do more than get dressed. I have to do something with this hair! I look like Medusa on a bad day in the middle of her period!' She kissed him lightly on the cheek and went from the living room, down the hallway and into the bathroom. The echo of her laugh remained in Bob's ears. It was the first time she had laughed since the kidnapping.

* * *

Lois went back to work the next day. Midge saw her come into the studio and ran towards her, hugging her as she walked to her office. 'Now look, Midge,' Lois said, 'I have anticipated everything you are going to say, so don't bother to say it. Okay? I know you and the rest of the guys here feel sorry for me, want Tony to return safe and sound and want the kidnappers brought to justice. I know all that. I also know that my being back here embarrasses you all somewhat. You don't really know how to handle me, don't know if I'll burst into tears or act like an emotionless robot. So don't worry. I'll just be myself. All you guys be the same.'

'Is this what's known as Lois Bruno Being Brave?' Midge asked.

'No. It's what's known as Lois Bruno being secure. I saw Tony yesterday.' She put up her hand before the woman could ask the inevitable question. 'It was in a dream. In what my folks and I call a vision. I saw him and he was in good health. He was clean and being cared for. I know you don't believe in those things, but that's what I saw.'

24

'I do believe in them,' Midge protested. 'I've always believed in them.'

'I didn't know that.' Lois smiled slightly. 'Anyway, I've seen him and it's given me great comfort. It's made me positive about the outcome of it all. I don't know *who* took him and I don't know *why*, but I know he is being well cared for and they'll bring him back to me soon.'

'I gotta admire your thinking,' Midge said.

'I *have* to think this way.' Lois put her purse on her desk. 'If I didn't I would go bonkers. I'd be another banana in the basket.' She looked around her office. 'I'm glad to see somebody watered my plants.'

'I did. Look, does Bob feel as positive about this as you do?'

Lois shook her head and started separating out a jumble of coloured pencils. 'No. Of course not. He doesn't believe in any of it. But – ' She paused and looked at Midge. 'But he knows I've been right about other things I've seen in the past, so he hopes I'm right about this one. He knows it gives me courage. He loves me, he wouldn't take it away from me.'

'Has he told you this? In so many words?'

'He doesn't have to. We talked about it a little yesterday over lunch. We went out for lunch, we discussed it and we agreed not to mention it. Not to mention the kidnapping and not to mention my vision.'

'How's it possible to do that? I mean, this has been such a terrible thing . . .'

'It must be out of sight, out of mind, Midge. Our lives must continue. We have to go on with our normal routines and pretend that everything is okay.'

'And the fact that Tony is nowhere around? How are you going to manage that?'

'We've decided to act as if he had gone to visit my parents. He's with them, in West Virginia. And when they get tired of him, they'll send him back. Look, did you tell Grahams to make that lamp up as originally designed? I can't recall what I said to you about it. It's okay, whatever they do. Oh yes, that awful MacArthur woman. Did she come by to see me? Did she leave the specifications of her floor plan?' She began rifling through a pile of folders on her desk. 'Didn't Alice take care of this last week? Christ, they'll be down my throat for sure.'

Midge stood there watching her for a couple more minutes, then headed for the door.

'Oh Midge,' Lois called out, 'thanks again for . . . for watering my plants.'

* * *

The farce of Tony being with his grandparents continued for three more weeks. The pantomime of not glancing at his closed bedroom door went on just as long. His name wasn't mentioned. At least not to each other. At least not aloud. But he was always there, always an invisible presence at the kitchen table, on the living room sofa, on the pillow in front of the television set. Bob's mother had embroidered that pillow for Tony. She had covered it with images of Bugs Bunny and Daffy Duck and Miss Piggy and He Man and several others that Tony watched every Saturday morning. Bob and Lois tried not to look at that pillow, tried stepping around it. Both of them wished the other one would put it away somewhere, yet neither would be the one to actually do it. It would break their agreement, break their trust in the future. Putting that pillow away would mean relegating their son to the past. Often Lois thought of an inscription in the graveyard back home: 'He is not dead, he is just away.'

* * *

And then, one day, a telephone call did come.

'Mrs Bruno? Mrs Lois Bruno?' a female voice came out of the receiver.

'Yes,' Lois replied.

'Mrs Bruno, this is Officer Santos. You were in my office a few weeks back.'

'Yes!' Lois said, and wanting to react normally to the news that was about to come, added, 'Your last name is Santos! We were right. We *thought* you were Puerto Rican.'

'Brazilian,' the woman said drily. 'I tried to reach you at your apartment and then I called your office. We have some information for you about your son.'

'About Tony?' Lois held her breath.

'We think we may have found him.'

'Oh, thank God!' Lois' voice broke. 'Thank God!'

26

'We need you to identify him.'

'Of course. How wonderful! Where is he? Is he okay? I mean,' Lois was halfway out of her office chair and heading toward her coat, the telephone cord stretching across the room. 'I'll be there as soon as I can. Is he in your office? I'll be right there.'

'Ma'am, your son is not at my office. Let me give you the address where I'll be expecting you.' She gave Lois a number and street that was way downtown, near the Battery.

'I'll just call my husband and tell him,' Lois said. 'He'll be so pleased!'

'Ma'am, I've already called him. I called him first. He will meet you there. So will I.'

Lois hung up without saying goodbye, struggled into her coat and almost ran down the hallway. She stopped at the reception desk. 'Janice, they've found Tony. I'm going to get him. Isn't that wonderful?'

'Wonderful, Lois. Gee that's great.'

'If anybody calls tell them I'll be gone for the rest of the day. I'm just wondering, do you think it would be faster to take the subway instead of a taxi down to the station? For some reason they have him on Windcross Street.'

'Windcross? That's way down. There's no subway stop really near there,' the girl replied. 'I'd take a cab if I were you. Wonder why they have him down there?'

'Some police red tape,' Lois said lightly. 'Anyway, I'm gone for the day.'

'Call me and let me know he's okay?' This from Midge who had heard the conversation and come out of her office.

'I will. I promise. Oh, I feel so relieved!' With that she was gone.

Midge looked at the receptionist. 'Where did she say they had Tony?'

'At a station house on Windcross.'

'Windcross?' A male clerk came up to the desk. 'I live in that area. There's no station house there.'

'There must be,' Janice replied. 'That's the address they gave her.'

'There's no station house there,' repeated the young man. 'What's down there is the morgue.'

When the taxi stopped in front of the building, Lois saw for the first time what kind of a place it really was. Fortunately Bob was standing on the steps, waiting for her. He opened the back door of the cab, then paid the driver. Neither of them said a word as they entered the building. Lois was shivering, her eyes were wide and she kept shaking her head, in short involuntary spasms. Bob had his arm around her shoulders. She was sure her ankles would go at any minute. She had lost all feeling in them, all feeling in anything below the insistent pounding of her heart.

Officer Santos was there. 'Thank you for coming,' she said to them both. 'It should only take a minute.'

'We have more than a minute,' Lois heard her foolish voice say.

With Officer Santos leading, they walked down a long corridor and halted in front of closed elevator doors. The policewoman pushed a button and while they waited, Bob gave his wife a tender kiss on the cheek. She didn't feel it. The doors opened and there were two men inside the elevator, both wearing white hospital coats. Lois looked at their faces but they didn't let their eyes make contact with hers. They had done this a hundred times. The only way to stay sane was to stay aloof.

The doors opened and they walked out into a small reception area. There was a black man in white trousers and a white hospital coat. He had a clipboard in one hand. There was a gold wedding band on his hand as well, shining in bright contrast against his black skin. Two tribal ritual scars marred his left cheek. He and Officer Santos conferred quietly for a few moments. Then the woman came over to the silent couple.

'We both think it would be best if you went in first, Mr Bruno,' she said. 'The body is badly damaged. Some of the features are missing. We, Dr Matinga and I, both feel Mrs Bruno should be spared the sight. Of course,' she sighed, 'It's up to you but we have to give you our recommendations.'

Bob nodded. 'I don't really want to go in there myself,' he said.

'We understand that,' the doctor replied. There was a thickness to his English, something from his African language that had refused to go away in spite of his degrees from British and American universities. 'It is never easy,' he said. 'I myself still find it distasteful at times. But it must be done,

28

sir. We must have an identification of the boy. If it's not your son then all the better. Now isn't that right?'

'I'm going in with you,' said Lois.

'No.' Bob led her over to a green plastic bench. 'It's not necessary. It probably won't be Tony and if it's not there's no need for you to see it. If it is Tony then I'll take you in.'

'Right,' she said and squeezed his hand. 'But it won't be. We both know that. You go in, then.' She seemed to shrink against the wall. 'I'll stay out here. I'll be all right. You just go on in.'

Officer Santos held out a box of Kleenex. Lois shook her head. 'I'll be all right,' she repeated. 'Bob, go in, get it over with and then we can go home.'

It seemed to Bob that the ten feet to the door of the room where the bodies were kept was ten miles. The doctor pushed the door open and the two men went inside. Bob had expected to see the walls lined with square metal doors and handles like on filing cabinets, and he expected he would have to wait while the body was rolled out of a hole in the wall. Instead there was only a metal cart, with wheels, sitting in the middle of the room. Overhead a spotlight picked up the details of the dozens of wrinkles in the cloth that concealed the small body underneath. Bob stood by the white draped thing on the table.

'Tell me when you're ready, sir,' the doctor said, his deep tones cutting through the rather frigid air.

'I'll never be ready,' Bob said grimly. 'Go ahead. Get it over with.'

The black hand moved across the white sheet and slowly pulled it down to reveal the small face . . . or, rather, what had once been a face.

Bob stared, then gagged and turned away. 'I can't,' he murmured, trying to swallow back some of the stuff that he felt rising up from his stomach.

'Sir,' the doctor said, 'you must. Please. Look back at him.'

Bob turned towards the thing on the table. He tried to be brave and macho and Italian about what he was looking at. The small boy's pale white skin had started turning black, but even under that blackness could be seen the marks of bruises and what looked like cigarette burns. The thin chest had a deep jagged scar under the rib cage. It reminded Bob of all the paintings he had seen of where the soldier's sword had pierced Christ's body. The face, or most of it, was gone. Either blown away or cut away or eaten away. He couldn't tell and he didn't want to know. The hair was darker than Tony's had been, or at least as how he remembered his son's hair colouring to be. 'The hair,' he said slowly, 'it doesn't look quite the same. Could what have happened to him . . . this terrible thing that happened to him . . . could it have altered the colour of the hair?'

'I doubt it,' the medical man replied. 'Hair keeps on growing for a while even after death. It rarely changes colour. Except under great stress, of course.'

'What had happened to him you wouldn't call great stress?' Bob looked at the African, glad to take his eyes from the thing on the table.

'Yes, of course it was great stress. The boy obviously suffered terribly before he died but I can't tell you for certain that the tortures would have altered his hair colouring. Have you seen enough?' Bob nodded and the doctor pulled the sheet back up over the dead boy's head.

Once outside, in the waiting area, Bob walked quickly over to Lois. He sat down beside her and reached for her hands. He held them tightly without saying anything. There were tears in his eyes. There was pleading in his eyes.

'Is it . . .?' Lois asked.

Bob looked at the doctor, then at the policewoman, then back at his wife. 'Yes,' he said hoarsely. 'That's Tony in there. They found him.'

In a flash Lois was up and out of the bench and running towards the morgue room door. She pushed it open and stopped momentarily to get her bearings.

Bob jumped up from the bench and shouted to the others. 'Stop her! For God's sake don't let her see him!'

Lois ran further into the room, heading straight for the thing that was wrapped in white.

'Lois!' Bob called as he started after her. 'Lois! Please don't!'

Officer Santos ran past Bob. 'Let me handle this,' she said.

'He's my baby!' Lois wailed. 'They've got my baby!' She reached the wheeled cart and put out a trembling hand, a hand unsure if it was going to caress the sheet or pull it back.

The policewoman was beside Lois now. 'Come on, Mrs Bruno. Let's go back outside.'

Lois lashed out at the woman, sending her sideways with one powerful thrust of her arm. 'No! I want my baby! My Tony! My little Tony!'

Bob was beside her. 'Come on hon, let's get out of here.'

She looked at him, her tears blurring his features in her eyes. 'That's Tony under there,' she said simply. 'That's our boy under there.'

He put his arm around her shoulder and exerted a slight pressure to turn her away from the thing on the table. 'Yes, hon. I know. Come on. Come on now.'

'No!' Lois screamed and her hand darted out and yanked away the sheet.

Officer Santos grabbed her and span her toward the wall before she had a chance to see the grisly face and the tortured body. Lois staggered against the wall. The policewoman pulled the covering back over the body. The unexpected thrust had knocked the wind out of Lois and she slumped and slid down into a sitting position on the floor.

Bob knelt beside her. He tried to lift her but she seemed as heavy as lead. Behind them Officer Santos and the African doctor rushed the covered body out through a side door.

'I want to see him,' Lois wailed. 'I want to see Tony!'

'No,' he said firmly. 'You can't see him! Lois, it's too terrible! You'd never be able to erase the memory from your mind. Never!'

'That's my baby!' Lois wailed. 'I want to hold my baby!' She tried to struggle to her feet but Bob held her down. She sat, her arms stretched out toward the door where the body had been taken, her face set in a silent scream. Then she took a deep breath, pulling in cold morgue room air and gave out a long, low moan that was laden with anguish, heartbreak and defeat.

They let her sit there, sobbing, for several minutes. Finally Officer Santos put her hands under Lois' arms and brought her to her feet. With Bob on one side and the policewoman on the other, they managed to get her out of the room and back toward the elevator in the waiting room.

The African doctor tried to comfort her. 'I am sorry,' he said. 'I am truly sorry.' He put out his left hand and pushed back a strand of hair that had fallen across her forehead.

Lois noticed his wedding ring again, like a swath of yellow sunlight against his black skin. 'Do you have any children, doctor?' she asked in a faraway voice.

31

'Yes ma'am,' he replied. 'Three.'

'I have a little boy,' she said in that same voice. 'I have a little boy. Maybe you could meet him one day. He's not here right now. No, he's away. He's visiting his grandparents. He's far, far away.'

*   *   *

Bob's parents flew from Florida and his married sister from Boston. Lois' mother and father came to New York immediately, as soon as Bob told them. Lois was an only child and so the tragic loss of their only grandchild was especially difficult for the elderly couple. They had wanted to stay in a hotel but Bob thought it would be better if they stayed in the apartment, with Lois. There was a sofa in Tony's room . . . what used to be Tony's room . . . that folded out into a double bed. There would be no problem.

When the funeral director had asked Bob when he wanted the service, he told him 'as soon as all the family gets here.' So, the day after their arrival, the small party gathered in one of the many side rooms of the Madison Avenue funeral parlour and the brief service was held. There were a few people from Bob's warehouse and his childhood lifetime pal Anthony Venutti and his wife Anne. Most of Lois' design studio were there: Midge among them. When the funeral director had asked him what denomination they were Bob had shrugged. 'I'm a lapsed Catholic and my wife's a lapsed Presbyterian. It doesn't really matter what kind of preacher does his thing.' The director used his professional judgement and had both a Catholic priest and a Presbyterian minister come in. If the parents didn't care he knew the grandparents certainly would. And he had been right, of course. The Duncans had been upset when they first were told that Lois was going to marry a Catholic and the Brunos demanded to know when Lois was going to convert to Catholicism. In order to defuse the problem, from the very start the young couple decided not to go to any church and to let their children, when they got to the right age, decide on whatever religion they wanted to believe in. This calmed both sets of grandparents, and each of them began calculating how they would influence the grandchildren when the time came. Mrs Duncan had hugged Mrs Bruno, then both women burst into tears on each others fall coats. Mr Bruno shook hands with Mr Duncan and both men noted that the others eyes were red.

The closed casket was waiting for them as the doors to the small 'chapel' were opened. Lois insisted on walking unaided to her chair in the front row. Her face was swollen from weeping yet she had refused to wear black. She and her mother had argued about it right up to the moment they left the apartment.

'Tony is not dead! I know that, mother! That will not be Tony in that casket. I'm not going to mourn my son. I'm not!'

'Then why have you been crying so?' the older woman wanted to know.

'Because somewhere my Tony is waiting for me and is frightened and needs me! And somewhere,' she continued, 'there is another woman, another *mother*, who waits for her child to come home but he won't come home because he's being buried this afternoon. He's being buried and his mother will never know what happened to him! She'll wait all the rest of her life for the phone to ring or the letter to arrive saying he is alive. And it will never come!' She clutched her mother closer to her and the tears fell rapidly again. 'Oh mother, the news will never come!'

Mrs Duncan murmured into her daughter's ear, trying to calm her, trying to understand what she was going through. That was Tony in the morgue. Bob had repeatedly told them he was positive it was Tony. He admitted the hair colouring was off but the doctor had assured him that hair can change colour, often does change colour, under stress. And Tony had undergone terrible stress. The bruises and the burns and the chest wound all proved that. He had been a frail child to begin with, small for his age and susceptible to colds. Taken suddenly away from his parents, held a prisoner and subjected to torture like that, it would make any child's hair colour turn. No, he assured all four grandparents, that *was* Tony on the .norgue table. He had no doubt of it.

'How are you going to convince Lois of it?' his father had asked.

'I'm not going to try,' he said slowly. 'Right now she is going through shock. After a while she'll come around to reason. She's an intelligent woman. She'll see reality on her own. My job is to make sure I'm beside her whenever she needs me.'

33

When the service was over Lois walked up to the closed brown wood and metal casket. 'Goodbye and God speed,' she said softly, 'whoever you are.'

Midge reached out and touched her on the elbow. Lois turned and smiled at her friend. Midge stretched out her arms and Lois fell into them, comfortable against the warmth of the woman's ample breasts. The other mourners parted and let Midge lead Lois up the aisle and out of the room. There was no graveyard to go to: Bob had ordered Tony's body cremated. No, he didn't want the ashes and he didn't care what the funeral parlour did with them. The child was gone, he and his wife didn't need any reminders of how they would miss him.

* * *

The Duncans stayed two more days before returning to West Virginia. Bob's parents had flown back to Florida immediately after the funeral, and his sister left the same evening. She had a husband and two children to take care of.

The first night they were alone in the apartment together, after all the relatives had gone, Bob saw Lois pour herself a rather large shot of Scotch. 'Are you sure you want another?' he asked.

She nodded. 'It's cold in here. This helps to take away the chill.'

'I can turn the thermostat up,' he said, and almost added, 'Then you won't have to drink that,' but he didn't.

She had her back to him, staring out of the window. 'That's all right. I don't mind a bit of a chill. Bob, have you figured it out yet?'

'What?' He watched her warily.

'What we are going to do about Tony? I mean, do we hire someone to sit here in case he comes home while we're at work? I've thought about that, you know. Both of us away, the apartment empty. What would he do? How would he find us? He doesn't have your phone number, he doesn't have mine.'

She couldn't see the frown on Bob's face. 'We're not going to do anything and we certainly can't afford to hire someone to sit around on their ass waiting for a visit that will never come.'

'Never come?' She wheeled around at this. 'Never? Is that

34

what you said?' He nodded. 'Never is a long time. I never use that word. It's too negative.'

'You just did.'

'I just did what?'

'Just used that word. Never. I thought you said you never used it.'

'I didn't. I said never is a long time. I ought to know what I said.'

'Look – ' Bob started. 'You said . . . Oh, never mind. It's not important.'

'No,' she said and walked rather shakily back to the half-empty Scotch bottle. 'It's not important. Nothing is important.' She poured another two inches of whisky into her glass. 'Not any more.'

'I'm going to bed,' he said. 'I think you should too.'

'I'm not sleepy. You go on. I'll stay here for awhile.'

'And do what? Drink some more?'

'Maybe.' She smiled. 'If I get thirsty. I'm going to wait awhile.'

'Wait?'

'Maybe they'll call tonight.'

'Who?'

'The police. That nice Santos woman. Maybe she'll call tonight and tell me they've found Tony. Did you like her? I thought she was a lovely lady. She wasn't very happy when I told her we thought she was Puerto Rican. She is Brazilian. Did you know that? I thought they were all the same. You know, Mexicans and Brazilians and Columbians and Venezu . . . Venezulwalians . . . or whatever they're called.' Her voice slurred. 'Never wanted to go to those places. Did you? I didn't. Bugs and straw hats and all that sun. All that horrible Goddamned sun!'

'I thought you wanted to go to Jamaica. You know we have tickets for two weeks there in February,' he reminded her. He almost asked her if she didn't remember the discussion they had had about Tony being out of school for two weeks, but he didn't. 'They've got bugs and straw hats and sun there too, you know.'

'I know,' she said and took another gulp from the glass. 'But the Jamaicans aren't the same as Brazilians and those other people.' She looked at him and her eyes had trouble focusing. 'We're going *where*? Where did you say?'

'Jamaica. Remember? We got the tickets weeks ago.' He almost added, 'before Tony was kidnapped.'

'Jamaica?' She laughed and sloshed some of the booze onto her dress. 'Nobody goes to Jamaica in February! That's in Long Island! I know that! Jamaica!'

'It'll do you good,' he said. 'By then you'll be ready for the sun and the beaches and the straw hats. It'll do us both good. Now come on to bed.' He walked over to her and put his hand on her arm. She shook it off.

'No. It won't do me any good. There is only one thing that'll do me any good. Only one thing. Wanna know what it is?' She tried to focus her eyes on him but he was just a blur. 'Only one thing do me any good. My Tony coming home. My baby. Back here. Right here. That'll do me good.'

Bob awoke about three and saw that Lois had not come to bed. He went into the living room and stood there watching her asleep on the sofa. She was still sitting up, her head lolled against the back of the couch. Miraculously the drink in her hand hadn't spilled. He shifted her around, stretching her legs out and putting a pillow under her head. Then he went and got a blanket and covered her.

'Tony is never coming home,' he said. 'Never. Trust me on this one.'

*   *   *

Four days went by, including a weekend of rapidly emptying Scotch bottles and an unread Sunday New York Times and then, on Tuesday morning, she announced she was going back to work. Bob held his breath, wondering what the next erratic move would be, but she calmly fixed their breakfasts, got dressed, combed her hair and left the apartment when he did. She got into her car, smiled at him, reminded him to bring home some cheese from the Italian deli near his warehouse, blew him a kiss and drove off. He glanced up at the sky, hunched his shoulders and made the sign of the Cross, an old habit from his childhood that still helped when he needed to express himself. 'Let's hope it's working its way out through her,' he said aloud. 'Jesus, let's hope.'

'Morning!' Lois sailed into the studio with a big smile on her lips and a wave at Janice at the reception desk. The girl stared at her but managed a return cheerful greeting through her surprise.

Lois stopped at the door to Midge's office. 'Morning, darlin',' she said. 'How are ya?'

'Fine.' Midge hadn't expected to see Lois for the rest of the week. 'I'm fine, but how are you?'

'Well, thanks. And rested. Rarin' to get back to work. I've had enough time off. The company needs me. In fact, I'm afraid to see what kind of problems you all have piled up on my desk.'

'Just little ones. Goodyear wants you to redesign the tyre and Boeing wants you to redesign their jets. But that's it, nothing major.' She smiled and looked at Lois, trying to see if there were any cracks in this back-to-normal facade. No one in the office wanted Lois there if she was going to crumble under their feet, have to be swept up with a broom and the pieces hauled off in a bucket, but if work would be good therapy then Midge, and everyone else on the staff, had pledged to make things as 'normal' as possible. 'You sure you want to be here?'

'Of course. Where else would I be? I've had enough of that empty apartment. I've been staring at its four walls far too long. Yesterday I found myself planning a whole new decorating scheme. You know, new wallpaper, new chair coverings, even new plants for the windows. When I caught myself doing that, I knew it was time to get the hell out and get back to reality.'

Midge grimaced. 'Unfortunately, this place is reality.'

'It is,' Lois agreed, 'and I need as much reality now as I can absorb. Look, I've been a real basket case and I want to apologize.' She went closer to Midge and touched her friend on the shoulder. 'You were there when I needed you. I appreciate it. I really do.'

Midge opened her arms and Lois went into them, happy for the haven her friend provided. 'You don't have to thank me,' she said softly in Lois' ear. 'You've been through one helluva lot. We all care for you and we suffered along with you. We want you to be happy and it bothered all of us that you were so down. Besides girl,' she said pushing Lois out at arms length, 'we loves ya! Haven't you got that in your cotton-pickin' head yet? We loves ya, chile!'

'And I loves y'all too, Miss Scarlett,' Lois said in her best

Hattie McDaniel voice. 'If the Yankees is gone and the plantation's been spared, I think I'll get back into my kitchen and get my work done.'

'The tribulations are passed, Mammy. This is a brand new day.'

'God I hope so, Miss Scarlett.' Lois pulled away and started out of the office. 'God, Midge, I hope you're right. I've got to believe that the tribulations are passed. I don't have the strength for any more tribulations.'

She jumped back into her job with a vengeance. As if to obliterate everything from her mind she worked feverishly on the waiting back projects and spent hours on the phone soliciting new jobs from former clients. There was a shoe store that needed a special revolving window display rack. Lois whipped one out for them in two days. A small hotel in the Berkshires wanted a new brochure, something to attract the yuppy crowd. Lois designed it in a day and a half. A bus company in Minnesota needed a revised logo. Lois had them repainting their entire fleet in less than ten days. She even managed to create a poster for an off-off-Broadway theatre group that was doing *Macbeth* with only five actors. She did it for free. For the fun of it. She returned to the apartment late almost every night. More often than not she and Bob went out to dinner as there was no time for her to cook. Bob didn't mind. It was good to have Lois out into the world, busy and interested in life once more. And, he noted, the level in the Scotch bottle didn't seem to be going down lately.

And she never mentioned Tony.

One night, in the middle of November, the downstairs entrance bell rang. Bob frowned and glanced at his watch. 'Who can that be?' he said to Lois. Both of them had been watching an old Bogie and Bacall film on television. 'It's almost eleven.'

Lois felt her heart rise up into her throat but she didn't say that maybe it was news about Tony. She had pledged to herself and to her Creator that she would not mention Tony any more. Not to Bob and not aloud. Still, it was all she could do to watch calmly as Bob pushed the call button and asked who it was.

'It's me, Midge,' the woman answered, her familiar voice coming through the small speaker next to the living room door.

Bob pushed the other button that released the downstairs door with a loud buzzing sound. 'Wonder what she wants?' Lois shook her head in reply. 'Odd,' he said. 'At this hour.'

In a minute Midge was ringing the bell outside in the hallway. When Bob opened the door she came bustling into the apartment, a large flat package under her arm wrapped in brown paper. 'Darlings!' she said and collapsed onto their sofa. 'God, what a night. I'm exhausted. I've been to an auction over in Jersey. Some old faggot who died and left a house crammed full of Victorian antiques and World War One dreck. The place was absolutely mobbed. You know, all the dealers and the decorators and most of the Greenwich Village loonies. I didn't even get a seat. I had to stand through the whole thing. Hey, I've been here almost a full minute. Isn't anybody going to offer a girl a drink?'

Bob went into the kitchen for some ice and tonic water and Lois searched the cabinet for the bottle of gin.

'So you bought something?' Lois pointed at the parcel Midge had on her knee.

'I did,' Midge sighed. 'Actually I bought more than I bargained for. I had hoped to find some wicker chairs – you know, to go with that table I found on Third Avenue? – and so when I heard there was to be that kind of stuff in the auction I hightailed it over there right after work. Ah, thanks Bob. You will get your reward in Heaven.' She took a long pull from the glass, draining almost half the liquid with the first taste. 'Delicious! Anyway, when I saw all those other people there I knew that any wicker would go through the roof. The smart set was onto the sale. But anyway there wasn't any wicker. I guess the old poof didn't like getting his behind scratched with a bent twig. But what there was was this most marvellous Victorian etching of a little girl playing with two kittens. You know the type, she's on the floor wearing white ruffles and a ribbon in her hair and the kittens are playing with a ball and some string. Hand-coloured it was, really lovely.'

'And that's what's in the package?' Bob asked.

'Oh no. That's downstairs in my car.' She finished the drink and handed the empty glass to Bob. 'A refill, if you don't mind. Anyway, I fell in love with the engraving. I know exactly where I'm going to hang it. Lois, you know that spot on my living room wall? Over the English nest

39

of tables?' Lois nodded. 'Right there. I'm going to put it right there. It'll go beautifully with the small watercolour of Niagara Falls that I got at that auction in Philadelphia a couple of months ago.'

'Then what's that thing in the brown paper?' Lois asked.

'Oh. This? This is for you. For the two of you.'

Lois' eyes widened in pleasure. 'Midge! How thoughtful of you! You shouldn't have.'

'Well, I really didn't.' She shrugged her shoulders and grinned. 'Don't let your egos get out of control. I wasn't even thinking of you people when the kitty print came up for sale. I'm afraid I wasn't paying a great deal of attention. There was this gorgeous hunk standing next to me in the tightest pair of blue jeans I've seen since Elvis Presley in *Love me Tender* and he started talking to me and so when I bid on the kitty picture I didn't know that I was actually bidding on *two* pictures! I thought the kitty picture was going a bit too high, but I did want it. It was a battle between me and some thin arty-farty type and I became determined to outbid him and I did. Wasn't that wonderful? Anyway, when I went to pay I discovered that I had purchased *two* pictures. One of them the kitty thing and the other, this one. It's nice and all that, but it isn't my style – know what I mean? Anyway, I don't have any place left on my walls to hang it. It's rather large. So . . . Bob, I thought you were going to get me another drink.'

'Let's see the picture first,' he said. 'Maybe it's not worth a second gin and tonic.'

'Beast! Anyway, on the way back to Manhattan I thought now *who* would like this thing? And your faces leapt to mind. It's your kind of thing. Really it is. I mean it's got Bob and Lois written all over it.' She held the parcel out toward them. They both reached for it at the same time.

The paper came off quickly. Lois was the first to gasp, 'Midge! It's wonderful! Oh look Bob, isn't it wonderful? Midge, we can't accept this! Are you sure? Are you sure you don't want it?'

'It's not my style,' the woman repeated. 'It's yours. Consider it an early Christmas present.'

'It's very nice,' Bob admitted. 'Thank you, Midge. It's greatly appreciated.'

Lois straddled the framed engraving across the padded arms of an easy chair. Bob turned the overhead ceiling light on.

As they stood silently admiring their unexpected gift, Lois reached out and put her arm around her husband's waist.

The engraving was in tones of black and white and grey. It was about two feet across and a foot and a half high, including the white area around the actual picture and the narrow gilded wooden frame.

It was a view of a large house. The house looked as if it was made out of rough stone blocks. Not cinder blocks or concrete squares, but rocks that had been individually hewn. The house had two floors with eight large windows on each level. The windows were in a row. Four on the left and four on the right. The line was broken on the ground floor by a large ornate doorway with much carving and scroll work around it, and directly over it was a balcony. There was a high pointed roof and from the very top and the very centre a flag was flying. Over it all were clouds and the artist's interpretation of rays from the sun.

The house sat exactly in the centre of the drawing on a large well kept lawn. There was almost eight inches of smooth lawn leading down from the house to the bottom of the picture. To the right was a small twisted tree, its trunk contorted, its branches bent and tilted at angles. To the left was a large grove of trees, several dozen of them growing closely together, their trunks and overhead branches forming a small forest of their own. At the bottom of the picture, on a two inch swath of white margin, the word 'CORRA' was engraved in old-fashioned script. There was nothing else in the margin, no name of the artist nor the publisher. No place of publication or printing date. Just the one word 'CORRA'.

'This must be very old,' Lois finally said. 'I mean it's not a new print.'

'I don't know,' Midge said. 'All I wanted was my kitties. My kitties are dated. It says 1868 on it.'

'Down there?' Bob pointed to the blank strip under the engraving of the house. 'It should give all the printing information down here.'

'I know but it doesn't.'

'It must be very old,' Lois repeated. 'Look.' And she moved the frame slightly so the ceiling light glimmered against the glass. 'See how rough the glass is. Look you can see the pit marks and some bubbles in it. New glass wouldn't do that. This has been framed a long time ago.' She turned the picture

41

around and inspected the other side of it. 'I guess so,' she murmured. 'It's been sealed with some kind of cloth. The cloth has been glued to a wooden back. They don't frame stuff like this anymore. They use nails and paper. Not cloth and glue.' She turned to Midge. 'This is really very old. Are you sure you want us to have it? Are you sure you want to give this away?'

'Course I'm sure. I'm not into old houses and stuff like that.'

'No.' Bob grinned. 'Kitties and auction-goers in tight blue jeans.'

'You got it,' she said, laughing, 'and not necessarily in that order.'

Lois turned the engraving around again and got down on her knees, the better to inspect it. 'It's so beautifully done,' she remarked. 'The lines are firm and clear. The blacks are not overused and the crosshatchings are delicate. The shadows are perfect and, look, many of the leaves in the trees have been delineated to pick out individual shapes and forms. Oh Midge, this is beautiful!' She crossed over to the sofa and gave her friend a kiss on the forehead. 'Thank you ever so much! It's just beautiful!'

'If it makes you smile darlin', then that's all the thanks I need.'

Bob was still by the picture. 'What do you think this "Corra" is? The name of the house? The location of the house?'

'No idea,' Midge said. 'Maybe it's the name of the family who owned the house. Corra.' She turned the word over on her tongue. 'Sounds Italian to me.'

'Could be,' said Bob. 'I knew some people whose name was Corrado. Could be Italian.'

Lois shook her head. 'The house doesn't *look* Italian. I think it's got to be something else. Swiss maybe. Or Austrian.'

'Could be German,' Midge volunteered. 'Or Swedish. They have large houses like that in Sweden. They build them big to keep out the cold. Maybe it belongs to those beer people.'

'Beer people?' Lois looked at her. 'What beer people?'

'You know, that family that makes their beer out in Colorado. What's their name?'

'That's Coors,' Bob laughed. 'I don't think this place belongs to them.'

'Just a thought.' Midge got up. 'I gotta go. Work tomorrow and all that. Besides I want to hang my kitties before I go to bed. Once I get started I'll probably be all night moving everything else in the apartment one or two inches to the left or right to balance it.'

'You don't have to,' Lois teased, 'you could give us that one too.'

'Your concern is touching,' Midge replied, giving Lois a peck on the cheek, 'but it ain't gonna work. I'll keep the kitties, you keep the Corra. See you in the office.'

'Thanks, Midge,' Bob said. 'It was very kind of you.' But Midge was out the door with a backward wave of her hand.

Lois went into the kitchen and, after digging around in the bottom drawer of a cabinet that was snarled with wire, pliers, string and rubber bands, she found the hammer and a medium sized nail. 'I was thinking I'd put it in the hallway,' she announced to Bob. 'We'll take down that Venice poster and put it there. What do you think?'

'Perfect place for it,' he replied. 'That way I can see it every time I come out of the bathroom.'

She made a face. 'Don't start knocking this picture! It's beautiful and I'm sure Midge paid plenty for it, even if she did buy it when she was more interested in that tight pair of jeans.'

Bob removed the thumbtacks from the poster he had bought when he was a college student on a trip to Venice, and took the large framed engraving from the living room chair and centred it on the hallway wall. It was the only hallway in their apartment, leading from the living room to the dining area, along to Tony's bedroom, then the bathroom and finally their bedroom at the very end of the corridor. Most apartments in that block of Manhattan were laid out like that and most people cluttered their corridors with small pictures, watercolours, photographs, posters and screw-on book and what-not shelves. Lois had decided she liked the 'clean' look better and so that poster had been the only item of decoration. They had talked about buying something 'really good' for the hallway, eventually. Now they both agreed, without even discussing it, that this unexpected and beautiful engraving was that something.

Bob made a pencilled mark on the wall and Lois hammered in the nail. Bob hung the picture. Both of them stepped back against the other wall and admired their handiwork. It was perfectly centred. It looked as if it belonged there.

After Bob had turned out the bedroom light, Lois said softly: 'You know there is something about that print that is so soothing. Don't know what it is. It just makes me feel good when I look at it.'

'I'm glad it makes you happy,' her husband said. 'It was very nice of Midge to give it to us.'

'Yes,' said Lois. 'She is a sweetheart.'

Bob didn't reply.

In the morning Lois's hand reached out and shut down the alarm five minutes before it was set to go off. She had always done that, always awoken just five minutes before the ringing got under way. She walked to the bedroom window to see what kind of a day it was going to be and frowned as she saw the snowflakes falling onto the parked cars below. She wiggled out of her nightgown and walked naked into the bathroom. Then she stopped, turned around and went to admire the engraving on the wall.

'Good morning, house,' she said. Her admiring gaze went across the front of the old mansion and she noted how each window had its own frame and latch. Then to the balcony with a small door hidden in the background. Then to the flag that was flying on a gable in the centre of the roof. She touched the spot on the glass over the flag and wished she knew what flag it was. Her fingertips ran lightly, caressingly, down over one side of the house and trailed down across the smooth front lawn. She let her fingers drift down to the lower right hand corner of the frame and then she stopped. She squinted, rubbed at the glass and then squinted again.

'What's this?' she said aloud, and rubbed at the glass again. She was trying to wipe away a smudge, a small dark patch that was just inside the lower right hand of the engraving. A smear of blackness that was only on the corner, less than an eighth of an inch onto the grass. She rubbed again, but the imperfection was not on the ancient glass, but underneath it, on the engraving itself. 'Damn!' she muttered. 'I don't remember you being there last night. Double damn!' She sighed and went into the bathroom and closed the door. As she threw cold water on her face she sighed again. The engraving had been so perfect in her mind, so beautifully done and now there was a flaw in it. 'You've got to stop looking for perfection,' she said to her image in the mirror. 'Nothing in this world is perfect.'

44

CHAPTER THREE

It was Thanksgiving Day, and the Brunos had been invited up to Connecticut to spend the day with one of Bob's old friends. He and Anthony Venutti had done twelve years of Brooklyn public schools together and had then both decided to go to City College for business administration courses. Bob knew he was going into his father's restaurant supply business and Anthony knew he would inherit his father's florist shops. They had made a promise, almost from that first day in the first grade, that because they were both Italian and from the same neighbourhood they would stay friends forever. Amazingly, they had. Bob had made another promise, this one to Anthony's mother, that he would never call Anthony by the nickname 'Tony'. Anthony's parents, trying hard to work up the social ladder, insisted their son always be referred to by his Christian name. 'After all,' Mrs Venutti was heard to say more than once, 'whoever heard of saying a Novena to St Tony?'

Lois had been introduced to Anthony and his wife Anne when she and Bob started going steady. She liked them both right from the start. Anthony was witty, in a dry sort of way, and Anne was dark and bubbly and interested in everything that was happening around her. Anne wasn't really her given name. Her Italian mother had called her Antonia but Anne had changed it very quickly once she started school. The Venuttis had come down for Tony's funeral and had sent a very elaborate floral piece. Lois had said little to them that day, just hugging Anne and holding onto Anthony's hand a little longer than usual. This day, Thanksgiving, was the first time the couples had seen one another since Tony's service.

Lois had been looking forward to it. It would get her out of the city, get her into open fields and houses with front lawns and snowflakes that didn't touch the earth already tinged with soot and pollution. She looked forward to gossiping with Anne and listening to what had been happening to whom. Also she was looking forward to Anne's home-cooked meal. Ever since Tony's disappearance, the food in the Bruno apartment had been frozen-efficient, take-out or pot-luck. Anne was a super cook and Lois remembered the previous Thanksgiving when she had outdone herself cooking not only a US-tasting turkey, but an Italian-tasting rabbit. She wondered what Anne would think up this year.

'I think I'll wear this,' she said to Bob, and he watched her put back the several dresses and suits she had first spread across the bed. She held up the knitted green wool skirt and matching top. 'What do you think? It'll be cold up there and it does look kind of festive.' She didn't wait for his approval but stepped into the skirt and started sliding it up around her waist. 'I haven't worn it since last winter.' She turned to him. 'Are you sure? I mean, it doesn't bulge where it shouldn't?' She opened the closet door and inspected herself in the full-length mirror, smoothing her hands over her hips.

'I don't know why it should bulge,' he replied. 'If anything, you've lost weight since last winter.' In fact his wife had lost several pounds in the last couple of months since the kidnapping. Lois was always complaining about not being able to lose weight but now that she had lost so much in such a dramatic manner she didn't mention it. The Weight Watcher cookbooks and the diet powders in the kitchen went unused. As usual, when something bothered her she didn't talk about it. This was the first time her weight loss had been mentioned.

Lois chose to ignore him. 'I guess it's still okay,' she said. She reached for the top and slid it over her head. She almost hadn't tried it on in the shop but when the clerk told her how fabulous that colour green was against her pale skin and her red hair she had to have it. She knew she looked good in it. She inspected the image in the mirror. 'Yeah,' she said to no one. 'I guess it'll do. Does brighten me up a bit.'

'Are you finished in the bathroom?' Bob asked. 'Because if you are, I'll go in and shave and take my shower.'

'No!' She put up her hand, holding him back. 'I've got to get my nail polish. It's in the cabinet. If I'm going to wear this dress, I can't wear this colour with it.' She held up her hand again, but this time to show him the colour on her fingernails. She hurried from the bedroom and Bob could hear

46

her open and close the bathroom cabinet door. Then there was a pause. A rather long pause.

'Bob,' she called out in a voice that sounded puzzled, unsure. 'Come here a minute.'

Bob, still in his pyjama bottoms, went into the hall.

'Look at this,' she said softly. Her finger pointed to a smear at the bottom edge of the picture.

'What?'

'It's changed.'

'What's changed?'

'That ink blob or whatever it is. Look at it. Doesn't it seem different to you?'

Bob looked at the spot. 'I don't see anything different,' he said. 'Looks the same as it always does.'

'No,' she said, 'no, no. It's changed somehow. It's not the same. It looks like it's grown, or something.'

Bob looked at it again, closer this time. 'I still don't see – '

'No, I'm right. It has. It's different. It's not what it was that first time I saw it.' She didn't look at him, but kept her attention on the small smear of black ink that lay on the white margin under the engraving and slightly onto the lawn itself. 'No, no, no,' she muttered. 'It wasn't that big before. It's larger.'

'How could that be?' he asked. 'Ink doesn't grow.'

'Maybe not, but this thing has.' She wet the tip of her finger and rubbed at it over the glass. 'It's under the glass,' she said with conviction. 'It's something there. Right there, underneath the glass.' She rubbed at it again, as if hoping to erase it without breaking the glass.

'Look, Lois, it's only your . . .' And then Bob stopped. He wasn't going to tell her it was her imagination. What was real and what was imagination had, since Tony's death, become a very sore point. In the beginning, he had accused her of too much imagination and she had lashed out at him, telling him that he was insensitive and unfeeling. There had been a row, and afterwards he was ashamed of himself for provoking her whilst she was under such terrible stress. He started his reply in a different way. 'It's probably the humidity in the apartment. You know how stuffy this place gets when we have the heat on all day. It must have something to do with old ink and old paper and something in the air. That's probably all it is.'

47

'Do you think so?' Her eyes were still on the tiny black blob. She shook her head. 'I don't know. I'm a graphics designer and I use paints and inks all the time, but I never – '

'You never used ink that was a hundred years old before,' Bob interrupted her, 'and used it on paper that was also a hundred years old. And,' he continued, 'had it locked up all those years between glass and wood.'

'Maybe you're right. But it seems awfully strange to me. I never heard of ink doing anything like that, especially after it's dried.'

Bob pushed her gently into the bedroom. 'Now you have to change your nail colour and I have to shave and shower and we have to get this show on the road.' He got her to the bedroom door. 'If you'll excuse me now, I have a date with a razor blade and a bottle of shampoo.'

'I don't know,' she said as she went into the bedroom, 'I didn't think that ink could . . .'

'Sweetheart,' he said, 'how many times have I told you not to think?' He got out of the way just in time to avoid being hit by the pillow she threw at him.

Lois sat back and relaxed on the way up to Connecticut. There was less traffic than on a work day, the mobs of commuters were staying home with their families. The snow which had been falling for the past week had ceased entirely with the dawn and the skies overhead were crispy and blue. The high-ways were clear and dry, for the maintenance crews had been out early. Lois snuggled into her coat and watched the scenery outside change from apartment blocks and store fronts to shopping centres, to open fields and finally to small towns with individual wooden houses and trees in the front yards and cars parked in the driveways and basketball hoops fastened to garages. It felt almost like home. She had phoned her parents that morning to wish them a happy Thanksgiving and she experienced a momentary twinge of envy when her mother told her she and her father were going to have dinner with the Thompsons. Mrs Thompson was almost a grandmother figure to Lois and she thought she could actually see the elderly woman bustling about her big farmhouse kitchen preparing the turkey, peeling the potatoes and testing the seasoning in the gravy. She missed Thanksgiving at home. Christmas too, for that matter. Those had always been special days – family days –

but after she met Bob those days had been spent with him. That was the way it should be, her mother had told her, and she wasn't to feel guilty about not being with her parents. After all, her mother had pointed out, she had a son and a husband and her own home with them. Tony and Bob were her new 'family' and Lois had a duty to spend her holidays with them now.

Tony. Lois wiped the image from her mind as quickly as it had entered it. She would not think about Tony today. Yet it was difficult. He loved gnawing the turkey drumstick and there was a photo of him, somewhere, on his third Thanksgiving with a huge turkey leg in his small hand and his little mouth trying to bite off a chunk of it. No. No thinking about Tony today. If Tony was still alive she hoped whoever had him would give him a drumstick. If. The newness of the word startled her for a second. She had thought 'if Tony'. It was the first time she had started to accept the possibility that he was really dead. 'If Tony . . .' That's something I'm going to have to resolve, she said to herself. The doubts would have to go, would have to be replaced by reality. Bob had been right when he told her she relied too much on her imagination. She had yelled at him and had started crying, but now she understood that he had been right. She had to get used to living in the real world again. A real world where it was entirely possible that Tony would never appear again. A real world without her Tony. A real world where her small son would only be a memory.

*   *   *

'Swedish meatballs, chop suey and flour tortillas,' Anne said with an impish grin. 'And that's only the first course. Wait till you see what kind of meat will be on the platter!' She took Lois' coat and then gave her another hug.

'You are joking, I hope,' Bob said. 'I'm allergic to Swedish meatballs.'

'Tough.' Anne replied. 'You no lika the meatballs you no getta the bird.'

'Darling!' Anthony laughed. 'That's a terrible imitation of Chico Marx!'

'That wasn't Chico I was doing, sweetheart, I was doing your mother.' Anne pushed her dark hair out of her face and laughed delightedly.

'She really loves my mother,' Anthony said quickly. 'They're really very good friends.'

'Sure I love your mother. I'd love to see her come out of that oven in there with an apple in her mouth.'

'She'd have to be basted in tomato sauce,' Anthony replied seriously. 'Apples aren't mama's style.'

'They're *acid* enough.' Anne smiled sweetly at her husband.

Lois reacted as they had hoped. 'But you and Mrs Venutti have always been close,' she protested.

'Don't mind us,' Anne said, 'it's just a family joke. Actually, I invited both mom and pop Venutti to dinner today.'

'She gave the invitation with her fingers crossed,' Anthony added.

'It worked, though. You don't see her over here telling me how much oregano to add to the Jello, do you?'

Bob grimaced. 'Oregano in Jello? Lois, are you sure you want to have dinner in this place?'

'Just pick the bits of oregano out of the Jello,' Anthony replied straight-faced. 'It's the slivers of chicken bone in the Waldorf Salad that you've got to be careful of.'

'Another minute of this,' Bob said loudly, 'and I'll take my bride back to that MacDonald's we passed near the freeway.'

'Take me with you,' said Anthony. 'I've peeked into Anne's kitchen. I know what's coming.'

'What *really* is coming now,' said Anne, 'is a punch bowl.' She guided them into the living room and they found comfortable places on chairs and the sofa. Anne had placed a large silver punch bowl in the centre of the coffee table. Next to it, nestling in a bowl of crushed ice were four crystal goblets. 'I thought champagne punch would be appropriate for today. Anybody mind? No? Good! Now let's settle down to some serious celebrating.'

Lois sipped her drink slowly, letting the tart, icy, still-bubbling liquid tickle all the way down. 'Superb, Anne,' she said.

'Really great,' Bob chimed in.

'And that's just for openers,' Anthony said. 'You haven't seen what's on the dining room table yet.'

'And they're not going to until we finish this punch,' Anne said. 'Come on, empty your glasses. Let's do the refills. This stuff won't keep in my Tupperware jug.' She gathered the glasses as they drained them and quickly handed them back, brimming and sparkling.

The conversation began with what Bob's business had been doing and then shifted, naturally, to Anthony's florist shops and the problems of getting cut flowers in the wintertime. Then Anne asked Lois about a mutual friend who was a professional actor and the talk turned to the latest Broadway shows, who had seen what or hadn't seen what and wished they had, and then to recent television programmes and the political problems in Washington. Somehow, in all that, the topic of art and illustration arose.

'Tell them about the engraving,' Bob said to Lois. 'The one Midge gave us.'

'Oh, yes!' Lois' eyes lit up as she thought about the print. 'Well, there's this woman at my office. Her name is Midge and she's a real character. She's always doing crazy things and I love her to death for it, and a few days ago she showed up at our place with this package under her arm.'

'Wrapped in brown paper,' Bob added. 'I mean here it was almost eleven p.m. and this dingy female has just come from an auction over in Jersey and she had this engraving for us.'

'Actually she didn't buy it for us,' Lois interjected. 'She had been bidding on another print and didn't know there were two items in the lot number. Anyway,' she grinned, 'her attention was not really on the auctioneer but on some hunk in tight jeans standing next to her. So she bid, overbid probably if I know Midge, and got two for the price of one.'

'Two hunks?' Anne asked grinning.

'Two works of art,' Lois smiled. 'I don't know whether Midge could have afforded the hunk or not. Anyway, she decided that the print she didn't want . . .'

'Didn't even know about . . .' Bob added.

'Didn't even know about,' Lois repeated, 'would be perfect for us. So she gave it to us and it's on our hallway wall and I love it!'

'What's it a print of?' Anthony asked.

'An old house somewhere,' Lois said, 'an old manor house from the looks of it. It's really quite a wonderful place. Two floors with windows running out along each floor. And there's a door with lots of carved wood around it and a balcony on the next floor over the door. And a big front lawn. I'll bet one quarter of the actual engraving is that big front lawn.

51

And some trees,' she added, seeing the print in her mind's eye. 'There's a small gnarled tree on one side of the house and a whole grove of trees on the other. The print is old. Bob and I don't have any idea how old, but the glass is that ancient kind with imperfections and tiny bubbles in it. And it was framed ages ago. With linen strips glued to the back. I think it's terrific. It looks just great in the hallway!' She looked at Bob for confirmation and he nodded and smiled at her.

'Sounds fantastic,' Anthony said. 'But why did your friend give it to you? I mean, from your description, it must be worth a bit of dough.'

Lois shrugged her shoulders. 'Midge is like that. She's so generous and good hearted that you don't ask her *why* she does things, you just accept them and say thank you.'

'Anyway, she's running out of wall space,' Bob put in. 'She had trouble hanging the picture she really wanted: some Victorian thing with a girl and a couple of cats.'

'Sounds like you got the better deal,' Anne said.

'I think so, too,' Bob said.

'Where was this engraving made?' Anthony asked. 'Does it say who designed it and where it was printed?'

'That's the funny thing,' Lois answered him. 'Every engraving I've ever seen had all that right there in the white margin under the picture, but this margin is blank. No artist and no publisher.' She took another sip of the champagne. 'There's just one word engraved there. "Corra". That's all it says.'

'Corra?' Anthony rolled the word around on his tongue for a moment. 'Sounds Italian to me.'

'*Everything* sounds Italian to you.' Anne made a face at him.

'But it does,' he insisted. 'I think there is a town in Italy called Corra. I'm almost sure of it. The word "corre" is Italian for "catch".'

'Not the same thing,' Lois said. 'This place doesn't *look* Italian.'

'You mean there's no Parma ham hanging in the windows?' Anne said.

'Nothing in the windows,' Bob said. 'Not even curtains. The artist left them blank.'

'I once heard of a ski resort in Yugoslavia called Corra.' Anthony was still trying to get the taste of the word. 'At least I think it was Yugoslavia.'

52

'Sounds like Switzerland to me,' Anne got up from her chair and started towards the kitchen. 'I gotta go in there and rattle some pans. You people finish that punch and then wait till you hear the gong . . . Anyway Lois – ' She stopped and turned back. 'You don't even know what "Corra" stands for. It could be the name of the house itself, rather than a *place*. Maybe the people who owned it were named "Corra".'

Anthony dipped the ladle into the punch bowl. 'Or maybe what you have is a rare early advertisement from the Corra-Cola Bottling Company. You know, the pause that refreshes.'

'On *that*,' Anne held her nose, 'I'm *hiding* in the kitchen. You people eat by yourselves. I don't want anybody to know that I'm married to someone who could stoop so low! Corra-Cola indeed!' She vanished behind the swinging kitchen door.

Lois grinned but continued the conversation. 'I don't think the engraving is European. I mean not mid-Europe like Italy or Germany. I think it's probably English. It *feels* English.'

'Corra?' said Anthony. 'That doesn't sound English to me. A couple of Rs and ending in A? No, if it was English it should end in "ton" or "wich". It should be Corra-upon-Avon or something like that.'

Lois shook her head. 'I know it should sound more English than it does, but I just *feel* that's where it came from.'

'Looks like you have a mystery on your hands. I'd say a visit to a good reference library is definitely in order.'

'I agree,' Bob said. 'Go somewhere and look it up and get the question settled once and for all.'

'And if it turns out that it's *not* Italian – ' Lois reached over and kissed her husband on the cheek – 'can we keep it anyway?'

'In that case,' Bob grinned, 'maybe in the bathroom.'

Lois punched him playfully on the arm and hoped, secretly in her heart of hearts, that the engraving was not Italian. She wanted it to be English and she didn't know why.

When Anne had reappeared from the kitchen and shouted 'Gong!' they went into the dining room. Anne had outdone herself again. Instead of a turkey she had managed to buy – and beautifully cook – a wild pheasant and a small suckling pig. There were mashed potatoes and candied yams and lima beans in some sort of cheese sauce, and baby carrots and leeks dripping in butter, cranberry sauce and two kinds of gravy, a small salad on a side plate, homemade whole wheat rolls and red wine, or white, and rhubarb or pumpkin pie and rich black coffee with fresh thick cream.

Bob and Anthony managed to push themselves away from the table after double helpings of almost everything. The four of them had drunk five bottles of wine and the men almost crawled to the comfort of the living room sofa and easy chairs. Lois helped Anne clear the table, scrape the dishes and stack them in the dishwasher. While the machine churned away they put the leftovers (and there weren't that many of them) in the refrigerator.

When they came out of the kitchen, the men were setting up a game of Trivial Pursuit.

'Oh, no,' Lois said. 'I hate that game! I never know any of the answers.'

'Anthony's been up all night memorizing the answer cards,' Anne said. 'I don't blame you if you don't want to play.'

Lois yawned. 'It's just that I've still got all that food in my stomach. All the blood that should be in my brain is down there working on the Thanksgiving meal.'

'Look, hon,' Bob said as he saw her yawn again. 'It's been a long day and we've still got a long drive back to the city. Why don't you lie down for a while?'

'I can't do that,' Lois protested.

'Why not?' Bob asked. 'Go on into the guest room. Take a nap. It'll do you good.'

'I didn't come up here to sleep,' she said to Anne. 'I came to see you.'

'Well, you've seen me,' Anne replied. 'Now go and lie down. Do what your husband tells you. I obey Anthony all the time.'

'Oh sure!' Anthony laughed.

Lois hesitated. She really didn't want to play that silly game and was feeling drowsy.

'Go on,' Bob said. 'Just close your eyes for an hour or so. We won't miss you.'

'Well, thanks a lot. But okay. I know when I'm not wanted.'

'You got it,' Anne said. 'Look, the guest room is right down the hall. You know where it is. Just flop out on the bed and let the food digest by itself.'

Lois caught herself stifling yet another yawn. 'Maybe I will, but I won't be long. You'll only have an hour or so to talk about me while my back is turned.'

54

'That'll be plenty of time to dish the dirt on you,' Anne said, smiling. 'Anyway Anthony is going to win the game with or without you. He cheats, you know.'

'Are you sure?' Lois could feel another yawn coming on.

'Out!' Bob pointed towards the hallway.

'Okay,' Lois kissed Anne on her cheek. 'Bob cheats at this game too. Let me know how it all comes out.' She walked across the room and turned down the corridor to the bedrooms. She knew which one was the guest room for she and Bob had spent several weekends with the Venuttis over the past years.

The room contained a large double bed covered with a white chenille spread that had a large red rose woven into its centre. There was a small table beside the bed with a lamp and a telephone on it. The patio doors were hidden by white and red draperies. In the summer Anne kept the doors open and houseguests could sit outside and soak up the wonderful Connecticut air, but now that it was winter the sliding glass doors were locked and the curtains drawn. Lois debated whether to take off her clothes or not, decided to keep them on, kicked off her shoes and stretched out on the bed. She stared at the soft pattern of the ceiling paper and smiled as she thought of her husband and her two good friends playing their silly adult game. It was good to be out of their apartment, good to be out of Manhattan, even if only for one day. It was good for Bob to get away too, she told herself. She started thinking about something else but the thought didn't continue, for in less time than she would have imagined she drifted into a deep sleep.

In the living room, the dice were thrown, the questions answered, the little coloured markers moved along the board.

'She seems okay now,' Anthony said. 'That haggard look she had at the funeral is gone. She looks rested.'

'She is,' Bob said. 'Going back to work helped a helluva lot. For a few days I was afraid she was hitting the booze bottle a little too hard, but even that stopped when she decided to get back into reality.'

'Does she ever mention him?' Anne asked.

'Tony? You know how she is. She doesn't like talking about things that are so personal. Once the service was over, she's hardly brought up his name at all.'

'Didn't you tell me,' Anthony asked, 'that at first she didn't believe Tony was really dead? That there was another boy in that coffin?'

'Yeah, I did,' Bob replied, 'but that idea seems to be gone too.'

'I can understand it.' Anne threw the dice and Anthony reached for a question card. 'If I had a child and he suddenly vanished the way yours did, I wouldn't want to believe the worst. I would hold out for a happy ending.'

'But I saw the body in the morgue,' Bob said, knowing full well they knew he had identified his son in that awful place. 'I know what I saw. It wasn't pretty and I'll never forget it, but I saw him. He was there and he was dead. One of the most difficult things I've ever done was to go out of that room and tell Lois that it was really Tony in there.'

Anne reached across the table and put her hand atop Bob's. 'We felt so sorry when we heard about it,' she said. 'We wanted to be able to do something, but there was nothing we could do. Friends feel so . . . so helpless at a time like that. We wanted to press a magic button or wave a wizard's wand and bring Tony back to life, but there wasn't a thing we could do to help.'

'Just being there was enough help,' Bob replied. 'Inviting us to dinner today has been a big help. You really don't know how much Lois needed today. There are times when I still see tiny cracks on her surface. Like with that picture her friend Midge gave us.'

'With the picture? What do you mean?' Anthony was about to throw the dice, but he stopped.

'Well,' Bob said and lowered his voice, 'I wasn't going to mention it to either of you but there is some sort of flaw in the engraving, some bit of ink blob in one of the corners and Lois is sure it has changed since we got the damned thing.'

'Changed?'

'Grown. She is sure the blob has grown.'

'Ink doesn't grow,' Anne said.

'I know,' Bob replied. 'But she thinks it has. What can I do?'

'Maybe it's some kind of fungus,' Anne suggested.

'A fungus? Alive and growing after all these years of being imprisoned in a glass and wood frame?' Bob shook his head. 'No. I wish it were something as simple as a fungus. I could deal with a fungus. What I can't deal with is Lois' strange quirks of mind.' He turned to Anne. 'Is there any more of that wine left? I could sure use a glass of it right now.'

Anne pushed back her chair and got up. 'I'll get you some. Anthony?' He nodded. 'Okay, I'll get both of you some. Look Bob, don't you get too upset with Lois about this engraving thing. It just might be a therapeutic way of letting off her emotion, her grief, over Tony's death. You know, not talking about Tony but finding something else to get upset about.'

'Sounds like first-year psychology to me,' Anthony said.

'It may be,' Anne replied, 'but if she refuses to accept Tony's death she could very easily find something else to worry about.'

'An ink blob in an old picture?' her husband said, doubting her analysis.

'Sure. Why not? Tony was the perfect little boy and now he's gone. Someone gives Lois the perfect engraving and she discovers a flaw in it. She'll complain about the picture when she won't talk about her son. She'll use that ink blot as a way of mourning over her lost child.'

'You've lost me on this one,' Anthony said.

'She's wound up,' Anne insisted. 'She's as tight as a two-dollar watch spring and nowhere to release her tensions. If she'd talk about Tony, which she won't, it'd be better. Instead she sees flaws in ordinary things and can't see the flaws in her own reality.' She turned to Bob. 'Am I making any sense to you?'

'Yes,' he said softly, 'you are. She *is* like a watch spring and I keep wondering when it is going to snap and spin out of control.'

Anthony rattled the dice in the cup. 'When I heard that Tony had been kidnapped, I was crushed. After all, I loved that kid too. You named him after me. You could call *him* Tony. My mother didn't make you promise not to. You two are blowing Lois' reactions out of proportion. Bob, it's natural you're concerned and Anne, you don't help things with your twenty-five cents' worth of amateur psychology. Lois has gone through a terrible time in her life, a really shitty time, but I know she's strong enough to come out of it on her own. She's an intelligent, educated and creative woman. She'll make it. Bob, don't go down the wrong trail with her, don't start thinking maybe she's going nuts. Remember where she's been in the past couple months and you'll see that she's made

57

incredible progress. If she wants to see an ink stain move, let her. She needs it and it doesn't mean she's flipping out.' He shook the dice cup again. 'Now, woman, are you going to get some wine and, man, are you going to relax and play this game?'

* * *

Lois stirred uneasily in her sleep. The rich food and the wine were playing tricks on her subconscious and there had been a series of short and upsetting dreams since she had fallen asleep. In one, she had been driving a large black car and it had stalled in the middle of nowhere and she had been forced to get out and try to find her way back through fields surrounded by high mountains. In another, she stood helplessly by and watched some men throw a girl down into a deep well. In another brief fragment, she was standing in front of her engraving when it exploded and burst into flames. She tried to put out the fire by throwing herself against it but she caught fire too. She had awoken, momentarily, after that one and glanced around the room. She recognized where she was and fell immediately back into sleep.

This dream was the worst one. She had gone somewhere with Tony, into a department store it looked like, and he had wanted to see the toys. She had told him they would find toys later. The boy had insisted, and while Lois stopped at a counter to admire some scarves Tony had run away from her. She began asking clerks and shoppers where the toy department was but nobody could tell her. She ran down aisles crowded with merchandise, then tried to get on an escalator that was going the wrong direction. She started calling his name. Then he started calling for her. She could hear his voice: 'Mommy! Mommy!' It seemed to be coming from an open elevator shaft. She ran to the edge and looked down. There, at the bottom of the pit, was her son. 'Mommy!' he called to her. 'Please, Mommy!' She pressed herself flat against the floor and tried to stretch her arm so it would reach to the bottom of the shaft. Her arm got longer and longer but the pit got deeper and deeper. 'I'm coming, baby!' she called to him and he answered. 'Mommy! Here I am, Mommy! Please, Mommy!'

She sat upright, suddenly, as if she was hinged at the waist.

58

She was wide awake now and the perspiration was rolling down her forehead. Eyes wide she stared around the room trying to locate where she was, trying to erase the image of the pit and her little boy at the bottom of it. And his voice. It had been so vivid. His little voice calling out for her. She put her hands over her eyes and tried to regulate her short stabbing intakes of breath. She was shaking and her legs were jerking in tiny spasms.

'Mommy!'

The voice came again. Lois stopped breathing.

'Mommy! Please, Mommy!'

Lois twisted her head in the direction of the voice. She wasn't dreaming now. She was awake and she was aware she was awake.

'Please, Mommy! Over here!'

The voice was coming from behind the curtains that led out onto the patio. A shock of electricity shot through her body and she felt herself swing her legs over the side of the bed. She felt her feet touch the carpeted floor.

'Mommy! Mommy!'

She ran to the heavy curtains and tried to push them back but they wouldn't budge. Then she fumbled for the pulls that she knew must be at the edge of the drapes. She grabbed the rope and yanked hard. The curtains quickly opened and the room was filled with early evening light.

And there was Tony. There was her son.

'Tony!' she whispered. 'My God, Tony!' She pulled at the door handles but they didn't move. 'My baby!' she shouted through her sudden flood of tears. 'My baby! I'm coming! My baby!' Again she pulled at the door handles but the glass panels refused to slide open.

Tony pressed his face against the clear door. He was crying too. His face was streaked with tears and they were washing away the dirt and grime that marred his skin. He was wearing the blue trousers and the woollen jacket she had dressed him in the day she had sent him off to school. His eyes pleaded with her. 'Let me in, Mommy! Let me in!'

She tried yanking on the doors again but they still didn't open. 'She must have these things locked! She's locked them, baby!' Lois shouted. 'Don't worry! Mommy's here!'

She staggered backward into the bedroom, searching frantically for something to smash the glass doors. The

59

telephone. She pulled it loose from its outlet and ran back to the doors. Tony was still there, sobbing and begging to be let into the house. Lois banged at the door with the telephone. Its bell jangled in protest but the glass didn't break. 'I'm coming, baby!' she shouted at Tony again. Then she backed up a few paces, took aim and threw the phone as hard as she could against the glass. There was a shattering sound and then somewhere an alarm went off. Lois tried reaching Tony through the hole she had created in the door. Her arm wouldn't reach. He was right there but her arm just wouldn't reach. 'Tony! My baby! Mommy's here, my darling. Mommy's here!' She shoved harder trying to break more of the glass with the force of her shoulder. The glass wouldn't crack, wouldn't break off any more.

'What the hell's going on in here?' Anthony stood at the entrance to the bedroom, Bob and Anne right behind him. 'We heard the burglar alarm, what's wrong?'

Lois turned hurriedly to face them, her arm still in the hole in the door. 'It's Tony!' she cried. 'Tony's out there. Open these goddamn doors, my baby's out there!'

The three ran to where she was standing and looked out. Tony wasn't there. There was nobody out there.

Lois stared out into the nothingness in panic. 'He was there!' she screamed at them. 'Tony was out there! He called me and I woke up and there he was and he was dressed in his wool jacket and he wanted to come in.' She stared at them. 'Do something!' She yanked her arm out of the jagged hole and they could all see the blood that was running down her arm and the places where her green woollen top had been unravelled by the shards of broken glass. 'Anne! For Christ's sake don't just stand there! Unlock these damn doors! I've got to get Tony!'

'He's not out there,' Bob said and grabbed Lois by the shoulders. 'He's not out there!'

'I saw him!' She sobbed and tried to wrench out of his grasp. 'I saw him! He was crying and calling my name! Bob, let me go! I've got to get these damn doors open! I've got to get my baby!'

Anne glanced at Bob, then at her own husband and went and undid the latch that held the doors. She slid one wide open. The cold Thanksgiving Day air rolled into the heated bedroom.

Lois tried to run but Bob steered her carefully out onto

the patio. With sharp hawk-like movements she peered into the emptiness of the back yard, searched the darkening garden shadows for signs of her son. Her eyes darted back and forth, under trees and around shrubs but he wasn't there. Because of the overhanging roof, there was no snow on the patio, no snow to hold Tony's footprints. Beyond the edge of concrete, short bushes grew closely together, blocking out of view any prints that might have been in the yard near the driveway.

'If I could have got those doors open,' she said in a softer tone. 'If those damned doors hadn't been locked.'

'Tony wasn't there,' Bob said tenderly. 'You dreamt it.'

'His little face was dirty, Bob, and he was crying. He said he wanted to come in and I tried to open the doors but they were locked, and even when I smashed one of them I still couldn't . . .'

She stopped and looked down at her arm. Blood had seeped through the wool of her sleeve and was dripping onto the patio.

'We'll have to take a look at those cuts,' Anne said. 'Get her into the bathroom, Bob.'

'He was crying, Bob, and he looked so cold and dirty and his little hands were making motions at me, wanting me to open those doors and let him come into the house. But I couldn't get the doors open fast enough . . . If I had opened those doors our baby would have been back with us. But I couldn't open them, Bob. I tried and tried but they were locked.' Bob turned her around slowly and started walking her back into the bedroom and over to the guest bathroom. 'The doors were locked. I didn't know how to open them.' She was mumbling now, going into shock. 'He was so dirty, Bob. His little face and hands were so dirty. He said "Mommy" and "please" and he wanted to come in.' Her voice began to slur as Bob and Anthony together steered her onto the closed toilet seat beside the washbasin and Bob knelt beside her. 'He still had on his warm jacket. I'm glad I bought him that jacket, Bob. You remember when we bought him that jacket? Do you, Bob? Do you?' Her voice was even more slurred. 'He said "mommy". He did, Bob. He said "mommy", he really did.'

Anne took a pair of scissors and cut upwards into the sleeve of Lois' woollen top. 'It's ruined anyway,' she said.

She pulled back the cloth and looked at Lois' wounds. 'She was lucky. The material was thick enough to catch most of the glass splinters. The cuts aren't deep.' She bathed the injured arm in warm water and then patted it dry with a clean towel.

Lois' head lolled on Bob's chest. 'What's the matter?' she asked through thick lips. 'Something the matter?'

Anne started out of the room. 'I've got some stuff in my bathroom to put on these cuts. You guys keep holding her.'

Anthony glanced at Bob. 'What do you think she saw out there?'

Bob shrugged. 'Don't know. Probably nothing. It was probably the tail end of a dream.'

'A nightmare, you mean,' Anthony replied.

'Let me know how much it costs to replace that door and I'll send you a cheque,' Bob said.

Anthony made a face. 'Don't worry about it. It's covered by insurance. What do you think made her do it?' he asked. 'You know it takes a helluva lot of force to break one of those doors. They're supposed to be unbreakable. Burglar proof. How did she manage it?'

Anne came back into the bathroom, a small basket of medical things in her hand. 'A mother's emotion is a powerful thing. When a mother sees her child in danger she can call upon some hidden strength and make miracles.' She began to rub Lois' arm with antiseptic ointment and put a Band Aid on one cut that was still bleeding. 'I read about a woman just recently who saw her young son covered up by a pile of concrete sewer pipes. He had been playing on them and they started to slide. She ran over to him, picked up those pipes as if they were made of cardboard and yanked her kid to safety. Afterwards, when they told her each pipe weighed over five hundred pounds, she couldn't pick one up no matter how she tried.'

'His face was dirty, Bob,' Lois muttered from somewhere far inside herself.

'A mother has a helluva lot of strength,' Anne continued. 'It's easy to see how Lois could have broken that door. It's a strength that comes suddenly and then dissipates as soon as the child is safe. That's probably what's hit Lois now, that sudden let-down off that energy high. She'll be all right,

she's just going to need a lot of love and understanding.'
She looked at Bob. 'From you!'

'She'll get it,' he said. 'I promise.'

*   *   *

The drive back to Manhattan was made almost in silence. Lois
had had some hot tea laced with brandy and had come out
of her shock as she sat with Anne's arms around her and
wearing one of Anne's old sweaters. No one had asked if she
felt better. No one had wanted to bring back a flood of
memories. Lois didn't mention seeing Tony to any of them.
Her eyes were still slightly glazed by the time Bob bundled
her into her heavy coat and helped her into the car.

Back in the apartment, Lois went into the bathroom and
took a shower. She inspected the deep scratches on her right
arm and was glad the woollen top had been as thick as it was.
She glanced at the matching skirt that lay in a heap on the
floor. The top was ruined and she knew she would never wear
the skirt again. She could never wear it without it bringing
back images of Tony's tear-streaked face. She kicked at the
crumpled outfit, hoping to kick away the memory. She carefully dried her right arm and, following Anne's instructions,
rubbed a new application of ointment into the scratches. She
looked at herself in the mirror over the washbasin. Her face
without make-up and her hair pinned up haphazardly looked
terribly old. Suddenly. She bent closer to the reflection, as
she lifted the skin under one eye, trying to smooth out the
wrinkles she saw there. She wasn't going to talk about
what happened to Bob again. He would say it was all her
imagination. Her lack of reality. Her losing her grip. Whatever. She wouldn't tell Midge about it, either. Some things
are better kept from others, even best friends. Midge wouldn't
think she was going crazy but she would think it strange, and
Lois didn't want people thinking she was strange. Strange was
for the bag ladies that went through garbage cans on New
York streets. Strange was for sideshow freaks; the lady with
the beard, the man with the crocodile skin. Those kind of
people. Strange was for psychics and mediums who claimed
they could see into the beyond, could communicate with the
dead. Yet, she had done that this afternoon. *If* Tony was really
dead as all the world insisted on believing, then she had

communicated with the dead. She had made contact with someone who was no longer in body but only in spirit. But Tony is not dead! the thought raced through her mind. She picked out the clips that held her long red hair in the shower and she ran her hands through her locks several times, letting her hair fall down around her shoulders, letting it fall free and alive. That's the key word. Tony is *alive*. Maybe that wasn't Tony in the flesh that she saw, maybe she had seen some sort of paranormal image of her little boy. Maybe he had astral-projected to where she was. It could happen. She had read about things like that. Maybe Tony had made an out-of-body trip to see her, to assure her that he was still alive. That would be a perfectly plausible explanation as to why when the doors were finally opened he wasn't there at all. Of course – she smiled at her reflection in the mirror – that's what it was. That's what I saw. It makes perfect sense when you understand it! When I tell Bob, then he'll understand and see that . . . She shook her head and the mass of red hair flowed around her face. Bob won't understand anything of the kind. He won't see the reality of it. *Her* reality of it. He won't want to see. That's fine. Then she'd keep her explanation to herself. If Bob ever grew more spiritual, then he would understand. But not yet. He's not ready yet. She ran her hands through her hair again and stared at the attractive young woman who stared back at her.

'He won't understand,' she said aloud to her reflection. 'But I know what I saw. I saw Tony. And Tony is alive.'

She picked up the wool skirt and opened the bathroom door. She went into the kitchen and tossed the skirt into the garbage bag beside the sink. Then she went back down the hallway towards the bedroom.

She stopped. She stared at the engraving. At the place where the ink blob had been. 'Had been.' She heard herself repeat her thought aloud. She stared again then called loudly, 'Bob! Bob, come here. Quickly!'

Bob ran from the bedroom to where she was standing. 'Now what?' he asked.

'That ink spot. It's moved! It's not where it was before!'

Bob looked at the spot and then back into his wife's face. 'I don't see any – '

'It has!' she insisted. 'It's moved! It used to be partially in the white margin but now it's managed to get completely onto the lawn. There – ' She pointed at the blob of dark ink. 'Don't you see it? Can't you see that it's changed?'

He looked at the engraving and then back at her. 'Lois, I can't see any difference from where it's ever been. Look, hon – ' He put his arm around her bare shoulders – 'this has been a tough day. A very trying day for you. You must be tired. I know I am. Let's get to bed. Let's discuss this in the morning. Okay?' He tried to steer her away from the picture, lead her in the direction of the bedroom.

'You don't see it?' Her voice rose as she looked from him back to the picture and then back to him. 'You don't see that it's *moved*?'

'I don't,' he said softly, 'I really don't.' He reached out for her and he folded her into his arms. 'It's been a long day,' he said.

Lois had tears in her eyes. 'What's happening to me?' she managed to say. 'What's wrong?' She was sobbing now. 'Am I losing my mind? Bob, what's *wrong* with me?'

CHAPTER FOUR

There were five of them around the table, that large highly polished dining room table that could seat two dozen guests when it was fully extended, and they waited for four others to arrive.

The enormous room had, at one time, been very elegant. It had a high-vaulted ceiling with three crystal chandeliers hanging from it. There were still bits and pieces of burnt candles in the holders of the chandeliers, as if the house had never been wired for electricity. But of course it had been, they just preferred the softer more uncritical glow of candlelight.

The large walls were decorated with oil paintings of men in heavy ermine-collared coats and women with long gowns and masses of curls. There were painted views of green valleys, of sailing ships floundering on high seas and others of girls with baskets of fruit and flowers. Most of these paintings needed cleaning, for years of dust and candle smoke had covered their sheen. The paintings hung at odd angles, as if over the years they had tilted on their own, out of boredom, and nobody had cared enough to straighten them again.

There were four large windows in this room. Windows that went almost from floor to ceiling but they were covered with thick dark green velvet drapes that shut out all light, even from the sun on a bright summer's day. The drapes had been closed years ago, blocking out the view of the wide, sloping front lawn but, more importantly, blocking out the view inside the house to any nosy neighbour or stranger who was brave enough to get that close to the windows. There was no smell of dust or closeness in the room because of the mound of jasmine incense burning from the golden lily-pad censer on the table.

The five at the table nodded when the door opened and three others came in.

'Where's Mountolive?' asked the oldest-looking man, the one with the white hair.

'He can't make it. Something came up at his shop.' This from the youngest person in the group, a moderately tall man with a thin body and a shock of thick hair. 'I'm to tell him what's been discussed,' he added.

'I suppose that'll have to do,' the white-haired man said.

'So there's only eight of us tonight. I'll tell cook,' this from a rather plump woman with streaks of grey in her dark hair. She was one of those people whose age is difficult to guess. She moved with the agility of a girl of twenty, yet some of the lines around her face showed she was really in her mid-fifties. She bustled importantly from the room.

The new arrivals took their places around the large table. They had left their heavy coats and scarves and gloves in the entrance foyer and were now wearing woollen sweaters, tweed jackets, woollen skirts and sensible walking shoes. They, too, were of indeterminate ages: anywhere from their early fifties to their late sixties. In the light of the three white candles in their individual holders on the table, it was difficult to see their features, difficult to make out lines and creases hidden in shadows. On the table, as well as the incense burner and the three candles, there was a well-thumbed book. On its black covers it had an odd symbol of triangles and tiny circles and a single flower embossed on it in gold. Much of the gilding had been rubbed off from the many years of use the book had seen. Also on the table was a single rose. A single rose on a stem with two leaves, and it was made of gold. It caught the flickerings of the candle flames and held them momentarily until they were tossed back into the darkness. Next to the gold rose, on a square of black velvet, lay a heavy triangular object of metal and enamel with silver inlay. There was only one design, in the exact centre: a single human eye, open with an iris of blue lapis and crushed diamonds. The eye didn't move, didn't blink, yet gave the impression that it was seeing and understanding everything that was happening in the room.

The lady who had left the room to talk with the cook now returned with a large silver tray. There was a silver tea service on it and a plate piled high with sweet pastries, muffins and flat oat cakes. There was also a silver creamer and a covered sugar bowl. Another woman, shorter and fatter than the first, followed right behind her with a tray of her own, this one with china cups, plates, silver knives and spoons and neatly folded linen napkins. The two trays were placed in the centre of the table and the cook left the room. The first woman took her seat with the others. No one spoke as each person reached for a cup, ate some food and sipped the warming tea.

The white-haired man broke the silence. 'I heard from New York today. The girl thought she saw her child last Thursday.'

'Thought she saw him?' One of the men stopped sipping his tea and stared. 'What do you mean *saw*?'

'She thought she saw him,' the first man replied. 'What other words can I use? She was visiting some friends for the American holiday and the child appeared at a glass door. She thought she saw the child.'

'Oh,' one of the women said. 'What did she do?'

'Tried to get him, of course,' the white-haired man replied.

'But she didn't?' another woman's voice rose questioningly.

'Of course not. But she's seen him now. She's sure he's alive.'

'That's good.' Another man spoke for the first time. 'So it's been worth the money we paid.'

'Aye,' the white-haired man who was obviously leading the group said. 'We paid and he delivered.'

'Surely we must all hope now that she's the right one,' a woman with what sounded like a French accent said. 'We've put her through a great deal if she's not the right one.'

'She will be,' the leader said. 'I'm positive of it. But there is still that one more test to give.' He looked at the youngest man at the table. 'Have you put everything in order for the voyage?'

The young man nodded. 'Tickets both ways purchased, and I have the telephone number of our contact when I get there.'

'Who have you told?' someone in the shadows inquired.

'Nobody, of course!' The young man's tone was defensive. 'Nobody at all. You know I wouldn't.'

The man in the shadows was not satisfied with the answer. 'Have you told Fiona? Does she know you're about to make the journey?'

'I just told you, I've informed no one. Especially not Fiona.'

'The final verification must be done quickly,' the French-sounding lady said.

'We still have time,' a man put in. 'We've taken this long, I don't see the need to rush things.'

The woman who had brought the tea things spoke up. 'He's already started to move. He's started up the lawn.'

'Oh,' the man sighed. 'I didn't know that. Then we must be quick about it.'

'Is it time for him to move up the lawn already?' a woman asked.

'Right on schedule,' said the white-haired man. 'Things have started into motion at last.'

'I will try to get across and be back within a week,' the young man with the red hair said. 'The analysis will be made before I get on the plane.'

'Our man over there will do it himself?'

'Not himself but he knows somebody who will do it. Someone he says he trusts.'

'I'll have to get the house ready,' the first woman said. 'Air it out and do up their rooms.' She looked around her in the gloom. 'And put this place to rights as well. It's been years since it's seen the daylight.'

'And the wee one,' a man asked. 'What about him?'

'He'll be on his way here in a fortnight.' The leader smiled and reached for another pastry. 'It's quite ingenious how they're getting him here. Completely without knowledge of the authorities.'

'His room is in order?'

'It's been ready and waiting for him for weeks now,' said the first woman. 'It'll suit him well, I assure you.'

'Then everything depends on the analysis?' a woman asked.

'On that,' said the white-haired man, 'and on getting her over here. New York assures me there will be no problem.'

'There's enough money offered,' the French lady chuckled. 'For that amount we can be sure the merchandise will be safely delivered.'

The first woman got up and started collecting the tea things and piling them onto the trays. It was the signal for the rest of them to rise as well. 'Frankly,' she said, 'I'm glad the time is approaching. We've planned it and planned it for so long that I was afraid the day would never come.'

'Aye,' said one of the men, 'we've waited a lifetime, it seems.'

The Frenchwoman went up to the young man. 'You're sure you haven't told Fiona about all this?'

He wanted to get angry but he knew the consequences of defiance to this group. 'I've told you all, more than once, that she doesn't have an inkling.'

'Fiona's mouth moves faster than her brain,' a man said. 'Sometimes her chin appears to be double-hinged.'

'Don't concern yourselves with her,' the young man said firmly. 'She's no threat.'

'I wouldn't want to have to uncover the old well,' the white-haired man said, looking straight into the young man's eyes.

The young man stepped backward, unconsciously and fearfully. 'Don't worry. I'll do the job exactly the way I promised.'

'Grand!' the first woman said. 'Then we can get on with all the rest of it.'

'Aye,' a man added. 'The Plan shall, at long last, be realized.'

'Aye,' a woman spoke up, 'and don't you know how all this would have pleased father.'

CHAPTER FIVE

Lois didn't mention seeing Tony after that. She kept her promise to herself. She was not going to bring it up so Bob could tell her it was only imagination. Nor did she tell Midge about it. The woman had asked her, on the following work day, how her Thanksgiving had been and Lois had merely smiled and started telling of the fantastic table Anne had set. Midge had asked her if she felt rested from the weekend and Lois had smiled again, and then lied, and said she was full of energy and rarin' to go. She thought that Midge had looked at her strangely, but she didn't comment on it. Tony was her child. Tony's apparition was meant for her. For her and no one else.

Each evening, as soon as she got back to her apartment she checked the blob of ink in the bottom right hand of the engraving. Often she looked at it even before she had hung up her coat or taken off her snow boots. Each morning before she went into the bathroom, she would stop and check the blob again. She would stand before the print, hall light on, and carefully inspect that smear of ink.

There didn't seem to be any change in it.

'Perhaps Bob is right,' she told her mirror one morning. 'Perhaps it's only the humidity and the age of the ink.' She rubbed the mild soap into her face and enjoyed the sensation when the warm water splashed it off. 'Inanimate things don't move,' she said to her image. 'That's what inanimate means. "Lacking power of motion." That's what the dictionary says and I guess that's what I have to go along with.' She started brushing her full red hair. 'It probably was all my imagination. I was too keyed up, too uptight. But I'm not anymore.' She shook her head as she continued to brush. 'I'm not any more. I've calmed down. I'm back in the real world again. I don't like it but I've got to accept it.' And she made a face at the face in the mirror.

The project currently on her desk had to do with redesigning a brochure for a festival of symphony music. Their previous year's brochure was so confused it read as if every orchestra was playing the same thing every night and all at the same time. Paying customers had arrived to hear Beethoven and got Berlioz. The management then got hell. This year they decided to have it reworked and Lois' company was awarded the contract. She enjoyed sorting it all out: dates, orchestras, selections, conductors, soloists, etc. Then she enjoying getting it onto paper and then that paper onto a sheet of shiny paper that folded itself into a six column brochure that could be sent through the mail. It took her a week to get it right: right in her mind and right in the eyes of the festival committee. They loved it, of course, and Lois was pleased. As far as she was concerned, taking an abstract idea and turning it into something that was solid and could be held and understood was one of life's great achievements. Maybe she only produced a brochure, or a table lamp design or a poster for a rock group, but it was the same creative force that helped the writer do a book, the painter a canvas or a composer the melody.

And it had another benefit as well: as long as she was immersed in a creative project it kept her mind off her missing child.

That evening, on her way home, she stopped at the liquor store and bought herself a bottle of fine single malt whisky. She studied the various labels and noted the strange sounding Scottish place names where the distilleries were located. Finally she chose one because of the odd name and the neatly designed label. Tonight would be a good night to celebrate. She had delivered the festival brochure and everyone had been happy. What better occasion to break open a bottle of the best Scotland had to offer?

When she came into the apartment she noted the red light on the telephone answer machine was lit. She pressed the play-back button and Bob's voice resounded metallically out of the box.

'Hi, hon. It's me. Look I'm going to be late tonight. That shipment of baking pans from Sweden came in all banged up. Christ only knows what happened to them, but I've got to make sure they're ready to be shipped back around midnight. I can get them out of here tonight if I hurry. Love you.' End of message.

'Nuts!' Lois said aloud and went into her bedroom to hang up her coat and get out of her office clothes. She'd been in them all day and as long as Bob wasn't coming back until late she might as well get into her robe and warm slippers and pamper herself with a tall Scotch and ice.

She walked back into the living room, her slippers flapping on the bare wood of the hallway and retrieved the brown bag from the liquor store. Going into the kitchen, she found a whisky glass and scooped some ice cubes from the automatic dispenser in the refrigerator. She twisted open the bottle, poured herself a healthy dose and then headed out of the kitchen, stopping long enough to take a deep pull of the wonderful amber liquid. She stood there, happily noting the effect the Scotch made on her insides as it ran over her tongue, down her throat and splashed warmly into her empty stomach. Nectar of the gods! she said to herself and walked out into the hallway. 'Hey,' she spoke to the engraving hanging silently on the wall, 'how are you doin' tonight? H'm?' She turned on the hall light and went over to the picture. 'Got any surprises for me? You been a good boy?'

Her eyes shifted automatically to the lower right hand corner. She gasped, straightened up, shook her head and bent down again to get a better view.

'You've moved!' she said. 'My God! You've moved again!'

She reached out to touch the frame but recoiled in horror. The blob *had* moved. It was not just lying on the edge of the picture but had moved farther up onto the lawn. It had moved at least an inch upwards, away from the white border. Upwards towards the house by at least an inch.

And it wasn't just a blob anymore. It wasn't a shapeless smear but instead it had taken on a form . . . a *human* form.

'No,' Lois said softly. 'No. Oh no!' She took another long pull on the Scotch. 'No. I'm only seeing things. It's my imagination.' She bent closer to the engraving, eyes wide in disbelief. She pulled back and shuddered. 'It's not my imagination,' she said loudly. 'It's not!'

There on the lawn in the engraving, about an inch up from the white margin, was the form of a man. He was about three inches tall and was dressed in a long black cloak. The cloak went from his shoulders down to the grass. She assumed it was a man even though she couldn't see his face because the figure wore a large hat with a wide floppy brim. He had his

72

THE NATIONAL LOTTERY

ESTIMATED JACKPOT
10 MILLION

A. 01 06 11 30 48 49
B. 03 05 12 23 33 47
C. 07 08 14 22 28 41
E. 16 17 25 33 37 44
F. 04 15 27 29 36 38

SAT 28 SEP 96
FOR 01 DRAW

012203   £ 5.00

RET NO.   100167
272-04765125-24247

records). At least 25% of the sales price of this ticket, net of 12% lottery duty, goes to The National Lottery Distribution Fund. Further information can be obtained from any National Lottery retailer. If additional help is required call 0645 100 000.

Name _____

Address _____

_____ Postcode _____

stralfors

SG **567011068**

THE NATIONAL LOTTERY

This ticket is issued subject to the Rules governing the game to which it relates. These Rules which set out the contractual rights and obligations of the player and the game promoter are available at the point of sale or from The National Lottery at the address below. This ticket is void if the entries on its face differ from the central computer entries corresponding to the control number hereon. To determine whether this ticket is a winning ticket, refer to the Rules. A prize must be claimed within 180 days of draw date by the holder filling in his/her name and address on the winning ticket and presenting it to a National Lottery retailer who will either pay such prize forthwith or direct the holder to a designated Post Office or National Lottery office. **At claimant's risk**, claims may be made by posting the ticket and a claim form to: The National Lottery, Tolpits Lane, Watford, WD1 8RN (retain copies for your records). At least 25% of the sales price of this ticket, net of 12% lottery duty, goes to The National Lottery Distribution Fund. Further information can be obtained from any National Lottery retailer. If additional help is required call 0645 100 000.

Name _____

Address _____

_____ Postcode _____

stralfors

SG **567011069**

THE NATIONAL LOTTERY

This ticket is issued subject to the Rules governing the game to which it relates. These Rules which set out the contractual rights and obligations of the player and the game promoter are available at the point of sale or from The National Lottery at the address below. This ticket is void if the entries on its face differ from the central computer entries corresponding to the control number hereon. To determine whether this ticket is a winning ticket, refer to the Rules. A prize must be claimed within 180 days of draw date by the holder filling in his/her name and address on the winning ticket and presenting it to a National Lottery retailer who will either pay such prize forthwith or direct the holder to a designated Post Office or National Lottery office. **At claimant's risk**, claims may be made by posting the ticket and a claim form to: The National Lottery, Tolpits Lane, Watford, WD1 8RN (retain copies for your records). At least 25% of the sales price of this ticket, net of 12% lottery duty, goes to The National Lottery Distribution Fund. Further information can be obtained from any National Lottery retailer. If additional help is required call 0645 100 000.

Name _____

Address _____

_____ Postcode _____

stralfors

SG **567011070**

back to her. He was just standing there, standing on *her* lawn in *her* engraving!

She ran into the living room and grabbed the telephone. Her fingers instinctively punched out the number of Bob's warehouse. She didn't care if he was farting about with some crap from Sweden. She needed him and she needed him now!

When Bob finally picked up the phone he said: 'Lois? I was back on the loading dock. What's up?'

She tried to steady her voice. 'I want you to come home,' she said.

'I will,' he said, and he laughed. 'Did you think I was going to run away to a desert island someplace?'

'I mean *now*,' she said, her voice still under control. 'I want you to come home right now.'

'I can't.' He sounded peeved. 'I'm just getting through the last of that damaged order and gotta get the export bills taken care of before the shipper gets here in an hour or so.'

'Bob, something has happened and I need you *here*.'

'Happened? What happened?' He paused. 'It's not . . . not Tony is it?'

Lois shook her head even though he couldn't see her. 'No, it's not him.' She couldn't bring herself to say the name. 'It's something else. I need you *here*, Bob.'

'Well what is it?' The peevish note in his voice had gotten harder. 'I told you I have to get this order out tonight.' He waited but she didn't respond. 'Lois, what's the trouble?'

'If I tell you on the phone, you won't come,' she said simply.

'Try me. What's the problem?'

She took a deep breath. 'It's the picture. The one Midge gave us. The ink blob has moved.'

There was a pause on his part now. 'Oh for Christ's sake, hon. Not that again.'

'I need you here,' she insisted. 'I can't take this by myself.'

'Hon, there's no use in us going over this again. Not now and not on the phone. I've got work to do here. You *know* that!'

'The ink blob has moved! Can't you understand that? It's changed! It's now like a man and it's up onto the lawn!'

'Have you been drinking?'

'Don't try to change the subject. Listen to what I'm telling you.'

'Have you been drinking? I asked you.'

'I've had a couple slugs of Scotch, but I'm not *drunk*. Jesus, Bob, give me *some* credit.' She started to whimper, she refused to cry. 'I need you,' she implored.

There was a long pause on his end now. 'I can't come home right now,' he said at last. 'I've got to stay here until this order is picked up. Maybe in an hour, maybe less. I'll be there as soon as I can.'

'And what am I supposed to do in the meantime?'

'Stay away from the picture,' he said and then added, 'and stay away from the bottle. I'll be home as soon as I can.'

'But Bob – '

'Sorry, hon,' and he hung up.

Lois stood there, the dead receiver in her hand. Then she slammed it back into its cradle. 'Damn you!' she said loudly to the machine. She stared around the living room. Only the table lamp near the phone was lit. Quickly she went around switching on the other lamps and then throwing the wall switch that turned on the ugly ceiling light fixture that they both hated and hardly ever used. She surveyed her handiwork. There wasn't a shadow anywhere in the room. 'Good,' she said aloud.

She picked up her half empty glass and went into the kitchen. She added a couple of ice cubes to the glass and poured enough Scotch from the bottle to raise the level almost to the rim. She lifted it carefully to sip from it but she spilled some onto the kitchen floor. She hadn't been aware of it but her hands were shaking. She took another sip, enough so she could walk and not slop the whisky over the sides of the glass. Then she went into the living room and put the glass down on the coffee table in front of the sofa.

She sat on the sofa and looked around the room. She wasn't going to think about the picture. She ran her hands through her hair. She always did that when she was nervous. She wasn't going to think about the picture. She reached for the glass, took a deep swig, and set it back on the table. She noticed the African violet that was growing near the window. There was a leaf that needed picking off. Good. She'd fuss with her plants, maybe water them, but she wasn't going to think about that picture. The leaf was nipped off, then she tested the soil. It was damp. It didn't need water. What else was there to do? She picked up the television remote control and punched on the set. Some politician was being interviewed. She pushed another channel. A commercial for dog food. She didn't own a dog. She tried another channel. Some men were riding horses across the prairie. She never liked Western films. Another push on the remote. A country singer. She punched the set off.

She went back to her glass. Another gulp of the warming liquid. She set her shoulders straight, gave her head a toss and marched into the hallway. 'Okay, you bastard,' she said as she took the engraving from the wall, 'let's see what in hell this is all about.'

She carried the picture back to the sofa, put it down and sat beside it. Yes. There was the figure. About three inches tall and wearing a long cloak and a wide brim hat. He was all in black, of course, there were no colours in this old print. There he was, out in the open for everyone to see. For Bob to see. When he finally managed to get his rear-end home he would see that she hadn't been imagining things. Bob would see with his own eyes that the blob had changed and had moved upwards and now there was a figure on the lawn, a figure that had not been there even yesterday. Bob would see that. Bob would have to admit the figure was there.

She reached for her glass and, taking shorter sips now, she studied the intruder. What was it? What *caused* it? This was a helluva lot more than humidity working on old ink. This wasn't anything to do with paper quality or fungus. This was something *weird*. This was something that had no logical explanation. Of course – and she took another sip – everything has a logical explanation. Nothing is so strange that it can't eventually be explained. She'd get the answer. She had several books in her office, they would tell her about engravings and ink and all that. Bob might know too. After all, Bob could be infuriating at times, but he was no dope. No, Bob might be able to explain it to her. She knew there was an explanation somewhere. She wasn't going to relax until she knew what that explanation was.

As Lois examined the figure, it turned slightly towards her. She screamed and dropped the glass, sending the whisky soaking into her robe and onto the sofa.

The figure had turned. There was a round smooth face with small dark eyes under the hat. She thought she saw a smile. Then the figure turned back again and the face was gone.

*   *   *

She had taken him over to the engraving and made him look at it as soon as he came into the apartment. She didn't even give him time to take off his coat.

'Well?' she demanded. 'Is there a little man there or isn't there?'

He rubbed at the glass, the way she had done dozens of times, and carried the frame over to the table lamp and examined it closely. Finally he looked up at her, a puzzled expression on his face. 'Yes,' he said slowly, 'there is something there. A blob of ink that wasn't there the last time I looked.'

'It's not a blob of ink. It's the image of a little man. It may look like just a blob to you, but that little fucker's got a face and he turned around and leered at me.'

Bob hung the engraving in its place in the hallway. He wasn't going to argue with her. If she wanted to call this blob a little man, if she wanted to believe it had a face, then it did. 'What are we going to do about it?' he asked her.

'Let's take it out of the frame. Let's examine it with a magnifying glass. Maybe we can scrape him off. He doesn't belong on that lawn. Not on *my* lawn!'

'No, we'd better not touch it. We might ruin it and it could be more valuable than we think it is. First thing in the morning, let's get it examined by an expert. There's bound to be several of them listed in the Yellow Pages. We'll call one and set up an appointment and have him take this thing apart.'

'But you do see it? You do see the man?'

'I see a blob of ink that could resemble a man, yes.'

'I thought at first I was going crazy.'

Bob didn't reply.

Neither of them went to work the next morning. They parked the car across the street from the small shop in the mid-Twenties near Park Avenue. It was an average neighbourhood for that part of town: a small grocery, several book shops, a bar or two, a second-hand clothing outlet and an antique shop with windows so grimy none of the 'treasures' inside could be seen. The art appraiser and expert was in a small room above the antique shop.

As they drove over they had rehearsed what they would tell the man. There was not to be any mention that the figure had moved. Only that they had suspicions that the figure wasn't part of the original design and could he verify that it had been added at a later date. Lois agreed there was to be no mention of the blob turning into a human form. A form with a cloak and a hat, and a fat face with beady eyes.

The man mumbled his name as he shook Bob's hand. It was a middle-European name, sounding Polish or Rumanian. He was way into his sixties and had thin grey hair on a thin grey head. He wore a rather grimy white shirt and a necktie that hung loosely around his thin neck.

'Let me see what you have brought me,' he said as he took the parcel and unwrapped the brown paper Lois had put around it. 'Ah,' he smiled, 'an engraving.' He put it onto a dark wooden table and turned on a small table lamp with a very large bulb. The sudden brightness flooded the area, making the glass in the frame reflect everything around it. The man took out a huge magnifying glass and began to examine the print. 'Very nice,' he said. 'Fine detail. Good sharp lines. Obviously European. Probably quite old.' He looked up at the couple. 'What do you want? An appraisal for insurance?'

'No,' Bob said. 'Not exactly. You see we bought this thing a few weeks ago and . . .'

'So how much did you pay?' the man asked.

'Twelve hundred dollars,' Bob lied.

The man nodded. 'Probably about right,' he said.

Lois opened her eyes in astonishment and stared at Bob.

'We thought so too,' Bob continued, 'until one of our friends who is in the antiques business looked at the print and said she thought the figure had been added at a later date.'

'This figure?' The man's finger pointed at the cloaked man on the lawn. 'Why would your friend, this antiques person, tell you that? Most unusual, if true.'

'I don't know why she did,' Bob went on, 'but she said she thought the figure had been put in by another engraver. That it wasn't there when the print was first made.'

'And if that's true,' Lois put in, 'then the print has been damaged and it's not worth what we paid for it. I mean, it's not in its original condition anymore and we should try and get our money back.'

The man shrugged. 'I never heard of such a thing,' he said flatly.

'We never did either,' Bob replied, 'but we were wondering

if you could somehow examine it and tell us if it's true or not.'

'I never heard of such a thing,' the man said again and turned the picture over. 'I'll have to take it out. Undo the original backing on it.'

'Will that make a difference in its value?' Lois asked.

'None whatsoever. A picture's value is in the work of the artist, not in the frame somebody put around to display it.' He brought the lamp closer to the picture and with a very sharp knife made a few swift incisions into the cloth that bound the back to the frame. 'This is linen,' he said flicking a bit of the cloth off onto the table. 'Applied with glue. See? There are tiny hairs in the glue. To hold it better, they put horse hairs in glue. They haven't done that for years. Maybe two hundred years, at least.' The linen parted easily under the sharp blade, then he began to pry around the edge of the frame. 'Here. See these?' They bent closer. 'Wooden pegs. Small wooden pegs holding on the back piece. They don't do wooden pegs anymore either. Takes too long. They use nails today. Pick up a nail, slam it with a hammer and frame a picture. No,' he sighed, 'the old ways have gone. From these pegs and from this linen, I'd say this was framed at least two hundred years ago. Maybe more.'

'You mean no one has touched the engraving in over two hundred years?' Lois asked.

'That's what I just said. Yes, young woman.'

'So if the figure had been added afterwards, it had to have been put there at least two hundred years ago?' This from Bob.

The expert looked up at him. 'If it's been in this frame for two hundred years then that's the way it would have to have been done.' His tone was that of an annoyed school teacher who had a dunce for a pupil. 'How's the forger going to do it otherwise? Crawl under the glass? Send in a termite with a pen in its jaws?'

'I was only asking,' Bob replied, slightly irritated.

The last of the pegs was worked free and the man removed the piece of polished wood that backed the engraving. Underneath it was a double layer of some shiny white material. 'Silk,' the man said before they could ask. 'The purest of all fabrics. They used to put this in frames to cushion the paper against the wood of the backing. See? It's still fresh. Hasn't

78

rotted at all. I haven't seen a picture framed this way in years. Very interesting.'

Both Bob and Lois held their breath as he carefully lifted the engraving itself away from the glass and frame and turned it over onto the table. Then he moved the light closer to the print, and picking up his magnifying glass he started to examine the figure. After a few minutes he frowned, went to a desk that was against the far wall, rummaged around in a drawer and came up with a jeweller's glass. He put the strap around his head and swung the black plastic cone over his right eye. He bent low over the engraving, moving his head ever so slightly, occasionally blowing lightly on the print to eliminate any motes of dust. After what seemed like a very long time, he straightened up, swung the magnifying lens onto his forehead and said, 'It's original. Nothing's been added.'

'Are you positive?' Bob asked, his voice rising.

'You come to an expert,' said the old man, 'and you're supposed to listen to what the expert says to you. I'm saying to you that this figure was there from the beginning.' He snapped off the table light. 'You want me to put this back together?'

'Wait a minute.' Lois was getting angry now. 'We don't want you to do any such thing. Not yet, anyway. I'm a graphic designer.' The man shrugged. 'I deal with art and lines all day. Show me *how* you know this hasn't been added at a later date.' She switched the light back on. 'You're the expert. You explain to me how you arrived at your conclusion.'

The man shot her a look, then handed her the magnifying glass. He repositioned his jeweller's glass. 'Here,' he said, pointing to the figure, 'these lines that make up his hat. They are short and deep and pure. The lines from the lawn, these lines that make it look like grass is growing, you don't see them *under* the hat. Don't see them raised up under there. If the hat had been added over the grass, you'd see what had been under there. You'd see the unevenness. But you can't because it wasn't done that way. And here – ' his finger grew like Gulliver's as it appeared under Lois' magnifying glass. 'By his cloak. The shadow of it against the lawn is made with the same exact lines that made the grass around it. I know about artists' lines. I know when one artist has done one part of a work and another artist has added something else. Like handwriting. Every artist draws a line in a different way than another artist does. This figure has been done by one man and it's the same man who did the grass and the house. You see what I'm telling you? There's no doubt about it.' He switched off the light again and this time removed the jeweller's headband. He was finished. 'Now can I put this back together?'

'But it *can't* be,' Lois insisted.

'But it is,' the man said harshly. 'Lady, what do you want from me?'

'When we first got this picture,' Lois said, 'there was no little man on the lawn. There was just a smear of ink. Down here.' She pointed to the lower right hand corner of the print.

'Lois, I don't think . . .' Bob started to say.

'And then over the weeks, this blob of ink has moved upwards, has changed form and is now this figure standing on the lawn.' Her finger struck at the cloaked creature. There was a satisfaction in doing it. It was the first time she had been able to touch it, to get back at it. 'And if it has been moving and changing, then it *couldn't possibly* match up with the other lines in the picture the way you have shown me.'

The old man looked at her. 'The figure was moving?'

'Yes.'

'And this you saw?'

'Yes,' Lois repeated. 'And this I saw.'

The man looked at Bob. 'Did you see it move?'

Bob looked at Lois and then back to the old man. 'No,' he said, 'I didn't.'

'Bob! You know this figure wasn't there when Midge brought this thing to our apartment. How can you say that?'

'I never actually *saw* it move,' Bob said carefully.

'So you too think it's moved?' the old man asked him.

'It looks like it's changed,' Bob said. 'It looks different.'

'Different!' Lois exploded. 'This little bastard invades our picture and you can only say it looks *different*?'

'Look – ' The old man held up his hands. 'You two want to have a domestic argument then go to somebody else's place. I've given you the information you've asked for. You don't want to accept it, get a second opinion. I'm an expert. I've been doing this kind of work for years, long before I came to America. I know what I'm talking about but your wife here, just because she got a diploma from some decorating school, thinks she knows more than I do.' He started pounding the pegs back into the frame. 'Maybe she does. Maybe I'm a numbskull. I say the picture is original and she says somebody got at it somehow and added something. So she's become the expert. Tell her to hang out her sign. Tell her to put her name in the Yellow Pages too.' He quickly assembled the backing onto the frame. 'Why bother sealing it up again? The next expert will only have to undo it.' He wrapped the brown paper around the frame and handed the parcel to Bob. 'So far I'm still the expert, so I'm the one who gets paid. That'll be seventy-five dollars. An expert charges money. In cash.'

Lois opened her purse and took out her billfold. She took out the seventy-five dollars and as she looked up to hand the bills to the old man she caught him making a circle with his finger around his right ear.

Lois wanted to throw the money at him, but instead placed it carefully on the table. She took the parcel from Bob and left the room, walking quickly down the stairs and back out onto the sidewalk. As they waited for a break in the traffic so they could get across the street to their car, Lois looked at Bob. 'I saw what that man did,' she said. 'That gesture around his ear.'

'Yeah,' Bob said. 'So did I. That old man thinks you're bananas. I warned you not to tell him about the figure moving. Now he thinks you're as crazy as a bedbug.'

'And do you?' she asked angrily.

He didn't reply, just took her arm as they made a rapid dash over to their car.

* * *

'We both thought we needed to approach this thing on a more scientific basis,' Bob said to the man who was in their dining room, moving the table and chairs around to make space for his equipment. 'Let's hope this brings some explanation.'

The man continued positioning the spotlights, arranging the height of the tripod legs and tilting the aluminium shades around the huge bulbs. 'I never thought when I opened up my studio I'd be taking pictures of a little guy under a sheet of glass. A little spook . . . Good thing I've known you since high school.' The photographer chuckled. 'Anybody else would call the funny farm wagon if you asked them to do this.'

'I thought of you right away,' Bob said. 'You were always

with the odd-ball bunch at school. I figured this assignment was right up your alley.'

'It is.' He grinned as he took the bulky 35mm camera out of its leather carrying case and started securing it to the tripod. 'I'm still into ghosts and all that stuff. I still subscribe to *Fate* magazine and get the monthly bulletins from the Psychical Research Society. If there is a way to catch that little guy moving, catch him on film I mean, then I've got one helluva psychic photo for my collection!'

'And you can do anything you want to with it,' Bob assured him. 'Just catch him moving, that's all we want.'

Lois had taken the engraving from the hallway and now stood ready to hang it on the dining room wall wherever Hal, the photographer, wanted it. They had decided on using the dining room because they could close the door and it was the one room in their apartment that they didn't use every day. That room and Tony's bedroom and neither of them had suggested using the bedroom.

The idea was simple enough. The engraving would hang on the dining room wall for two days. During that time Hal's camera would be pointed at it. The shutter was on a timer and every fifteen minutes it would open and snap a photograph. Hal had attached an extra large film holder to the camera, giving it enough film to take one picture every fifteen minutes for forty-eight hours. Each time the shutter clicked the floodlights would be turned on. Bob and Lois agreed not to open the dining room door during that time. Nothing was to disturb the camera and lights once the timer started.

Hal positioned the engraving on the wall. Lois winced as he pounded a nail into her wallpaper making a hole where there hadn't been one before. He set the camera onto the picture, made sure the spotlights didn't reflect off the glass, checked the timer with his own wristwatch, then led them from the dining room. He closed the door and, jokingly, made the sign of the Cross over it.

'Let's hope it works. God, I hope it does!'

'Something has to work,' Lois said. 'I can't take much more of this.'

For two days the dining room remained closed. While they were at work and while they were in other areas of the apartment the lights came on, the camera shutter whirred and the lights went off. Every fifteen minutes. In the evening, they could see the light stream suddenly out from under the door, and then just as suddenly vanish again.

On the second night, they sat on the living room sofa, having a drink. 'I'm dying to go in there and peek,' Bob confided to Lois.

'Don't you dare!' she ordered.

'Glad we didn't leave the whisky in there,' he smiled.

Lois took a sip from her glass and looked in the direction of the closed dining room door. 'That guy in the engraving gives me the creeps every time I think about him. There is something about him that's terrible and evil.'

'I thought you didn't believe in the concept of good and evil,' Bob said. 'I thought you believed that everything was neutral energy, how human beings used it.'

She nodded. 'Yes, but that little creep isn't human. He's got to be powered by something. He's being manipulated by somebody, somewhere.'

'You don't know that,' Bob remarked.

'I don't have to know it. I just feel it.' She took another sip from her glass. 'I don't know what is controlling it. I rather doubt if it's anything as sophisticated as a micro chip. But there is a reason he's appeared under that glass. There is a *reason* that this is happening to us.'

Bob raised an eyebrow. 'Somebody's out to get us?'

'I don't know,' she replied. 'Out to get us or get *to* us for some reason. Maybe it's a message, some sort of psychic message we have to figure out.'

'Wouldn't it be easier for whoever is doing this just to leave a message on our answering machine?' He grinned at her.

She grinned back. 'You know what I mean.' She stiffened slightly as the whir and flash of light came from behind the dining room door. 'I've been thinking about it and was wondering if it doesn't have something to do with . . .' She paused, unsure as to how to progress with her train of thought.

'With Tony's death?' he asked.

She shook her head quickly, annoyed that he should have brought up her son's name. 'No. Not about that, but about our future, maybe a warning about something that is going to happen and we should know about it and be prepared.'

'You got all of that out of an ink blot moving up the grass?'

'It could be,' she said softly. 'It could be a warning, a

psychic notice to keep us on our toes. A message to become more aware.'

'Aware of what? And why like this? It would have been so much simpler to mail us a letter.'

She ignored that. 'It's shaken us. If the figure has done anything so far, he's disturbed us. Made us notice him. Made us aware of his presence. He's heightened our sense of perception, if you will.'

'That sounds too metaphysical,' Bob wasn't smiling.

'What do you want?' she shrugged. 'What's under that glass *is* metaphysical. It's a psychic happening. You *have* to give it that label. It sure as hell isn't normal.'

'No,' Bob replied. 'I've gotta admit your little creep is not normal, but I can't buy the idea that he's some kind of Delphic oracle wearing a floppy hat.'

'We're going to have to wait and see,' she said, glancing at the dining room door. 'Tomorrow should give us more clues.'

Hal arrived just before noon the next day, Saturday, and started taking down his equipment. All three of them had immediately looked at the engraving to see if there had been any movement on the part of the cloaked figure. It didn't appear as if there had. 'If he did move,' Hal said, 'even the slightest bit, we'll see it when we develop the film.'

They rode to Hal's studio in his van and waited in his cardboard and plastic garden bridal setting while the negatives were being developed and then printed. When he called them to come into the back room he had a disappointed look on his face.

'It didn't move,' he said. 'I've compared them all, compared the first shot with the last one taken and there isn't a bit of difference. Damn! I was hoping.'

'So were we,' Lois said.

'You're sure you've seen this guy change positions?' Hal asked them again.

'I've seen him do it,' Lois said. 'He turned and looked at me while I was watching him. Bob never saw him do that. Bob just saw him in a new place, that's all.' They had told Hal this before but it felt good to confess it all over again in light of this failed photo session.

84

Hal shrugged. 'Sorry. I really hoped it would come out the way you both wanted it.'

'Not your fault,' Bob said. 'What do I owe you?'

'Nothing. Forget it. This was one of those fun assignments that I like to do on spec. Anyway, I stood to gain a helluva lot if the little jerk had been caught on my film.'

'That's very nice of you,' Lois said. 'We owe you dinner sometime. Okay?'

Hal shrugged again, he was still disappointed. 'Sure. Dinner would be great.' As they started for the door he said, 'You call me if he moves again. Will you? I mean, I'd love be there to see it or at least compare the photos we took today with new ones that proved he had moved his position.'

In the cab back to their apartment, Lois was very quiet. It hadn't worked. There was no proof that this figure had really moved. Maybe it was her imagination. No. She knew it had grown, had changed shape, had moved up onto the lawn. Then there was that other nagging doubt. Bob had said it aloud. She'd not been able to do so. Bob had said that maybe the little man had to do with Tony. That had been her first thought, too, but she dismissed the idea as ridiculous. She was connecting everything unusual with Tony. Any coincidence, any strange feelings, even overheard snatches of music made her connect them with Tony. Her mind needed a rinsing out. She needed to pour hot water and a good detergent into her brain and swish it around until these crazy thoughts about Tony had been washed away, until every stray bit and piece of still-clinging memory had been shaken loose and flushed away.

Yet what if Bob had been right? What if the horrible little man in the picture *was* a message about Tony? What if the man had appeared to tell her about her son and she was too dense, too uptight, to interpret the message? Bob said Tony was dead. Bob had identified the body. Yet she felt that Tony was still alive. Sure, she'd gone to the funeral, had sent out thank-you notes afterwards, had closed the door to his bedroom, yet there was this feeling, this deep inner knowing that her son was still alive. Somewhere out there, maybe inside one of the scores of buildings the taxi was rapidly passing. Maybe if she stopped the taxi in front of that building over there, the one with the shoe store on the ground floor, and maybe if she went in and took the elevator to let's say the tenth floor, and maybe if she walked three doorways down on the left side of the hallway and knocked, the door would open and there her Tony would be. Maybe.

Back in their apartment, Lois wearily set about moving the dining room table and chairs into their original positions. She scowled at the nail in the centre of the wall. She'd have to find something to hang on it, to cover it over. She walked back into the hallway and straightened the engraving. In their hurry to get to the studio she had hung it slightly crooked.

She stopped.

The figure had moved. His hat was at a slightly different angle, his cloak touched the ground in a different way and his right foot, until now hidden, was now slightly forward as if in the process of taking a step.

'Bob!' she called. 'Come over here! He's done it again. He's changed!'

Bob, who had been trying to catch up on the news in that morning's *New York Times* came into the hallway from the living room. 'Where?' he said. 'Show me.'

She pointed and he whistled. 'Can you see how he's changed? Can you see now that it's got a human form . . . that it's shaped like a little man in a cloak and hat? Can you see that *now*?' she demanded.

He whistled again. 'Hon, I've got to admit it. The blob has changed. It *does* look like a man now. You were right.'

'And *see*,' she spoke quickly, 'he's got one foot in front of the other now. Just as if we've caught him about to take a step. See that foot? It wasn't there before.'

'Should we call Hal? Have him come back with his camera?'

'No. That's not important anymore. There's been enough change to show both of us something strange is going on under that glass. You know, he must be smarter than we think he is.'

'What do you mean by that?' he asked.

'Well, he held his old position for two days while the camera was on him. He's only moved now that the camera has been taken away. It's almost as if he knew what the camera was doing. Almost as if he didn't *want* to be caught on film.'

'Then . . .' Bob paused for the right words '. . . then not only is he alive under there but he must also have the power of reason. He can think. He can react. What have we got ourselves into?'

Lois' voice started to quiver and she fought back the urge to scream and run from the apartment. 'There's something alive under that glass, Bob. Something alive and intelligent and horrible!'

CHAPTER SIX

'What time you leavin' for lunch?' Midge stood in the doorway to Lois' office. 'There's a new place over near Bloomingdale's that sounds pretty good. Betty over at Arttex told me about it. I've got to get some pantihose at Bloomie's anyway.'

Lois shook her head. 'Sorry, hon, but I'm not having lunch today. I'm going to spend a few hours at the public library.'

'The library? Whatever for?'

'That damned picture you gave us,' Lois made a face. 'I want to know where it was made. Any *normal* engraving would have all the info right on the bottom margin but no, you had to go and find one that was blank.'

Midge smiled. 'You don't expect me to do anything normally, do you?'

'No, but it would be nice to have some sort of clue. You know how curious I am. I can't have that thing hanging in my house and not know anything about it.'

'Make up a story,' Midge suggested. 'I did once in San Francisco when I found this old brown photograph of a man wearing a long white beard. He was sitting between two skinny and ugly ladies wearing long skirts and pious expressions on their faces. I thought they were neat, so I brought them home and hung them in the bathroom. When anyone asked I said they were my great-uncle and his two wives. I told everyone they were Mormons and that one night the wives poisoned him and they threw his body into a canyon. It was wonderful. I had instant ancestors. Go on,' she grinned, 'make up a story. Say that place is your family home and when your cousin the ninth Duke of Armpit dies, you'll inherit the title and will have to go back there and live in the family seat.'

'I don't think so,' said Lois. 'I don't believe I want people to think I'll someday be the Duchess of Armpit. No,' she said getting up from behind her desk, 'both Bob and I want to get the facts on that place. It's almost become an obsession.'

'Then aren't you glad I gave the thing to you? It's brought some excitement into your life.'

'Midge, you don't know how much excitement it's brought. But do me a favour, if you buy any more mistakes at an auction, give them to somebody else. Okay?'

'Gratitude, gratitude,' Midge moaned as Lois put on her coat. 'That's all I ever get is gratitude.'

'You'll get something stronger next time,' Lois warned. 'And you won't be able to hang it on your wall and call it an ancestor.'

The main reading room of the New York Public Library was half-full. Lois was surprised to see so many people seated at the long polished tables reading under the individual green lamp shades. Then she looked again and saw that many of them were threadbare characters with grimy fingers and cheap overcoats who were in there just to get out of the cold. She smiled as she remembered her father's contention that every library should have a room with beds instead of tables so that those people who just wanted to get in out of the weather wouldn't take up the places of those who had really come for the books.

She had already handed in her book requests. She had gone through the card catalogue and had asked to see a gazetteer of Italy, one of Austria and one of Yugoslavia. Those were the three countries where everyone seemed to think her house might be. She had also asked for a list of towns in Great Britain because she secretly hoped she might find Corra somewhere in the British Isles.

The small square with the number she had been given lit up and she went to the desk to claim the large and dusty volumes. She wondered if the clerk would say anything about asking for such unexciting books but the woman only looked at her number and shoved the books at her. Lois supposed she had long since lost interest in the books she was paid to hand out. The collection was one of the largest in the world

and the librarian would be consulted by some of the oddest
people in the world. A gazetteer of a remote place like
Yugoslavia must have seemed an ordinary request indeed.

Lois carted the volumes to a vacant seat at one of the
tables and put the books on it. Then she removed her coat
and draped it over the back of the varnished chair. She took
a pen and notepad out of her purse and reached for the
volume on Italy. Bob was sure Corra was there, so was his
friend Anthony. She hoped they were wrong. Might as well
get that over with first.

She turned to the Cs and her finger ran down the list. There
was a Corciano and a Cornuda and a Cortona but no Corra.
She closed the book with a smile of triumph on her face. Good.
The place wasn't in Italy. She knew it wouldn't be.

Then the book on Austria was consulted. The only place
even close was Carnuntum, an old Roman settlement on the
Danube. Another smile as she shut that one. The Yugoslav
book was even quicker. Cikat and Cres and Crikvenica but
no Corra.

Then her hand went out, trembling slightly now, for the
volume on Great Britain. The index, in typically British
irritating fashion, was divided into England, Ireland, Scotland, Wales and the islands. Nothing like Corra in England.
Nor in Ireland. Then there it was. In the middle of the 'C'
column for Scotland. Corra. Written clearly and plainly in
black ink on white paper. Corra.

She turned to the section of maps and, of course, some of
the pages were missing. There was no map of Scotland there
at all. She frowned and got up, then picked up all the books
and returned them to the desk clerk. 'I've got to go back out
to the card catalogue,' she told the woman. The woman
didn't even glance at her. 'Do I keep the same number,' Lois
continued, 'or do I get a new one when I come back in?'

The woman still didn't look up at her. 'Keep it,' she said.
'Show the guard on the way out.' Lois didn't bother to say
thank you.

She found the catalogue number for a detailed map of
Scotland and while she was in the room she also requested
a couple of books on Scottish history. When she went back
to the reading room to wait for her books she saw the woman
wasn't there. In her place was a young bearded man with a
long feathered earring in his left ear. Lois wondered if they

had shoved the unsmiling woman into the large square box they used to send the books up and down to the stacks and if someone had already filed her away under 'indifferent'.

When her books arrived she took them back to her seat. To her delight her coat was still there. This was, after all, New York City. She opened the map and found the reference for Corra. Then she turned to the indicated page and followed the letter and number across the squares in the map.

Then there it was again. Corra. A place in small print, surrounded by green open spaces. Her finger ran south and she came to a stretch of blue water labelled Solway Firth. Then there was a strange sounding town called Kirkcudbright. Then, running her finger northwards, she stopped at the town with the largest print of all. Dumfries. She said the name softly, letting it rest easily on her tongue. Then she noticed the broken lines that divided the area from the others around it. Those were the county lines and she quickly figured out that her Corra was in the County of Dumfries and Galloway. Her eyes went back to the tiny printed name. Corra. How strange to see it somewhere else, somewhere other than at the bottom of her engraving.

She reached for one of the history books and started turning the pages, scanning quickly for a mention of her town. She found Dumfries, and quite often too, especially when reference was made of border wars between the English and the Scots. She read some of it and was amazed and then amused at how they kept raiding each other's cattle, kept sacking each other's castles and kept burning each other's villages. Poor Dumfries was always in the middle of it, its citizens getting sacked one time, its citizens doing the sacking the next. Horses and death, churches and hangings, princes and dungeons. It was a wonder anybody survived to write about it.

Then there it was: 'At this time the Queen's forces joined with the private forces of the Earl of Corra. His large estate was used to quarter both men and beasts. When the battle had finished the Earl's only son lay mortally wounded. Hearing of their defeat the commander of Howard Castle penned a treaty that . . .' Lois stopped reading.

The Earl of Corra, she said to herself. His large estate. She flipped through a few more pages, then, finding no further mention, opened the other book. She tried to find the approximate place in this book that would cover the same period in history. At last she found the reference: 'Hoping to enlarge his already considerable holdings, Roger Grenville, the Earl of Corra, offered the Royal troops the use of his house and lands. The Earl, one of the most powerful men in the area, was related to the Howards through the marriage of his eldest sister Adelaide. In spite of plans carefully drawn up by himself and others, the attack upon the English forces was swiftly routed. The Earl's son and heir was thrown from his horse and was soon dead.'

And there, in a black and white line drawing about as big as her thumbnail, was 'The standard of the Earl of Corra.' A flag. The Earl's flag but also Lois's flag. She was sure of it. She quickly opened her purse and took out the enlargement she had made from one of Hal's negatives. The flag on the roof of her house and the flag in the margin drawing of the book were one and the same. Roger Grenville's house, the Earl's house and her house. No question about it!

She closed the book in triumph. Italy huh? Yugoslavia huh? Oh no! She grinned broadly. Her house was exactly where she had hoped – where she had known – it was going to be. Her house was in Scotland and she was damned glad of it.

* * *

Lois spooned some more gravy over her mashed potatoes. She pushed the bowl towards Bob, but he shook his head. 'So anyway,' she said, 'I got out a couple more books and tried to read as much as I could about the Earl of Corra and his family. Their surname was Grenville. His lands had been given to his grandfather by some Scottish king and . . .'

'You mean English king,' he interrupted. 'Scotland and England are the same country. Have the same Royal Family.'

'Not back then, they didn't,' she said. 'The Scots had their own kings and queens and princes and stuff and the English had theirs. They were always fighting each other. The Scots, I mean. One family killed off the leaders of the other family and then a third party would come along and the first two enemies would unite to get rid of the third and then, when they'd done it, the first two would go back to murdering each other.'

'Nice people,' he said reaching for another slice of bread.

'Don't say a word against them,' Lois said with a grin. 'The

way you Italians were always killing each other off? Wars and murders and Lucretia Borgia?'

'So I concede a point,' he replied, 'but tell me about your Earl.'

'Well he was a great friend of Mary Queen of Scots and when she went into England to see her cousin Elizabeth, he got involved in several minor clashes with the English over trying to get her back. I guess it was her mother who gave them the land in the first place.'

'Mary's mother?' he asked. 'Where did she get the land to give him?'

Lois shrugged. 'Who knows. Probably took it from some enemy. I'm sure she didn't buy it from a real estate agent and then hand it to him.'

'I'm sure,' he agreed.

'The house was built about that time, about 1530. It's real old. Anyway, around the early eighteen hundreds the Earl got into several fights with the Church of England. He was a Catholic and he didn't want to change his religion.'

'Wait a minute.' Bob put up his hand. 'How could he get land from Mary's mother in fifteen something and still be around in the eighteen hundreds? What did he live to be? Three hundred years old?'

'No,' she shook her head, 'not the same earl that got the land. His grandson or great-grandson or something. The family was still in the house and they were still fighting the powers in London. Anyway, if you'd let me finish, it seems he didn't want to go to the English church and there were a bunch of others who felt the same way. They wanted the old religion, as they called it, but by that time the English ruler was insisting everyone go to the same church.'

'That was Elizabeth the First.'

'No, silly. Elizabeth was long dead by that time. I don't know who was king of England then. It's not important.'

'It was to the queen,' he said.

'I'll ignore that. Anyway, things really heated up and soldiers were sent in to burn down the Catholic churches and monasteries and stuff and so the Earl and his friends got together and drew up a plan to defeat the troops from London. It didn't work.'

'What didn't?' Bob was actually starting to get interested in this disjointed story.

'His plan. It didn't work. There were too many English soldiers and not enough Scotsmen and they were taken by surprise and had to fight on open land instead of the hills and forests they had expected to fight on, and then his son fell off his horse and was trampled to death.'

'The Earl's son?'

'Yes. And so the Earl went back to his house – my house – and I guess he just lived out the rest of his days there. There is no mention of him afterwards, but there was something about some members of the family being accused of witchcraft and being burnt at the stake.'

'The Earl's family?'

'Uh-huh. I suppose things like cousins and stuff.'

'So who lives there now?'

'I don't know. Probably distant cousins of the Earl. I couldn't find any mention of the place after the witchcraft trials.'

'So the people who lived in your house were witches?' he laughed. 'That sure as hell doesn't surprise me. Maybe that's why you like the place so much. Maybe you were one of those witches in a past life and maybe they burnt you and you want to go back and see if your broomstick is too damaged to fly.'

'Oh, you're so funny!' she said. 'You know – ' She paused. 'I do feel as if I've been there before. I think that's what I feel. I recognized the place as soon as I saw the engraving. Perhaps it's some gene still lurking in my Scottish blood. I didn't know *where* it was but I felt I knew it.' She sipped the last of the wine in her glass. It had been a good meal and she was pleased she was able to have it ready by the time Bob came home. Somehow discovering that her house was in Scotland had calmed her, had relaxed her. She even *wanted* to play the role of wife and cook that night. 'I'll bet if I went in it, I'd know where things were. Like the living room and the library and the kitchen. I bet I'd know what was behind a door before I opened it. It's a spooky feeling but at the same time a comforting one.'

'Well,' he said, pushing his chair away from the table, 'I doubt if you'll ever get to see it.'

'Why not?'

'It's in Scotland, that's why. You live here, in the US of A. And when we take our vacations we go to nice warm places like Bermuda and Jamaica. We don't go to places like Scotland. Not in February.'

93

'Someday maybe we could take a summer vacation,' she said quickly. 'You could change things at your place. You don't always have to take your vacation in the winter. You don't have to sun yourself every year.'

'The schedule was set up years ago,' he replied. 'You know that.'

'Sure – by your father so he could get down to Miami every year. *You're* the boss now, you know. You could change it.' She rose and started clearing the table. 'We don't have to look at palm trees every time we go away.'

'But you *like* the sun,' he said. 'You always enjoy the islands.'

'Sure I do, but . . .'

'But what?'

'But maybe this time I'd like something different. Maybe this time we could go to Scotland and see my house.'

'We've got tickets for Jamaica, you know that.'

'They could be changed,' she said softly.

He shook his head. 'Everything's set up. The flights, the deal on the beach house, everything. You know that. If I changed things now I'd lose money.'

She was still busying herself with the dishes, saying aloud the thoughts she had formed since leaving the library. 'We could always fly to London, then take a train up to Dumfries and then go look at the house. If you still insisted on sun we could fly over to Spain or Portugal.'

He stared at her. 'And what about Jamaica?'

'It'll be there,' she said simply. 'It's not going anywhere.'

'No, our plans are for Jamaica and Jamaica is where we are going.'

'Plans can be changed,' she said, her voice low.

'These can't. Look, hon – ' He went to her and touched her lightly on the arm. 'Don't let's get things stirred up. Everything was fine about Jamaica until this afternoon. If we pull out now then Anthony and Anne will have to find another couple to share the rent on the beach house. I can't do that to them.'

Lois sighed. When it was first suggested that their friends go with them and share the luxury oceanside villa she had thought it a wonderful idea. Now she wasn't so sure. 'I don't see why I have to go someplace just because Anthony and Anne are going.'

'But it was *our* idea!' Bob was getting annoyed. The

conversation had gone far enough. 'If I pull out now, Anthony either finds somebody else at the last minute or else I pay our share anyway and we lose the money. Because of that damned picture.'

She sighed, deeply. 'It would be nice to see that house. My house.'

'Scotland in February, baby,' he said soothingly. 'After two days, you'd hate it.'

'I suppose so. Maybe some other year then.' She looked at him. 'Maybe the vacation after Jamaica?' She put it to him as a question and waited for the answer.

'Sure,' he said, kissing her lightly on the forehead. 'Sure. The vacation after Jamaica.'

CHAPTER SEVEN

The little man under the glass hadn't moved in over a week. Every day Lois inspected him before she went to work and examined him as soon as she got home. Bob did the same and they both agreed: he was standing slightly off balance with his right foot ready to take a step forward. When he would take that next step was anybody's guess.

Midge and Lois finally got around to having lunch at the new place near Bloomingdale's. Because it had recently opened and because it had been 'discovered' by the creative in-crowd, they had a drink at the bar while waiting for a table.

'This place feels like a class reunion,' Lois said as she sipped her Scotch on the rocks. 'I recognize about half the faces but I can't put any names to them. Now that guy over there, the one in the brown sport coat with the green tie, I'm sure I've seen him before.'

'Snyder Graphics,' Midge said glibly. 'He's been in our office a few times. The girl he's with is a PR person for the Amherst Theatre chain. I did some stuff for them once. I don't remember her name.' She laughed. 'I see what you mean, faces and no names.'

They continued to watch the others while they chatted

about things that were happening in the office. Midge said that she was slightly behind in the restaurant menu she was designing. 'I took it home with me last night and I was sure I was going to work on it, but I got sidetracked. Didn't do a damn thing with it.'

'What did you do? Watch that mini-series called *Desire Me*?' Lois shook her head. 'Really, I don't know how you can watch such drivel.'

'No, I didn't watch that show. I read the book and hated it. As a matter of fact I got absorbed in another book and forgot to turn the set on at all. Did you see it? Did they show that great scene where the heroine and the truck driver make love in the butcher shop? On top of the skinned carcasses of beef?'

Lois laughed. 'I don't watch stuff like that. What were you reading that was so fascinating? Your diary?'

'God, I wish!' Midge said. 'No, it was a book I found.'

'Did you find one of those sales again?' Midge was always going to auctions and in her mind, Lois could see the stack of books Midge piled up in the corner of her kitchen, books she had thought were great bargains and promised herself someday she would read.

'No,' the slightly older and heavier woman said, 'I found this book. I really did. Last night I took the Madison Avenue bus downtown and sat beside a teenage girl. You know the type – lots of make-up and frizzy hair and a purse jammed with lipsticks and combs and cigarettes.' Lois nodded. 'Okay, when she got up to leave she left this book on the seat. I noticed it just as she was getting off the bus and I yelled at her but she didn't hear me. The driver just shut the door and drove on, of course.'

'Of course.'

'So I took the book home. Anyway, it turns out to be a book of ghost stories. Really neat things about haunted castles and headless riders and footsteps heard from the floor above. I *love* that kind of stuff!'

'I don't,' Lois replied quickly. 'It's all so stereotype. I mean, every ghost is mourning for a lost child or a lost lover, it's a bore.'

'Well, I think they're just great. There was this one story about a woman who lived in a castle somewhere in England, and one night when her husband wasn't home she heard the door to her bedroom open.'

'The hinges squeaked and it woke her,' Lois said.

'Right. So she fumbles for a match and lights the candle on the bedside table and there is this *thing*, this apparition just kind of glowing there, sort of floating off the floor. She wants to scream, of course, but no sound comes out of her throat. So she takes a better look and she sees that this is the ghost of a woman. The ghost has on long skirts and wears her hair in high curls and – '

'And is the ghost of her husband's first wife and she didn't know the guy had been married before.' Lois finished the story for her.

Midge scowled at her. 'You've read it.'

'No.' Lois smiled and took another sip of her drink. 'That's why I *don't* read that stuff.'

Undaunted Midge continued. 'Well, anyway there is another one. It seems this old man went to . . .'

At that moment the maitre d' came over to them saying their table was ready. They left the bar, carrying their drinks, to a table near the wall. As they had already placed their order, the first courses were waiting for them along with the butter and soft rolls. As soon as they sat down, Midge started in on her shrimp cocktail and Lois began spreading her pâté. They munched for awhile in silence, their eyes darting round the room to see who else was there that they knew but didn't know.

Midge sat back, pushing the empty glass slightly away from her. She dabbed at her lips with the napkin, making sure she didn't remove her lipstick at the same time. 'So anyway, as I was trying to tell you, in this other story that really raised the goosebumps on my arm, there was this old man who went to an antique shop and saw a picture he liked. I think it was an engraving. So he paid for it and he brought it back to his house. Well he hung it on the wall and admired it but then one day he noticed something funny down in the lower corner. The right-hand corner as you look at the thing.'

Lois stopped spreading the last bit of pâté. Her hands with the knife and the bit of bread hung motionless in midair. 'He saw something *funny* down there? What?'

'It was like an ink stain and he was positive it hadn't been there when he first bought the picture. So the next day he looked and the stain had changed. It had moved up the picture.'

'Wait a minute.' Lois put her knife and bread on her plate. 'What kind of a picture was this? I mean, what was the subject matter of the thing?'

'A house,' Midge said. 'An old house, some big old place with a lot of windows and a lot of lawn.'

Lois stared her friend directly in the eye. 'Bob has told you, hasn't he?'

Midge stared back. 'Bob has told me what? What are you talking about?'

'He did, didn't he?'

'I haven't seen Bob,' she said. 'What the hell are you talking about? You gonna let me finish telling you the story or not?'

'About the figure in the engraving. The one you gave us. He told you, didn't he?' Lois angrily picked up her napkin, wiped her fingers and stuffed the napkin back onto her lap. 'He made a promise to me that he wouldn't tell a soul and I made the same promise to him. And now he's gone and told you about that little bastard under the glass! I don't know which is the bigger bastard: the little man or Bob!'

'Now wait a minute!' Midge reached out and put her hand over Lois'. 'I really don't know what in hell you're talking about but Bob hasn't told me anything. I haven't seen him. When could I see him?'

'He could have talked to you on the phone,' Lois replied, still angry.

'He could have but he didn't. You don't think I would have told you if I'd had a telephone call from your husband?'

'Well then, how did you know about the figure under the glass?'

'I just told you,' Midge said. 'I read it in that book the kid left on the bus. Christ, Lois, what's the matter with you?'

'You're positive,' Lois insisted, 'you're positive Bob didn't breathe a word of this to you?'

Midge looked at Lois in astonishment. 'Look, hon, I was in the process of telling you about a story I read in some book and you started going strange on me. I don't know what you're accusing me and Bob of doing, but you're wrong. Okay?'

'I want to read that book,' Lois said quickly.

'Sure,' Midge said, 'when I finish it I'll bring it to work.'

'No,' Lois said. 'I want to read that book *today*. Now!' She rose from her chair and stood beside the table.

'Sit down, for God's sake,' Midge whispered. 'I'll bring it over to your place after work tonight.'

'Now!' Lois' voice rose. 'I want to read it *now!*'

'Look, you're embarrassing the hell out of me,' Midge said angrily. 'Sit back down and eat your lunch. We'll get the book later.'

'I don't want to eat my lunch,' Lois said loudly. 'I want that book. Come on!' She grabbed Midge by the arm, trying to pull her up out of the chair.

'Lois, I'm trying to eat my lunch! You're making a fool of yourself.' Midge stared around the room at all the faces that were staring at them. 'Sit *down!*' she hissed.

But Lois wasn't going to sit down. 'Come on,' she said, 'let's go to your place. I want to read that book.'

Midge rose to her feet, her face turning red from all the attention Lois was causing. 'What about our food? We've already ordered.'

Lois took two ten dollar bills from her purse and threw them on the table. 'That ought to pay for it,' she said. 'Come on, let's go.'

As Lois hustled Midge from the restaurant, guiding the woman by a firm grip on her arm, the maitre d' came flustering over to them. 'Is there a problem, ladies? Is everything all right?' Midge started to apologize but Lois just moved her faster out the door.

The cab ride down to Midge's apartment was made in almost total silence. Midge had stopped asking questions Lois didn't intend to answer. Lois' mind was racing quickly, miles ahead of the cab and its traffic. When they got to the building, she told the cabbie: 'Wait here. We won't be but a minute.'

They took the elevator to Midge's floor and Lois fidgeted while Midge found her door key and they both went in. Midge went straight to her bedroom and came out with a book bound in blue boards. 'Here,' was all she said.

Lois took the book and looked at the title embossed on the cover. *Unexpected Tales* compiled by Esmund T. Whittlesby. She turned the first few pages and saw that the book had first been published in 1877, then reprinted several times. This edition was dated 1922. She turned to the table of contents.

'It's the one called "The Mezzotint",' Midge said curtly.

Lois scanned the list of stories, found the title and shut the book. She tucked it under her arm and started out the apartment door. 'Come on,' she said, 'the cab is waiting.'

On the drive back Lois kept the blue volume clutched tightly in her hands. She didn't open it, didn't try to read the story. Not yet and not there, in that cab. She wanted to be alone when she read it. She didn't know how much Midge knew about her engraving and her little man and she didn't want Midge chattering away while she read.

'Driver, I'll get out here,' she said to the cabbie. 'You can continue with my friend to her office.'

'Here?' Midge broke her silence. 'You're not going back to the office?'

'No. I want to read this. I can walk from here. It's only a couple of blocks over.' She had the door open as soon as the cab had come to a stop at the corner and climbed out. 'See you,' she said and started closing the door. She stopped, pulled it open again and smiled at Midge. 'I know you think I'm buggy, but maybe I can explain everything later. Maybe. Thanks, Midge.' There was another smile and she shut the door and hurried around the corner.

Inside her own apartment, she kicked off her shoes and hung her coat and scarf in the closet. She went into the kitchen and put some ice cubes into a tall glass, and poured a liberal quantity of Scotch over the cubes. She came back into the living room and, taking the blue covered book into her hands, she fluffed some cushions on the sofa and settled back against them. This story, this work of fiction, just might have the clues she and Bob had been looking for. She turned to the correct page and started to read.

THE MEZZOTINT

There had been a slow and steady rainfall all that afternoon and my rooms were damp and dark because of it. I had made a small fire in the grate but it had done very little to remove the shadows that seemed to lurk in each corner. I was not happy in this, my new living quarters. I was accustomed to more elegant surroundings and a proper sitting room and sleeping quarters. My dear wife, who had been my dear companion for so many years, had been placed in the churchyard only two months before, and I could no longer bear to live in the same house where we had spent such happy times. My few friends considered it a rash gesture on my part but I sold the house and sold most of the possessions we had accumulated over the years. I had found this smaller accommodation and had saved back only those household items that I deemed necessary to refurnish my new quarters. I took very few things with me, for each item held the memory of my dear love.

It was because of that that I found myself walking in the mist that afternoon. I needed a cushion for the large easy chair that I like to sit in when I read. I had not wanted to keep any of the cushions from my home, for my wife had embroidered and sewn each and every one of them herself. As I walked down a side street, a street not clattering with horses' hooves and the rattle of carriage wheels against the paving stones, I realized I had never been there before. I thought, in all the years that I had dwelt in this city, that I had trod each of its alleys and walks by that time. But this was a street that was new to me and I entered further into it with mixed emotions, not unlike that of discovery combined with reluctance.

Then there it was, in a shop window. I can't recall if I was more fascinated by the wonderful carved and gilded frame or by the grandeur of the house itself. It was a magnificent picture and a strong desire to possess it came over me in an instant. Almost as if I was moving against my will I found my footsteps heading towards the shop door, then found myself inside that very shop.

The proprietor was an old man, white haired and thin, even older than myself. He greeted me with a bow, and when I told him I would like to see the picture in the window he seemed to hesitate for a moment. Then he bowed again and went to collect it.

He took it over to a table where there was an oil lamp. Turning up the wick, I examined the object of my interest. It was an engraving. It was exceedingly well drawn and well burnished. The subject matter was that of a large house that sat in the centre of an immaculate stretch of lawn. I could not discern what architectural style the house was in, for it seemed to be both Georgian and Italianate. There were only two floors to the house and both of them were lined with large windows. There were eight windows on each level, four on one side and four on the other with a large door on the ground floor and a small balcony directly above it. A tiled roof spanned the house and there was a banner of some sort flying from a mast on a small cupola on the roof.

101

The lawn was magnificent. It was unbroken by trees or bushes or cultivated circles of plants that are so fashionable on front lawns today. There was, on the right side of the house – and by that I mean to indicate the right side from the viewer's point of view, a small gnarled tree. On the left side of the house there were several large trees, a grove one could almost call them, and they were densely and darkly drawn.

I lifted the frame closer to the light to see the markings in the white space between the image and the frame but it was blank. There was only one word engraved there: CORRA.

I asked the proprietor the provenance of this picture, calling his attention to the fact that neither the artist nor the publisher had seen fit to sign their work. He shook his head and stated that he knew nothing about its heritage, that it had been brought into his shop one day by a young woman who had wanted to sell it. She had said she found it in the attic of a house she had purchased and had no use for it on her own walls. But, the old man remarked to me, it was a well-executed art work; and then he turned it around to show me how securely it had been mounted to the antique gilt frame. The back had been fastened with strips of linen over wooden pegs and that, he assured me, was evidence itself that it was not newly created but probably at least a century old.

I asked him the price and then held my breath, fearful that his response would be far greater than my purse would allow. He quoted me a low figure, so low, in fact, that I asked him to repeat it, thinking I had misunderstood the old gentleman. I gladly paid his asking price. He wrapped the engraving well to keep out the elements and I quickly carried it back to my living quarters.

I hung it on the wall of my one large room. I placed it exactly opposite from my reading chair and, I must admit, I got great pleasure from glancing up at it from time to time as I lifted my eyes from a printed page.

Then one morning I noted something rather peculiar. In the lower right hand corner of the engraving a small smear of ink had appeared. Thinking it was something on the outside of the glass, I wiped it with a damp cloth, but I could not erase it for the stain was under the glass, indeed on the engraving itself. I scowled at it and felt saddened, for I had truly come to love that picture and had considered it perfect. Now this stain had arrived to mar that perfection.

Two days later, as I was reading the morning journal, I glanced up at the engraving and saw that the stain had moved. It was no longer just a small blot in the corner but had changed its form and was now up upon the lawn itself. I rose from my sitting position, removed the picture from the wall and carried it to the window where I could examine it by sunlight. Yes, my eyes had not been playing tricks on me: the spot had grown and changed. I wondered what could make the ink react in such a manner and even thought of returning it to the old man in his shop for a refund, but I knew this was not his responsibility. He had no knowledge of this engraving apart from the fact that it had been discovered in a dusty attic. No, the purchase had been mine and I would have to live with it.

And live with it I did even when, over the next few days, the blemish under the glass changed shape again and took on the definite form of a man. I could not believe what my eyes told me. There he was, standing openly and clearly upon the lawn of my house. (I had taken to calling it 'my' house, for over a period of time I had come to feel that possibly I had dwelt there in previous existences.) The man, this intruder on my front lawn, was dressed in a full length cloak that fell from his shoulders to the ground. He wore a wide-brimmed hat that concealed his neck and head.

A short time after its first appearance (I regret now that I did not make punctual entries in a diary), the figure moved again. He moved up the lawn a little further. He had ceased his movement with one foot in front of the other as if poised to take another step. I was fully cognisant that there was nothing I could do to stop him.

Over the next few weeks the silent and unwanted visitor moved upwards towards the house. There was no sign of this movement upon the engraving itself: indeed, in each new position I found him he seemed to be perfectly blended with the lines of the original engraver's hand.

Then one morning he reached the house. All I could do was wait to see what would next transpire. I only had a day or two of anticipation when I noted that one of the lower windows had lifted open during the night. The window on the ground floor adjacent to the massive front door. This window had always been shut before. Now it was open, yet the others remained closed.

I sat up all that night, watching from my chair across the

103

room, with only the glow of a single candle to illuminate the scene. Just as I was about to nod off I caught him in movement. He turned and glanced quickly, first to one side and then to the other. There was only a glimpse of his face but it appeared to be round and fat and with small piercing eyes. He did not look back at me, but rather raised himself slightly over the window sill, pulled himself inside and vanished into the house. Needless to say my emotion was that of absolute incredulity. My intellect was unable to admit what my eyes had offered as being true. I sat there for the remainder of the night, wondering if he would make a reappearance at the window. He did not.

Several days elapsed and there was nothing different about my engraving, nothing that an unknowing stranger could perceive. There was no one on the lawn, the house had not been disturbed. There was just one sign that my mysterious visitor had been there: the window on the ground floor remained open.

On the last day of February (I remember the date well, for I had attended a birthday celebration for an old friend), I returned to my rooms and saw the little man again. He was standing at the window, looking outwards onto the lawn. Now, for the first time, I could see the round face and those small eyes. He had a stub for a nose and his mouth was grim and unsmiling. I sat in my chair and I waited for what might next transpire.

He did not keep me waiting long. He climbed out of the window and landed easily on his feet on the grass. Then he reached back into the house and lifted something from the floor. Clutching it in his arms he turned back towards me.

I was thunderstruck, for next to his wretched cloak he carried a small child. I could not tell if it was a male or female child because he had it wrapped in such a fashion that only its face was visible. It was not an infant, however, for from the size of it as it lay in his arms it was probably about five years old. I'm sure it was old enough to have been able to walk by itself, had this creature permitted its little legs to touch the ground.

I reiterate, dear reader, and ask you to understand my total impotence in this matter. There was absolutely nothing I could do to stop this fiend from completing his deed.

The next day he started down the lawn, not in the direction he had first used, but down the left side of the house, at an angle and towards the grove of trees at the side edge of the engraving. Each day he got farther and farther from the house and nearer and nearer to the trees. Each day his body changed position, first one foot from under the cloak, then the other. Even the movement of the hem of his cloak changed as he proceeded. Also subject to change was the arms and legs of the innocent child. I could make out differences in the bulges under the blanket in which the unfortunate youth had been wrapped. It seemed, as it appeared to me, that the victim was moving its arms and kicking with its legs in protest.

Then one day the man reached the grove of trees and even as I watched he slipped silently into them. Then I noticed, on still another day, some slight movement as he walked through them. Then he reached the edge of the engraving and, still holding the child in his arms, vanished out of the picture completely. He never returned. Nor did the child, and one day, months afterwards, I happened to notice that someone had closed the window.

CHAPTER EIGHT

Bob looked up from his desk. 'Lois! Hi, hon!' He saw the expression on her face. 'What's the matter?'

'Put your coat on,' she said tersely. 'I want you to buy me a drink.'

'Buy you a drink? I've got booze here in the office and, speaking of offices, why aren't you in yours?'

'Put your coat on,' she repeated. She handed him his coat from the hook on the wall. 'I have something I want to show you.'

'Can't you show me here?'

'You're going to need a drink when you see *this*,' she said. He looked at her. 'You're not smiling. Something is wrong.'

'I'm not smiling, you're right. Let's go.'

They left his office building and walked the two blocks to the neighbourhood bar where Bob sometimes had a quick lunch. At that time of the afternoon they were the only customers, with the exception of a pair of elderly black women in a rear booth drinking beer straight from the bottle.

Bob got two Scotches from the bartender and brought them to the booth Lois had settled into. 'Now what's this all about?' he asked as he slid in across from her.

Lois reached into her purse and brought out the book of ghost stories. 'Read the story that starts on page ninety-seven,' she said.

'You brought me away from my work and out into the cold to read a story? I don't believe it.' He stared at the cover. 'What's with you?'

'Midge gave it to me. She found it on a Madison Avenue downtown bus. It's either a helluva coincidence or else you told Midge the whole story.'

'Story? What story?' He raised his voice somewhat because one of the ladies in the back booth had put some money in the juke box and Aretha Franklin wailed out through the musty, neon-lit air. 'What do you mean, told Midge?'

'About the engraving. About the little man under the glass. You promised me you'd tell nobody. Remember?'

He glared at her. 'Of course I remember. And I didn't. I haven't seen Midge since the day she brought that damned thing. How could I tell her anything? You know at times, Lois, you can be real annoying.'

'Then it was a coincidence,' she sighed. 'I believe you. I'm sorry. If it wasn't a coincidence then it must be another sign.'

'You sure you're okay?' he asked.

'I'm okay,' she said.

'Let me see the book.' He wanted to say a lot more but decided it wouldn't do to get his wife upset in a public place, even in a public place as seedy as this one.

'Page ninety-seven,' she said.

He nodded, opened the book and glanced up at her. 'You want me to read this thing now? All of it?' She nodded. 'To myself or aloud?' he grinned. She didn't reply so he started reading. He read straight through the few pages of the story, not stopping even to pick up his glass of whisky. Lois' eyes examined his face as he read, trying to see his emotions, trying to gauge where he was in the story. He finished reading, closed the book and pushed it across the table to her. Aretha Franklin still wailed.

'Well?' she asked.

'You're right. It's a helluva coincidence.' He let out a long breath, one he had been holding since about halfway through the story. 'I mean even down to the name Corra.'

'But what do you think it means?'

'I don't know what it *means*,' he said. 'It is an interesting story, rather badly written, I thought. Kind of so-so Victorian bullshit.'

'That's not what I want to know,' she finished her drink. 'Why do you think what happened to the old man in the story is happening to us? I mean, he bought his picture back in the days of horses and oil lamps. That was a long time ago. Why is it all happening again? Why is the spooky man moving across our paper lawn *again*?'

'Well, first of all,' Bob said, 'you are confusing two important points. The man and his picture are fiction. You and I are real. So you can't say it's happened *before*. It never happened before. That's just a story.'

'How do you know? Why are you so sure it's fiction?'

'It says so right here.' Bob reached for the book and opened the cover to the frontispiece. 'Look. "Tales compiled by Esmund T. Whittlesby." It doesn't say they are *true* stories.'

'It doesn't say they are fiction either,' she returned. 'That Whittlesby guy went around finding ghost stories and then published them in book form. Some could be true and some could be fiction. He just doesn't say which are which.'

'Yeah, but look, Lois – ' Bob thumbed through the pages. 'This for instance. "It was then that I turned to see the spirit floating down my staircase. I knew I had to do something to stop it before it entered the drawing room where my dear mother lay so weak and ill . . ." I mean, come on, this lady has to stop a ghost from giving her mother another heart attack? That's not fiction? It is to me.'

Lois held her ground. 'It could be true. Lots of people see ghosts. You know that and so do I.'

He took a sip of his whisky. 'I don't know that,' he said.

'Because you don't *want* to know it,' she replied, rather angrily. 'You've never wanted to know about those things.'

He reached over and put his hand on hers. 'Look hon, let's not get back into that old argument again. Not now. I've got work to do this afternoon. You go on home and I'll bring something in from the Italian deli for supper.'

'That's all you are going to say about that story? I don't believe you!'

'What do you want me to say? I said it was badly written and is a bunch of crap! What can I add to that?'

'You must at least have some opinion as to why the man in our picture is behaving exactly like the one in this book. I mean, we have both treated this as being the most natural thing in the world. Some little bastard is crawling up an engraving on our wall, and we act as if *everybody* has a man moving under their glass.'

'I've played it cool because of you,' he said, choosing his words carefully. 'I didn't want you to get more upset than you already are.'

'Oh, it's been done for *me*? Poor crazy old Lois? I don't need your sympathy, thank you. I can manage on my own.'

'I doubt it sometimes,' he said, his voice low.

'Well,' she said evenly, 'there are times when I have doubts about you too. Sometimes I feel like Ingrid Bergman in *Gaslight* where she thinks Charles Boyer is trying to drive her mad.'

'That's unfair,' he said.

'Maybe to you it is, but not to me.'

At that he got up. 'You want another drink?' She shook her head. 'Okay then, I'm going back to work. I'm not going to sit here arguing with you.' He started buttoning his coat and walking towards the door.

'Bob!' Lois called after him. He stopped and turned back towards her. 'We're not going to Jamaica in February. We're going to Scotland. To Corra.'

He walked quickly back to the booth. 'Now wait a minute,' he said angrily, then glanced at the two black ladies who were listening to him now that their records had been played. He lowered his voice. 'We have discussed this and we have agreed that we will *not* change our holiday plans. There are several good reasons why, and you know each and every one of them. I'm not going to argue this with you. I'm not going to argue this with you *here* or any place else.'

'What about the man in the picture?' she flared back. 'What are you going to do about *him*?'

'Screw him!' Bob said loudly and walked out of the bar.

Lois sat for a while, turning her empty glass in her hands, wondering how she was going to convince Bob to change his mind. She had to convince him. There was no other way.

It made perfect sense to her. If the little man in the story had started the very same way as he did inside her picture, and if he was wearing the same clothes and moving up the same lawn, and if it – not *if* but *was* – the very same house, then even though it happened over a hundred years ago it must be happening *again*. It must be happening right now!

She went to the bar and ordered another shot and more ice, then sat down and made fresh circles with the bottom of the tumbler. For some reason the little bastard was doing it all over again. Why, she didn't know, but if he was acting exactly as he did in the story, then he would reach the house, a window would open and later he would appear with a child and carry it into the trees. Not just into the trees but completely off the edge of the engraving. He was about to steal another little kid and carry it into oblivion, into nothingness. What was there once he had left the engraving itself? Nothing. How could anyone hope to save a child who was being kidnapped into thin air, into absolute non-existence? The events were happening all over again. At this very moment he was moving closer and closer to the house. Closer to that innocent little boy.

Her heart stopped. She took a deep breath, wondering if it would ever beat again. She drank the whisky quickly. 'Jesus!' she said aloud, then relaxed slightly as she felt the muscle inside her chest start working again. 'I never thought of that,' she whispered. 'I never put the two of them together. Oh my God. Suppose he's after Tony? Suppose that's where they've taken my Tony and that little bastard is going to steal him away from there.'

She started to cry. She could feel the warm tears start building up on her eyelids. The two women in the back booth were leaving and as they passed her one of them stopped. 'He's not worth crying over, honey. Don't waste your time. I cried over my man when he left and now I'd cry if he told me he was coming back.' She patted Lois on the arm. 'Lots of fish out there in that sea.'

* * *

When Bob returned to the apartment, Lois was in the kitchen munching a sandwich. 'Hey,' he said, holding up two white paper bags, 'I told you I'd bring some supper from the deli.'

She walked out of the kitchen, almost brushing against him

but pulling just far enough away so that their bodies didn't touch, and she took her sandwich into the living room.

'Do you want any of this rigatoni or what?' he called to her. She didn't answer. He looked into the living room. 'I said are you going to have some of this stuff or not?' She shook her head, picked up a magazine and started flipping the pages as she ate. 'Oh, I get it. You're not talking to me.' He paused. 'Okay. Fine with me. You want to play at being three years old, go ahead.' He went back into the kitchen and put the Italian food on a platter. Then he marched silently into the living room and took a magazine for himself and just as silently returned to the kitchen. He ate quickly and irritably. There was no sound from his wife.

About a half hour later, he came into the living room and switched on the television. 'There's something I want to see,' he said. She shrugged, got up from the sofa and went into the bedroom, closing the door. He watched two programmes he wasn't really interested in plus half of a movie he couldn't make head nor tail of and finally switched off the set and went into the bedroom. He undressed in the dark and, putting on the grey sweatshirt he always slept in, got into bed.

They lay like that for awhile. Neither of them speaking, each knowing the other was awake. Finally she said softly: 'Bob, we've got to help that little boy.'

He had been waiting for her to speak first. 'What little boy?'

'The one inside the house. We have to stop the man from taking him again.'

He sighed. 'That was fiction. Understand that.'

'You don't know that. Anyway what's happening to our picture is not fiction. It's real and it's taking place now.'

'The kid getting grabbed is over and done with. It's ancient history. Let's not discuss this anymore.'

She sat up and turned towards him. Even in the darkness he could see that her face was streaked with tears. 'That figure is moving along the engraving now. Right now. That means the kidnapping is going to take place again. Very soon. It's happening to the engraving so it must also be happening on the front lawn of that house in Corra. Now! At this very moment.'

'You don't make sense,' he said.

'What does make sense in all this?' she demanded, her voice rising. 'I can't explain it any other way. You know what

110

I'm talking about. My *feelings*. My *hunches*. You know my hunches on these things are usually right.'

'Okay, I'll give you that point. Your batting average is pretty high on some things. But – ' He reached out and touched her hair. 'We're still going to Jamaica.'

Lois turned swiftly and slipped out of bed. She stood there looking down at him. 'I can't believe you could be so cold. There's a little boy over there who needs our help!'

'I think you're the one who needs help,' he said and then started to apologize. 'I really didn't mean that. I'm sorry.'

'That's twice today you've told me I was going crazy!' she shouted. 'Twice! Is that what you want? You want me to go crazy?'

'Look, hon,' he started pleadingly but she hurried from the room slamming the door behind her. He waited about five minutes, hoping she would come back on her own. When she didn't he got up and walked into the living room, still wearing just the sweatshirt. Lois was leaning against the wall, staring out into the dark street below. He put his hand on her shoulder but she shook it off and moved away from him. 'I said I'm sorry,' he said. 'It was stupid of me.'

'You don't care how you hurt me,' she yelled.

Stunned by this outburst, he put a finger to his lips. 'Not so loud. You'll wake the whole building.'

'I don't care!' she yelled again. 'You don't care what happens to me or to anybody else! It's always you and what you want and when you want it!'

'Look, I said I was sorry.'

'There's a child out there about to be taken from his home and probably murdered. An innocent kid who can't defend himself and we have been given a sign from above to help him, and you refuse. You want to sun your ass in Jamaica! A child has been given to us to save and you won't lift a finger to help.'

'Would you please lower your voice,' he said, his own voice loud now too. 'Jesus Christ! Does everyone in Manhattan have to hear you?'

'Everyone in Manhattan should know how heartless you are!'

He stopped and stared at her. His eyes widened. 'I don't believe you,' he said softly. 'Jesus, I don't believe you.' Lois watched him warily. 'That kid in the picture. You think it's Tony, don't you? You think that by going over to Scotland you're going to get Tony back. I'll be goddamned.'

She came at him, suddenly, striking at his chest and shoulder with her fists. He managed to grab one of her arms and swing her away from him, then with his free hand he slapped her sharply across the face. 'Calm down now for Christ's sake! Calm down!'

She crumpled against him as if she had been a marionette and someone had cut her strings. He gathered her in his arms and almost carried her back into the bedroom and put her into bed. She didn't say anything else to him after that and soon he could hear the slow, steady breathing that told him she had fallen asleep. He propped himself up on one elbow and stayed like that, looking at her. There was just enough light coming through the bedroom window to see her face. What was wrong with her? He'd never struck her before. He didn't believe in men hitting their wives, but it was the only thing he could do to calm her. Had Tony's death twisted her that badly? Was Tony's kidnapping really driving his wife crazy?

He got up and went into the bathroom. He didn't bother to turn on the light and his single steady stream splashed into the water in darkness. On the way back to the bedroom he stopped and looked at the engraving hanging on the wall. 'What are you up to now, you little fucker?' he whispered at the image under the glass.

Then the little man turned and smiled at Bob. As he smiled he lifted one arm and made a gesture like cutting a throat.

CHAPTER NINE

Lois served Bob his coffee and two slices of buttered toast. She hadn't mentioned last night. Hadn't apologized for screaming and hitting him. Bob knew that she never would. 'I don't want that damned thing in the house any longer. Get rid of it today,' she said. 'Take it out and burn it.'

'Burn the engraving?' He raised his eyebrows. 'It's worth some money.'

She sighed. 'That figures. I ask you to do something and you argue about it.'

He was tempted to say something, but knew all it would do was rekindle the still smouldering ashes from last night's argument. 'I'll take it to the office and leave it there, if that's what you want.' He watched her face. 'I'll wrap it good and put it in the back warehouse. It won't take up much space and it'll be out of here. Okay?'

'I would prefer that you destroy it,' she said calmly, 'but if you think it's worth some money, then fine. Do that. Take it and hide it but get it out of my sight.'

'The man in that appraisal shop said it was worth about twelve hundred dollars. Remember? You don't want to burn something that valuable. I'll take it to Christie's or somebody and put it up for auction. Okay?'

'As long as it's out of here,' she said. 'I never want to see the damned thing again.' She walked from the kitchen and into the bedroom. When she came back out she was wearing her coat, scarf and snow boots. 'I'm not eating any breakfast. I want to get to the office early. Got things to do,' she said. With that she walked out of the apartment. Bob could only sit and listen to the front door close behind her.

Lois didn't take her car even though it had snowed overnight. She stuffed her hands into the deep pockets of her winter coat and walked the fifteen blocks to her office. This has gone too far, she told herself as she waited at the first crossing for the light to change. That engraving has started to ruin our marriage. I wish Midge had never given it to us. She started toward the opposite corner. I don't know *why* it came to us the way it did and I don't know what I can do about it. I've seen the little bastard under the glass, I've seen him move. I know there isn't anyone under there. Not really. There couldn't be. What this is is some sort of psychic sign, some warning of what is about to happen. I've read enough books. I've seen enough movies. I know what it really is. But what can I do about it? A delivery truck went by and if she hadn't jumped quickly she would have been sprayed with the slush it churned up. She walked on. It does them a lot of good to give me signs like these, she muttered into the wind. I mean, what can *I* do about them? I'm here in New York and the house is way over in Scotland. *I* can't save that kid. I can't go charging over the ocean and wait as some little

113

creep climbs through a window in some old house in a town I never even heard of. I really don't know why you guys wasted your time telling me about it. She looked up at the sky as if expecting the spirits who had sent her this message would be floating above the brown bricks of the Arundle Carpet Company. All she got was snow in her face. Maybe I *am* going bananas. Maybe Tony's death has sent me skidding. And now I've got that kid in the engraving confused with Tony. No, no . . . there is no kid in my engraving. The kid is in the ghost story. For all I know there may never be a kid in my engraving. It may only be in the story, only in that old book of fictional tales. She underlined the word *fictional* in her mind. It felt better that way. I can't do this to Bob. She waited for another light to change then started across the street. He's a good man and a good husband. He's as upset over losing Tony as I am. I keep forgetting that fact. Tony was Bob's son too. Not just mine. I have to look at this thing from his point of view as well. First he loses a son and then his wife starts going bonkers. 'No,' she said aloud, 'Bob is too important to me to let this continue.' A man wearing a dark overcoat and carrying a briefcase looked at her.

'You say something, lady?'

She shook her head. 'Sorry.' She turned at the next corner. It wasn't the turn she usually made but she didn't want the man to think she was trying to pick him up. I've got to be a better wife, she said to herself. I've got to make a lot of things up to Bob. He doesn't deserve to have his family crumble around him like this. Not like this. Not with a dead child and a crazy wife. Whatever is happening in that picture will happen whether I do anything to stop it or not. If it's fate, then I am helpless to save that child. Just like the old man in the story, all I can do is watch it happen. Well I'm not going to watch. She tucked her scarf determinedly deeper into her coat collar. When it happens – *if* it happens – I won't be there to see it. She stopped and looked at her reflection in the glass window of an office supply store. You are going to stop this crap right now, she said to the face reflected back at her. Make up your mind. Right now. You're going with your husband to Jamaica.

* * *

'And do you remember the time that Eddie Lipski wore that witch's hat to class and Miss Upton pretended she didn't notice?'

Bob laughed and speared some more salad onto his fork. 'She was determined not to give him any attention at all. How she managed to conduct the entire class that day is a miracle.'

'And Eddie was pissed!' the man across the restaurant table said. 'He was sure old lady Upton would have a fit and when she didn't it just made Eddie all the more angry.'

'So the next day he came into the classroom with a raw hot dog sticking out of his fly!' Bob laughed again and said, 'I haven't thought of that in years.'

'And then Miss Upton's only comment to him was, "Eddie, too bad you were born with such a little one. My butcher sells that size for about three cents apiece." I've never seen a kid get redder in the face before!' Bob's luncheon companion was laughing so hard now that he almost spilled the wine in his glass. 'Whatever happened to Eddie anyway?'

'He runs the meat section at Safeway Supermarket on Delancy!' Bob was laughing just as hard as Sam was. 'If Miss Upton is still alive I wonder if she buys her meat there!'

Sam Rothberg set his wine glass on the table and wiped the corner of each eye with his napkin. 'We had some crazy times at that school,' he grinned. He smiled at his old friend Bob Bruno. 'God, how many years ago that was.'

'Too many,' Bob replied, 'but they were great times. We even managed to learn something.'

'In spite of Eddie's hot dog.' Sam laughed again. This was the first time since Bob's wedding that he had been alone with Sam. He and Sam had run together in the same pack at high school, had gone to football games together and once, without knowing it, had even dated the same girl. While Bob had gone into his father's restaurant supply business, Sam had gone on to college and had managed to earn a psychiatrist's degree. Now he ran a rather successful clinic in Brooklyn. Most of his clients were welfare cases so his fees came up front and were promptly paid by the government. He didn't get rich women with phobias about their place in society but rather women strung out by poverty or unable to cope with their kids on drugs. After the steaks and French fries had been served, Sam looked at Bob. 'Okay,' he said with a smile, 'what's on your mind? You didn't invite me to this plush place to talk about old times.'

Bob shrugged. 'I was afraid you'd be clever enough to pick that up. I *do* have a problem that I'd like to talk about with you. I don't intend to pick your brain for free,' he added quickly. 'I expect to get your bill.'

'You said when you invited me that you were paying the tab in this place. That's enough for me. So shoot. What's on your mind? Is it Lois?'

Bob's eyes widened. 'How did you know?'

'Professional guess,' he smiled. 'What's the matter? You two not having a sex life?'

Bob shook his head. 'No, not that. That part's fine.' He paused. 'Well, almost. No, it's kind of a long story.'

'You take as long as you want,' said the psychiatrist. 'I'll keep drinking this fine wine as long as you pay for it.'

'Well,' Bob began, 'a friend of hers, a girl who works in her office, gave her a framed engraving. Gave it to her as a gift. She got it with another picture at an auction and didn't want it.' Sam nodded. 'Lois really liked it and we hung it on the wall in our hallway. Then one day Lois thought she noticed something different about the picture.'

'Different?' Sam carried a bite of steak to his mouth. 'How different?'

Bob took a deep breath and told Sam the story. He started with the blob in the corner and worked all the way up through the little man appearing on the lawn, then the book of ghost stories and ended with Lois' insistence that the event was happening all over again and that *they* were being given some kind of sign from heaven to go and save the child inside the house.

'Where does Tony's death fit into all this?' Sam got to the heart of the problem with just one question.

'She thinks the kid in the picture could be Tony. She hasn't said it in so many words but I know that's what she thinks. We went up to Anthony Venutti's place for Thanksgiving and Lois had her worst spell so far.' Sam's eyebrows raised. 'She thought she saw Tony outside on the terrace and she broke a glass door trying to get at him.' Bob shook his head. 'It was all pretty grim.'

Sam put his fork on his plate. 'You know, it doesn't sound too good. It could be that Lois is on the verge of a nervous

116

breakdown. I mean, I think she's a great lady but a *normal* person doesn't go around seeing little men under glass and thinking it's all happening because God is showing her a sign.'

'I know,' Bob said quietly. 'I understand what you're saying.'

'Is she under a lot of pressure at work?'

'No more than usual.'

'And you say your marriage is okay?'

'I guess. As good as can be expected under the circumstances.'

'This little man thing that she thinks she sees. You've seen the engraving. Do *you* think it's changed any? I mean, have you noticed any movement of the figure?'

Bob took a deliberate sip of wine and set the glass carefully onto the white tablecloth. He looked Sam straight in the eyes. 'No,' he said, 'I haven't seen it move. Of course not.'

Sam picked up his fork. 'Well then, I think what you have is a sick lady on your hands and the sooner you get her into some kind of therapy, the better. I couldn't see her, of course, because she's a friend but I could give you the names of a couple of doctors you can call and set up an appointment. Lois will have to agree to the sessions, obviously.'

'She won't. She doesn't think anything is wrong with her.'

Sam emptied the last of the wine in the bottle and signalled to the waiter for a fresh bottle. 'Then you're going to have to insist,' he said. 'You're going to have to get her to start taking regular sessions. If not, my friend, you may end up with a real basket case on your hands.'

*   *   *

Lois and Midge left the office together that night. Bob had telephoned saying he would be late. Something about doing an inventory. Midge suggested they stop at a deli and eat at Lois' place. They bought some brown bread, a pound of sharp yellow cheese and two fat Polish sausages that Midge just *had* to try. They added a six-pack of beer before they got to the checkout counter.

Midge put the sausages into a pot of boiling water and stirred at them with a fork as if that would make them cook faster. 'These things smell great,' she said as she leaned over the pot to inhale the vapour. 'My grandmother used to make sausages that looked like these. I just hope they taste like Grandma's. Doubt it, though.'

'I know what you mean,' Lois said. 'I've eaten my way through a ton of stuff here in New York hoping it would taste the same as it used to back in West Virginia. It never does.'

'Maybe our tasters have gotten older.'

'I don't think it's that,' Lois replied. 'Our memories are playing tricks on us. We only *think* that Grandma's apple sauce cake was as wonderful as we remember it. In reality it was probably just another cake like anybody else's.'

'Ah!' Midge shook her index finger at Lois. 'But it was Grandma's cake, and she had made it and we loved Grandma and she loved us. That's where the taste came from. That's why the cake from Spindelman's on Second Avenue doesn't taste like Grandma's. Mr Spindelman doesn't love us.'

'Thank God for that,' Lois said, grinning. 'Have you *seen* Mr Spindelman?'

Midge got the plates out of the cupboard and started setting the silverware on the kitchen table. Having space for a table in the kitchen was one of the main reasons Lois and Bob had rented this apartment. Most people Lois knew ate on stools at a Formica counter top. The dining room, just as it was back home, was reserved for special occasions. Having Midge in for a quick snack was not considered special.

'Oh shit!' Midge was looking on the shelf that held the spices and condiments. 'I thought you said you had brown mustard.'

'You didn't ask me about brown mustard,' Lois said.

'Yeah, I did. In the deli and you nodded.'

'Well, I must have misunderstood. Anyway, we don't. Bob used the last of it the other night and I forgot to get some more. There's some hot French mustard in there. Put that on the table.'

'No, no, no!' Midge grabbed her coat that she'd flung across one of the kitchen chairs. 'Can't have Polish sausage without brown mustard! Can't put French on it. It won't taste anything like Grandma's with French.' She buttoned up her coat. 'I'll only be a minute. I'll make a dash to the deli and be back before the sausages are ready. Anything else we need?' Lois shook her head. 'Bye. Be back in a flash.'

Lois continued to set the table. She put napkins beside each plate and set two English pub beer glasses beside them. Then her salt and pepper shakers in the shape of Garfield the cat. A cousin had given them to her as a joke wedding present, but she loved them. She considered them among the best

118

presents she and Bob had received. Then she went to the stove where the sausages were furiously boiling. She turned down the flame and waited until the water calmed down somewhat. She thought they were almost done. She heard the apartment door open and didn't bother to turn around as the footsteps came across the living room, down the hallway and into the kitchen. 'Did they have Grandma's taste in a mustard jar?' she asked. When there was no reply she turned around.

The scream that rose in her throat froze before it reached her lips.

Two men stood in the doorway. Each had a ski mask over his head. Each had a gun in his hand.

Lois felt her legs weaken and then her body began to crawl with a million pinpricks as visions of being mugged or raped crashed into her consciousness.

One of the men, the taller of the two, grabbed her arm and yanked her through the doorway. He turned her in the direction of the living room and pushed her along the hallway until they were by the sofa. Then he shoved her onto it. She had still not been able to utter a word.

'Where is it?' the tall one said, his voice slightly muffled by the mask.

Lois managed to stammer: 'Where is what?'

'You know what I'm talking about,' the man said gruffly. 'Where is it?'

'Oh God!' Lois heard her voice breaking as she tried to reply through her fear. 'I don't know what you're talking about.'

The smaller of the two went over to the desk by the television set and pulled out the drawers. He turned them upside down, scattering papers and photographs and rubber bands and letters everywhere. Then Lois heard him move down the hall, into their bedroom. She heard the same sounds of drawers being yanked from their runners and things falling.

'It's not here,' the man said, returning to the living room. Lois felt a little stronger. 'If you'll tell me what you're . . .?'

'Then just hold her,' the tall one said.

The other man went behind the sofa and put his hands heavily onto Lois' shoulders. She struggled but he was stronger than she was and he pressed her down into the cushions.

Her eyes grew wide as she watched the man in front of her take a leather box out of his overcoat pocket. He snapped open the lid and her eyes grew wider as she saw him remove a small, clear glass syringe.

The man behind her shifted one of his hands and grabbed her right arm. She was wearing a sweater over a short-sleeved blouse and he quickly pulled up the sleeve of the sweater, exposing her arm up past her elbow. Then the man with the syringe bent over her, pointing the needle at her skin.

'No!' she yelled but the man behind her stretched out her arm. He forced it into a rigid position. Her arm ached where he tightly gripped her.

'Don't move!' the tall man ordered. 'It'll be easier if you don't move.'

'Tell me what it is you want! Please don't hurt me.'

'Don't move, he told you,' the man behind her said, and his fingers sank deeper into the flesh.

Then the needle found what it had been looking for and plunged swiftly and almost painlessly into a blue vein. Lois was too shocked to speak, too terrified to jerk away. All she could do was watch the syringe fill rapidly with her blood and then wince as the needle was withdrawn.

The man behind her released his hold on her. The man in front of her slipped the gorged syringe into the leather case, snapped it shut and put it back into his overcoat pocket. Then, moving quickly, they went to the door, opened it and were gone.

Lois sat there in a daze. She was too stunned to think clearly. She managed to get to her feet and go over to the door. She slammed it shut and threw the two bolts and twisted the catch lock. She turned around and surveyed the mess over by the desk. Then she looked down at her arm. Yes, it had all been real. There was a small puncture in the bend of her arm and it was still leaking tiny drops of blood.

Then there was a pounding on the door. Lois screamed. It was the first time she had been able to release the sound that had been building up inside her. The pounding came again.

'Lois, open the door! It's me. Midge.'

Now Lois ran to the door, fumbled with the bolts and the catch lock and embraced the woman as she came into the apartment. 'Oh Midge! It was awful!' and she started to cry.

'Wait a minute. What are you talking about?' Midge's gaze went around the living room and she saw the mess by the desk. 'Jesus honey, what happened? Are you all right?'

Lois was slamming the bolts in the door again. Then she leaned against it, still crying. 'I thought it was you, Midge, but there were two of them and they had masks on and one of them had a hypodermic needle . . .'

'Hold on, hon.' Midge reached out and Lois went willingly into the safety of her arms. She put her head on the woman's shoulder and kept crying as Midge made soothing noises in her ear and lightly caressed her hair. When the heavy sobbing had abated, Midge led her gently to the sofa and sat beside her as Lois took several gasping breaths. 'Okay babe, now tell me what happened. Did they hurt you? What did they want?'

Lois shook her head. 'They didn't hurt me, try to rape me or anything, if that's what you mean. They were looking for something. They did the desk first and then in the bedroom. I haven't been in there yet. I don't know what it looks like.'

'What did they say?'

'I don't really recall.' Lois took another deep breath, trying to make her breathing return to normal. 'They didn't say a lot. One of them asked me where "it" was and when I asked them what they wanted they didn't tell me. Then the other one took out this hypodermic thing and while the other one held me down they drew out some blood. Look!' She pointed to the red spot on her inner arm. She still hadn't pulled her sweater sleeve back down.

'Christ, hon.' Midge examined the spot. 'Does it hurt?'

'No. It didn't even when he did it. I guess I was in such a state I couldn't feel it. And then they left.'

'Was that all? What did they take?'

'Just my blood, I guess. They didn't seem to find whatever it was they were looking for. I mean, they didn't have anything in their hands when they left.' She shuddered. 'It was spooky, Midge. Real spooky. I mean, all they seemed to steal from here was my *blood*.'

* * *

Bob came home just as soon as Midge phoned him. He found both women still on the sofa but Lois had stopped crying and had washed her face.

'It was all my fault,' Midge said. 'I should not have left the apartment door open when I went to the deli. It was a stupid thing to do.' She patted Lois on the arm. 'I'm sorry, hon.'

'Nonsense,' Lois replied. 'It wasn't your fault. They'd have got in one way or another.'

'And you don't want me to call the police?' Bob had wanted to call them as soon as he had talked with Lois, but she had vetoed the idea. What was done, was done, she had told him, and anyway what could they complain about? That the thieves had taken a tube full of her blood? 'They didn't harm you or hit you or mistreat you in any way?'

'Just scared the hell out of me.' She felt the prickly sensation in her body as she remembered the masked faces suddenly in the kitchen doorway. 'I was too frightened to scream. I relaxed a little bit when I realized they didn't want to hurt me. In fact the man who took my blood told me it would be easier on me if I didn't move. It's almost as if he didn't want me to be hurt.'

'And you can't give any better description of them than that? That they wore overcoats and ski masks and one was taller than the other?'

'I can't,' she said. 'It all happened so quickly that there was very little to remember.'

'I should never have gone for that damned mustard!' Midge said. 'I should have stayed here with you.'

Lois managed her first smile. 'It had nothing to do with you being here or not. In fact, I'm glad you weren't here. They might have hurt both of us then.'

Bob went into the kitchen and poured himself a drink. On his way back he looked into the bedroom. He rejoined the women and said, 'Bedroom looks like a tornado hit it. What the hell do you think they were looking for?'

Lois reached out for his glass and he handed it to her. She took a slow, deliberate swig. 'I have a theory,' she said, glancing first at Midge and then at her husband. They both waited. 'It's just an idea, mind you, and I know you'll both think it's silly but maybe, just maybe, they were after the engraving.'

'The engraving?' Midge's voice rose. 'You mean that picture I gave you? *That* engraving? That piece of junk?'

Bob looked at Lois. 'I think you're wrong.'

'Why would they want that thing?' Midge asked. 'What's so special about it?'

Bob was still looking at Lois. 'You haven't told her?'

'No.'

'Told me what?' Midge demanded. 'What haven't you told me?'

'It's too long a story to go into,' Bob replied. 'She'll tell you later. Sometime.'

'What's wrong with now?'

'Not just yet, okay, hon?' Lois said. 'I really don't feel like going into all of it now.'

'Okay, but I don't like being accused of causing whatever happened to you tonight. I mean, I did give that picture to you and if you think the robbers were after it, then this is all my fault for giving you the damned thing in the first place.' Midge got up and went into the kitchen. They could hear her putting ice cubes in a glass. 'But if that's what they were after,' she said as she walked back into the living room, 'why did they look in the desk drawers for it? It's too big for that. Why dump out the stuff in the bureau drawers? That picture wouldn't fit in those drawers.'

'Maybe they didn't know what size the picture was,' Lois said. 'Or maybe they thought we had taken it out of the frame and rolled it up. It would fit in a bureau drawer if we rolled it up.'

'Did they look for it on the walls?' Bob asked. 'Did you see them looking around the place first?'

Lois shook her head. 'I didn't. I was in the kitchen. They had time to look at the walls and see that it wasn't hanging there.'

'That old thing I gave you? I still can't believe it.' Midge rattled the ice cubes in her glass.

'And I have another theory,' Lois said, getting up from the sofa and walking toward the window. 'I know you're not going to like it, Bob, but it sticks in my mind and I can't get rid of it.' She turned and looked at him wishing she didn't have to say it. He watched her carefully. 'I think,' she resumed, 'that whoever it is that wants that picture – and I don't think either of those two men want it, I think they were paid by someone – whoever wants it wants to keep me from going to Corra. Wants to frighten me away from that house and the child inside it.'

'Oh for Christ's sake, Lois!' Bob exploded. 'Not that again! Please, dear Jesus!'

'See?' Lois said. 'I knew you wouldn't want to hear it.'

'I don't want to hear it because we have discussed it so damned many times! Stop beating a dead horse!'

Midge raised her voice. 'Would either one of you two shouters like to calm down and tell me what this is all about?'

'No!' Bob replied rudely. 'It's none of your business.'

Midge coloured. 'Well . . . then I'll stay out of it.'

'Fine, you just do that.'

'Whoever wants that picture,' Lois went on, 'hopes that by stealing it I won't see what happens. I won't see the man getting into the house and then stealing the little boy.'

'You don't know it's a boy,' Bob said, in the same tone he had used on Midge.

'Yes I do. I know it's a little boy.'

'And I suppose you know who the little boy is?'

'Yes,' she nodded. 'I do. It's my son.'

Midge spoke up again. 'What the hell are you two talking about?'

Bob glared at her and then ignored her. 'Please, Lois! Not that same bullshit again! I can't take much more of it.'

Lois' only reply was to hand him her empty glass. 'Fill this up,' she said, 'I need another drink.'

Seething with anger, Bob took her glass, then had second thoughts and threw it on the floor. 'You don't need a drink, you need help! You need to see a shrink and have him drive those crazy ideas out of your head! That's what you need.'

Midge scrambled off the sofa and went over to Bob. 'Now wait a minute,' she said, 'Lois has been through a helluva lot tonight and I don't think it's fair for you to talk to her like that. You may be her husband, but I'm her friend and I think you're acting like a horse's ass.'

'That's okay, Midge.' Lois walked past them both. 'You don't understand. You haven't been here when we've had conversations about this before. He won't change. He never tries to see my point of view. He's a macho Italian who's never wrong. Don't mind his screaming. I don't even listen to it any more.' She headed for the bedroom, then turned in the hallway. 'I'm going to take a Valium or two and I'm going to bed. I'm exhausted and I don't want to carry on this conversation. The stuff is still in the kitchen, Midge. Why don't the two of you eat it? I'll throw it out tomorrow morning if it's still there.' She turned and went into the bedroom, closing the door.

124

'You want another drink?' Bob asked Midge. 'One for the road?'

'No, thanks. I'd better get home.'

'I'm sorry I was rude to you.'

'That's okay.' She smiled. 'You had your reasons.'

He watched her as she put on her coat and snow boots, then he undid the latches and the lock on the door. Midge stepped into the outer hall and Bob followed her, leaving the door slightly ajar.

'Midge,' he said softly, 'what am I going to do?'

'I don't know,' she replied. 'It sounds like you got one helluva problem.'

'She's getting worse. More irrational every day and of course today didn't help matters any. Has she said anything to you about going to Scotland?'

'She's mentioned it a couple of times in the office but she still plans on going to Jamaica with you.'

'She wants to go over there, you know,' he said. 'She thinks Tony is still alive. She thinks he's in that house. She thinks what happened in that ghost story is happening all over again but this time the little man will carry Tony out of there. She's got it all confused in her mind.' He sighed. 'She's got our Tony and that child all mixed together.'

'You know what I think you should do?' Midge said.

'No. What?'

'I'd go off to Scotland and I'd find that damn house and I'd make her understand that there is nothing to all this. If she were there – right there – the reality of it would force her to understand there is nothing in all her fears.'

'But I've got tickets for Jamaica. Everything's set up.'

'Change them,' Midge said simply. 'If you don't get that girl over to Scotland soon, she may never be in a condition to go anywhere again. You delay and the woman you married will slip away from you forever. If you don't take her to Scotland then you'd better take her to a mental hospital.'

There was a loud gasp behind them and both of them turned quickly. Lois was standing in the doorway wearing her nightgown. From the expression on her face it was clear she had overheard their entire conversation.

CHAPTER TEN

The pilot had announced there would be quite a lot of fog over the English Channel several minutes before they landed, but Lois kept her nose pressed to the window anyway, hoping for her first glimpse of the fabled green English countryside. But the pilot had been right, there was nothing to see down there but billowing masses of white stuff.

She had left New York's Kennedy Airport covered in grimy weeks-old snow and shouldn't have been surprised when she saw London's Heathrow Airport was covered with the same. After all, it was the second week in January. The entire world froze in January, with the exception of strange places she had never wanted to visit like Chile, Australia and Ethiopia.

The trip had been Bob's Christmas surprise for her. They had dined out on the night of the twenty-fourth and during the meal he had taken a slim brightly wrapped package out of his suit jacket pocket. He had handed it to her just as she was about to take the first sip of champagne. He had asked her to wait and open the gift first. When she saw it was a round trip air ticket to London she burst into tears and almost knocked over the brimming champagne goblet in her haste to jump up and hug him. He looked embarrassed as people at other tables glanced in their direction. Lois was so pleased that she showed the tickets to two tables of complete strangers and when they applauded Bob for his gesture, he modestly rose and did a theatrical bow.

The trip to England didn't mean the trip to Jamaica had been called off, he had told her. They were still going down there with Anthony and Anne and they would still have their two weeks in the sun. The plans were that they would go to London for three days and nights (the hotel was included in the special deal he got from the travel agent), then they would take the train north to Scotland. They had reservations for three days at a hotel called the Waverley in the town of

Dumfries. They would rent a car (Bob had driven on 'the wrong side' of the road before) and they would go to Corra and see the house. They'd spend all three days there, if that was what Lois wanted, and then they would return to London and take the plane back to New York.

She had listened to him recite the itinerary as if it was a Shakespeare sonnet. Her eyes never left his and they were misted in pleasure, thankfulness and love. When he had finished she reached across the table and put her hand on his. 'This is so sweet of you,' she had said. 'How can I ever thank you enough?' He had replied: 'Just stay in love with me. Just be my Lois.' On Christmas morning they awoke late, their naked bodies still entwined under the warm woollen blankets.

They walked from the plane down a long corridor and then started following the signs and arrows telling them to turn this way and that. They walked briskly with the crowd, some of whom were laden with hand luggage and babies and extra fur coats. Bob carried his briefcase and Lois carried the engraving. She had unwrapped it when Bob brought it back to the apartment the night before their flight and both of them had seen that the little man hadn't advanced another step. He was right where he had been before he was consigned to the Siberia of the warehouse. Lois wrapped the picture – frame and all – in a double layer of waterproof plastic and then a layer of plastic bubble-wrap just in case the airlines had insisted on it being checked. But they let her take it aboard and she placed it in an overhead compartment. It was covered in two layers of brown wrapping paper and tied all together with thick white string. She was determined to take the engraving back to Corra. To compare the house in the picture with the actual house on the grounds. And if the people living in Corra wanted the picture to hang on their own walls she would give it to them. She thought it only fitting that the picture should finally return to its source. Bob didn't voice one word of objection when she told him her plans.

They stood in line for twenty minutes until they finally had their passports examined and stamped. When they got to the baggage area, their luggage (two blue ones for her and an old brown one for him) was waiting. Bob found an available wheeled cart and they put everything on it and pushed it towards the exit that was marked with a large sign saying: 'Nothing to Declare'.

'Just a moment, sir. Madam.' One of the uniformed guards stopped them as they were about to move out into the noisy cavernous airport lobby. 'Sir, if you don't mind,' and he put his hand on their baggage cart.

Bob smiled at the guard. It was an old trick his father had taught him: if someone wants to talk to you and he's wearing a uniform, you smile. 'Yes?'

'What do you have in there?' He pointed to the brown paper wrappings.

'A picture,' Bob replied.

'An engraving,' Lois added.

'May I see it?'

Bob shrugged. 'Of course.' He looked at Lois and shrugged again.

'Would you come this way, please?' The guard walked ahead of them and then held a side door open. Bob wheeled his luggage cart into the room. 'Would you place that parcel on the table please?' Bob obliged the man. 'Would you open it, please?' Bob started fumbling with the knots on the string until Lois brushed him aside. She had made the knots and she knew how to unmake them. Quickly she got through the paper and the sheets of protective plastic and the engraving lay open and upwards on the table. The guard looked at it for a minute or so. 'Where did you get this?' he asked.

'In the States,' Bob said. 'Actually, it was from an auction in New Jersey.'

'Why do you have it with you now?'

'You see down here?' Lois tried to control her annoyance at this minor official, 'down here where it says "Corra"? Well, we are going to Corra and we wanted to take this up there and compare it.'

'That's all?' the man asked.

'That's all.' Lois set her mouth in a firm line. 'There's no law against bringing this in, is there?'

'I won't be but a minute,' the guard said and left the room.

'Well for Christ's sake!' Bob muttered. 'Now what?'

'Who knows? It's probably his first day on the job and he's trying to make points.'

After an interval where neither said anything to the other, the door opened and the guard returned. Now he had another man with him, a balding man in civilian clothes. The man gave them a brief nod, flashed a badge pinned on the underside of his suit lapel and without comment went over to the engraving and started examining it. His eyes took in each detail. His hands fondled the frame. At one point he took out his handkerchief and wiped at something on the glass. Finally he turned back to them. 'I'm sorry,' he said, 'but you can't bring this into the United Kingdom.'

'What?' Lois exploded. 'That's the most ridiculous thing I ever heard of. It's only a picture you know. It's not a bomb!'

'I know what it is,' the plain-clothes man said, 'and I can't permit you to bring it into the country.'

'But it's an *English* picture. It was made here. It's not as if it were being imported. It's being returned. Returned to where it was made.'

The man shook his head. 'You don't know that. There's nothing here that says the engraving was done in England.'

'We've checked it out,' Bob said, 'there's only one Corra where it could have come from and that is in Scotland.'

'Scotland is still part of Great Britain, isn't it?' Lois asked with just a touch of sarcasm.

'Unfortunately yes,' the man replied. 'You will have to leave the picture here. We'll give you a receipt and you can claim it when you leave, when you take it back to the United States.'

'I'm not leaving this here with you!' Lois' voice grew louder. 'I didn't bring this thing all the way across the ocean just so you guys could impound it. Get me your law book. Show me chapter and verse where it says this picture can't be brought into your country!'

'Lois, please . . .'

'Please, hell!' Lois shouted. 'This is ridiculous! This is just damned fool red tape, something to keep these guys earning a salary.'

'Madam, I assure you . . .' the guard started.

Lois turned on him. 'You can't assure me of anything. I want to see your Goddamned law and if I don't agree with it then I'm going to my embassy and get *them* to straighten out this crap!'

'Madam, if you're trying to threaten me, then that's an entirely different matter. I *can* show you chapter and verse, as you call it, as to what happens when one of Her Majesty's civil servants are threatened.' He smiled at her now, for the first time, then he took out his handkerchief and wiped the perspiration from his receding hairline. 'We shall give you

129

a receipt and you can claim this object when you leave the country. Now I think this discussion should be brought to a close.' He nodded to the uniformed guard and the guard started picking up the engraving and all the plastic and paper that had been around it.

'No!' Lois grabbed the picture from the startled guard. 'No, dammit! Keep your hands off this!' She brought the frame to her chest, cradling it. 'This is mine. You've no right to it.'

The two men stood stock still. Bob reached out to take the picture from her. 'Come on, hon. Let's do as they say. Give me the engraving.'

She twisted away from him and staggered back against the wall. 'No, Bob. Don't let them take this. Don't let them touch it!' She started to cry and she pulled the frame even closer to her chest. The tears streaked down her face.

'Look,' Bob said, 'can I have a word with you guys?' He pointed towards the door. 'Out there?'

The guard glanced at the plain-clothes man and when he nodded all three left the room. Lois didn't bother to glance up and see them go. They were in another corridor, different from the one they had used to enter the room. The two officials waited for Bob's explanation.

'My wife is sick,' he said. 'Emotionally sick. She's also tired. It's a long trip over here and she hardly slept on the plane. She's under medical supervision. I can give you the name of her psychiatrist in New York, if you want it.' They continued to look at him. 'We lost our little boy a few months ago. Our only son. He was murdered. Kidnapped and murdered. She still hasn't gotten over it. Maybe she never will. She's got some crazy idea that the house in the picture contains her son. She somehow thinks that place up in Corra is where the kidnapper has our little boy hidden away. She thinks if she can get into the house, she'll rescue him. I've told her Tony's dead. Hell, I even identified the body but it didn't matter. She's sure he's alive.' He watched the expressions on both faces. 'That's why we're here. To put this thing to rest once and for all. It's not my idea, it's her doctor's. He says it's the only way she can be cured. I'd much rather be lying on a beach someplace instead of being here in London. Especially in January.'

'So the picture she's hugging in there is like she's hugging her dead child?'

Both men remained silent, then the guard spoke up: 'It's

not my decision to make, sir, but I would think in light of the circumstances surrounding the case that . . .'

The balding plain-clothes man nodded. 'In light of the circumstances, I must agree with you.' He reached into his coat pocket and brought out a printed pad about the size of a deck of cards. He filled in some of the blanks with his ballpoint pen. Then he signed the memo. 'Let me have your passport,' he said to Bob. He took the passport and peeled the memo from its smooth backing and stuck the piece of paper onto the last page of the blue book. 'You may bring in the picture,' he said as he handed the passport back. 'But you must also bring the picture *out* with you. You must have that picture in your possession when you leave the country. I'm making a special concession to you on this and I trust you'll appreciate it.'

Bob glanced at the official order, then put his passport into his pocket. 'I do appreciate it,' he said. 'Thank you.'

The two officials turned and walked down the hallway. Bob went back through the door into the room. Lois was busy at the table, carefully rewrapping the engraving. She looked up when he came in. 'Well?' was all she said.

'We can keep the picture.'

She visibly relaxed. 'What did you tell them to make them change their minds?'

He grinned. 'Nothing. I slipped each one of them a fifty.'

*   *   *

'They have arrived,' the man with the white hair said as he glanced at the others around the table. 'They got in this morning. Heathrow.'

'Good,' said the Frenchwoman. 'That means they should be here soon.'

'Well, for my part everything's in readiness,' the plump woman with streaks of grey in her hair said. 'I'm sure you've all noticed how clean and sparkling this dining room is. Took me all of last week to get it done.'

'Aye,' said the other man, 'and the entrance way as well. You've done your work well. It makes this place looked lived in again.'

'That it does,' the white-haired man said. 'It hasn't looked this good in years.'

131

'Well,' replied the plump woman 'There's a *reason* now.'
'Aye,' he answered, 'too bad father isn't here to witness it.'

* * *

The rest of the first day and all of the second one went by
in a blur of London tourist sights and sounds. Neither of them
had been to the British capital before and so everything was
new in their eyes, everything was exciting and must be stared
at, commented on and photographed. They rode in a red
double-decker bus. They oohed at the Changing of the Guards
and aahed at the interior of St Paul's. They wandered down
separate corridors in the British Museum, Bob looking for
the medieval armour and Lois looking for the Egyptian
mummies, but they stood hand in hand as they admired the
Elgin Marbles. They ate a cheap lunch standing up in a pub
and dined elegantly French in a restaurant near Hyde Park.
They liked the speed of the underground but enjoyed the
back seat space of the huge black taxis. They watched
street entertainers at Covent Garden and were entranced by
Rigoletto at the London Coliseum.

The second night, after they had returned to their hotel
room and were together in bed, Lois reached under the
covers and put her hand on Bob's abdomen. 'Thank you
again for this trip,' she whispered. 'It's been like a fairy tale
coming true.'

He slid her hand farther down his body. 'You're welcome,'
he whispered in reply. 'I did it because I love you. I've
always loved you.' He felt her hand caressing him between
his legs. 'And I love it when you do that too.' He grinned in
the darkness as her fingers touched tighter, expanding flesh.

'You're all I ever wanted in a husband,' she said. 'You've
been wonderful for me.' Now she could feel his hand between
her thighs. She pushed it away, up to her breasts. 'No,' she
whispered. 'My period started a couple of days ago.' He
sighed. 'I know it hasn't been easy married to me,' she said
and then moaned slightly under the probings of his fingers.
'These last few months have been very upsetting for you. I
know it and I'm sorry.'

'Don't talk,' he said softly in her ear. 'Just let's hold each
other. Like the old days. Like we used to.' He started to say
something else, but stopped to hold his breath in anticipation

of what he knew was about to happen as she slid down beneath the covers, the warmth of her mouth swallowing him completely.

*   *   *

They had agreed, even before they left New York, that this last full day in London would be taken up with 'important' things. Bob wanted to visit a restaurant supply house he had corresponded with for years and Lois had wanted to go shopping. Not necessarily to buy anything. Just to shop. She tried to explain the difference to Bob and he had laughed and shook his head.

Breakfast over and The Times glanced at, they caught a cab in front of their hotel. Lois told the driver she wanted to go to Selfridge's department store.

She had explained to Bob, when they were making their plans, that Selfridge's was founded by an American and according to many of the jet-set, it was a better store than Harrods. She'd hit Harrods in the afternoon, she told him.

The cab pulled into Oxford Street, went a few blocks through clogged traffic that reminded both of them of Fifth Avenue at Christmas time and finally stopped at the big grey columned building with all the flags out front.

'Have you got enough money?' Bob asked her as she got out of the car.

She nodded. 'If I run out I've got some plastic.'

'Oh, Gawd!' he groaned. 'I forgot about those over here.'

'I haven't, and I've been saving mine. This is shopping day!'

'I thought you weren't going to buy anything.'

'I'm not, but a girl can't shop with no cash or cards. That's no fun. The fun comes when you see something you must have and then you reward yourself for not buying it later on by buying something else you simply must have.'

'You'll be okay?' he said, still holding the door open.

'I'll be fine. I speak the language over here, you know.'

'Back at the hotel for tea?' he tried to affect an English accent.

'Raw-ther,' she replied in the same bad imitation. Then Bob closed the door and the cab drove on.

Lois pushed through the revolving door and the scents from a dozen perfume counters hit her nose. Outside it was cold and smelled of exhaust fumes, suddenly she had entered a world of warmth and Chanel No.5. She took a deep breath. Just like back home.

She walked slowly through the various departments, down the labyrinth of aisles, counters and rooms adjoining rooms. She fingered textiles in one place, held a Spode china plate to the light in another and toyed with the idea of buying a pair of ostrich leather gloves. She put them back: she didn't need gloves, she was just shopping. She took the escalator up to the women's better dress department and almost succumbed to buying a stunning slick number in navy blue with white stripes. The saleswoman agreed that it looked 'smashing' on her. She didn't need a new dress, she told herself. She took the escalator to the basement and spent at least a half hour examining the amazing range of kitchen gadgets she wanted but didn't need. Things like a cheese grater with a handle, a plastic tube that spewed little curls of crushed garlic onto a plate and a clear glass mug with a plastic plunger that brewed a single cup of fresh coffee. She sighed: she didn't need any of those things either.

She decided to go back up and look at the dinner ware and crystal again. There was a Royal Doulton figurine that had fascinated her. Maybe she could make just one purchase this time. After all, she had done exceptionally well by not buying any of the other things she liked. As she took the escalator up from the basement to the second floor, she glanced at the people beside her, those descending on the other escalator. Her breathing stopped.

There was a little boy who looked just like Tony! He was holding a woman's hand and he was washed and warmly dressed. Then he was gone.

Lois was so startled that she almost stumbled when the escalator reached the floor. A man behind her grabbed her arm or she would have fallen. She murmured a thank you and walked unsteadily until she found a chair for sale. She sat in it, trying to control the flutterings of her hands. Now get a hold of yourself . . . don't act like a fool. That wasn't Tony! Tony is dead. He's dead and cremated. I know you don't want him to be dead, but he *is* dead. You must accept that fact, girl. You've got to get your act together. It's either that or a psychiatrist. You heard Bob and Midge say that. You know they were right and they love you. They only have your best interests at heart. She sat there for a few minutes, grateful that no sales person had asked her if she wanted to buy the chair. She got up and was pleased to feel her legs solidly obeying her each step forward. She didn't think about the porcelain figurine. She needed to get out of that store, needed to get some fresh air even if it was filled with carbon monoxide. She found the escalator marked 'down' and rode to the street floor. A patch of brilliant fuchsia caught the corner of her eye. It was an entire counter filled with silk fuchsia-coloured scarves. One of her favourite colours. Now she really needed one of those.

As she examined the weaving of the scarf the woman with the little boy passed her again. This time they were walking, this time the woman stopped to inspect a selection of umbrellas.

Lois stood near the scarves, holding one in her hand, yet not looking at it. She was looking at the little boy. He was the height her Tony had been and even though he was wearing a warm winter coat she knew that underneath it his little body must be like Tony's. He wore a brightly knit stocking cap and it was pulled down around both ears. She didn't know what colour his hair was but he was fair-complexioned and she was sure under that cap was a shock of red. His eyes were large, like Tony's, but she couldn't see what colour they were. Tony's had been blue. A beautiful butterfly-wing blue.

She put down the scarf and started edging her way towards the umbrella display. She was only a few feet away when the woman tugged on the child's hand and when he didn't respond she swooped him up into her arms and rapidly walked away. Lois followed as best she could, wondering what colour the boy's eyes really were. Just as they reached the revolving door, the boy turned around in the woman's arms and stared directly at Lois. His eyes were blue. Butterfly-wing blue. Then the pair vanished out of the store and were swallowed up by the crowd milling along the sidewalk.

Lois walked briskly towards the door but was beaten to it first by two young girls pushing baby buggies. Neither girl could have been more than nineteen and each had a child, and each child was covered with blankets and paper bags and plastic toys. While Lois fumed the two young mothers fumbled to get their kids and their buggies out of the entrance

135

way. When she managed to get to the sidewalk, there was no sign of the woman and the little boy.

She walked a few blocks, trying to crane her neck over the crowd, trying to see if she could spot them. She didn't know if they had gone right towards Marble Arch or left towards Oxford Circus. Finally she passed a pub and went in. 'What the hell,' she told herself, 'I couldn't catch up with them anyway.' She ordered a large dose of single malt whisky, straight up and no ice, and took the glass over to an empty table by the window. As she sat there, forcing herself to relax, she gazed out at a green world. The pub sat on a corner and the window was set in green glass. Everyone that went by looked like they were dressed for St Patrick's Day. But Tony is dead. He was cremated, his ashes scattered. Life must go on. *My* life must go on. She sipped the amber liquid and was glad for the heat it spread around the lining of her stomach. Finally, she set the empty glass on the small table in front of her. Now for Harrods, she told herself.

A green Tony stared in at her. She jumped up and glass and table went toppling onto the carpeted floor. 'I'm sorry!' she said to the man behind the bar and then, stepping over the table, she ran out into the street. She turned the corner. He wasn't there. She walked to the green window and touched it lightly with her hand. Tony had been there! She felt it. She knew it. That had been Tony and he had recognized her and that woman must have recognized her because of the way she had scooped him up and hurried from the store. Yes, it *was* Tony. Tony was alive and in London! But where? Oh God, but where?

She twisted one way and then the other. Finally she decided to follow a side street, leading away from the crowds on Oxford Street. She almost ran to the next crossing and looked both directions. No, there was no sign of the woman and the little boy. *Her* little boy. She hurried across the street and now she was running, running to see if they had made it around the next corner. They had to be somewhere. They couldn't have disappeared into thin air.

Then there they were. Across the street. Halfway down the block to the next corner. There stood the woman and there stood the little boy. Both of them were staring at her, staring through the continuing traffic. Waiting for her.

Lois pushed past other pedestrians, almost knocking one

elderly lady to the ground and banging her shin on another of those baby buggies.

The little boy was holding out his arms to her. He was right across the street and holding out his arms. His mouth was moving. She couldn't hear his voice over the noise of the cars but she knew he was saying 'Mommy.' She *knew* it!

'Mommy's coming,' she shouted. 'Tony! Mommy's here!'

She dashed into the street. There was a thumping sensation against her left hip and she felt herself being pushed sideways, being pushed off her feet, being pushed into the hard dirty road. She didn't have time to scream.

The only sound she heard was of brakes screeching, then a grey-haired man wearing a chauffeur's cap was kneeling down beside her. 'Hey! Missus!' he said. 'Are you all right?'

He put his hands under her back and raised her into a sitting position. Already the cars and taxis behind them were honking for them to get out of the way.

'You just ran right out in front of me, missus,' he said. 'Good thing I swerved or I would have hit you square on.' She moved her legs and he helped her to her feet. 'You bleedin' or anything?'

She shook her head. 'I'll be all right,' she said. 'Just got the wind knocked out of me.' She brushed at the grime on the side of her coat. 'It was my fault. I didn't look where I was going. I wanted to . . .' And she pointed to the other side of the street. 'He's gone,' she said with a whimper. 'My baby's not there.'

The rear window of the limousine slid down and an old lady dressed in black furs called to the driver. 'Is she all right?'

'Yes, mum,' he said. 'Shaken up a bit, though.'

'Well then, let's be on the way. We'll be late.' She closed the window and watched while her driver helped Lois onto the sidewalk. 'It's astonishing how people dash out in front of other people's cars,' she said to her travelling companion, a lady equally as old and equally as richly furred.

'She must be drunk,' the second lady said.

The first lady harrumphed: 'Either that or she's an *American.*'

CHAPTER ELEVEN

In the morning their taxi took them through Hyde Park, on their way to Euston station. There was a noon train to Dumfries, in Scotland, and they wanted to get first choice of the first-class compartments.

Bob glanced at Lois seated beside him. 'What's that on your coat?'

'Oh, just some dirt.' She brushed at the spot.

'How'd you get that?'

'Yesterday. Shopping. I knocked up against one of those trash bins in the street. Some guys were repairing a store front and I got too close to the garbage pile.' She brushed at it again. 'Stupid thing to do.' She looked at him but he was staring out of the window, watching the strollers in the park, strollers even on a cold and overcast day like today. She hadn't told him about almost being run over by a car. It would have upset him. She also didn't tell him that she thought she had seen Tony. That would have upset him even more. No, she wasn't going to ruin their last few hours in London with the news that she had seen Tony. And she *had* seen him. She was sure of that. She hadn't gone to Harrods, even though she told Bob she had. She had gone to the bar at the Hilton and, surrounded by the warm American-feeling atmosphere, she had turned everything over and over in her mind. She had nursed the same Scotch for almost two hours and the waiter hadn't urged her to reorder or move on.

She had considered, of course, not going to Scotland. She had thought about staying in London and searching for Tony and the woman. At first it seemed the sensible thing to do, then she remembered nothing in this made any sense. Everything so far pointed towards Scotland. Corra and that house. Corra and that awful little man under the glass. Corra and her baby. Yes, it would all come together when they got to Corra. She would have her child back once she got inside

138

that house. She knew that. She was positive of that. It made no sense to stay in London. Tony might have been here today but he would be at Corra waiting for her. No, it was time to move on. Time to stop wasting time playing the tourist and move on.

At the station they found an empty baggage cart and loaded their suitcases on it. Lois carried the engraving, wrapped in bubble plastic sheeting and brown paper, in her hand. They found the right platform and when the gates were opened they walked alongside the sleek and shiny train until they found the first class coach. Lois went in first and Bob handed the luggage up to her. They chose a compartment in the centre of the coach and Bob quickly had everything inside it. Lois placed the engraving carefully in an overhead rack.

'Isn't this wonderful?' she beamed. 'I mean look at this place! Red cloth-covered seats, sliding glass and wooden doors, funky little wall lights and even red curtains at the window. Just like in the movies,' she laughed delightedly.

'You almost expect Marlene Dietrich wearing a trench coat to open the doors and ask for a light.' Bob grinned back at her. Just then came the announcement that the train was about to leave and the stops it would make along the way. The voice also told the passengers where the restaurant car was located and then spieled off a long list of things available from the buffet car: everything from peanuts to something they thought sounded like patsies.

'What's a patsy?' she asked.

He shrugged and then with a slight lurch the train started to move. 'Right on time,' Bob said after consulting his watch. 'Good old British reliability.'

'And nobody in here with us. I'm glad. I want to enjoy this trip without having to be nice to strangers.'

'Just keep being nice to me,' he said to her.

'You got it,' she grinned.

They watched office buildings whiz by, then some clean and not so clean industrial areas rushed past and eventually everything was green fields lightly scattered with snow. Each time they came into a station and stopped for passengers, they read the place names aloud: St Albans, Milton Keynes, Rugby ('Rugby? I didn't know there was a town with that name.' 'Neither did I.'), Stafford, Nantwich and Wigan.

It was at Wigan that the man got off the train. Neither of

them noticed him but he had boarded in London and had sat in the compartment next to theirs. He had made sure they were aboard when he first got on and re-checked that they were still there when he got off. He kept his hat on all during the journey because they might have recognized him if they had seen him without it. They had watched him wipe his handkerchief across his balding forehead in the customs' room at Heathrow Airport. Now, as at that time, he was dressed in plain clothes.

At Preston the doors to their compartment opened and a small, elderly woman asked: 'May I sit in here, please?'

'Of course,' Lois smiled. 'We don't own the room, we're just renting it for the journey.'

The woman laughed lightly and sat down beside Lois. 'I'm just going as far as Carlisle,' she said. 'My grandson is meeting me there. I don't like to travel on the train alone. All these terrible people roaming around free nowadays. An old lady isn't safe anymore.'

'Just like New York,' Bob said.

'Oh, you're Americans! How delightful! I haven't had a chat with Americans for years. We don't get them much where I live. Nothing to bring them to a little place like my village. We did have a lot of you during the war.' She smiled at Bob and then at Lois. 'Oh yes, a lot of you Yanks were over here then. I learned how to dance the boogie-woogie and how to say "yes ma'am" and "no ma'am" through my nose.' She laughed. 'It was a fast time, I must say. Of course,' she smiled, 'I was younger then. That helped.'

Lois stood up and by moving the engraving to one side, brought a small overnight bag down from the luggage rack. She opened it and then took out something and held it in her closed hand. 'If you are into boogie and all that,' she grinned, 'have I got something for you!' She opened her hand and extended it to the old lady.

'Chewing gum!' she laughed delightedly. 'Blimey, I haven't seen American chewing gum in years!'

'It's yours,' Lois said. The woman shook her head. 'Please take it. I've got more of it.'

The lady took the package, put it to her nose and took a deep breath, then snapped open her purse and dropped the gum inside. The old purse snapped shut. 'If it's all right with you, I will have a piece later. My dentures shouldn't be seen chewing gum in public.' She laughed. 'Terribly sweet of you.'

For the next hour all three chatted away as if they were old friends. She asked questions about the States and they asked about her life. It was what she didn't say, or how she avoided saying it, that intrigued them both. Apparently the little old lady had been quite the bold young woman in her day.

'We're coming into Carlisle,' she said. 'That farmhouse we passed. I always use that as my signal. When that house goes by I start getting ready to get off.'

'We get off at Carlisle too,' Bob said. 'We change trains there for Dumfries.'

'Oh, yes you would,' the lady said. 'This train is going on to Edinburgh and the one from Carlisle is a local up to Glasgow.' She rose and started buttoning her coat. 'Can I help you with any of this? I mean all I have to carry is my handbag.'

'No, no bother, thank you,' Bob said. 'We can manage.'

The train pulled into the station and came to a smooth stop. The woman held the compartment door open while they took out their luggage and then stood on the platform while they took their things off the train. They looked for an empty baggage cart but there was none in sight. Bob picked up two of the suitcases and Lois tried to carry the other one and balance the engraving at the same time.

'Here, let me help you with that.' The woman reached out and took the engraving from Lois. 'I'll show you where you have to go to get your train. It's up and across that bridge there.' She pointed to an overpass inside the terminal. 'My grandson always meets me there. It's near the car park.' She started ahead of them and the two Americans followed.

All the lights were on in the terminal. It was only a little after five but the blackness of the Scottish winter made it look like midnight outside. They walked up the stairs, then across the ramp, and back down the stairs on the other side. Then they were led out into a section of platforms where the wind blew coldly at them and flecks of snow clung to their clothing. The woman consulted a flashing television screen that said 'departures' over it. She motioned and they followed her farther down the passageway where a not so new engine waited to pull several equally decrepit coaches. 'This is your train,' she said.

141

They found the coach marked 'first class' and Lois got on to help take in the baggage. Bob got on with the last one and, after putting them all in the luggage rack, he came back to the platform for the engraving that was still in the old woman's hands.

But the old woman wasn't there.

Bob stood on the train steps for a stunned second, then turned and ran back to where Lois was waiting. 'She's gone!' he shouted.

'Who's gone?'

'The old lady. She's got your picture!' With that he turned and ran down the corridor of the coach and out onto the platform. He looked to the left. It was all darkness and icy wind. He decided on the right and he began to run alongside the train, heading back towards the main waiting room and the footbridge they had crossed over. There were few people there and Bob was thankful he didn't have to push others aside. He ran and craned his neck trying to see around steel columns. At times he would stop and quickly look behind him in the hope that he had passed her and hadn't seen her.

A sign read 'car park'. He remembered the woman had said her grandson would be waiting for her there. He ran in the direction of the arrow on the sign, through the main terminal building, past an orange juice stand, a newspaper kiosk and three young men with guitars and beards and dirty sandals sitting on the floor.

Outside in the car park it was completely dark. There were just a few cars there. As he ran past he glanced into them. All of them were empty. He continued to run in the direction the arrows were pointing. He assumed it was up and onto the city street. He stopped to get his breath and glanced up. There she stood, at the top of the ramp. She too had stopped and she still had the brown paper parcel in her hands.

'Hey!' Bob shouted, and could feel the warmth of his breath as it rushed back across his face. 'Lady! Wait a minute!'

The old woman faltered for a second, then turned and dashed out of sight. Bob ran up the ramp and found himself in an intersection of cars and pedestrians and noise. He twisted his head one way and then the other, trying to figure which way she had gone. Then he saw her. Across the road, about to turn down a side street. Bob didn't even bother to look, but dashed out after her. There was a squeal of brakes and a city bus driver shouted something Bob didn't understand. He turned down the side street. She was about two blocks ahead of him. 'Hey! Lady!' he shouted again, but she didn't stop. Jesus Christ, he thought. How can one old bitch run so fast?

At the next corner she turned left. When he got to the corner he did the same. He followed behind her, always two blocks back, always two blocks short of grabbing her. Then she seemed to disappear. She had been there, in front of him, and then she was gone. Bob continued to run until he reached the spot where he had last seen her. There was a board fence along the sidewalk. One of the boards was missing. She must have slipped behind the fence. Bob scraped his chin and bruised his knee as he moved his bulk through the narrow opening. Now he was in a field, a grassy area of weeds and patches of snow and rusting soft drink cans and scraps of newspaper.

There she was, at the far end of the field. How in hell she could run that fast and sustain it he didn't know. He was getting winded and he considered himself in good shape. He was at least forty years younger than she was. What kind of an old woman was this? Another thought entered his head: *was* it a woman? Maybe it was a young athlete wearing one helluva good disguise. The woman reached the fence on the other side of this open area. She glanced around at Bob, then raised one arm and pulled herself up to the top of the fence. Still clutching the engraving, she tumbled off onto the other side. Bob, still not stopping, was amazed.

He got to the fence and it was all he could do to pull himself up and over even using both hands. He landed on softer ground, ground that gave in slightly as he ran across it. Then he smelled the salt. There was sea water somewhere out there. He couldn't hear it, but he could smell it.

The moon, which had been lying lazily behind cloud banks peeked out onto the landscape below and silhouetted the running figure in front of Bob. She was heading into blackness. In fact, on this side of the fence everything was pitch black.

'Hey!' He tried to shout, but he didn't have any wind. He stopped and watched as the figure ran to the left, paused and then started running to the right. Bob started after her but specks of moonlight showed him she was no longer carrying

143

the package. He slammed on his brakes and ran down to the spot where he thought she had paused. Now he could hear the waves lapping ever so softly against the grassy shore. He took three or four deep breaths trying to pull fresh cold air into his scorched and aching lungs. Where was it? Where did it land? It had been just about here that she had got rid of it.

Again the moon was favouring him. He caught a glimmer of wet paper riding the waves. Not caring about his shoes or his pant legs, he waded out into the icy, ink-black water. He reached for it, almost stumbled on something against his foot and reached again. This time he grabbed it. He could feel the paper and the string and he hauled the package towards him. Finally he stood there, knee deep in water, clutching the engraving.

He sloshed ashore. The wind whipped his wet trousers around his shins. 'Jesus Christ!' he said aloud. 'What the fuck was that all about?' Nobody answered him. It was silence and blackness everywhere. He had lost all sense of direction and couldn't find his way back to the fence. 'Shit!' he said, and started slogging towards a small light in the distance. 'Shit!'

As he got closer he saw it was a single light bulb burning in a back kitchen window. It seemed to be the only house around, or at least the only one with electricity. He made it to the back door, worried about his icy feet and the possibility of a snarling watchdog.

After he knocked he waited for what felt like ten minutes before the door cautiously opened. The man who peered out said nothing.

'I'm lost,' Bob told him. 'Do you have a phone?' The man nodded. 'Could you call me a taxi? I'd be very grateful.'

The man opened the door a little wider. 'Where do you want the taxi to take you?'

'To the train station. In Carlisle. My wife's waiting for me.' He paused and took a deep breath. It was the first time he had thought of Lois and what she might be going through by herself back there. 'It really is urgent,' he said. 'I'll pay you.'

The door opened completely. 'You're a Yank,' the man said. 'Get in here out of the cold.' When Bob came into the warm but sparsely furnished kitchen he saw there was a woman seated at a small table. 'My wife,' the man said. 'What were you doing out there?' His gaze went down to Bob's muddy, wet trousers. 'This is the wrong time of the year to go fishing.'

144

Bob thought of telling him about the old woman and about the parcel he held in his arms but thought better of it. 'I hitched a ride with some guy whose tyre had a flat. I started walking back to town but I guess I took the wrong shortcut. I wandered into some water.' He looked at the mess from his knees down. 'I'm dripping on your floor. I'm sorry.'

The woman spoke up. 'Don't you worry. Andrew, call the man a taxi and I'll make him a nice cup of tea.'

'Don't go to any bother,' Bob protested. 'My wife must be climbing the wall wondering what happened to me.'

'You just sit down there,' the woman said. 'By the time the taxi driver gets here you'll have had time to drink your tea.'

In a few minutes Bob had a warm mug of tea in his cold hands and when he told them it was the best cup of tea he'd had in years, he wasn't kidding. 'If only I could do something about my feet,' he grinned.

'When you get to your hotel,' the old man said, 'you put your feet in a basin of cold water. Not hot, mind you, but cold. It'll take away the chill.'

'I don't know when that will be,' Bob said. 'We were planning on going to Dumfries tonight. We have hotel reservations up there.'

The man took out his pocket watch and then glanced at the wooden clock on the mantel. 'You'll never make Dumfries tonight. The last train has already gone. None till six in the morning.'

Bob sighed. 'Oh wonderful!'

'Stay on in Carlisle, why don't you?' the woman suggested. 'Have a warm bath and take the morning train. Nothing's so important that you can't tarry a bit, is it?'

'We are on a tight schedule,' Bob said and took another sip of tea. 'I've got each night planned out.'

'Oh you Americans!' the woman laughed. 'Always got to know where you're going. You'd live longer if you'd just let things take their course.'

'Maybe I'll have the taxi take us straight to Dumfries,' Bob said, ignoring her remark. 'That way we'll still be on schedule.'

'It's some fifty miles,' the man said.

'Will you be coming back and inspecting the Solway during the daytime?' the woman asked.

'The Solway?' he repeated. 'What's a solway?'

The man grinned. 'Yank, it's the water you got soaked in. You went wading in the Solway Firth. Didn't you know that?'

'I never heard of the Solway Firth,' Bob said. 'What is it? A river?'

The woman laughed. 'No, it's not a river. It's an arm of the sea. It's a good thing you didn't wade out too far or you would have been sucked out into Scotland.'

'Aye,' the man said. 'The Solway is the water line dividing England from Scotland. On this side is us and on the other side is them. Good thing you didn't let go your grip on that package. It would have been halfway to Scotland by now.'

CHAPTER TWELVE

When he hadn't returned in time for the train to leave, Lois decided she wasn't going without him and in a mad scramble, aided by two passengers and a ticket collector, she managed to unload their luggage. She didn't budge from the platform, but sat there guarding their possessions and shivering.

She breathed a sigh of relief when she saw him coming, brown paper parcel in hand. 'What on earth happened?'

'I don't know,' he replied after giving her a tight hug. 'That old lady is a better runner than Sebastian Coe. Damn, I never saw anyone travel that fast. I chased her to the edge of the ocean and that's when she threw the picture in.'

'In the water?' Lois' voice rose in concern. 'Why did she do that?'

'I don't know. I don't know why she did anything she did. It's weird.'

'But is it all right? The picture, I mean. Did you check it?'

He handed it to her. 'You check it. It's damp on the outside but with all that plastic stuff you put around it, I'm sure it's dry underneath. It didn't have time to get really wet. I hauled it out of there just minutes after she threw it in.'

But Lois didn't want to see the damage if there was any. Also, she didn't want to see that little man. Not now. Not after everything that had happened in England so far. 'I'll look later,' was all she said. Then she noticed his still-damp trouser legs. 'But what about *you*? Oh Bob, I'm sorry. I was so anxious about this damned thing that I forgot about you! Are you all right? Were you hurt?'

'I'm fine,' he gave her a smile. 'My lungs were aching like hell after that Olympic dash, but a lady gave me a cup of tea and I calmed down a bit. Warmed up too. A lady in a little cottage near the sea. Her husband called me a cab. Speaking of which,' he picked up the two heaviest suitcases, 'is waiting right outside the station at this very moment. There are no more trains to Dumfries until tomorrow. So, the driver has agreed, for a sum, to take us to Dumfries. Right to the hotel. It's silly to blow our schedule and stay in this town tonight.'

She picked up the other case plus her own small overnight kit, managed to tuck the engraving under her arm. 'I agree. Let's get out of here. This station gives me the creeps.'

Bob led the way to the car park. The driver, when he saw them emerge from the station, drove up to meet them. He put the cases in the trunk (he called it 'the boot'), but Lois insisted the engraving ride in the back seat with them.

The ride north was done in darkness. They were passed by few cars and there was almost nothing to see from the taxi windows. Lois sat huddled close to Bob, holding his hand, giving him warmth. 'I don't understand why that old woman acted the way she did,' she said. 'I mean, we treated her as a friend. I gave her some chewing gum and she repaid us by stealing.'

'I don't know if she *was* an old woman,' he replied. 'She ran like a young man, a young man in damned good physical condition.'

'You don't think – ' Lois formed her thought slowly – 'that she intended to steal the picture from the very beginning? I mean that she sat with us and was nice to us only because she wanted that picture?'

'How did she know what was in the package? We didn't tell her what was in there. We didn't unwrap it and show her the damned thing.'

'That's true,' Lois sighed. 'Maybe she just thought that because we were Americans whatever we had inside the package had to be valuable. So she just kind of took the first thing she could grab and ran.' She looked at him. 'What do you think?'

147

'I don't know, hon. I can't give you an answer because the whole thing is as screwed up in my mind as it is in yours. All I *do* know is that we've had nothing but trouble ever since Midge gave us the blasted thing. I'll be glad to leave it with whoever is living in that house in Corra.'

Lois didn't reply. Her thoughts were already on the next three days. The three days that would take her to Corra, get her inside that house and get her reunited with her Tony.

'I know the Waverley, yes sir,' the driver said suddenly. 'Fine hotel it is too. Nothing fancy, but then nothing in Dumfries *is* fancy. You been there before?'

'No, our first time.'

'Lovely place, Dumfries. Old churches and buildings. Even some ruined castles on the outskirts of town. Nice walk along the water, if you like that sort of thing. Peter Pan's father used to walk there.'

'Peter Pan's *father*?' said Lois, dumbfounded.

'Yeah, you know. That writer fellow. Barrie, that was his name. He said he got his inspiration for Peter Pan by walking along the riverbank in Dumfries.' At that moment the headlights of the taxi picked out a sign that said 'Welcome to Dumfries'. There were street lights, after a few blocks, and they illuminated small red brick homes, store fronts and empty bus shelters at the edge of the sidewalk. The driver continued with his thrown-in-for-free guided tour: 'Robbie Burns lived here, too. You ever read any of his poetry?' He didn't wait for an answer. Those that have read him say he was good. Old-fashioned English, you know, but a real master of his craft. Know what I mean?' They murmured that they did. 'Now we're coming to more or less the centre of the town. See that place there? The one with the clock tower and sitting in the middle of the street? Midsteeple, we call it. Over three hundred years old. Used to be a prison, it did, and when Robbie Burns died they had his body on view there. Lots of old buildings here go way back, they do. Of course lots of others got destroyed.'

'Destroyed?' Lois asked. 'You mean earthquakes?'

The driver laughed loudly. 'Oh no, missus. Not earthquakes. This isn't your California. They got destroyed by the English. The English came in here and burnt the bloody place more than once, they did. They rounded people up and took them as prisoners and they killed a lot of them too.

148

Elizabeth did that. The queen and her soldiers, did those things.'

'Elizabeth the Second?' Lois glanced at Bob and grinned. 'You're not talking about Diana's mother-in-law are you?'

Again the driver laughed. 'Oh no, missus. I mean the *first* Elizabeth. She was always fighting with the Scots across the Border and poor Dumfries lay just across it. So anytime there were any goings and comings Dumfries got the brunt. Went on for years, these raids and battles. Even after the old queen died and Mary Queen of Scots' own son took over, they were fighting and killing one another. Burnings and raids and hostages and all kinds of bloody hell.'

'It's a wonder Dumfries survived,' Bob remarked.

'Aye, that it is, but the Scots are a tough bunch. Don't let those kilts they wear fool you. The whole world knows you don't mess with a Scotsman when he's got a tilt to his kilt.'

'And you,' Lois laughed, 'You've got to be a Scotsman yourself.'

'Aye, and proud of it. My ancestors did a lot of English bashing. Course,' he laughed again, 'a lot of them got bashed in return. Those English are a tough lot too, don't you know. They didn't create an empire by sitting on their backsides and sipping tea all day.'

The taxi passed a darkened movie house, a furniture store, a large granite sandstone building that was city offices, a couple of tall churches and some small hotels until it pulled up at a corner. It was almost like being at the end of the earth. There were no lights ahead or on either side of them.

'This is it,' the driver said. 'The Waverley. Looks dark in there. I suspect they've closed the place up for the night. You might have to pound on the front door.'

'They close their hotels in Scotland?' Lois couldn't believe it.

'Aye, some of the smaller ones, they do. They take a count of the keys that are out and they know who's back and who's still prowling the pubs. When most of their customers are back, they lock the doors. Don't you do that in America?'

Bob laughed. 'I don't think they ever lock the doors at the Waldorf Astoria or the Plaza in New York.'

'Then how do they keep the place secure?'

'They have a night staff, people behind the desk and running the elevators all night.'

'Lord!' The driver got out of the car and started to unlock

149

the trunk. 'Think of the expense! No wonder a Scotsman can't afford to take a holiday in your country.'

Bob reached into his billfold and brought out several British banknotes. 'Here. Thanks for everything. We've enjoyed it.'

The man looked at the amount. 'Hey. I can't take this. It's too much.'

'I'm giving you a healthy tip, that's all,' Bob replied. 'It's dark as hell as well as being cold and you did us a favour. Plus you made us laugh. That's value well worth paying for.'

'Well, I thank you. It was a pleasure meeting you and an honour to serve you.'

'I enjoyed meeting my first Scotsman on his home turf.' Lois smiled at him. 'Thank you.'

The driver motioned to the hotel. 'Well, at least you're in safe hands over here. So far the second Elizabeth and her bunch haven't seen the necessity of attacking Dumfries.' He grinned, got back into his cab and drove into the blackness.

Bob took a couple of the suitcases and went up the narrow front steps. He tried peering through the glass in the door but couldn't see a thing. So he knocked, lightly at first, then when nobody answered, much harder. 'I can't believe they'd shut down a hotel,' he said irritatedly. Then he came back onto the pavement and walked a few yards towards another entrance. 'Lois, there's a light on this side. Maybe we've got the wrong door.' He bounded up another set of stairs and when he knocked, the door swung open by itself. He looked inside. It was crowded with people, all men, many sitting or standing at a bar. Behind the bar were whisky bottles, glasses and soft lights reflected in mirrors. In the back of the room pool balls clicked against one another and a television set with the picture on but the sound turned down flickered silently. He walked into the dark, smoke-filled room and as he did every eye in the house was upon him.

On the other side of the bar a very attractive young woman, long blonde hair and large blue eyes, dried her hands on a towel and came down to where he was standing. 'Can I help you?' she asked.

'Yes. My wife and I have a reservation in the hotel but it seems to be locked.'

She smiled. 'Oh yes, Mr Bruno. From America. Yes, we do have your reservation. We thought you'd be here much earlier. We wondered what happened to you.'

'What happened you wouldn't believe,' he said and gave her a tired smile in return. 'It was right out of a Stephen King novel.' He pointed towards the door. 'My wife and the luggage are outside.'

'Oh, of course. You just wait now and I'll go and open the front door. You came in the pub door.' He nodded and looked around the room again. All eyes were still on him. 'I won't be but a minute.' Then she was gone through an archway behind the bar.

'You want some assistance?' a man asked him. 'Need a hand with your things?'

'No thanks,' Bob replied, 'we've managed so far.'

'Just thought I'd ask.' The man went back to his pint of ale.

As they signed the register at the small alcove that served as a front desk the blonde girl said: 'My name is Fiona. My mother and father own this place. On their behalf, allow me to welcome you to it.'

'Why thank you,' Lois said. 'It's good to be here. For a while we didn't think we'd make it.'

'Oh, I know what you mean,' the girl said. 'The train service is getting more terrible each passing year. Sometimes some of our guests get so disgusted they get off the train and take a taxi. Can you imagine?'

Lois laughed. 'Yes, I can imagine because that's what we did. We missed our connection at Carlisle – ' She shot a look at Bob – 'and rather than stay overnight down there we decided to come on up by car.'

'You did right,' the girl said, then stopped. 'But then, oh dear, does that mean you haven't had any supper? And here with the dining room closed and all, being as it's so late.'

'We haven't eaten,' Lois said. 'We hadn't thought about food.'

'Oh dear,' Fiona shook her head. 'Here let me give you your key and you just go on up those stairs there, turn to the right and go through the heavy door and down the hall. When you get to the big mirror, go right again and your room will be at the end. It's facing the street, lovely view that. Then when you've had a chance to wash your face, you come back down to the pub and I'll have something for you to eat. Can't promise you much, being as it's so late and all. How about sandwiches? Cheese and maybe some roast beef?' They

151

nodded. 'Good. Now you two run along and come back in about fifteen minutes. Tea?'

'Could I have a drink first?' asked Lois.

Fiona beamed. 'What would you like, dear?' When she heard Scotch and water she beamed again. 'For two? Wait a moment.' She was gone and in a moment she was back. She handed them the glasses. 'Take these on up to your room with you. It'll help to remove the chill. No charge. Compliments of the management.' Then she was gone again.

When they found their room they were surprised to see it was about twice the size of the room they had had in London, and at about one-fourth the price. There were two double beds, layered in blankets and unmatching spreads. There was a wooden wardrobe closet against one wall and a large oak bureau with Victorian brassware handles. There was a television set and a portable electric heater. An overstuffed chair that matched none of the above sat near a small table in a corner. The room itself was on a corner so there was a view out onto the main street, (almost directly above where the taxi had unloaded them) and a smaller side street. Some kind of large flowers were embossed across the wallpaper and, to Lois' relief, behind a white door was a full bathroom and shower.

'This place isn't so bad,' she said when she came out of the bathroom, having combed her hair and touched up her make-up. 'Lots of wonderful hot water in there.'

When he had finished in the bathroom they left the room, carefully locked the door with a large key on an even larger plastic holder, and went down the stairs to the pub. On a small table in the room's only quiet corner were four plates with sandwiches (cheese, ham and cheese, hot, broiled sausage and cold roast beef), plus a pot of tea.

As they ate in silence, they looked about the room. Many of the men had gone by this time and the others had divided themselves into groups of two or three. They leaned on the bar, wearing their woollen overcoats and scarves and flat tweed caps. Lois supposed most of the coats had been purchased years before as none of them were new and all looked like they could use a good dry cleaning. Their shoes were thick-soled and dark. Their scarves were in sombre colours, like their work-worn hands. She thought their attitude, as well as their clothing, was that of men who have

152

never had things easy, who had struggled to earn the clothes they now wore and the pints of beer they now drank and who would go to their graves without ever having most of the things so many Americans took for granted.

'This looks like a working man's pub,' Bob said, picking up on Lois' thoughts.

'It's not the Plaza,' she agreed, then added: 'but you know what? I prefer this place to the Plaza. No, I really do. I feel at home here. These guys can come here and relax and inside I know that I can too. Does that make any sense?'

'It does. You never like the ritzy places, but don't forget you're also tired and just glad to be off that train and in this warm hotel.'

'Aye,' she said trying her Scots imitation, 'that I am.' She took another bite of her ham and cheese sandwich and washed it down with some tea. 'That I am.'

One by one, but sometimes in pairs, the men buttoned up their coats and pulled their hats down farther onto their heads and went out into the winter night. As the last few straggled towards the door, Fiona started turning off the lights around the room. One of the men, younger and taller than the others, stopped at their table. 'Fiona and her folks were concerned when you didn't show up on the train. She's happy now that you're here.'

'That's awfully sweet of her.' Lois gave him a sincere smile. 'You know, we're not used to this kind of treatment, and never from a hotel back home.'

'I've never been to the States,' the young man said. 'I hope to someday. Fiona and I plan to take our honeymoon there,' he laughed, 'providing I can save up the money.'

'Oh?' Lois looked closer at the young man. 'You and Fiona are an item?'

'Aye,' he nodded, 'we are engaged, if that's what you mean. I'm sorry – ' He reached out his hand. 'I am forgetting my manners. My mum would whale me if she was here. My name is Malcolm Travis. Pleased to make your acquaintance.'

'I'm Lois Bruno, and this is my husband Bob. Nice to meet you, too.'

'Fiona is a pretty girl,' Bob said. 'Looks like you're a lucky guy.'

'I know that.' He grinned. 'She could have any fellow in Dumfries but she's chosen me.'

153

'You ought to have great-looking kids,' Lois said.

He turned bright red, even redder than the hair atop his head. 'I haven't got that far in my thinking,' he managed to say, 'that's for God to decide. In the future.' His blush didn't fade.

'I'm sorry,' Lois said, even though she wasn't sorry at all. 'I shouldn't have said that. We Americans just come out with things.'

He managed a laugh. 'I know. I've met a few Yanks before.' He paused giving himself time to change the subject. 'Will you be in Dumfries long?'

'Two or three days.' Lois said.

He shook his head. 'What on earth can you find to do for three days here?'

'Well, we won't be here all the time. We are going to rent a car and go down to Corra in the morning.'

Again he shook his head. 'Corra? What's in Corra? You can run from one side of the village to the other in five minutes. Do you have family there?'

'No,' she kept talking, 'there's a house we want to look at.'

'To buy? You want to buy a house in Corra?'

'Not buy,' Lois said, 'just look at. There's a house there I want to see.'

'I've been to Corra many times,' Malcolm said. 'Perhaps I know the one.'

'I can't tell you where it is exactly,' she said. 'We're just going to go there and look around.'

'Well, if I could be of any help . . .'

'Thanks,' Bob said, 'but we'll manage.'

'I'm not doing anything tomorrow. I could go with you. I could be your guide.'

'I don't think so,' Bob replied.

'There are many old houses around there. Perhaps I could help you save time.'

'We really don't need a guide.' Lois noted a hard edge in Bob's voice.

'I'd like to do it,' Malcolm insisted. 'You don't have to pay me. It would be interesting to go with you.'

Bob put his cup down on the table. 'Look,' he said in an even tone, 'we appreciate the offer but we want to do this on our own. Understand? Now if you don't mind . . .'

'Bob!' Lois said under her breath.

Malcolm stepped away from the table and fastened the top button of his coat. He looked hurt, but then his features softened. 'It's all right. I understand. You Yanks like to do things alone, like swimming the channel.' He smiled at Lois. 'But if you need me for anything while you're here, I'm available. I don't have a steady employment at the moment, so when you need me . . . if you should need me . . . just tell Fiona. She knows where to find me.' He reached into his pocket for his knitted gloves. 'I enjoyed talking to you.' He turned and waved to Fiona, who was stacking dirty glasses onto a tray. She waved back and Lois felt the cold had grown sharper when he opened the door and went into the night.

* * *

The next morning, they had what the menu called 'a full Scottish breakfast,' consisting of fruit juice, hot porridge, two eggs any style, two sausages, two strips of bacon, a slice of tomato, toast or rolls and butter with jam and tea or a choice of coffee black or coffee white. 'It's to keep your blood warm while you're out on the hill tending your sheep,' the young waitress had replied laughingly when Lois protested over the amount of food.

'Back in New York, I usually just have toast and coffee,' she said.

'Aye,' the girl replied, 'but what's the conditions of your sheep?'

'Now you've got a point there,' Lois laughed. 'My sheep have seen better days.'

After breakfast Fiona told them their rented car had arrived. She had them sign the agency papers and gave Bob the key. 'We'll just put it all on your bill,' she said, 'the garage manager is a friend of mine.'

Lois went to their room to get the engraving. It was still wrapped in its protective plastic and brown paper. When they got to the car, Malcolm was standing nearby.

'Morning,' he said and gave them a grin.

'Morning, Malcolm,' Lois replied. 'Beautiful day.'

'That it is,' he answered. 'Lovely. Not supposed to snow today. That's what the radio says.'

'Good.' Bob forced a smile as he got in behind the wheel on the right side of the car.

'Sure you know how to drive on our side of the road?' Malcolm held the door open for Lois but was talking to Bob. 'Not the same as in the States.'

'I know,' Bob's voice was dry. 'I'm already behind the wheel. I can see the difference.'

'You've driven before on our side?' Malcolm asked.

'Yes, he has,' Lois answered for him, 'we spent a month in the Bahamas. Bob drove there. He's a very good driver.' She gently slid the engraving onto the back seat before sitting in the front.

'I could always go with you.' The red-haired young man insisted. 'I could do the driving and that way you could both relax.'

'I'm relaxed,' Bob said evenly, 'very relaxed, thank you.'

'I know Corra. I know people down there.'

'Look buddy,' Bob's voice was even more restrained, 'will you take your hands off the car and let us get on our way.'

Malcolm stepped back. 'Oh. Surely. Just trying to help.'

Bob turned the key in the ignition, put the car into first gear and it made a series of little rabbit jumps before coming to a complete stop. He muttered something and Lois suppressed a giggle. Again the key was turned, the gear was changed and this time, with a lighter foot on the accelerator and a surer hand on the gear stick, the automobile began to purr as it moved smoothly ahead.

Fiona had supplied them with a hand-drawn map of how to get from the hotel to the southern part of the town where they would join up with highway A711. From there it was straight down to Corra. Lois had learned from experience not to talk to Bob when he was driving while trying to follow instructions, so as they pulled onto A711 and started down the narrow paved roadway, she said: 'I think you were a little harsh with that kid. He doesn't mean any harm.'

'You mean Malcolm? I wasn't harsh with him, I just told him we didn't need him.'

'Yeah, but it was the *way* you told him. You were a little rude.'

'To hell with it,' he said. 'Something about him I don't like.'

'I thought he was kind of cute.'

'You would.'

The sky was clear and coloured a crispy blue and white.

There was no lying snow so the farmyards and pasture lands were firm and unmuddied in tones of pale green and yellow-brown. Lois watched in fascination as they passed small stone houses and cultivated fields bristling at ground level with shoots of winter wheat. Her designer's eye liked the way the smoke floated into the wind after it left the round pipe-like clay chimneys on the slate roofs. She gasped in pleasure at a bend in the road where a stream gurgled so noisily over the rocks that she was sure she could hear it even inside the car. She actually squealed in pleasure – and made Bob smile – when she saw her first flock of sheep. 'Oh! Look at those adorable little black faces! And those wonderful woolly coats!' Several of the sheep stopped grazing long enough to lift their heads and stare at them. 'Bob, aren't they adorable?'

He grinned. 'Know how they're best?' She shook her head. 'On a platter with potatoes, carrots and mint sauce.' She made a face and punched him on the arm. 'I mean, look at them. They've got it made. All they have to do is walk around and eat grass and let their hair grow. What a neat life.'

'Yeah, but in the spring the little lambs get killed and eaten. I mean, there is some risk at being a sheep. Especially a boy sheep.'

'That's true. The girls are home free. Got nothing to worry about except having lambs each year and letting their hair grow. Hardly anybody eats old sheep.'

'They call it mutton,' she said.

'You know what? One of those old ewes back there, you know who she reminded me of?' Lois shook her head. 'One of the fat ones in a white fluffy coat with the farmer's blotch of colour smeared on its back? Know who it reminded me of?' She waited. He laughed: 'Your friend Midge.' Now she punched him harder. 'I swear to God, I'm sure I saw Midge wearing a coat that looked just like that.' Again, he laughed.

'You are horrid!' she said, but she was also laughing. 'Poor Midge. She can't help it if she's a little overweight. I'll admit that some of the outfits she wears don't have a lot of style, but she's a good person.'

'Uh-huh. She's good. But that ewe is better. I'd much rather have her with horseradish sauce than Midge any day.'

'I sent her a postcard from London,' Lois said. 'I hope she gets it.'

'You sent that old sheep a postcard?'

She punched his arm again. 'Will you stop it?' Then she leaned over and kissed him lightly on the ear. 'Love you,' she said.

'Me too,' he said.

The car came up over a hill and there was a road sign with an arrow: 'Beeswing.'

Lois squealed again. 'Beeswing! Isn't that the most wonderful name for a town? Oh, I adore it! Imagine living in a place called Beeswing!'

The roadway continued for a few more miles. Only three automobiles passed them on the other side, then there it was. A sign straight ahead. Corra.

Lois took a deep breath as they passed the marker. 'Oh boy,' she said. 'Here we go.'

'Welcome to Corra,' Bob said. 'You wanted it. You got it.'

'I'm ready,' she said but she wasn't smiling. 'Let's get this over with.'

The village was hillier than the rest of the terrain had been and was no more than a couple of streets crossing each other. They went through the place and were on the other side before they knew what they had done. Lois' eyes had searched for her house. They had flickered over small brick cottages, a petrol station, something that might have been a church or a town hall and then the highway had divided and they were out in pasture land again. Bob pulled the car off the road. 'I think we went too far. I'm going to turn around.' Lois agreed and he made a U-turn and drove, slower this time, back to the centre of the tiny village. He went down the one main street, both of them looking for the house. It wasn't visible. 'I'm going to turn here,' he said and made a right off the main road. They were back in pasture land again.

'The house *does* have a lot of land around it,' Lois said. 'It's probably a little ways out of town rather than being right in it.' Bob grunted his agreement and kept the car moving slowly but steadily down this narrower road. Again, nothing.

'Why don't we go back to the main drag and take the other direction?'

'Sure.' He retraced his route back to the centre of the

village and took the only other road that led away from it. Again, his foot rested lightly on the accelerator. Again, no sign of their house. 'I can't imagine where it would be,' he said. 'The damn thing's big enough. It should be sticking out like a sore thumb.'

'Let's go back and ask somebody.' She knew how he hated to stop and ask directions. This stubbornness had caused more than one argument on their vacations together.

Surprisingly, he agreed. 'Yeah. I suppose that is the best thing at this point.' Because the road was so narrow it took a bit more manoeuvring to turn the car around. They drove in silence back to the crossroads that called itself Corra and Bob stopped in front of a grey stone building with a pub sign: 'The Bonnie Prince'. They got out and Lois took the engraving out of the back seat. When they entered the tavern they saw they were the only ones there. There wasn't even anybody behind the bar.

Bob leaned against the bar and waited a few minutes. 'Hey! Anyone home?' There was a bit of a noise like someone putting a lid on a metal pot and then the sounds of footsteps from the back room. 'I think I roused somebody,' he said.

A tall, thin and very plain woman came through a doorway behind the bar. She wore no make-up and her hair fell limp around her narrow shoulders. 'Pub's closed,' she said.

'I just want some information,' Bob said.

'I'm here to sell beer not information. The pub's closed. Come back at eleven.'

Lois decided to handle this. 'We are looking for a house here in Corra and we need to ask someone where it is.'

'A house? Whose house?'

'We don't know who lives there. It's just a house.'

The woman wiped her hands on her soiled apron. 'You don't know whose house but you want me to tell you where it is?'

'More or less,' said Bob.

'If you don't know the family's name how do you expect me to know what in the devil you're talking about? Come back at eleven. When we're open.' She started towards the back room. 'My husband will be here then.'

Lois looked at the clock over the bar and saw it was not even ten o'clock yet. 'Please,' she said, 'we've come all the

way from the United States and we don't have much time.'
She put the engraving atop the bar. 'Look. I have a picture
of the house. Maybe if I showed you the picture you'd know
where I'm talking about.' She started undoing the outer
wrapping before the woman could protest.

The thin-lipped woman watched her, and sighed when Lois
got down to the second layer of protective plastic. 'I hope
this is not going to take all day,' she said.

Lois worked at the clear tape that secured the plastic
bubble-wrap, then worked the picture out of one end of the
wrappings. The glass in the frame reflected the red lights in
an overhead lager sign. 'This is the place.' Lois turned the
engraving so the house was facing the woman.

She looked at it, wrinkled her brow and then pursed her
lips. 'It says "Corra" down here,' she remarked.

'Right,' Bob answered, trying to keep the sarcasm out of
his voice. 'That's why we are looking for it in Corra.' He
paused. 'Rather than in Tel Aviv.'

His irony was lost on her. 'No,' and she shook her head.
'No. I never saw that house. Not here in Corra.' She shook
her head again. 'No. This place is not around here.'

Lois felt like a balloon that was losing its air. 'Are you
sure?'

'I've lived here all my life,' the woman said.

'But I mean are you sure? You don't recognize this place?'
A tone of desperation had crawled into Lois' voice. 'We've
come all this way . . .'

'Not my fault you made the trip,' the woman replied,
'but I'm telling you I don't know this house. Never saw it
before. It surely is not in Corra. Not *this* Corra. Maybe
somewhere else called Corra, but not this one.'

Lois' voice was getting higher. 'But there are no other
towns in Britain called Corra.'

The woman shrugged. 'Again, it's not my fault. Come back
when we're open if you wish. Maybe some customer will
know the place. I doubt it.' For the first time she smiled at
Lois. 'But you can try.'

They walked back into the chilly morning air and both
heard the noise the bolt on the pub door made as it slammed
behind them. 'A real sweetheart, that one,' Bob said.

Lois was fussing with the wrappings that had been around
the engraving. 'I can't understand why she doesn't know

160

where the house is. She's lived here all her life. She must have seen the place.'

Bob opened the automobile door and Lois put the engraving and all its many protective layers onto the rear seat. What had once been a neat package was now a large pile of cast-off paper, string and plastic sheeting. 'Why would she say she didn't know the house if she really did? That doesn't make sense, hon.'

'It doesn't make sense. I agree. But I think she was lying.'

'You think she recognized the house but she's deliberately not telling you?'

'Yes, I do.' Lois' mouth was a straight line. 'She's hiding something.'

'Look, hon . . . I understand where you're coming from, but there is always the real possibility that the word Corra doesn't really mean this little lost dump. It doesn't have to be the name of a *place*. It could be the name of the people who owned the house or some kind of code. Anything.'

'They put the word "Corra" on there because it meant *this* place. I told you the name of the people who owned the house was Grenville. Their family crest is flying over the balcony. I compared them with that book I found in the library. The family lived in this area of Scotland. They were big shots here.' She sighed. 'I told you all this. We've been over this. Corra isn't the artist's name and it isn't some kind of code. It's the name of a town. This town. That house is somewhere around here. We've come this far and, dammit, we're not going back until we've found it.' She started to get into the front seat, then changed her mind. 'We don't have to wait an hour for the owner of that joint to talk to us. This is not some deserted movie set. There are other human beings around here. Other people who should know where our house is.' She reached into the back seat and took the picture out again. 'Come on. Let's find some warm bodies and start asking questions.'

'I just don't want you to get upset,' he said.

'Upset? I'm not upset. Not yet. Huh-uh. You know me better than that. I'm angry now and I intend to find this place even if we have to beat the bushes by ourselves.'

But it didn't work that way. Inside the small grocery store the owner shook his head. So did three of his customers. They didn't know of a house like that around Corra. At the gas station the kid with the greasy rag in his back pocket shook his head. He hadn't ever seen that place. Two elderly women, limping along together, one carrying a wicker basket of freshly ironed clothes, took one glance at the engraving, shook their heads and continued on their way. A young woman pushing a bundle of pink blankets in a pram, also shook her head. An elderly man with a pair of small scratching dogs did the same.

'Damn!' Lois was near tears as they headed back to their parked car. They silently got into the automobile and before Bob turned on the ignition he asked softly: 'Now what?'

Lois slumped down inside her coat. 'I don't know,' she replied. 'Looks like I screwed up, doesn't it?'

He put his hand out and took one of hers. 'You didn't,' he said. 'It's not the end of the world.'

She tried to smile at him. 'Well this place sure as hell is.'

'We've still got palm trees in Jamaica next month.'

'Maybe by that time I'll be over my disappointment. I was sure the house was here. I was so hoping it was. It would have meant so much to me if the house had been here.'

He knew she was talking about Tony. He also knew she would never put it into words. Bob turned the key and the engine started up. 'Where to now? Back to Dumfries?'

She burrowed deeper into her coat and into her private thoughts. 'Might as well.'

As he drove to the end of the street and readied to make the turn back onto the main highway, the old man with the two small scratching dogs waved his cane at them.

'He wants us to stop,' Lois said quickly. 'Bob, see what he wants.'

The old man, trying to remain upright on his cane in spite of the two dogs that wanted to go in opposite directions, made his way over to the car. Bob rolled down his window.

'About that house,' the old man said. 'There is a body who might be able to give you some information about it. Do you know Beeswing?'

'You mean the town back towards Dumfries?' Bob asked.

'Aye, the very one. Well, there is a retired school mistress who lives there, name of Miss Partridge. She's taught most of the folks in the region. Used to put pupils from Beeswing and Corra in the same building. Didn't need two separate schools. Know what I mean?' He peered in at

Lois and she could smell the snuff that made his teeth as brown as his ragged moustache. 'There's no soul in these parts Miss Partridge doesn't know. If she doesn't know them,' he grinned, 'they're not worth knowing. Know what I mean?'

'And you think she might know where this house is?' said Lois in a very relieved voice.

'Aye, she might. Can't give you a bank's guarantee on it, but she might.'

'What's her address in Beeswing?' Bob asked. 'What street does she live on?'

The old man showed his brown teeth and a dark liquid tried to dribble down his chin. 'Oh, there's no numbers in Beeswing. Just you ask for her when you get there. Everyone there knows where she resides. Know what I mean?'

'Thank you very much,' Lois beamed up at him. 'You've been a great help.'

'Tell Miss Partridge when you see her that it was I, Tom Mehagan, that sent you by.'

'Will do,' Bob smiled at the man. 'And thank you, Mr Mehagan.'

'Isn't any bother,' he said. 'Glad to help out a Yank. They helped out me and mine during the last great war. Know what I mean?' He pulled the leashes on his two mangy pets. 'Good luck.' He turned around and wobbled down the roadside.

'Now that was neat of him,' Bob said. 'Want to take a drive to Beeswing?'

'You bet I do!' All her gloom and disappointment had vanished. 'See? I always get my prayers answered.' She grinned, then pretended she was spitting snuff juice on the floor. 'Know what I mean?'

Finding Miss Partridge's house in Beeswing was much easier than finding the house in Corra. The first person they asked – in the picture postcard little village – knew exactly where the woman lived. Down that way, turn past the large oak tree and it's the third cottage past the corner. You can't miss it.'

Bob knocked on the door as Lois looked about her. Miss Partridge's cottage was small, even smaller than the two cottages on either side. There was a neatly hedged front lawn and pickling jars whose mouths were pressed to the ground showing where flowers had bloomed during the summer. Miss Partridge would have flowers next summer as well. There was a bootscraper fixed into the cement of the two foot square step that also served as a porch. A blue door had a Christmas wreath hanging lopsidedly on it, its ribbon faded from the snow and winter sun.

Bob knocked again. 'Maybe she's not home,' he said.

Lois' gaze continued along the side of the house to the shrubbery that separated it from the neighbouring cottage and she saw the eyes. They were staring out the window, peering through sheer cream curtains. 'Somebody next door is giving us the once over,' she said.

Bob looked in the same direction. 'Yeah. Strangers in this town must be a rare event.' He knocked again, harder, this time.

The eyes vanished from the curtain and in a few moments the door of the house next door opened and a middle-aged woman wearing a coat but with bedroom slippers on her feet came out onto her small cement stoop and started brushing at non-visible dust with a broom. She moved the broom but kept her eyes on them.

'Is Miss Partridge at home?' Bob called to her. The woman shrugged, didn't reply, and kept staring and moving the broom. 'Thanks,' Bob said. 'Appreciate the courtesy.' Then to Lois under his breath: 'Old bag!'

The door finally opened and a thin hand, made of translucent skin and enlarged blue veins, signalled to them.

'Come in quickly,' a tremulous voice said, 'or you'll catch your death of cold out there.' She stepped to one side and Bob pushed open the door and entered the cottage. Lois was right behind. 'Close the door. I can't afford to heat all Beeswing.' Lois did as she was told.

'Miss Partridge?' Bob stretched out his hand. 'My name is Bruno, Bob Bruno, and this is my wife, Lois. We're from the States.' He had found that bit of information freely given as usually a big help.

'I'm sure,' the old lady said. 'There. Those two chairs. Sit in them, please. I'll take this one over here. The cushion in the seat is a blessing.' She walked slowly to the chair and sat in it. Her feet didn't touch the carpeted floor. They guessed she was no more than five feet tall and the way she fixed her hair – straight back and twisted into a bun –

didn't add anything to her height. She had on grey wool slippers and long wool socks. Her skirt, of a dark tartan plaid, reached almost down to her ankles and she wore three sweaters: a blue turtleneck, a yellow V-neck and a brown buttoned-up cardigan.

'Do you know how old I am?' she asked suddenly.

Lois hated questions like that and always tried to give back an answer that would flatter the senior citizen asking it. 'I'd say about sixty-five,' she lied.

'Ninety-seven!' the woman said proudly. 'Nobody else in my family lived past seventy-five.'

'That's wonderful,' Bob said. 'Really impressive.'

'I was born right here,' she gave more un-asked-for information.

'In this town?' Lois smiled.

'In this village and here in this house. This house was my grandfather's house. He bought it from the money he got after being demobilized when the Duke of Wellington defeated Napoleon. That was in 1815, it was. My father was born here and I was born here. They expected my children to be born here as well, but I didn't have any need for children of my own. I was too busy taking care of everybody else's wee ones. I was a teacher, you know. Taught for years.'

'Yes, we heard that,' said Lois. 'In fact a gentleman by the name of Tom Mehagan told us about you.'

'Who?' Lois repeated the name. Miss Partridge laughed, showing a few teeth still straggling around the edges of her gums. 'Young Tommy Mehagan! What a rapscallion that child was! Full of pepper and I had the devil's own time trying to get him to read, I did. Stubborn child! Course, not having no real father and all didn't do the lad any good either.'

Lois wondered when she had last seen 'young Tommy' but decided not to let her get started on any new reminiscences. 'Miss Partridge, the reason we're here is that we're trying to locate a house, an old house somewhere near Corra. We spent all morning over there driving around and asking people about it, but nobody seems to have any idea where it is. Then Mr Mehagan suggested we come here and talk to you. He said you know everything there is to know about this part of the world.'

'He did, did he?' The old woman sounded pleased. 'Coming from Tommy that's grand praise.' She looked from one to the other. 'A house you say? Whose house?'

'That's the problem. We don't know who lives there now. Years ago it belonged to the Grenville family. I have a picture of it in the car and if you would just look at it for a moment maybe you could tell me something about it.' Lois got up from her chair. 'I'll only be a second.' She went out.

'There was only one school building for the two villages,' Miss Partridge said suddenly to Bob. 'All the pupils sat in the same room, they did, and while the wee ones were doing their exercises I would be learning the bigger ones their exercises. There was a fire in '37. Whole place went up and the roof went in. Whoosh! Just like that. Ever see a building on fire?' She looked at him and he nodded. 'I get cards from America at Christmas time. Many of my pupils have gone there to live. Here, let me show you some. I have them all in that drawer over there.' She started to get up, slowly and with great difficulty, and Bob sighed with relief when Lois came back into the cottage and Miss Partridge sat back down.

'Here. This is the house I'm trying to locate.' Lois rested the engraving on the old woman's lap.

Miss Partridge looked at the picture and then up at Lois. 'Why, of course, I know that place!' she said. 'It's the old Barlow place. The house of the Barlow family. They were descended from the Earl of Corra, you know.'

'Here in Corra?' Lois said excitedly. 'I mean *there* in Corra?'

'Of course. Wonderful old house. I was in it when I was a girl. They used to have lawn parties in the summer on Mrs Barlow's birthday. I went there one year with Elsie Stanley and I'll never forget it because there were some soldiers there who only spoke French. It was just like in a novel. They were so handsome in their uniforms but our parents had forbidden us to talk to them because . . .'

Lois hoped her interruption would not be too rude.

'Miss Partridge, where exactly is this house? Can you give us the address? Or draw us a map?'

'Draw you a map where the house is?' The old woman shook her head. 'Oh, I couldn't do that.'

'Why not?' Bob asked.

'Why, this place doesn't exist anymore. Heavens child, this place is only a memory now. The house burnt to the ground years ago.'

* * *

Lois pulled even farther into her coat on the ride back to Dumfries. Bob didn't try to talk to her and she didn't volunteer any conversation. It's not fair, she kept saying to herself. All this way and all this expense and the house doesn't exist anymore. So Tony isn't there. He's never been there. The place burnt years ago. So why all this 'message' nonsense? Why all these 'signs' that I should come to Scotland? It's a goddamned dirty trick, she said to herself, hoping the spirits or whoever the bastards were that had been playing these games with her would hear her. It's not fair and I don't think it's amusing. In fact, I'm so disappointed in you guys that I never intend to listen to you again! You got that, you bastards? 'Never!'

'Never what?' Bob asked, and only then did she realize that she'd said the last word aloud.

She coloured. 'Nothing. I was talking to myself.'

On a normal day he would have made some comeback about where they put people who talk to themselves, but today he didn't. Today was not a normal day.

As they drove towards the Waverley Hotel they stopped for a red light. Malcolm was waiting at the corner to cross. 'There he is again,' Bob muttered.

He stuck his head in the window when Lois rolled it down. 'How was your trip? Find the place, did you?'

'No,' Lois replied with a long sigh. 'It doesn't exist anymore. It was burnt down years ago.'

'More's the pity,' he said, 'but are you sure?'

'We talked with a schoolteacher in Beeswing. She gave us the facts.'

Malcolm smiled. 'That would be Miss Partridge now, wouldn't it? She was my teacher for a while when we lived near Corra. Grand old girl . . . what are you going to do now? Stay on a while in Dumfries?'

'I don't see any point in it,' Lois said. 'We'll probably go up to Edinburgh tomorrow.' She hadn't discussed it

167

with Bob but she knew he'd be glad to get away from here.

'Many old houses are gone now,' Malcolm said. 'Lovely ones too. Some burnt down and others just fell down by themselves. It takes a lot of money to keep up a big place. There's not been much money up here for a long time. Getting worse too, you know, what with the unemployment and the young men going south seeking work.'

The light changed and, of course, a horn instantly blew behind him. Bob lifted his foot from the brake and the car glided down the street and came to a stop in the parking lot beside the hotel. They got their room key and stood looking at each other. 'What'll it be?' Bob said. 'Bathroom or bar?'

'Bar,' she said grimly. 'I can pee anytime.'

Even though it was not quite noon, the little pub was almost full. A tour bus had stopped for lunch and it seemed as if everyone there except Fiona and the Brunos were speaking German. Fiona poured them each a Scotch and they stood at the end of the bar, sipping slowly and watching the noisy visitors.

'It's a damn shame,' Lois finally said. 'We came all this way and spent all this money . . .'

'You want to talk about it now?' he asked. 'You up to it?'

'Sure. It's had time to sink in. I must have acted like a real basket case back in New York. Losing Tony, thinking I'd seen him, then getting that fucking picture and all my imaginings got confused with it. Then those crazy muggers who only took some blood. I was all mixed up in my head.'

'Look, hon, you don't have to talk about it. I understand.'

'But I do have to talk about it. I've got to bring it out of my head and into reality. I can't keep scrambling everything together. It's not fair to you.'

'You don't hear me complaining, do you?'

She smiled at him. 'No. You've been marvellous all through this. You really have. You understood where I was coming from when even I myself wasn't sure. I mean you even took time off work and spent a bundle just to get me over here so I could see for myself how wrong I was. It's a helluva husband – and friend – that would do that.'

'You forget, I also happen to be in love with you,' he said softly. 'That's a factor too.'

'I've never forgotten that.' She smiled at him again. 'It has always been uppermost in my mind. I couldn't have gone through any of this without your love.'

'Another drink?' he asked, and Fiona brought two more. 'I'm going to say something – ' He spoke slowly. 'And I just want you to listen. Don't get angry and don't clam up. Okay?' She nodded. 'I know you were hoping to find Tony alive and well in that house.' He put out one hand. 'Now don't answer. I asked you to listen. I know that deep in your heart you wanted to believe that our son is still alive and being held prisoner in that mansion. Midge's goddamned engraving and that goddamned ghost story didn't help matters any. You still hope Tony is alive. Now that the house is gone, you hope he's someplace else: the States, Canada, who knows where? I would like to hope he's still alive. I really would. He was my son, too. I loved the little guy. But as much as I'd like to have him back, I know he's gone. Gone forever. I saw his body. That image still haunts me. Sometimes it gets into my dreams and awakens me.' She reached out and touched him on the cheek. 'But I know he won't be coming back and I know you will never find him in some old house. I know that.'

'I know that, too. Now,' she said. 'I didn't tell you but I thought I saw him in London. The day I went shopping. It wasn't him, of course. It was all in my head and I didn't tell you because I didn't want to upset you. We were having such a good time.' He just looked at her, and didn't comment. 'I can go back to New York now and start living again. I haven't been living for the past four months. This trip has crossed the Ts and dotted the Is. I'll be okay now.' Again the smile. 'I promise you that.'

Fiona came to their end of the bar. 'If you want lunch, you'd better go in now. Most of the bus people have cleared out. Try the steak and kidney pie. It's grand!'

The crusted pie *was* 'grand' and they washed it down with frothy mugs of real ale. They talked about friends in New York and about Bob's business. They wondered what Midge was doing and if Bob's father was keeping his old bones warm in the Florida sun. They talked about the black-faced sheep on the road and the idea of buying a farm in Scotland for a second home, and Lois even laughed several times. What they didn't talk about was Tony and the fact the house was gone.

They went to their room after lunch and curled up together on the large bed and fell asleep. After an hour or so Lois stirred, and saw that Bob was awake and looking at her. 'I've been thinking,' he said.

'Oh? That's a first.'

'Yeah. We've come all this way to see that house and we didn't even consider seeing the land where it once stood. I mean, we should at least see the grounds of the place. Don't you agree?'

'If you want to,' she said, 'but I don't see much point in it.' Actually, she never wanted to set foot in Corra again.

'I mean you're a designer, you know how things look or should look. Let's find the site of the place and compare it with the landscape in the engraving. We've come all this way.'

'If you want to,' she repeated, then added, 'but I don't see what it will accomplish.'

'If you see that the landscape couldn't possibly be the same as in the picture then it will do a lot of good. It'll cross another of those Ts you were talking about.'

'How are we going to find the spot?'

'Miss Partridge. We'll go back and ask her. She can draw us a map. Hell, we can even load the old girl in the car and have her direct us to it. I'll bet she's not been out of that cottage all winter.'

'I guess,' Lois said. 'Sure. Why not? We don't have anything else to do this afternoon.'

The ride back to Beeswing seemed to take less than fifteen minutes. Bob made all the right turns and came to a stop in front of the old woman's cottage. They walked to the front door and Bob knocked. They waited for an answer and when there was none, he knocked again. 'It takes her a while to get her engine started,' he said.

The door to the cottage next door opened and the neighbour lady started across the lawn towards them. 'What do you want this time?' she asked.

'We were here this morning,' Lois said. The woman nodded. 'We want to see Miss Partridge again.'

'You can't see her,' the woman replied. 'Nobody can see her.'

'What do you mean?'

'Miss Partridge can't talk to anyone. She's dead, God rest her soul.'

'Dead?' Lois was shocked. 'But how can that be? We talked with her just this morning. She was fine this morning.'

'What happened?' Bob asked.

The woman shook her head. 'I don't know. I don't stick my nose in other folks' affairs. Some men came and took her body away. It was less than an hour ago.'

'Some men?' Bob's voice rose. 'You mean hospital people in an ambulance?'

The woman shook her head again. 'Just some men. In a big car. Strangers they were to me. You know Miss Partridge was all alone. Poor soul didn't have any family. Don't know who those men were. Don't know why they cared for her remains.'

Lois was still in shock. 'Don't you think that was a little unusual? To put a body in a car? Is that how you do things in Scotland?'

The woman looked at them, from one face to the other. 'I can't tell any more than what I know. You'd be best advised to go elsewhere for your information.' She started back towards her open front door, then stopped and turned back towards them. 'Just a wee word of warning,' she said. 'Don't hang on here in Beeswing and Corra. It's not good to be foreigners around here.'

Still not believing that the eccentric old lady was dead, they went back and got into the car. Bob started the motor and they headed back towards Dumfries. As he pulled out onto the main highway, Lois turned around to see if the engraving was riding safely in the back seat.

'Oh my God!' Lois let out a short high scream that so startled Bob he almost ran off the highway. 'Oh Bob! Look at this damn thing!'

He stopped the car and turned around. 'Shit!' he said.

It was quite obvious. The little man under the glass had crept two inches farther up the lawn, two inches closer to the house.

CHAPTER THIRTEEN

The plump woman with the ample bosom and the salt and pepper hair lit the candles in the silver holders on the table. The book was there and also, near it, were the gilded rose and the triangular amulet. The metal items caught the colour in the flames. Eight of the other people were there, only one chair remained empty. They waited for tea to be brought in.

'They got Miss Partridge today,' one of the old men said softly. The others nodded their heads. They had all heard the news. 'Poor old soul,' the man continued. 'I'll miss her. She was harmless.'

'She knew too much,' said the woman with the French accent. 'She knew more than most around here.'

'She would have said nothing,' another man said. 'She's kept the secret too long to blab it now.'

'Her mind was wandering,' another said.

'Still no reason to kill her,' the first man replied. 'They could have just warned her.'

'You didn't warn Miss Partridge,' the Frenchwoman said with a grim smile. 'She always did exactly what she had a mind to. To tell her not to do something was the very same as begging her to do it.'

'The Americans brought it all about,' the first man said.

'Aye. The Americans.'

'They visited her this morning.'

'*We* brought it about,' a younger male voice said, 'for it was *we* who brought the Americans over here in the first place.'

The Frenchwoman shrugged. 'We knew there would be casualties.'

'But did it have to be Miss Partridge?' The young man asked sadly. 'I had her in school. She had been my teacher.'

The first man adjusted his glasses and looked at the young

man. He shook his head of white wiry hair. 'Malcolm, we have all known and loved the old woman but lamenting won't bring her back. You know we didn't expect her to get involved with *the plan*. The important thing is that we continue with *the plan*.'

Malcolm didn't look at any of them, just kept his gaze at the reflections of light on the table in front of him. 'Sometimes I wish I'd never heard of *the plan*.' He rubbed at his eyes. 'Sometimes it's a heavy cross to bear.'

'Well it got you a free trip to New York City, didn't it, my young laddie?' the buxom woman said as she opened the door to let in the cook with the tea tray.

'You got to fly in an aeroplane,' said the white-haired man, 'and you saw sights none of us have ever seen before.'

'Yes but to do that I had to attack a helpless woman.' Now Malcolm glared at the elderly faces around him. 'I burst into her flat like a thieving jackal and drained her of her very own blood. I'm not proud of that, on my honour, I'm not.'

'But it was worth it, wasn't it? The blood proved that she was truly the one. It proved it without a doubt,' the white-haired man continued. 'The American woman is the right choice.'

'Part of *the plan*, Malcolm.' Another man patted Malcolm on the shoulder. 'T'was all part of *the plan*.'

'Well, they're leaving tomorrow.' Malcolm's gaze went slowly around the table. 'They say they're off for Edinburgh. Then the States. So where's *the plan* now?'

'It's all working,' the Frenchwoman said.

'Aye,' said the buxom woman as she poured the tea. 'We know what hotel they will be in. We know when their aeroplane reservations are for. I don't see it as a complication.'

'But the delay!' Malcolm insisted.

' 'Tis no delay, my lad,' the white-haired man replied. 'It's all been taken into consideration. It's part of *the plan*.'

'Is father still moving up the face of her picture?' A man grinned. 'Love to watch him do it, myself.'

'I haven't been able to inspect the picture,' Malcolm said. 'They've taken it with them when they've gone out.'

'Couldn't you just sneak into their room and take a peek? When they aren't around?' The woman with the tea pot smiled. 'Give it a look? For us?'

Malcolm shook his head. 'I don't know. Fiona keeps the pass key on her most of the time.'

'Did the American bring the book with her?'

'I haven't seen it.'

'Probably in her suitcase,' the Frenchwoman said. 'Be nice to have it back in our own library again. It belongs here. It was one of father's, you know.'

'Aye,' the white-haired man said. 'We'll ask her for it when she gets here.'

'When she gets here?' Malcolm's voice rose. 'Didn't I just tell you that she's off tomorrow for Edinburgh and then the States? How do you expect to get her *here*? She's already been here, or at least she's been very near. She probably passed this house half a dozen times in the car today.'

The white-haired man stood up. 'You haven't been informed of everything involved in the completion of *the plan*. So if you've finished with your tea, and it appears that you have, I'd like you to take a little stroll with me. I'd like to give you the next instalment of your part in *the plan*.'

'My *next* part? I thought I was finished. I thought I did my part.'

'Not quite, my boy. We need you for a couple more pieces of the puzzle.'

'Once the American woman gets here,' said the Frenchwoman, 'you'll be free of all of us if you choose.'

'Yes.' The woman with the tea pot reached for his empty cup. 'Free to do what you want, like marry Miss Fiona.'

'That is still on, isn't it?' the Frenchwoman asked.

Malcolm reddened under his red hair. 'Aye,' he said shyly.

'Let's get the American here, Malcolm, and then we can start planning what to wear to your wedding.'

*   *   *

Malcolm walked into the small front lobby of the Waverley Hotel. 'Hello,' he said to Fiona. She glanced up from the ledger book she was writing in. She had it open on the reception counter and had a pile of bills and receipts beside it. 'You're not done yet, love?'

174

'Not quite. Dad did a lot of paying out today. Seems half the people that walked in here had a bill in their hand.' She smiled at him. 'Just be a second, though.'

'Are the Americans in their room?' he asked, hoping his tone was nonchalant.

'Aye. They're pretty tired. It's been a long day for them, what with that teacher dying and all.'

'Did they tell you about it?' He wondered how much they had told her. 'Were they there when it happened?'

'No. It seems the poor soul had only been gone for an hour or so before the Americans returned. Mrs Bruno was the most upset, I think. She seemed to think the old woman might still have been alive had they not visited her.'

'What?' Malcolm's voice rose.

'Yes. Mrs Bruno thought maybe they overtired the old soul with their questions and all. She said the woman wasn't moving too fast when they visited her. She wonders if afterwards the old dear might not have tried to contact somebody else.'

'Somebody else?'

'For more information about that house. You know, the one they came to find. Burnt down years ago, more's the pity.' She added up a column of figures and wrote the answer in the ledger book. 'Maybe the old lady thought she could give them more information. She went to the neighbour and made a phone call. Didn't have a phone of her own, you know.'

'Oh?' Malcolm pretended to examine a tourist map that had been hanging in the lobby for months. 'Who did she call?'

'I don't know.' Fiona erased a number and put in a new one. 'The men came shortly after but she was dead by then.'

'How did you hear that?' He tried to keep his voice level. 'The Americans tell you?'

'Oh no. They didn't know anything more than she had died. It was chatted about in the pub tonight. Some folks from Beeswing were in. They were telling it.' She closed the book and smiled at him. 'There. That's done for the day.' She put the ledger and the receipts in the black metal safe that was in the corner under a pile of newspapers and a

175

case of empty Coke bottles and slammed the door. She took her coat from off a peg, slipped quickly into it and then, with one last glance around the deserted lobby, she switched off all the lights, except one that was directly over the door. She opened the door, waited for him to go out first, then closed it and locked it. She slipped the key into her coat pocket.

They walked in silence up the silent street in the direction of the town square. He reached out for her hand and she gave it to him. His hand was warm and felt good in hers. As they passed darkened shop windows they could see their reflections in the glass, highlighted by the yellow burning street lamps. When they reached the top of the incline – nobody ever called it a hill – they saw there were several teenagers hanging around the Victorian cast iron fountain. Illuminated water splashed from long-necked cranes, down onto fat, water-spitting fish and bounced off the heads of chubby cherubs astride mythical sea creatures. Not far away, standing high and dry on his marble pedestal, Dumfries' favourite son, Robert Burns, watched everything that was going on.

'The embankment?' Malcolm asked. She smiled. They started walking away from the fountain, then down to the river's edge and across a small suspension bridge that swayed under their feet. It had been built many years before so that factory workers living on the other side of the river wouldn't have so far to walk to their jobs. The grasslands of the embankment were silent as well. In the daytime there were dogs and babies and schoolchildren and an occasional tourist. Now, where James M. Barrie had conceived Peter Pan, Malcolm took Fiona in his arms and kissed her.

'That was grand,' she said softly. 'Do it again?' He did, but when he pulled away she knew something was wrong. 'What's troubling you?'

He shook his head. She could almost see him in the darkness. 'Nothing. I guess I'm just tired.'

'From doing what?' she teased. 'Not from too much employment, that's for sure.'

'Just from things,' he sighed.

'What sort of things?' She reached up and drew his face down nearer to hers. 'You're not saying you're tired of me, are you?'

'No, of course not.' And as if to prove it he gave her another kiss. 'I've got things on my mind. That's all.'

'Malcolm – ' She tried not to let the peevish tone creep into her voice. 'If you can't tell *me*, who can you tell?'

'I can't tell anybody,' he said. 'Not you. Not yet. Not a soul.'

'Have you a secret?'

'Aye. You could call it that.'

'Malcolm, if we are going to be married I don't think we should have any secrets one from the other. We're supposed to share things.'

'I know.' His hands, which had been on her soft yellow hair, moved down her cheeks and came to rest on her shoulders. 'It's all going to be over soon.'

'What will? You know how I hate secrets.'

The hands moved downwards, stopping at the top button of her coat. 'It's something that I have to work out,' he said. 'I can't tell you now, so don't ask.' His fingers began to unbutton the coat, then slipped inside and sought the tips of her breasts. 'You've got to understand that I've got worries. You just have to accept it.'

Her body began to vibrate under his touch and she reached out with her own hand and sought for warmth inside the folds of his coat. Her hand was on his belt buckle and it itched to go farther down. 'I don't like seeing you bothered like this,' she said.

He moved her hand down. She didn't have to make the decision. She could feel him hardening under her grasp. 'After we're married,' he breathed in her ear. 'After we're married, things will be different.'

She pulled away from him. 'I've heard this so many times before.' She pulled away even farther. She was no longer touching him, nor he her. 'When, Malcolm? When will this marriage be?'

He reached for her, the pressure in his trousers demanding. 'Soon. I promise you.'

She turned sharply and started buttoning her coat. Out over the river a seagull that should have been asleep squawked at nothing. 'We've been engaged for almost three years now, Malcolm! Three years! For three years you've been telling me "soon".' He could see her eyes blazing. 'I want to know *when*. I think I deserve to have a definite date.'

'When it's all over and taken care of,' he said quietly.

'When *what's* all over and taken care of?' she insisted, her voice getting louder. The unsleepy seagull squawked again. 'When what's all over? I don't understand.'

'I don't expect you to,' he said with a sigh. 'I *can't* expect you to.'

CHAPTER FOURTEEN

Bob stopped shaving and looked at his wife, who was down on her knees peering under the hotel bed. 'I haven't seen you wearing it since we got to Scotland.'

'I didn't put it on while we were here,' she replied, 'but I did wear it in London. Remember when we went to that fancy French place? Well, I had it on then.'

'And it's not in your jewellery box?'

She shot him a look. 'If it was in the box would I be down on all fours looking under the bed?' Bob went back to his foam-covered jawline. 'It wasn't a valuable brooch. I found it in a little antique place on Third Avenue, but I liked it. It went well with black.' She straightened up. 'Oh well, gain a little then lose a little, I suppose.'

'I had a friend in New Orleans,' Bob said over the sound of running water, 'who used to say that possessions were only rented, that we never really *own* anything. He said he never saw a hearse going to the cemetery with a U-Haul-It behind.' He laughed and stuck his head, now being towelled dry, out of the door to get her reaction.

'Very funny!' But she was grinning. 'You about ready?' She glanced around the room making sure everything was packed into the three suitcases and the overnight case. She grimaced when she glanced at the engraving. It was leaning against the bed. Bob had wrapped it and tied it. She didn't even want to touch it. She had wanted to leave it at the hotel, to give it to Fiona's parents as a gift. They could hang it in one of the bedrooms and she would be free of it. Either that or throw it into the sea. That's where it belonged, at the bottom of a very deep ocean. But – it seemed to her there was always a 'but' – Bob had showed her his passport and the official paper stuck onto the inside back cover saying they must take the engraving back to the States with them. 'If we don't have it when we leave,' he said, 'we might not get out ourselves.' So she had agreed to drag it along with them for the rest of the trip. But – and this was now *her* 'but' – as soon as she got back to the apartment she would have Mr Santiago, the superintendent, throw it in the incinerator and she would stand there and watch him to make sure he did it. Bob had to admit it was probably a good idea.

Fiona was at the front desk as they paid their bill. 'Did you enjoy your stay?'

'Yes,' Bob said. 'Very much. The hotel is very comfortable.'

'To use an English expression, everything was "loverley".' Lois said.

'I'm pleased,' the girl said. 'Will you be going to Edinburgh straight away?'

'There's an 11.37 train,' Bob answered. 'We'll be on it.'

'And how many days will you stay then, in Edinburgh?'

'Just three,' he said. 'We both have jobs to get back to.'

'I've never been to the States,' the girl said. 'I've always wanted to, though. Perhaps when Malcolm and me get married we'll have our honeymoon in the States. I have an aunt, my mother's sister, living in Boston. We'll spend some time with her. Perhaps we will come to New York City and visit you.'

'I think that's a great idea,' Lois said. 'We have an extra bedroom. You both would be more than welcome.'

'At the moment it's just a dream,' Fiona said softly. 'We haven't set the date yet, let alone where we are going on our honeymoon.'

'Well, remember you have friends in Manhattan,' Bob said.

'Right,' Lois agreed, and then wondered why Bob had changed his mind about Malcolm. Yesterday he had been a jerk. Today he and his future bride were invited house guests. 'Oh, just one thing, Fiona. I can't seem to find a brooch that I was sure I had with me. I've looked everywhere in the room for it and I wondered, if it turns up, if you could send it on to me. I mean, it's not really valuable, but I did

179

like to wear it. It's kind of Victorian with angels and ribbons in silver and a red heart stone.'

'A ruby?' the girl's eyes widened.

'No,' Lois laughed. 'I wish it was. No, it's just an old piece of costume jewellery, but I would appreciate it being returned to me if one of the maids finds it.'

'We'll be at the Admiralton Hotel in Edinburgh,' Bob said. 'If you find it you could send it up by first-class mail and we'd get it before we left.'

'The Admiralton. Right. I know where it is.'

'Thanks, hon.' Lois reached out and took Fiona's hand. 'We didn't really get what we came for, but you have been awfully sweet.' She kissed the girl lightly on the cheek.

* * *

After small Dumfries and even tinier Corra, the city of Edinburgh seemed like a giant carved from dirty red stones massively astride a range of rugged hills. The cab from Waverley railway station took them out into wide avenues filled with cars, streets lined with shops and department stores, and sidewalks clogged with pedestrians. The taxi stopped at red lights, blew its horn at people who dodged between the traffic and switched on its wipers as dust-filled raindrops suddenly splattered blindly onto its windshield.

They pulled up in front of the Admiralton and the driver just sat there. Bob paid him exactly what the meter read, then opened the door quickly, grabbing two of the suitcases and running through the rain with them to the front door. He ran back, water now streaming down his face, grabbed the other suitcase and the overnight bag and made his second dash for the hotel lobby. Lois jumped out, the engraving held like an umbrella over her head, and ran through the rain after him. They turned to see the driver mumble something as he got out and slammed the back door of the cab.

They scanned the huge lobby for a porter, then picked up their luggage and carried it over to the reception desk. 'Dirty town, surly cabbies, no porters and rain,' Bob said. 'Reminds me of home.'

Their room was half the size of the one they had at the Waverley and three times the price. One large bed, one dresser, one built-in closet and a bathroom just a little larger than the closet. Lois looked dispiritedly around, then went into the bathroom for a towel. She rubbed it across Bob's wet hair and then wiped his damp face. He laughed and kissed her, then took the towel and went to the one window and looked out. 'It's stopped,' he said. 'Look, you can even see the sun.'

She went to the window. Yes, the sun had come out. The sky was blue and the straight lines of the ancient castle stood in brightly etched relief on its position of power on the city's highest hill.

In less than five minutes they were out of the hotel and among the crowds on the sidewalk. There had been a brochure, in their room, about tours of Edinburgh and they followed the map until they came to a street that seemed to be exclusively reserved for buses to park. One of the large Mercedes monsters had a sign in the window: 'Holyrood Palace'. They hopped aboard it. For the next hour they wandered through history like delighted children in never-never land. The palace was crammed full of things they wanted to touch, wanted to inspect and wanted to own. All they could do was wonder silently as the guide took them from room to room, each with treasures more elaborate than the others. They saw where the Queen sits when she is in residence and gives a dinner party. They saw the chairs she uses for receiving her subjects, still embroidered in the red, gold and silver initials of her grandfather and grandmother. They saw crystal chandeliers, walls covered in enormous oil paintings, and oriental carpets bigger than their entire apartment. They admired lacquered chests from China, gilded furniture from France, marble fireplaces from Italy and tapestries from Germany. Neither of them had ever been in a place like this before. It went against the grain of everything their American teachers and politicians had preached against monarchs, power and inherited wealth. This luxury hadn't been earned. Democracy and free enterprise had not purchased this opulence. The kings and queens who used this place had not been elected by the people. It wasn't the way things were done in the USA. And they loved every minute of it.

The tour bus took them through back streets and finally deposited them in the enormous courtyard of the castle. The wind blew crisply and they pulled their coat collars tighter as they hurried past the uniformed guards at the bridge over the empty moat and joined a group waiting for the next tour to begin.

Again, they were transported into a fascinating, unreal world. Here were stones that had been laid down centuries before any Pilgrims even thought of taking a boat from Plymouth. Here were stone steps, here were cannons pointed at the city in the valley below, here were collections of uniforms, cases of medals, books listing the names of servicemen killed in battles, the apartments where Mary Queen of Scots lived and the window high in the stone wall (and to Lois this was just like a fairy tale) where she lowered her infant son in a basket to safety with friends who stood far below. Then, as if neither of their digestions could take another rich mouthful, there was a small room shimmering with diamonds and emeralds and rubies that were the Scottish Crown Jewels. They staggered from the castle back out into the darkening afternoon. The rain had come again, but in the form of a dreary mist.

'I don't know about you,' Bob said, 'but I don't want to look at another inch of history. I need a drink.'

'Darlin', you must be readin' my mind.'

They walked quickly through the funnel-like entrance of the castle grounds and then started running because the rain suddenly poured out of the skies as though God was emptying a bathtub. Holding hands, they ran for half a block down the Royal Mile when Bob turned sharply to the right and Lois followed. They were in a narrow alcove, squeezed between two old stone walls. 'Here,' he shouted over the noise of the torrent, 'in here.' She followed him down a few steps and then gratefully into a large dark room. When their eyes accustomed to the gloom, the first thing they saw was an old woman with shoulder-length white stringy hair wearing a high cone hat. She sat gloating at the head of a centre table. The walls were splashed with garish impressions of a smiling satan and some kind of magical amulet. A green goat's head grinned at them from a rear wall, surrounded by the signs of the zodiac in golden paint.

A man touched Lois' arm and she jumped. 'Welcome,' he said. 'Would you like a table?' They nodded and, still looking all around them, were seated at the back wall with the grinning goat just two feet above their heads. The man handed them menus and silently went away.

'What is this place?' Lois asked, glancing around at the weird things – nailed, framed, painted – hanging around the large room.

'It's called the Witchery,' Bob said reading from the menu. 'It says that the corner we just passed, passed in a hurry through the rain,' he laughed, 'was where they used to burn witches. Years ago, of course. And this place is supposed to be haunted.' He smiled, 'at least that's what it says here.'

Lois relaxed a little. The old woman in the witch's hat at the centre table was a store dummy. She saw that now and wondered if customers ever deliberately sat at the table with the awful thing. 'Catch the waiter's eye,' she said, 'this place would drive anybody to drink.'

They were the only people eating in the place and the waiter, when he brought their Scotches, told them they were between the lunch and the dinner crowd. If they were hungry, most of the items on the menu were still available. For an appetizer they ordered 'Magic Mushrooms'. For her main course Lois chose 'Old Mother Long Nose's Secret' while Bob decided on a cold roast beef and cheese plate with the name 'Auld Nick's Platter'. They each had a mug of room-temperature Scottish ale to wash it down.

Lois wiped the last of the crumbs from her mouth with her napkin, set down her empty glass mug and said, 'That was exactly what I needed. Now a trip to the ladies' room and the afternoon will be complete.'

'It's over there,' Bob said. 'I saw the sign when we came in.'

Lois rose and walked past the bar in the direction Bob had pointed. There was a map on the wall and she glanced at it. 'Haunted Sites of Scotland' the legend said and she let her eyes glance across it quickly. She stopped, leaned closer and after a minute came back to the table.

'I thought you had to go,' Bob remarked.

'I did, but come over here. There's something I want you to see.' He got up and followed her. She stopped at the map. 'Look at that,' she said. 'Just look at that down there.'

Bob squinted in the shadows and tried to read where she

183

was pointing. 'Dumfries,' he said aloud. 'Howard Castle is supposed to be haunted. So what?'

'Not Dumfries!' She glided her finger down the glass about an inch. 'There. Where I'm pointing. Look what it says.'

Bob read it, then glanced up sharply at her. 'I'll be damned,' he said and went back and read it again. 'Corra. The house of the notorious black magician, Aleister Crowley. Known as "666" and "The Beast", he performed diabolical rituals there. Wow!' Bob looked at Lois again. 'That's your house,' he said, pointing to a small thimble-sized illustration over the words he had just read. 'It's the same view. Just like in the engraving. Well, son-of-a-bitch. What do you think of that?'

'I think,' Lois said, 'that some people back in Corra weren't telling us the truth. They didn't *want* us to find that house. But can you believe it.' She looked at the map again. 'We found the damned place after all.'

'Wait a minute. This is Edinburgh, not Corra. We haven't "found" anything. That old school teacher said the house burned down years ago. This is probably an old map.' He searched the bottom border for a date. 'It was printed in 1981.'

'Uh-huh,' Lois said, 'and Miss Partridge said the place had burned down years ago. Nineteen eighty-one is not years ago.'

'I agree, but so what? The map has been reprinted, that's all.'

'No. I think the house is still standing and we should go back there and find it on our own.'

'Wait a minute. We are not going back there. We are going to stay two more days in Edinburgh and then we are going back to the United States . . . and to a normal life. Remember? Remember when we had a *normal* life?'

'We've come all this way . . .'

'Yes, and we've still got a long way to go. Right now, let's go back to the table and have another drink.' He grinned. 'I mean after you have a pee. That was where you were headed when you got sidetracked by this map.'

'I don't have to go anymore,' she said and came back to their table with him. Soon there were two new Scotches in front of them. 'Aleister Crowley,' she shook her head and had a faint smile. 'Of all people.'

184

'I've never heard of him.'

'He's dead now, but he was a real character,' Lois explained. 'An Englishman who thought he had all the secrets of the devil. He was into rituals and chanting and candle burning. You know, all the spooky occult stuff. He called himself "666" because it says somewhere in the Bible that the Beast of the Apocalypse will have that number.'

'How do you know so much about him?'

'My folks had a couple of books about him,' she replied. 'I read them when I was a teenager. I remember being very impressed with the man's eyes and his nerve. I mean, to go around telling everybody you were the master of the universe and you had all the answers – that took a lot of nerve.' She laughed. 'He was a real put-on. He used to spell magic with a K. Magick. That was his special word. Everybody else knew about plain old magic but he knew all about it with a K.' She stopped and frowned. 'I'll bet I know why the locals didn't want anybody to find that place today. Crowley probably performed his Black Mass there. Dirty old man.'

Bob waited, then asked: 'What's a Black Mass?'

'You know what a regular Mass is. At least you should, your mother dragged you to church enough times.' He nodded. 'Well when Crowley said his Black Mass he said it backwards.'

'Backwards? The whole thing?'

'The whole thing. Word for word. In Latin, of course, because the Mass was only said in Latin in those days. And – ' She leaned forwards and lowered her voice even though they were the only customers in the restaurant. 'You'll like this, for an altar he used a naked woman.' She sat back to watch the expression on his face.

'He used a *what*?'

'A naked woman. Had her stretch out on a table that he called an altar and he stuck candles up her you-know-what and lit them during the ceremony.'

'I *am* impressed,' Bob said. 'And to think I wasted all those years going to Mass said by Father Maggiano.'

'Oh, he was big on sex,' Lois continued. 'He'd screw anything in skirts. Even sometimes anything in trousers. Didn't matter to him. He was master of the universe, he could do no wrong.'

'I can just see Father Maggiano's face if Tessie Valvecchio

185

threw herself naked on his altar. Her holder would require one helluva candle.' He laughed at his own joke. 'What was the purpose of all this backward mumbo-jumbo?'

'To summon up the devil, of course. To make contact with Satan. Also it was a good excuse to have sex. When the ritual was almost over he'd pull out the candles and have intercourse with the woman right there. In front of everybody.'

Bob shook his head. 'I don't think Father Maggiano could have done that. Not in front of everybody, and especially not on special Sundays when he celebrated three Masses before noon . . . But, Lois, I'm really surprised at your folks having books around the house like that. I mean, stuff that little kids could find and read? Your mom and dad never struck me as the kind to read porno.'

'Oh, they took the books away from me when they discovered I'd read them. They didn't buy them for pornography, anyway. They bought them because they both were interested in the psychic and the occult. You know that.'

'So what did they do with the books? Throw them away?'

'My father? That old Scotsman? He never threw anything away! He put them downstairs in a cupboard and locked them up. But I found the key,' she grinned, 'and I read them again just before I graduated from high school. Reading Tarot cards and doing astrology and all that stuff was very "in" when I was in school. Funny, but I never thought of those books as being pornographic. They were just mystical. I read them to see if I could learn anything, not to get sexually aroused. Anyway – ' She patted his hand. 'I have you for that now.'

'Lady, you are weird. You are even kookier than I thought! Listen – I got a great idea. Let's get out of this place and go back to the hotel. On the way we can buy some candles. I'll be the priest.'

She laughed. 'Me weird? Wait till I tell Father Maggiano what you want to do! He'll start you praying yourself out of Purgatory while you're still alive!'

* * *

'Darlings! I can't believe it!'

Bob and Lois stopped dead in their tracks in the large hotel lobby. 'For Christ's sake,' he said, 'it's Midge!'

The woman almost ran across the carpeted marble floor to hug them. 'Isn't this great?' she cried. 'I mean, of all the hotels in this town and I pick the very one you are in! I can't believe it!' She released Lois from her bear hug and stepped back. 'Can you beat it? I mean, isn't this just too weird for words?'

Lois came down from her momentary shock. 'Midge? You here? Now I'm the one who can't believe it.'

'Yeah,' Bob added, 'what are you doing over here? You should be in New York.'

She shook Bob's hand and gave him a quick kiss on the cheek. 'Well, I had some vacation time coming and, after all that talk of yours about Scotland this and Scotland that, I just decided to come over and check it out for myself. I got this great tour package from Wilson's Travel – you know the one, Lois, right down the hall from our office? – and when they asked me what kind of hotel I wanted I just said oh, I don't know, something not too expensive and rather central, and they looked in their big book and this place, the Admiralton, was the first on the list, being as it began with an "A" and so I said, well, hell, what's the difference? I never knew, I mean never even *dreamed* that this was the very same hotel you two would be in.' She gave Lois another hug. 'I mean, isn't this just about the most amazing coincidence you ever saw? Now we can all see Edinburgh together. If you haven't already seen it, of course.' She stopped to take a breath. 'How long have you been here, in this city, I mean?'

'Just since today.' Lois smiled at her friend. 'Gosh, it's good to see you! Did you get my card? I sent you one from London.'

Midge shook her head and a large mass of blonde tight curls waved across her scalp. 'Probably didn't have time to get there before I left. Well, what do you think? I mean, you haven't said a word about my new hairdo. I had it cut short.' She turned slowly for their benefit. 'I know it's still winter and the back of my neck feels like a cold douche bag, but curls are in this year and Mitzi-Marie, who does my hair at the salon? You know who I mean Lois, I *always* go to her, anyway, she said why didn't I try them? The curls, I mean. She said if I was going on a trip the last thing I wanted was a hairdo that I had to fuss with, and you know she was

187

absolutely right. No fuss to these at all. Didn't even get messed up on that Goddamned plane trip over here. Was your behind sore, hon, after you got off the plane? I thought mine would never be the same again. So how are you? Tell me, what have you done? I'm just dying to hear about everything!'

They went to the hotel bar. Midge asked for a Singapore Sling but when the waitress just looked blankly at her she decided on a Scotch and water, like the Brunos had ordered. She reached across the small table and clutched both Lois' hands.

'Now fill in the blanks. What have you been doing and did you see the house?'

'No,' Lois replied softly. 'We couldn't find it. They said it burnt down years ago.'

'Oh, what a friggin' shame! After all the fuss you went to.'

'But – ' Lois lowered her voice so anyone at another table couldn't hear her. 'I don't think it did burn down. I think the people in that little burg didn't want us to find it. We saw a picture of it just this afternoon. On a map in a spooky restaurant, and there was the house – my house – as plain as anything. Listed as one of Scotland's haunted sites.'

'The same house that's in the engraving I gave you?'

'Yeah,' Bob replied with a touch of sarcasm in his voice, 'the very same one and thanks again for giving us that damned thing, Midge.'

She ignored him. 'So what are you going to do? Going back to that town again or what?'

Bob didn't give his wife time to answer. 'We are not going to do anything. We are going to go back to the States the day after tomorrow. I've got a warehouse that needs me and Lois has a studio that needs her. This vacation, if you can call it that, has about come to an end.'

Lois took a drink from her glass. 'Midge,' she said in that same soft, secretive voice, 'I'm going to tell you about that engraving.' She glanced immediately at Bob. No emotion crossed his face. 'It's jinxed. That picture is all fucked up and one thing I know for certain now is that it's not me who is going bananas, it's that picture! It's haunted or cursed or has the hoodoo-voodoo or something on it, but I know now that it isn't me. And you know what else? I'm damned glad I found out.' She leaned back against the red velvet that padded the pub bench. 'A figure has appeared on the engraving. You didn't know that. A little man on the lawn. Intelligent reasoning says he isn't real, but he *is* real and he *really* is moving up towards the house. There is a force, a psychic energy if you want to call it that, that's making that creature move. And,' she put her face closer to Midge's, 'it's being done for a reason. It's being done to get our attention. Bob's and mine.'

'But we are not going to let it get our attention,' Bob said evenly, 'we are going back home and forgetting the whole thing.'

Lois glanced again at her husband. 'I need to tell *some-one* about this or I'll explode, and you are like a big sister to me.'

Midge grinned. 'Watch that "big" stuff. Just let me be your sister.'

Lois smiled at her friend. 'I didn't want to tell you what was happening when we were in New York, but now I think the time has come to bring it all out in the open. If we are not going to pursue this any farther, then there's no use pussy-footing around it.' This time she didn't look for confirmation from Bob. 'What's happened has happened and no amount of secrecy is going to change things. First of all, let me start with the little creep who appeared under the glass.'

'I know all about him,' Midge said.

'Bob told you?' Lois' voice rose.

'I did, hon. The night those guys busted into the apartment, I told Midge. I *had* to.'

'But you thought I was going crazy. Right?'

Midge searched for the right word. 'Well . . . maybe not *crazy* . . .'

'So Bob told you. I figured he had, even though he said he hadn't. Oh well.' she took another sip of her Scotch. 'Then you gave us that book of ghost stories. Remember?'

'I don't remember that I *gave* you the book. You kind of storm-troopered it away from me.'

Lois shrugged. 'Whatever. Anyway I went to the public library and found out that the only possible Corra was here in Scotland. I felt that what had happened in that ghost story was happening all over again. I didn't know why, I just *felt* it.'

'So that's why Scotland became so important all of a sudden.'

'Right. I had to get over here and see for myself if that little creep was actually moving up the lawn towards that house.'

'But first you had to *find* that house,' Midge was one step ahead of her.

'Right. But when we got there we couldn't find it because everyone lied to us about it. That's jumping ahead. First of all, when we landed in London some custom officials gave us a hard time and refused to let the engraving into the country. Bob took them aside and bribed them.'

'That true?' Midge looked at Bob and he nodded.

'Then on the train trip up here we sat next to the sweetest little old lady who turned out to be one of the fastest running octogenarians of all the Queen's loyal subjects. She grabbed the engraving and ran with it. Bob chased her and would have caught her but she threw the picture into the sea. Thank God I had it wrapped in all that waterproof plastic.'

Again from Midge to Bob: 'That true?' Again he nodded.

'Then when we finally get to Corra everybody gives us a bum steer and finally we hear about some retired school teacher who is an expert on the area and when we see her she tells me the house was burned down. Then that very afternoon, Midge I mean it couldn't have been more than three hours later, we drove back to question her again and she was *dead*.'

'Dead?' Midge drew in her breath. 'You mean like in kicked the bucket?'

'Exactly,' Lois said without smiling, 'but the bucket wasn't even there. Some strange men had come and taken her body away. Even the neighbour lady . . .'

'Who was a real bitch,' Bob interjected.

'Who was a real bitch,' Lois repeated, 'threatened us. She told us to go away and not come back because the area wasn't a safe place for foreigners.'

'Oh great,' Midge said, 'come home to Beautiful Britain.'

'Exactly,' Bob replied.

'Now then this afternoon,' Lois wasn't finished with her story, 'we find out that this very house – my house – is listed as one of the haunted sites of Scotland and hasn't burned down after all.'

'You don't know that,' Bob said. 'The house *could* be gone. That map was just a tourist gimmick.'

'Then why list it?' she asked quickly. 'Why put it on a newly printed map if the place no longer exists? That doesn't make sense and you know it.'

'She's got you there,' Midge said.

'Now on this map it said the house in Corra had been the house of Aleister Crowley.' Lois sat back waiting for this choice piece of information to sink in.

'Who?' was all she got from Midge.

'He was a notorious black magician,' Lois explained. 'He thought he had a direct telephone line to the Devil. *He* lived in my house! He and his crazy followers with their backwards Mass and their naked women with candles shoved up their twats.'

Midge made a face. 'Please! No more details. I think you've already told me more than I want to know.'

Lois stood up. 'I want you to come upstairs with us right now and look at the engraving. I want you to see it for yourself.'

'I haven't finished my drink,' Midge protested.

'Bring it with you. The hotel won't mind.'

On the way up to the room Lois realized she hadn't said a word about seeing Tony in that department store in London. She had been fully prepared to tell her friend everything, yet the story of Tony and almost getting run over wasn't mentioned. Was there some reason for still keeping Midge slightly apart from things? Was there yet, far back in the reaches of her sub-conscious mind, the hope, desire, dream, fantasy, *necessity* that maybe Tony was still alive . . . and in that house? Would she carry this with her forever? Would the thought of it never go away?

Bob unlocked the door and they went into the room. Midge glanced around. 'God, I thought my room was small. Good thing you two are friends.'

Lois went over to the engraving, put it on the bed and started undoing the string, then the brown paper and finally the plastic sheets. 'Here,' she said. 'See for yourself.'

'Jesus Christ!' Midge exclaimed. 'Look at that little bastard! He's just about a half inch away from the house!'

Lois looked and then pulled back. She closed her eyes. It was all supposed to be over by now. Why was it continuing?

'And look here,' Bob whispered. Lois opened her eyes and looked to where Bob was pointing. A window on the ground floor was open, next to the front door.

'It's never been open before!' Bob said shakily. 'Oh shit, hon. Somebody's opened the window for the little creep.'

'From the inside,' said Lois. 'It had to be from the inside. Whoever is in there wants him to come in, and he'll do it, too. He'll get into the house and he'll take the child. Just like in the ghost story! He'll steal the kid and carry it off into those trees over there and then just vanish off the side of the frame. He will, Bob! Like he did in the book. He'll kidnap Tony and we'll never be able to find him!'

'Hon – ' Bob took her hand. 'I think you'd better sit down.'

She pulled away from him. 'Sit down? How can I sit down when that bastard is planning on stealing my son!'

'Sit *down!*' Bob ordered. 'For God's sake, don't start on that again.'

Midge helped Bob put Lois in the one easy chair in the room. 'Look, Lois baby,' the older woman said, 'you'd better take it easy. Things have been rough. You've gotta cool it a bit.'

'How can I cool anything knowing what's going to happen?' She tried to get up but their hands on her shoulders kept her down. 'That creep is going to get into the house. The window has been opened for him. Just like in the book. And then he'll reappear at the window and he'll have Tony in his arms and he'll jump out onto the lawn and then he'll go to the left hand corner . . . into those trees . . . and that will be the end. The end of everything.' She started to cry and Midge reached for a box of Kleenex the hotel had put atop the dresser.

Bob hovered near his wife. 'Do you want another drink? Maybe a couple of aspirins?'

'No!' She got up suddenly almost knocking him off balance. 'Know what I want? I want to go back to Corra! I want to be there when he comes to the window. I want to take my child from his arms!'

'That was only a ghost story,' Bob said, though he no longer sounded convinced. 'Goddamnit Lois, that's why we have to get the hell out of this place! That's why we've got to get you back to the States. You're losing reality.'

'Reality?' Lois yelled back at him. 'A little child . . . our Tony . . . is going to be kidnapped . . . and you stand there shouting at me about "reality"? There is no reality. Not when Aleister Crowley's mixed into it.'

'Oh fine,' Bob threw up his hands and walked away from her. 'I thought you told me he was dead. How in hell can *he* be involved in this?'

'I don't know.' Suddenly she calmed down and sat back in the chair. 'He was a great psychic. He had tricks and secrets that few others possessed.'

'Oh come on,' Bob said.

'He'd studied all his life, made it his business to know things and made it his business to make these things work for him. Like right now. Whatever he's doing, he's making that little man under the glass move around.'

It was Midge's turn. 'Crowley is dead, Lois.'

'Sure. The body is dead but the energy survives. The energy survives and Crowley had more energy than a dozen men. It's only natural that when they buried his body they didn't bury the energy with it. You can't bury energy. You can't destroy energy. Energy *is*. It exists. It doesn't decay.'

'Have you been listening to Uri Geller?' Bob asked her.

'Uri's on the right track. He knows about energy. He knows how to manipulate it. You don't,' she glared at Bob. 'And what's more you don't want to know.'

'You've got it right for once. I *don't* care.'

Lois was silent for a moment, then her eyes widened. 'You know what? You know what I just realized? I mean it's been there in front of me all along and I didn't put two and two together . . . That little bastard under the glass, you know who he is?' She didn't wait for their responses. 'It's Aleister Crowley himself. It is! The face. I saw his face and his face was round and his eyes were deep and dark and I'll bet if he took off his hat he would be bald. Don't you see?' She turned from one to the other but they just stared at her. 'The creature under the glass is Crowley! That's exactly who it is. He's come back to his house and he's going to go into it and he's going to take out a little child and do some hellish thing with it.'

'How could that be?' Midge asked. 'Okay, maybe somebody is playing a trick on you, but with a microchip or something hidden under there. Maybe the whole thing is being done by a computer. That's possible. Computers do everything.'

Lois shook her head. 'Computers can't do what Crowley did.' She suddenly got to her feet. 'We're going back to Corra,' she announced. 'First thing in the morning we're going back there and we're going to put an end to this mess.'

Bob came closer to her but she pulled away from his touch. 'Midge is probably right. Somebody is pulling a trick on you, a damned dirty trick, but it's still not real. You can yell and rant all you like but in no way are we going back to Corra. We have one more day in Edinburgh and then we take the plane back to New York.'

'But suppose the baby *is* Tony?' She said this very calmly, looking Bob directly in the eyes. 'Suppose *something* is trying to tell us that Tony is still alive? Still alive and inside that house and if we don't get there and save him he'll be killed?'

Bob put both hands on her shoulders and shook her. 'Tony is dead, Lois! He's dead. I saw the body. We cremated him for Christ's sake! Tell her, Midge. You were there.'

'But this could be an *omen*,' Lois insisted. 'This could be some sign that Tony is not dead. That he's still alive and in that house and needing us!'

'Tony is dead!' Bob shouted. 'Aleister Crowley is dead!'

'The dead can return. That's what ghosts are all about. Midge, you understand what I'm saying, don't you?'

'Look, I don't want to get in the middle of this. I just thought it would be fun to come over to Scotland for a few days and see some of the places you've been talking about. I didn't come here to get into a marital battle.'

'It's no battle. We were brought over here for a *purpose*. I know that. I *feel* that. I've always listened to my hunches and I've always followed my instincts and now they tell me that Tony is alive and in Corra.'

Bob started towards the door. 'I can't take any more of this. I'm going down to the bar. If you want to see me, see me there. Maybe people are right. Maybe you are flipping your wig. I'm at the place now where I don't give a damn.'

He had the door half open when Midge yelled, 'Wait! Get back in here. Look. Look at this thing now!'

While all three of them watched in horror, the man in the print turned his face toward them. A small hand appeared from under the cloak and he doffed his large floppy black

194

hat. They could all see his round face, his bald head. Then he smiled, replaced his hat and saluted them with a touch of his brim. Before any of them could say a word, he turned, scurried up the last bit of lawn, hoisted himself over the sill of the open window and disappeared into the house.

* * *

Lois looked at the four small pink pills Midge offered her. They were sedatives, she was told, prescribed by her doctor when Midge had sprained an ankle last winter. 'They get rid of pain and they put you to sleep.' Lois swallowed all four at once.

'You could have waited,' Midge said. 'I was going to tell you to just take two.'

'Two won't do it,' Lois answered. 'Not now.'

'So what does this mean?' Bob stared at her, not knowing whether to be angry or concerned. 'You're going to cop out for the rest of the evening?'

'Right.' Lois didn't bother to look at him, she was upset with him and the little creep who was inside her house. No use trying to explain her feelings to Bob any longer. No use trying to get him to change his mind, to go back to Corra to find the house. 'I'm going to bed. It's been a long, rough day.'

'What about supper?' he asked.

'You read the language here. Order from the menu.'

'I mean, are you going to go out and have supper?'

'No. I don't want to see anybody. I don't want to go to a restaurant. I don't want to make any decisions about meat or chicken or fish. I just want to be left alone.' She almost added: 'And I don't want to see either one of you,' but she didn't.

'Well, Bob, I'm free to dine,' Midge said. 'Unless you want to eat alone.'

'Good idea.' Lois turned down the covers on the bed. 'The two of you go on without me. I'll be fine by myself.'

'Those pills work fast, hon,' Midge said.

'Good. That's what I want, some fast oblivion.'

Lois got into her nightgown, and, not bothering to brush her hair, slipped between the crisply ironed sheets. She plumped at the pillow, made sure her neck was just right on it, then closed her eyes. Midge hadn't been kidding. The pills worked fast and in two minutes she was asleep. Sometime much later, she awoke and glanced at the clock: 3.15 a.m. Still groggy with the effects of the sedative, she felt the other side of the bed. It was empty. Bob hadn't come to bed. He and Midge were probably closing the bar downstairs. She fell back into an even deeper sleep.

'How do you feel?' Bob was sitting on the edge of the bed, fully dressed and smiling at her. Midge was standing beside him.

'You sleep well?' she asked.

'I guess so.' Lois shook her head hoping to shake away a few of the cobwebs that still clung to her brain. 'Yeah – ' She tried to smile. 'I guess I needed that.'

'I've ordered breakfast up here,' Bob said. 'I figured you wouldn't want to get dressed and go downstairs.'

'You figured correctly.' She yawned and stretched her arms. 'God, Midge, what's in those powerful pink jobbers? Little men with baseball bats?'

'I told you they were strong. I take two and I'm out like a light.'

'They even leave you with a bit of a buzz.' Lois sat up and moved her legs, with some effort, over to the side of the bed and then pulled down the blankets. She stood up and looked at the other side of the bed. Bob's side. It hadn't been slept in. With a quizzical expression in her eyes, she asked, 'Where did you sleep?'

'I took a single room for the night. I didn't want to disturb you.'

'It was my idea,' Midge said. 'I thought you'd rest better that way. You really needed it.'

'A single room? Oh. Okay.' She went into the bathroom and closed the door. That was odd. In all the years they had been together, Bob had never slept apart from her. She looked in the mirror. There were new lines around her eyes and across her forehead. She just knew there were. She couldn't make them out clearly yet, but they'd be there for all the world to see very soon. She washed her face. Then she smiled at the reflection in the mirror. 'Sweet of him,' she said aloud. And, yes, it was sweet of Bob to have been so considerate of her exhausted condition that he took a single room so as not to disturb her. She'd been a bitch. She knew she'd pushed Bob

just about as far as she ever had before. He was really angry
with her. She couldn't blame him. He was right, of course.
No matter what that little bastard did inside the house, it
wasn't her concern. There was nothing she could do to stop
him taking the boy out of the house and into those trees.
Nothing. The old man in the ghost story was unable to do
anything except watch in horror. What could she do? Destroy
the picture? Break the glass and slash the paper with a razor
blade? Maybe she would hit the little man but maybe she
would hit the little boy as well. Go back to Corra and wait
for the man to come out of the window? But what if he wasn't
at the house? What if he was only in the *drawing* of the house?
So what good would come from making the trip back to
Corra? If the man and the child (she refused this morning to
think of the little boy as her Tony) were existing *only* on that
sheet of inked paper then finding the real house and waiting
outside the real window wouldn't do a bit of good. Bob was
right. She put on her lipstick and felt better. And it was so
thoughtful of him to take a single room and be that concerned
about her.

Breakfast over, plans were made for the final morning in
Scotland. While Midge and Lois went shopping, Bob was
going to tour a glass-making factory on the outskirts of the
city. He thought there might be a possibility some of his
restaurant glassware could be made there, and at better prices
than he paid for Belgian or Italian glass. They would meet
back at the hotel, by 12.30, have a drink in the bar and then
find a restaurant. Midge had read about a place on Castle
Street that served excellent scampi and fantastic lamb cutlets.
So it was decided.

The women wandered idly down Hanover Street looking in
the windows of the small, elegant shops. They admired a pair
of Chinese vases in one, dreamed aloud over a full-length mink
coat in another and made note of the prices of single malt
whisky in a third. By the time they arrived at Prince's Street,
the main shopping avenue, they figured they had saved ap-
proximately twelve thousand dollars by *not* buying the items
they liked. 'All in all not a bad shopping day,' Midge grinned.
'I rarely do not *not* buy this much, not even in New York.'

'It takes will power,' Lois laughed. 'Those vases would
be perfect in my apartment, but I'm proud of both of us.
We really economized!'

'Good for us,' Midge said.

'Absolutely,' Lois agreed.

They crossed the street and tried to admire the monstrous metal gingerbread, curlicued Victorian hodge-podge that was the monument to Sir Walter Scott. As designers they were appalled but as tourists they were fascinated. 'Lord,' Lois said, 'how long's it been since you've seen that much happening on one single space?'

'Quite a while.' Midge laughed. 'Does anybody still read what this guy wrote?'

Lois shook her head. 'I doubt it. I've never read any of his novels.'

'Can you imagine what this thing would be like if it was a monument to Stephen King?' Both of them laughed at the same time. 'It would be dripping with metal and marble people-eating cars and slobbering dogs and little girls breathing spikes of fire. I don't think Mr King wants a monument,' Midge continued. 'He's happy taking the cash instead.'

As they crossed the elevated stretch of cement and steel known as Waverley Bridge, they quickly did up the top buttons on their coats for the sharp Scottish wind suddenly whipped at them from all sides. To get a bit warmer they linked arms and strolled in the centre of the sidewalk making others walk around them. At the end of the bridge, the hills loomed mightily and they stared up at the massive red stone buildings that demanded attention. Four or five storeys of enormous windows with curtains, drapes and cupids with ribbon cornices. Flags flew from roof tops. Some doors had coats of arms emblazoned over them and all around cars and people struggled to make the hill, to turn left or right, to persist in the pilgrimage until they had reached the top. Lois and Midge turned left, passed a cathedral and climbed some stone staircases and passed the Festival Fringe Centre. The climb levelled off at 'South Bridge' and they were able to get their breath.

'God, I'll bet the people who live here have muscular legs,' Midge panted.

'And I hope they have strong hearts, too,' Lois was just as exhausted.

Midge nudged her, panting. 'Over there, on that corner, I do believe the sign says "pub". What do you say?'

'My throat feels like I just crossed the Sahara,' Lois exaggerated. 'I say go for it.'

They started for a traffic light with coloured stick men telling people to walk or stop. A red man with his arms at his side and his feet together meant "don't walk" while a green man taking giant steps sideways gave pedestrians permission to walk. Midge halted in front of a store that advertised tailor-made kilts. 'I wonder if they supply the man to go with them?' she mused. Lois didn't answer. 'Do you think you get your choice of hairy black legs or hairy red legs?' She turned to see if Lois was smiling. She wasn't.

She was staring, staring at a black car that had stopped right beside her at the corner, waiting for the light to change.

In that car, in the back seat of that car, Tony looked out at her.

'Oh no,' she said, 'Oh God no. Not again!'

Tears had streaked the child's face. His eyes were red from them. He put his hands against the side window and she could see his mouth forming the word 'Mommy!' over and over again.

She managed to regain her voice. 'Tony!' she screamed and ran to the car.

The child looked at her. He tried a brave smile. They were so close at last. Just a metal door and a window between them after all this time.

'Tony!' she yelled and tried to open the rear door. It was locked. 'Tony!' she screamed. She began to pound on the side of the car, she let her purse fall to the gutter as she used both fists to beat at the metal monster who refused to give up her child.

Midge came running. 'What the hell's going on?'

'They've got Tony!' Lois was sobbing now. 'They've got my baby! I want my baby!' She started pounding on the driver's side-window. The driver, almost obscured by coat collar, scarf and low-slung hat didn't even glance at her. 'Let him out!' she yelled. 'Let him out!' She ran to the front of the car, still beating at it with her clenched fists, trying to slay the monster barehanded.

Then the light changed. Midge heard the driver shift gears and grabbed Lois' coat sleeve, pulling her aside. The car, free of the unwanted attacker, moved smoothly forward. The boy in the back seat managed to get himself turned around, managed to give Lois another sorrowful wave from the rear window.

'You better get out of the middle of the street.' Midge held her steady as the rest of the traffic moved around them. 'Come on, let's get to the sidewalk.'

Lois shook herself free. 'No! No! They've got Tony! Don't you understand? They've got my baby!'

Midge tried again, gently taking her arm and turning her to where a group of curious pedestrians were now gawking.

Lois swung out with her free arm, hitting Midge in the side, making her lose her grip and almost fall onto the street. Then Lois started to run, to run up the middle of the traffic, dodging cars and a messenger on a motorbike and trying to get to the next corner where another traffic light had stopped the black car. Horns honked but she didn't hear them. Behind her brakes squealed but she ignored them. A man in a red delivery truck shouted something at her but she didn't notice. All her strength and energy was aimed at one point: the spot where the black car had stopped again.

There was a large truck in front of the black car. When the light changed the truck would have to shift into gear and the black car would have to sit there and wait until the truck was through the intersection. She kept her eyes on the tall square box that was the truck, telling it not to move, praying for it to remain still.

Pushing herself beside the cars lined up behind the black car, dirtying her coat on fenders and bumpers, she made her way up the row and finally was able to touch the trunk of the car. Tony was still staring at her, his face still lined with tears, his small hands pressed against the back window.

'I'm here, darling!' she shouted. 'Mommy's here!'

The child mouthed a greeting or a cry for help, she couldn't make it out.

Then the light changed, the truck moved out effortlessly and the black car glided calmly behind it. She stood there, in shock, watching Tony's face recede from her one more time.

Behind her a horn blew. 'Hey missus,' a masculine voice shouted, 'get out of the street!'

She stepped to one side and the man pulled his blue Volvo sharply around her. So did the green Ford and so did the cream VW which followed it. She stood there, staring into empty space, trying to see the top of the black car that had carried off her child.

'What's wrong?' It was a woman's voice. 'You can be terribly hurt this way.'

Lois looked down. A grey-haired lady had rolled down her window on the passenger side of a grey Daimler.

'They . . . they . . . took my baby,' she managed to stammer.

'Who did?'

'Up there.' She pointed. It was difficult to speak. 'They stole my baby. They have him in the car.'

The woman turned to the elderly man at the driver's wheel. 'Gerald, what shall we do?'

As car horns honked behind them, the man said, 'Well, we can't sit here.'

'I asked you what should we do?' the woman said.

'And I told you we can't sit here. Tell her to get in, I suppose.'

'Poor thing.' The woman motioned for Lois to get in the back of the car. Lois quickly obeyed. The Daimler jumped forward in the direction the black car had gone.

'My baby,' Lois managed to say through her tears. 'Up there. Big black car.'

'Who took your child?' The woman was horrified.

'Don't know,' she muttered. 'He's in the back seat of the black car.'

'We should call the police,' the man said.

Lois leant forward in panic. 'No. Please. No time for that. Follow the car. Please follow the car!' She started crying again.

'I've heard of things like this happening in the cinema,' Gerald muttered.

'Then do it!' the woman commanded.

'Chase the other car?' His voice rose.

'We've got to help her.'

'Suppose they got guns?' He still remembered scenes from the cinema.

'You used to be in military service,' the woman replied crisp.y. 'You know how to react if they start shooting.'

'Please,' Lois pleaded. 'Up there. The black car.'

The man pressed the accelerator down and the car shot forward. 'In the Suez I had a rifle of my own.'

'The lady's in distress, Gerald.'

'We will be likewise if they start shooting.'

'Please,' Lois urged him on. 'The black car behind the truck.'

'It's called a lorry over here,' Gerald said under his breath.

'You just drive,' the woman said, 'the English lessons will keep.'

The truck kept the black car fenced in and within eyesight for block after block. At times a few of the cars in front of Gerald's car would turn off and he was able to get closer. At other times, when they had to wait for the light to change, other cars would crawl between them and put the black car at an even greater distance.

'It's mid-morning,' the woman said soothingly. 'A terrible time for traffic.'

Lois nodded.

'You're an American?' The woman tried a little conversation to calm Lois down.

Lois nodded. 'New York,' she replied.

'And they just grabbed your son and drove off with him?'

Lois looked at the lady who was genuinely trying to help but didn't want to go into the whole long story. 'Yes. We were shopping. They just grabbed him.' She anticipated the next question. 'I don't know why.'

They were now on the outskirts of the city. Shopping areas gave way to dark metal factories, then small houses with large fields around them. There were trees in the distance, up ahead, black branches with tattered leaves against a clear grey horizon.

They passed an industrial park and the truck, which had been Gerald's point of reference, turned left and disappeared behind a stone wall. 'Damn!' Gerald said.

The black car, free now, shot forward, taking full advantage of the open space in front of it.

Gerald gunned the accelerator and his grey vintage Daimler followed. The black car, clearly visible many yards ahead of them, purred evenly over a slight hill, then rounded a curve. Gerald's manoeuvres were just as well executed.

'Where's your husband?' the woman asked.

'The hotel, I suppose,' Lois answered. 'Please, can't you go any faster?'

Gerald glanced in the mirror. He thought he was doing pretty well as it was. 'I've almost got it to the floor now,' he said.

'How old is your little boy?' The woman kept talking.

'He's only six. He's . . .' She broke off. Now there was no other vehicle between the black car and Gerald's grey one. 'There he is! In the window! See? Can you see him?' She shouted.

'Yes, I see him,' the woman responded. 'He's got red hair. Just like yours.'

Lois took a deep breath. Thank God, the woman *also* saw Tony. Until that moment she didn't know if she was hallucinating this whole thing. Her past actions and Bob's comments had filled her with terrible doubts about her sanity. 'You can? You can see him?'

'Of course,' Gerald said. 'The child looking out the back window. Is that your son?'

'Oh yes. Oh yes!' And more tears came, silently this time, but they still came.

The woman patted her hand. 'Don't you fret. We'll catch him. Won't you, Gerald?'

'Certainly will!' He gripped the steering wheel harder and lowered his head like a professional race driver. He was beginning to enjoy this chase. 'I haven't had this much fun since chasing the wogs in Suez.'

Just as he said that, the black car made an unexpected turn to the right, and vanished behind a line of tall trees. Gerald slowed down at the entrance to the side road, deftly manoeuvred the turn and churned up pebbles as he kept his eye on the narrow country road in front of him.

Lois groaned. 'I thought we'd lost him.'

'We've still got him in our sights,' Gerald grinned. 'Bloody bastard can't get rid of us now.'

The woman made a clucking sound at his language but made no comment.

'Damned difficult road, this,' Gerald said, holding the wheel even tighter. 'Dirt and bumps, mostly. Give him credit though, he keeps up his pace.'

They could see the black car was just a few yards ahead, kicking up stones and spewing dirt at them from its back wheels. The pebbles made little pinging noises as they bounded off the Daimler's hood and windshield. 'Get him to pay the bloody paint job too,' Gerald muttered.

Tony waved at them and Lois waved back. She didn't know if he could see her or not but this signalling was at least some form of communication with her child. In a few minutes, when they managed to overtake the car and force it to a halt, she would be reunited with him! Oh please, please dear Jesus. Let me reach my baby! I'll do anything you ask, dear Jesus, anything. I'll even go back to church. I promise, and I'll take Tony with me and if you want him to be raised a Catholic like his father, then yes, sweet Jesus, I'll even do that. Oh please, dear God! Oh please!

The black car slowed down. Gerald slowed behind it. The black car turned to the left, went a few yards and turned left again. Gerald made the first left, saw the car make the second but when he turned there was nothing there at all.

The car had vanished. Tony had vanished with it. Out here in the middle of nowhere, with no possible means of exit, the black car had evaporated.

Gerald came to a full stop. 'I don't understand,' he said.

'He's gone again!' Lois cried out.

'Now don't you worry,' the woman soothed her, 'They can't be too far away.'

Lois opened the car door and jumped out. She started running down the narrow road, running to the spot where the car had been. Gerald and the woman shouted at her but she refused to hear them, didn't need to hear them. All she needed was her son. He had been so close. She left the roadway, slipped into a ditch then back up the other side. There were bushes everywhere, some as tall as she was and all of them dense with winter-surviving leaves and dried berries. She shoved her way into them, shielding her face from the short, sharp branches. She pushed past them, yanking at her coat when it caught in the brambles. In front of her was an open field with grazing sheep, then the ground swelled into a hill and behind that an even higher hill of rock and scrub and patches of snow. Her eyes swept the area, taking in the openness and the vastness.

Then she saw him. He was standing all alone on the first hillock. His red hair shone in the winter dullness and he was wearing the same blue trousers and jacket she had put on him the day he vanished from school.

'Tony!' She started running towards him. Her shoes stubbed against rocks and tears clouded her vision. She waved her arms at him, imploring him not to move, to stay there till mommy could reach him.

The child waved back. He didn't run to her, just stood there watching her approach. Several sheep stopped pulling at grass long enough to stare as she ran past them.

Behind her she heard a horn blowing and the voices of the elderly couple calling for her. Let them. She had no intention of turning back now. She and her baby were about to be together.

Then Tony turned and started running himself, but he was running in the opposite direction, running away from Lois. She stopped for an instant, dumbstruck by his action.

'Tony!' she screamed. 'Stay there, baby! Stay there!'

The child took another look at her and disappeared around the hill.

In seconds Lois was in the exact spot where he had been standing. She stopped to breathe and as her lungs filled with the crisp country air she searched the hillside in front of her. It was steep and rocky where he had gone and as she scrambled quickly across it she wondered how his little legs could have managed the rough terrain. She slowed down. The rocks were larger now and thickly scattered. Walking was difficult, running was impossible. She sought more air into her lungs. 'Tony!' she called. 'Here's Mommy! Come to Mommy!'

Then she saw him again. He was on a ledge several yards above her. He stood there looking down at her. He didn't wave or cry, he only watched her.

'How did you get . . .?' she started to shout, but decided to conserve her energies. She looked for the path he must have taken, and not finding one began her own trail through the boulders and thistles towards his ledge.

Tony looked down at her.

She was scrambling now, at times almost on her knees as she grasped rocks and trees and roots to pull herself upwards. Her fingers started leaving red stains wherever they touched. She couldn't feel them. All she could feel was the searing in her lungs and the overwhelming desire to hold her baby close to her again. The ledge was directly above her. Tony still stood there, not moving. She reached up and held onto the stone shelf as her feet fought for some kind of support on the ground. She started pulling herself upwards, inching her hands out onto the ledge until both her elbows lay atop it. Then with a burst of strength that came from deep within

205

her, she managed to throw herself farther onto the flat stone surface, then swing her legs on as well.

Tony was gone.

She started crying again. This time in the sheer frustration of it all. She wiped her hands across her face and then wiped her coat. She saw the bloody tracks her fingers made but it didn't matter. Nothing would ever matter again until she was with her child.

'Mommy! Over here, Mommy. Over here!'

She whirled around to where his voice was coming. There was a narrow passageway between two enormous rocks. A passageway big enough for a child easily to slip through. She ran to it and called his name several times and each time the answer came back. 'In here, Mommy. In here.'

She looked at the space between the boulders, then got down on her hands and knees and inserted herself into the space. She wiggled back out and ripped off her heavy winter coat. She untied the laces of her clumsy walking shoes and kicked them off her feet. Then she got back on her knees and crawled, holding her breath and contracting her muscles, until she made it through the passage.

She stood up. She was in some kind of opening in the face of the hill. It wasn't exactly a cave but it had obviously been formed when those boulders outside had broken away. Enough light came from the entrance that she could clearly see around her.

There he was. Standing by the far wall. Watching her and smiling and holding out his little arms.

'Oh Tony! Thank God!' She rushed to him, reached out her own arms and fell back screaming. Where Tony had been standing now stood a large hairy thing with small feet and claws for fingers. Its face was two round eyes and a snout that dripped a dark liquid. It opened its mouth and she could see the teeth and the black tongue. 'Mommy!' Tony's voice came out of the thing's throat. 'Over here, Mommy. Over here!'

* * *

The police car's headlights picked out her form as she wandered along the edge of the highway. She was coatless and shoeless. Her face was scratched from briars and her chin was a dark purple where she had struck it as she fell in the

206

cave. Her fingers had stopped bleeding but the officer on duty duly noted in his report that she had dried blood under each of her nails.

The couple in the Daimler had immediately reported her missing to the Edinburgh police and said she had been chasing after her kidnapped child. Bob and Midge rushed to the station as soon as the police phoned their hotel.

Bob filled out some forms and signed them, then he and Midge took Lois back to the hotel in a cab. She didn't look at either of them, didn't say anything, only shaking her head when they asked her if she was hurt or had been raped.

'The police said the couple who drove you reported they saw Tony too. Did you really think that was Tony in the back seat of that car?' Bob asked.

Lois nodded.

'That's what you told me when you started banging on that car,' Midge said. 'I didn't have a chance to get a look at anybody in the car. I told Bob if Tony was in there, I didn't see him.'

'Can't you explain any of this?' Bob asked. 'Or won't you explain? Is that it?'

Lois put a grimy hand over her eyes.

'You almost get yourself killed in the middle of the street. You convince innocent strangers to speed after a car. They get out into the middle of nowhere and you jump out and go chasing off across the fields and the police have to come and bring you back to town.' Bob's voice rose as he repeated her actions. 'And now you don't want to talk about it? Midge and I stay in that hotel, half crazy with worry about you, and you refuse to explain yourself. Jesus, Lois! I don't know what the hell I'm going to do with you. I really don't.'

'I think you should save that until she's feeling better,' Midge said.

Bob glared at her and then at his wife. 'She's not *ever* going to feel better. This bullshit is going to go on and on and one day something serious will happen and innocent people will get hurt. I mean, look, for Christ's sake. She got that old couple to race after a disappearing car! It was bad enough when she got these crazy ideas by herself, but now she's starting to involve perfect strangers in them.'

'I still don't think you should get angry,' Midge said coolly. 'At least not now.'

'Look,' Bob's tone was sharp, 'I've got to live with her. You don't.'

Back in the hotel room, Midge helped Lois get undressed and waited patiently for her as she took a shower. Midge blow-dried Lois' hair and brushed it for her, while Lois just sat and stared at the blackness outside the window.

The doctor arrived after getting Bob's call. He had been recommended by the police, and he spent about fifteen minutes with Lois in the bedroom alone. Bob and Midge were waiting in the hallway when he came out. 'She's in shock,' he said. 'Her ordeal was too much for her. That and the cold with no shoes or coat. I had her take one of these.' He handed a small paper envelope with pills to Bob. 'And if she gets hysterical later on, give her one with a little water. There is one thing, by the way. Who is Tony?'

'Tony?' Bob's voice was wary. 'Why?'

'She says she almost had Tony, that this Tony person was almost close enough to hug.'

'I don't know any Tony,' Bob said slowly. 'Nobody by that name who is alive at any rate.'

'Well, I suggest you get her back home,' the doctor said, 'back to the States. She needs to be in familiar places, needs the consolation of reality. Her own reality is pretty shaken. Is your hometown over there called Corra?'

'No,' Bob looked the medical man directly in the eyes. 'Why? What did she say about Corra?'

'Just that she wants to go back there. She says this Tony is there waiting for her.'

CHAPTER FIFTEEN

They began by praying. They sat on stiff hard-backed chairs that had been arranged in a circle. When the prayers stopped, a small white Bible was passed from hand to hand and each person raised it to their lips. Those lips were about all that could be seen of any of them, for they wore white satin-like pointed hoods over their heads. Two holes cut out for eyes, one slit widened for lips and a small gold cross embroidered over where their foreheads should be. The rest of their bodies were hidden in floor-length robes of the same shiny material.

The room they sat in was their church, with a vaulted ceiling and an arched window. The window didn't have stained glass, however, but opaque yellowish panes designed to let light in and keep inquisitive eyes out. The walls of this room were hung with small icons, hand painted on slabs of wood. They depicted events in Christ's life as told in the New Testament. The walls themselves had been painted in huge, gaudy, primitive scenes of the boy Jesus in the temple, the man Jesus tending his flock, the martyred Jesus appearing to his disciples. At the far end of the room, in an alcove, was a wooden altar. Atop it stood a large painted statue of the crucified Jesus, his wounds horribly detailed in bright crimson paint. Around his feet dozens of votive candles burned, casting their light up onto the battered and beaten legs, making it look as if Jesus was descending into hell rather than rising into heaven.

In the circle one of the sitters, impossible to identify if it was a man or a woman, removed a large silver cross from a cloth bag. Then the person brought it up to his lips, kissed the huge, red uncut gemstones in its centre and passed the cross to the next seated person. When the cross made its way back to the first sitter, it was placed reverently back into the sack. 'Blessings upon us from the Lord Jesus,' a masculine voice came from under the mask. 'He is love. He is faith. He is purity.'

'And He loves us,' said another masculine voice from somewhere in the circle.

'And He prays for us.' This time a woman's voice.

'And He blesses us in our endeavours.' A man.

'He shines His light upon us and makes us strong.' Another man.

'We will work to please Him.' Still another man.

'With the Lord on our side how can we possibly fail?' This, now, from a woman.

'Amen,' from them all. 'Aye. Amen.'

There was a silence that lasted almost five minutes. It was difficult to tell if they were praying or meditating or just keeping quiet. Finally a man spoke. 'The American woman is in Edinburgh.'

'We know,' a woman said. 'She and her husband and a friend are playing like tourists up there.'

'They're leaving tomorrow? As planned?' This voice sounded like a teenage boy.

'As far as we know,' the same woman's voice replied. 'We haven't any news that would indicate otherwise.'

The teenage boy again: 'But how are we going to be certain they really *do* leave?'

'Yes. What will we do if they decide to stay on?' a man's voice questioned. 'You know, come back to Corra and make contact with *them*.'

'We have ways,' the man guarding the cross said. 'Don't forget Ian and Morgan are up there. They will pay them a call if necessary. If they don't leave tomorrow we have ways of frightening them back to their own country.'

'What are *they* doing to keep them here? That's what I want to know,' a female voice said. 'I can't believe *they* would just sit idly by and let them take a plane back to the States. Not after everything *they* went through to bring them over here in the first place.'

'There is not much *they* can do at this point,' replied the man with the cross. 'The woman's husband seems bent on getting back to New York. His wife usually does what he tells her to do.'

'I don't trust him,' a woman said. The satin hood shimmered in the colours from the candle flames. 'I saw him one afternoon on the street in Dumfries. He doesn't look right to me.'

'Nonsense,' the man replied. 'He's just a dupe for them. A dumb Italian Papist who doesn't know when he's being manipulated.'

'And that woman with them . . . what's her name?'

'Midge,' someone said.

There was laughter around the circle. 'What kind of a name is Midge?'

'Yes,' a man said when the laughter stopped, 'what's her part in all this?'

'Just a friend, we guess. We haven't been able to discover anything about her.'

'I don't like her,' a woman said.

The man with the cross shook his head. 'I don't know why you're all carrying on so. Don't we have faith in the Lord? Don't we all agree we have Him on our side?' He looked around the circle of hooded Believers. 'Don't we all agree that through *Him* we can destroy *them*?'

The murmur of acknowledgement echoed in the room.

'Then let's forget the Americans,' the man said. 'They are leaving tomorrow. They are no longer important. We must continue to put our energies on our original goal.' He picked up the cloth bag, removed the silver and gemstone cross and held it high above his head. 'He will help us destroy *them* and their satanic stronghold of evil once and for all.'

CHAPTER SIXTEEN

Bob got out of bed slowly, so as not to disturb Lois who was sound asleep. Whatever the doctor had given her really worked, for she hadn't moved all night, just lain there flat on her back, lips slightly parted and breathing normally. He went into the bathroom, shaved and then got dressed. Closing the door quietly after him he took the elevator to the lobby floor. The public telephones were at the far end of the large reception area, near a room all done up in Georgian furniture with paintings of stags and mountains and fierce warriors in kilts. Bob marvelled that the lobby could be so big when the guest rooms were so small.

'Yes, that's right,' he said to the person on the other end of the line. 'Bruno. Bob and Lois. We were supposed to leave today but my wife is very ill. She's in no condition to travel.' He listened for a minute. 'Yes, I know there will be a penalty for changing the reservations but in this case it can't be helped. My wife is under doctor's orders.' He listened again. 'I don't know when. Just leave the departure date open. When she's well enough to fly back, I'll make the reservations.' The person on the other end of the line said something and Bob nodded. 'Thanks. I appreciate your concern. Goodbye now.' He hung up and left the booth, taking just a few steps to where the house phones were. He dialled a number. 'Midge? I'm downstairs. Lois is still asleep. Want to have some breakfast? Okay, I'll be in the lobby.' He went to the newsstand, looked over the morning papers and bought a copy of the *Scotsman*. He took it over to a semicircle of high-backed leather chairs near the window, sat down and started to read.

'Are you Mr Bruno?' a voice said beside him.

He looked up. There were two men there, men in suits and ties and topcoats. He had never seen them before. 'Yes,' he said slowly.

'Mr Robert Bruno? Your wife's name is Lois Bruno?'

Bob nodded. 'Yes,' then, 'what's this all about?'

As if they were dancers and meticulously choreographed, in unison they stuck their right hands into their right coat pockets and whisked out leather sheaths which they flipped open, faultlessly, and flashed him their shiny metal badges. They gave him a second to examine them, then they closed the sheaths, expertly returned them to their pockets and put their hands at their sides. Barishnikov couldn't have done it better.

'CIA? What does the CIA want with me?' Bob searched their impassive faces, finding nothing.

'It's about your wife, sir.' The one in the lighter brown topcoat spoke first. He seemed to be the older of the two. 'We have knowledge that she is seriously ill. *Mentally* ill.'

Bob wanted to get to his feet but the two were standing so close and were so overpowering that he stayed where he was. 'Now wait a minute. My wife has been under a lot of strain lately but I don't think she's mentally ill. She had a rough day yesterday and she's still asleep. The doctor gave her some knock-out pills.'

'Did she tell you what happened yesterday?' The younger one spoke now, his topcoat was a deeper brown. Bob wondered if the CIA supply room had run out of the lighter colour.

'She told me about chasing a car and about getting lost out in the country.' He shrugged. 'I don't understand much of it but she slept peacefully last night. She'll be all right today.'

Light-coat spoke. 'We have it on good authority that your wife is mentally ill and, being as that is so, she should be taken back to the United States where she will be able to have the proper treatment.'

212

'Uncle Sam does not like to have his unbalanced citizens paraded for other people to see,' dark-coat said. 'Her place is not in a foreign hotel room but in an institution where she cannot upset innocent non-nationals.'

Bob began to seethe. 'My wife is not upsetting anyone. I'll admit she's been acting a little strange lately but she's not so bad that she needs to be admitted to an institution. Jesus Christ, what's with you guys? Don't you have anything more important than my wife to occupy your time?'

Light-coat reached into his breast pocket and took out a small notebook. He flipped the pages importantly.

'Yesterday she caused a disturbance in the streets of this city, Edinburgh. She disrupted traffic. She refused to get out of the middle of one of the city's main thoroughfares, she beat upon vehicles which were the property of private citizens and she commandeered a vehicle, driven by two elderly British subjects, and forced them to pursue a second vehicle which they did, far into the countryside where they lost sight of it.'

Dark-coat added: 'She could have caused a serious accident, not only to herself but to the nationals of this country.'

Bob's voice rose in anger. 'Wait a minute, you guys. She thought she saw our son. He was kidnapped last year. Anyway, she's never done anything like this before so I don't see what the big deal is.'

'She has done something similar before,' dark-coat continued. 'In London, last week, she caused a traffic jam and almost a vehicular accident when she ran directly into the path of a British subject's limousine.'

'I never heard about that,' Bob lied. He wasn't about to give these guys any points.

Both men shrugged their padded topcoat shoulders in unison. 'We have had her under observation since she entered Heathrow Airport.'

'Bob? Are you ready for breakfast?' Midge stood beside the men, a puzzled look on her face.

The men nodded curtly to her, then took three steps away from him towards the lobby door. 'Please keep in mind, Mr Bruno,' one of them said, 'that your government wishes you and your wife to return to your home as soon as possible. Failure to comply may necessitate our facilitating your travel arrangements.'

'And another thing,' the other one added, 'Uncle Sam

doesn't like his citizens getting involved in the politics of other countries. He looks upon it as a serious breach of American patriotism.'

'Involved in *politics*?' Bob stood up and walked over to them. 'What the fuck are you guys talking about?'

'Interfering,' light-coat said.

'In the politics of another nation,' dark-coat added. 'It is not looked at with appreciation.' As if starting back into their dance routine, they turned together, nodded at Midge, said 'Ma'am,' and made a perfect exit.

'What was that all about?' Midge asked as she watched them leave.

'I don't know. They were CIA goons.'

'They acted more like the KGB.'

Bob nodded. 'Bastards! They said Lois is crazy and I must take her home. It wasn't a request. It was an order.' He glanced out the window but there was no sign of them on the street. 'Bastards!' he said again.

* * *

Lois slept until almost two that afternoon. When she awoke she looked at Midge, who was sitting on the edge of the bed and Bob, who was standing at the foot of it. She smiled sheepishly. 'Good morning,' she said.

'It's more good afternoon,' Midge smiled. She reached out and smoothed Lois' red hair. 'Did you sleep well? Do you feel better?'

'I don't know yet,' she said. 'I don't feel tired but my tongue feels like dwarfs have been playing football on it.'

'Here, let me help you.' Midge held out a dressing gown and Lois got out of bed and slipped her arms into the sleeves. She winced. 'You okay?' Midge asked with concern.

'Yeah. Just that my arms ache, right here.' She massaged the muscles in her upper arm. 'My fingers too. They're sore.'

'You had a rough time,' Bob said.

'I'll be okay, you know me.' She put her hand quickly to her jaw. 'Now *that* hurts!'

'You must have fallen and bruised it,' Midge said soothingly. 'It looked a helluva lot worse yesterday.'

'I don't know if I even want to go into the bathroom and

214

look in the mirror.' She shuffled towards it and then stopped and gave Bob a light peck on the cheek. 'I'm sorry,' she whispered.

'I'm just glad you're okay today,' he said. 'It wasn't easy on any of us.'

'I know. All I can do is promise it won't happen again.' She gave him another quick kiss. 'Still love me?' He nodded. 'In spite of everything?'

She stopped and looked quickly around the room. 'Did you say it was afternoon? Already? Lord we'd better get this stuff packed up or we'll miss the plane.'

Bob touched her on the shoulder. 'We're not going back today. I cancelled the reservations. I thought it was for the best. We'll go back when you feel better.'

'We're not going back today? Not leaving Scotland?'

'Does that make you happier?'

'I don't know.' She looked at him and then at Midge. 'I really can't say. What'll we do with the time? Stay here in Edinburgh?'

'We don't have to do anything, do we?' Bob replied. 'I mean, we can just wander around and take it easy and when you feel like it, we'll go home.'

'I think that's best, hon,' Midge said. 'The office will understand.'

'What about you? Are you going to stay here too?'

'I've got two weeks,' Midge replied. 'Nothing I have to get back for.'

Lois broke into a big smile. 'Wonderful! Then we will have a vacation. No more craziness from me. I promise. Starting right this very minute.' She walked into the bathroom and closed the door. They could hear her singing.

'I guess you've made her happy,' Midge said to Bob. 'She needed that.'

'So did I,' he replied. 'I really don't know how much more she can take. At least I've got her mind off going back to New York right away.'

'You think, now, she'll want to try and find that house again? Will you go with her if she insists?' She stared at him. 'Will you?'

He shrugged. 'I'll have to. I don't see any other way to get it over with.'

Midge started to say something else when there was a knock

at the door. 'Who the hell's that?' she asked. 'Not more CIA goons, I hope.'

'Better not be,' Bob remarked as he opened the door. 'Yes?' he said to the couple who waited in the hallway. Then: 'Well, hello! A delegation from Dumfries!' He held the door wider as Malcolm and Fiona came into the room. They smiled at Midge and Bob shouted at the bathroom door: 'Honey? Are you decent? You have visitors.'

'What are you talking about?' came her voice from the other side of the door.

'Get dressed and come on out. You'll see.'

There was a pause of about a minute as the four stood there before Lois opened the bathroom door and peered out. 'Well, for heaven's sake!' she laughed with pleasure. 'What a surprise! What are you two doing here?'

'Malcolm found your brooch,' Fiona said, 'and we thought it best if we brought it to you, straight away.'

'Yes.' Malcolm dug into his overcoat pocket and pulled out the brooch. He opened his hand and extended it to Lois. 'I was afraid, if we posted it, you wouldn't get it before you leave.'

'And then to have it sent over the water to the States,' added Fiona. 'Anyway, it was a wonderful excuse for me to get away from the hotel for an afternoon.'

Lois took the brooch and examined it. 'Yes. It's mine. I thought I'd lost it forever. Where did you find it?'

'It was behind the dresser in your room,' Malcolm replied. 'When I heard you'd gone without it, I searched the room and there it was. It must have fallen from the top over the back of the dresser somehow.'

'I thought we looked there,' Lois said with a frown. 'Bob, didn't you look behind the dresser as well as under the bed?'

'Yes, but obviously I missed it. There wasn't a lot of light behind there. It must have been in shadows. Anyway, the important thing is that you've got it back.'

Lois hugged Fiona. 'And I have a chance of seeing two old friends again. It was so sweet of both of you, really.' She pulled away. 'Oh, I'm forgetting my manners. This is my friend Midge from New York. She and I work together. Midge, this is Malcolm and Fiona. From the Waverley Hotel in Dumfries.'

'Hi,' Midge said.

'What can we do to repay you for this?' Bob asked. 'Are you going to stay in Edinburgh long? Could we take you to dinner tonight?'

'You're not going back to America this afternoon?' Malcolm asked.

'No,' Lois replied. 'I wasn't feeling too well yesterday and . . . ah . . . Bob decided I needed the rest so he cancelled our flight for today. Wasn't that sweet of him? He knew I didn't want to go back to New York. Not just yet.'

Malcolm's eyes narrowed slightly. 'So when will you be returning?'

'I don't know for sure,' Bob said. 'Whenever Lois feels like it. Probably in a few days.'

'Good!' Fiona smiled broadly. 'That means you can come back to Dumfries and see it properly this time.'

Lois shook her head. 'No. I don't think so. Not Dumfries. Not again. I think I did all that I care to do down there.'

'Oh?' Malcolm looked at Bob. Bob pretended he didn't see the look.

'I don't think we can stay so late as for dinner,' Fiona said. 'The last train from here to Dumfries leaves about ten o'clock. But you could come with us and see Mrs Scully. Malcolm and I are going and I'm sure she'd have room for three more.'

'Who's Mrs Scully?' Midge asked.

'Oh,' said Fiona, 'she's a very famous medium in these parts. Everybody knows of her. She's on the telly and sometimes there are stories about her in the newspapers when she helps the police solve their crimes. She's quite respectable, you know.'

'Right,' Malcolm added. 'I've been to see Mrs Scully three times and each time she's told me things that came true.'

'Is she a witch or what?' Bob questioned.

'Oh no,' Fiona shook her head, 'she's not into evil things. She holds meetings once a fortnight in her flat . . .'

'Seances,' Malcolm corrected her.

'Yes, seances, one a fortnight in her flat and all kinds of things happen. I've never been, but Malcolm has told me.'

'I could call,' Malcolm said, 'and see if there is space this evening. Her sessions usually last about an hour. Then you folks can go on and have supper and we can catch the last train home.'

Midge was delighted. 'Hey, that sounds like a neat idea. A seance in scary old Scotland. Give us something to talk about to the bunch at the office, Lois.'

Lois wished she could read Bob's expression correctly to see what he really thought of the idea. She didn't want to upset him again and she knew what he thought of all this medium stuff. Psychic bullshit he called it. Her eyes searched his. But if this woman was that good, then there was a possibility that she could tell her about Tony. Maybe this woman could pick up on Tony and see where he was and see . . . oh God did she really want the truth . . . to see if Tony was dead? Her voice had a tremor in it as she said: 'Bob, what do you think?'

'I think it's a great idea.'

'You do?'

'Sure. Maybe she can tell me what's been happening at my warehouse so it won't be such a shock when I get back.' He grinned. 'Anyway, I know you *love* this sort of stuff and as I said earlier, this is *your* vacation, your time to relax.'

She looked at him with pure affection. 'Oh, that's wonderful! Sure, Malcolm, we'd love to go!'

The four of them left the room and went down to the bar in order to give Lois time to dress and fix her hair. When she joined them they all had to agree that she looked radiant. She said she felt 'good' and was 'anxiously' waiting to see what the medium would tell her.

They killed another hour in the bar, which was easy because Midge regaled them with stories of when she was living in San Francisco and of some of the crazy psychic people she knew out there. There was a medium who 'read' cooked spaghetti. There was a man who 'talked' with cats and dogs and there was another man (and this brought loud laughter from the group) who had his female clients lie down on his bed while he 'opened their sexual chakra'.

'Did he do it to you?' Bob asked.

'Honey,' she replied, 'mine has never had a chance to close down!'

Bob followed Malcolm's directions as he steered the rental car out of the main part of the city and into a neighbourhood of Victorian houses all joined wall to wall, each with little gardens and differently painted faces in an attempt to display some individuality. 'That one over there,' Malcolm said, 'the one with the burning candle in the window. And, see, there's somebody going in the front door now.'

Bob parked as close as he could get and, with Malcolm leading the way, they went up onto the small front porch and followed behind him when the door was opened.

'I'm Mrs Scully.' A small woman in her mid-thirties extended her hand to Lois.

'And I'm Lois Bru – '

'No last names, please,' the woman interrupted her.

'Okay. Well, I'm Lois and I'm from the States. This is my husband. It was awfully nice of you to let us come at the last moment like this.'

'Not at all. You're friends of Malcolm's. That's all the reference I need.' She gave Malcolm a light kiss on the cheek and he introduced Fiona and Midge and Bob. 'You'll have to excuse me,' she said, 'but I'd better go and see that the room is being set up properly. At the last session the chairs were so close together that not even a ghost could have got through them. Not even a thin one!' She went through a hall doorway and closed it behind her.

Malcolm led them into Mrs Scully's living room. There were a dozen other people already there. Some chatted quietly with others, some were reading magazines and some sat alone, nervously twisting their wedding rings.

'She's so much younger than I thought she'd be,' Lois said. 'So much smaller too. I was expecting an old woman with grey hair and an enormous cross bouncing off her bosom, like in the movies.'

'Oh, she's very down to earth,' the young man replied. 'No hocus-pocus stuff for her. She's for real. She's been investigated by the Society for Psychical Research in London and it's been rumoured that Uri Geller telephones *her* for information.'

'Really?' Midge said, 'now I am impressed.'

A side door in the living room opened and Mrs Scully smiled at everyone. 'Won't you come in, please?' They filed past her. Lois saw that there were three rows of metal folding chairs arranged in a semicircle, theatre-style. 'Sit anywhere you please,' the medium said, 'except that chair up there.' She pointed to a large leather armchair facing the folding chairs. 'That's mine. I know it looks more comfortable than those metal things,' she laughed, 'but you can't have it.'

219

Lois, Bob and Midge sat together in the second row. Malcolm and Fiona took chairs at the far end of the first row. The chairs were almost all occupied and there was a bulky woman in front of Lois who blocked most of the view. Lois had to move her chair closer to Bob's in order to see clearly.

Mrs Scully closed the door to the hallway and then threw the brass bolt to lock it. She did the same to the door that went into the living room. Then she turned down the small overhead glass chandelier and everyone watched as she lit three tall tapering white candles that were in ornate holders beside the leather chair. The medium sat in the chair and, through the dimness of the room, looked at the sitters.

'You all know who I am,' she said, 'so there's no need for introductions. I don't know who you are, with the exception of three or four of you who've been to see me before. And even then I don't know your last names. I only want to know your first names, your Christian names. When I used to ask for the complete name others were quick to accuse me of hiring detectives to search out all the information I could before the client came for a sitting. I don't need that.' She smiled through the semi-darkness. 'I don't go in for trumpets that float through the air and flowers that suddenly apport into your laps and bells ringing and perfume filling the air. Let the others do the Hollywood special effects.

'Now that I've told you what I don't do, let me tell you what I do. In a few minutes I shall induce myself into a deep trance. At that time, usually, my features will alter, my breath will quicken and my voice will change to that of a younger woman's. I wish I could keep the younger part after the session is over.' She chuckled and several of the audience snickered. 'This younger woman who takes me over is called Mara. Now she takes me over with my permission. This is not some demonic possession thing, but a conscious willing of myself into Mara's capable energies.' She paused to let that sink in. 'Mara is the only one that I permit to take me over. Other entities have tried, and I've fought them – each and every one. So please don't think you are going to be in the presence of any evil spirits. I simply won't have it and they know it.' Another pause to let that information sink in as well. 'I don't know very much about Mara because I'm never here at the same time she is.' Mrs Scully smiled. 'One day

I'd like to meet her and chat over a nice cup of tea. From what *others* have reported when Mara has been here is that she was born in what today is called Norway and died there about 235 years ago. You'll notice her accent when she speaks English through me. Mara has told people that she is a *willing* messenger on the other side. Rather than go into another dimension and lose all earthly contact, she has chosen to relay information from those who have departed to those who're still on this earth. She uses my body energy and my vocal cords like you would use a telephone. If she has a message for anyone here, she will use my voice – my telephone equipment if you will – to deliver the message. Because I am not here, because Mara has control of what is physically me, I cannot know in advance what messages she will bring, nor do I recall afterwards what has been said. I cannot promise in advance who will get a message and who will not. That is not up to me. That is up to *them*, those Mara is in contact with, on the other side. The messages do not originate with me. I am only the physical *medium* they use to send their words. I am not the source of the information, merely the radio transmitter through which their sounds are amplified. Do you all understand?'

Everyone murmured that they did.

'Good. Now I ask you three things before I begin. The first is when Mara speaks to you, answer her. The second is please do not talk at any time unless you are talking to Mara, and *please*, do not make any loud or sudden noises. They could be very detrimental to my health.' Again her smile. 'Do you understand?'

Again, everyone murmured that they did.

Mrs Scully settled back into her comfortable leather chair and took several deep breaths. Then her breathing became heavier and louder, each intake of air as though she was gasping for life and each exhale of air like a dying woman's death rattle. Then Lois noticed the medium's features begin to contort. Her eyes seemed to get smaller and her mouth seemed to stretch farther across her face. Lois knew it couldn't be, but she watched in fascination the transformations of the woman's face etched by the light of three tall candles. Mrs Scully's body contorted quickly, violently, suddenly, and then relaxed.

'Good evening,' a young woman's voice said out of Mrs

221

Scully's lips. 'I am Mara.' The voice waited. 'Good evening, I said.'

'Good evening,' several in the audience hastened to say in greeting.

'I hope you will understand my poor English,' the voice said. 'When I was on earth and when I had my own body I spoke in the language of my own people.' Mrs Scully's closed eyes searched the faces seated several feet away from her. 'Can you all understand me? Understand my speaking?'

As if on cue, everyone replied that they could.

'Good.' Mrs Scully's distended mouth smiled. There was more heavy breathing and after a long pause: 'Is Clara here? I have a message for Clara.'

The bulky woman sitting directly in front of Lois raised her hand. 'Yes,' she said, 'my name is Clara.'

'Clara, I have here a message from Walter. Do you know who Walter is?'

'Yes,' the woman whispered.

'Speak up, please,' the voice coming out of the medium demanded. 'I must have the energy of your voice to respond to you. Do you know a Walter?'

'Yes.' The woman's voice was louder but unsteady. 'Walter was my husband. He's dead now.'

'Yes,' Mara answered. 'I know he's dead. That's why he's over here and you are not. He is telling me . . .' There was a pause as Mrs Scully tilted her head to one side as if that would help her hear better . . . 'He is telling me that you have been approached by a lawyer. Is that correct?'

'Yes.' The woman's voice was soft again.

'Speak up!' Mara demanded.

'Yes. I have been. Just last week.'

'Good,' Mara said. 'No, not good that the lawyer has contacted you, good that you came here this afternoon. Your husband, Walter, wants to tell you that he is fine and not to worry about him but he also wants to tell you not to sign those papers the lawyer left with you. Do you understand?'

'Yes,' the woman said rather loudly. 'But Chester, his brother, had them drawn up. We could both make a great deal of money if the plans go through.'

'And you could also lose your house if the plan fails.' Mara's voice was harsh. 'Isn't that the truth?'

'I – I don't know,' the woman stammered. 'Well, yes, I suppose so but I never thought of that.'

'It's time you *did* start thinking,' Mara said sternly. 'Walter says the trouble is that when he was alive he took care of all the business in the family and you were unaware of what was happening.'

'That's true,' the woman replied.

'So now his brother sees a chance of making some money out of the estate Walter worked so hard to leave for you, and you are ready to sign it all away. Am I right?'

'Yes. I suppose so. When you look at it like that.' The woman was shaking now and Lois wondered when she would fumble for a handkerchief in her purse. 'I didn't consider all the possibilities,' she said. 'Tell Walter that. Tell him I'll be careful. Tell him I won't sign.'

'Good.' Mara's tone was softer now. 'I'll tell him. He'll be happy.'

'Thank you,' said the woman and then out came the handkerchief.

There was another long pause as everyone stared at the rigid form of the medium in her chair. Then she straightened up and looked, with closed eyes, at the sitters in the room. 'Lawrence or Torrance?' There was no reply. 'Is there a man here whose name sounds like Lawrence or Torrance?'

An elderly gentleman at the end of Lois' row raised his hand. 'Dorrance,' he said. 'My mother named me after a school chum of hers.'

'And did they call you Door for short?' Mara asked with a laugh.

'No.' The man grinned. 'Everyone called me Bud. It was much easier.'

'Bud. Yes, I will call you Bud too. I have a Rosemary over here who is anxious to get a message to you.' Bud let out a gasp. 'Yes, I can see you know who I'm talking about. Well she wants to tell you . . . was she your wife?'

'Yes,' Bud said, and his voice clouded over.

'She says she has been concerned over you ever since that last day in hospital. She says she was out of her body for those last minutes when they tried to revive her. She says she was in the room, standing beside you and watching as they cut into her throat and put that tube in there. But she wants you to know that she felt no pain. No pain, Bud, will

223

you understand that? You thought the doctors were killing her, when in fact she had already left the body. She asks you to please erase that scene from your memory, Bud. Please understand that she slipped away in peace and harmony and the doctors did everything they could for her. It was her time to go. She *wanted* to go. Can you understand that?'

'She had cancer.' Bud turned to those who were in the row with him. 'It was in her throat. She suffered so much.'

'But in the end . . . no, fifteen minutes *before* the end . . . she had stopped suffering. Bud, she did not pass away in pain. It was easy and joyful and she is waiting for you to join her over here. Can you understand that?' Bud said that he could. 'Will this information make you feel better?' Bud said that it would, then he, too, reached for his handkerchief.

Mrs Scully's body relaxed with a sigh and Bob took Lois' hand, squeezed it and smiled at her. Lois smiled back and glanced at Midge who was staring with complete fascination at the medium in the large leather chair. She turned to see Malcolm and Fiona. They too were holding hands and watching the unconscious psychic in front of them. Then the medium's body stiffened and Mara asked about an Annie in the group and when a woman identified herself, Lois found her mind beginning to wander. She didn't really care about Annie and her message. It was fun to see something like this but after two or three of such communications to complete strangers the novelty had started to wear off. Mara then singled out another woman, a Constance, and as the voice and the message droned on Lois started feeling light-headed. She closed her eyes and shook herself trying to make the sensation go away. Somebody named Philip was now trying to convince somebody named Suzanne that the grandchildren somewhere would be all right doing something that Lois kept tuning out on. She didn't want to tune out but she couldn't listen, couldn't concentrate on what was being said or anything that made sense. She closed her eyes and pressed her hands against her temples. Maybe the pressure outside would take away the pressure she felt mounting up inside. Hadn't Malcolm said these sessions only lasted an hour? Surely an hour was almost up. God, how she wanted to get out of that dark stuffy room and get outside. To have a drink. To breathe again.

Then suddenly she felt herself being jerked to her feet.

She opened her eyes. Everyone was still seated. The medium was still in front of her. Lois felt a stabbing pain in the back of her throat. Then the voice came out of her lips. 'What am I doing here in this circle of fools?' Lois put her hand up to her mouth. It was a man's voice. Harsh and demanding and arrogant. She hadn't felt her lips move yet the voice had come out of her body. 'And who are you?' Lois felt her hand pointing at Mrs Scully. 'What are you doing leading this group?' the man's voice demanded. 'Who gave you my throne?'

Bob reached up and grabbed Lois' arm, trying to make her sit down.

'Don't you touch me!' the voice inside Lois boomed. 'How dare you touch me?' Lois, her eyes shut tight, looked around the room. 'Most of you are new to me,' the voice continued. 'I don't recognize you. Where are my regulars? Where are my followers?'

There were murmurings from everyone and they stared from Lois to Mrs Scully and back to Lois again. The medium continued to sit in her chair, eyes closed, hands as if in prayer.

'What's been going on in my absence?' the harsh, masculine voice demanded. 'I thought I laid out everything perfectly clear. I thought I mapped out exactly what had to be done after my transition. Well?' Lois turned her head, scanning the small group.

Bob reached for her again. 'Please,' he whispered. 'Please, Lois, sit down.'

Lois swatted his hand away. 'And now what's happened to the plans? What's happened to the organization? Do you all understand how long it took me to set everything up? Do you all understand what mental as well as physical effort went into leaving you the legacy I did? Do you?'

Mrs Scully rose slowly from her chair. Her eyes were still tightly closed. She started walking towards Lois.

'You draw up plans and you have meetings,' the voice thundered on, 'and yet you stay locked in that infernal place not letting even the breath of a fresh day inside. What happened to my daily welcoming of the sun? What happened to my ritual of renewal? How do you expect the word to get out to non-believers? How do you expect to grow with new members when everything is stifled behind stone walls?'

Malcolm suddenly stood up, his eyes wide with terror. He pointed at Lois, his entire body trembling. 'Who are you?' he demanded. 'Who *are* you?'

Before the voice inside Lois could answer, Mrs Scully began to cry in a high child-like pitch. 'Mommy!' the voice inside the medium wailed. 'Corra, mommy! Corra!'

Fiona let out a scream as Lois and Mrs Scully reached for one another in a powerful embrace. Then they both fell to the floor, noisily scattering the sitters and the metal folding chairs.

CHAPTER SEVENTEEN

The second-class rail car was almost empty. Malcolm and Fiona sat close to one another without anyone watching. The lights inside were dim. British Rail didn't try to make these inland shorter trips as comfortable as the longer 125s that were full of tourists and businessmen. Fiona sat by the window, yet the pitch black of the Scottish night gave her nothing to see. She had talked of nothing else but Lois' possession at Mrs Scully's and then of Bob's reaction to it afterwards. 'He blamed *you* for it, Malcolm! The cheek of it! His wife goes bonkers and you get the blame!'

'I know,' Malcolm said. 'He called it a set-up. That's a Yank term. It means something arranged in advance to happen.'

'I thought a set-up was a glass and some ice cubes in a pub.' She remembered an American tourist asking for it at the Waverley.

'That's a set-up as well,' Malcolm said. 'The Americans have done strange things with our language.'

'They're strange people all the way around if you ask me,' she replied. We go to all the trouble of taking that brooch up to them and then he accuses you of manoeuvring everything at the seance. It's not fair.'

He gripped her hand tighter. She had slipped it into his coat pocket and he had held it ever since the train pulled out of Edinburgh station. 'He was just over-reacting,' he said. 'You heard what Lois had been through yesterday. Chasing that car and all.'

'I suppose he blames you for that as well?'

He smiled. 'No, I don't think so. But she's not a well person, you know. She has been having her troubles.'

'How were you supposed to have manipulated them over to the seance? Tell me? How? If it was your doing, what if they hadn't wanted to go? What does he think you would have done? Hit them over the head and taken them to Mrs Scully's by force?'

'Will you calm down?' He kissed her on the forehead. 'It's no skin off our nose. We'll never see those people again.'

She looked up at him. 'Don't be so sure. That Midge person told me they would probably be coming back to Dumfries, especially after Mrs Scully brought up Corra in the seance. God, that was weird!'

Malcolm's eyebrows raised. 'Oh? Midge said that?'

'Aye. She told me that Bob was going to bring his wife back to Corra and try to locate that house because it was the only way he could get his wife normal again. Midge told me he couldn't chance returning to the States and having her go on and on about it all the time. They were in Scotland and they were going to resolve it before they left.'

'H'm. I didn't know that.' A smile of satisfaction flickered across his lips. Fiona didn't see it. With her one free hand she was wiping the moisture from the train window, trying to discover how far along they were into their journey. It had been easier than he thought. The group would be proud of him. Taking the brooch from Lois' bedroom had been easy. The Brunos had been out. He had lifted the key from the rack while Fiona was tending the bar and in three minutes had taken the piece of jewellery and had replaced the key. He knew she would miss the brooch, if only because of its size. It had been amazingly easy to get Lois over to Mrs Scully's. No trouble at all. It had all worked quite nicely, thank you. Now they would finally get to the house. Now his part in all of it was finally over.

As if reading his mind, Fiona started in again: 'It still amazes me that you found that silly brooch of hers. They looked everywhere for it. I even went into the room with the maid afterwards and we searched. Then you went in alone and found it behind the dresser. What are you? Some

227

kind of psychic? Are you competition for Mrs Scully?' She grinned at him.

The guard came by for the tickets and after he had gone, Fiona said, 'You know, I kind of like that Lois. She's a dear sort. Not like her husband, I'm not fond of him at all.'

'I wouldn't get too attached to Lois if I were you,' Malcolm said and then immediately regretted it.

She looked at him. 'Why? What on earth do you mean by that?'

'Nothing. It's just that she'll be going back to the States soon . . .'

'I know that. No, no, Malcolm you meant something different. I can tell by the tone of your voice.'

He struggled for words. 'Just that I think you're pinning too much on the friendship. You know, planning to visit her in New York and all.'

She didn't take her eyes from his face. 'What's wrong with Lois? Why can't I like her if I want to?'

'Nothing's wrong with her,' he faltered. 'It's just that . . .'

'That what?'

'That . . .' He gave up. 'Come on Fiona, let's change the subject.'

'I'm not changing anything! You made a serious statement, my young lad, and I demand to know why you made it.' She saw his face grow slightly crimson but no explanation came from him. 'Well? I'm waiting.' She had put her hand back in his coat pocket after the guard had gone by. Now she pulled the hand out and shoved it into her own coat pocket. 'You have no right to be against Lois. Her fool of a husband perhaps, but not Lois herself.'

He decided on the macho approach. 'Look, I don't think it's any of your affair.'

She leaned away from him and against the window. 'Oh? So now I'm not to know things, am I?'

'I didn't mean that,' the macho tone hadn't worked.

'So now I'm supposed to say "yes, please and thank you" and not be expected to know why. Is that it?'

'Fiona, it's not your affair, that's all. You're carrying this too far and . . .'

'I'm carrying nothing! Look, my hands are empty.' She took them out of her pockets and showed them to him. 'They're empty. They're not touching you. They're not grabbing you. They don't even have an engagement ring on them, they don't.'

He sighed. 'Please don't start that thing again.'

'Thing? Thing?' she repeated loudly. 'You call our marriage a thing?'

'Please, you don't have to make so much noise. I asked you not to start on that again.'

'Start what? The marriage thing as you refer to it? Hah!' She turned and stared out of the window. 'This girl here – ' She pointed to her reflection in the glass. 'You see this girl? Well she is not interested any longer in your marriage thing, as you call it.'

'Aren't you being a wee bit dramatic?'

She whirled back around at him. 'Dramatic? No I'm not. You know what I'm being? I'm being me. I'm tired of plans that don't ever happen and tired of being put off month after month waiting to set a date. All my friends are getting married and some of them already have babies. What do I have? A man with no job, a man who won't explain what's delaying our wedding and now a man that tells me who to like and who not to like and says his reasons are not my affair? That man I'm going to trust? That man I'm going to cling to? I have me pride Malcolm. Oh aye, I have me pride.'

He touched her shoulder but she knocked his hand away. He stared at the back of her head and then down at the floor. It was hell when she got into one of these moods. Once she hadn't spoken to him for eight days. Now he had gone and done it again. It was time to be honest with her. He had delivered what the group had wanted. Lois was coming back to Dumfries, to Corra. His part in it was over. As from tonight he was finished. He and Fiona could now arrange their marriage. He was free and he must also be free to tell her. 'I want to explain to you,' he said. She didn't turn around. 'Fiona, if you are going to be my wife there is something you must know. There is something that I haven't been able to tell you before, but I can now.' She shrugged her shoulders and kept her gaze out the window. 'We couldn't set a date for the wedding before because I was involved in the plan. Lois Bruno is the plan.' He took a deep breath. 'There. I've said it. I promised them I wouldn't but I've said it.'

She turned slowly, her eyes searching his face. 'I don't

believe you,' she said softly. 'Malcolm – not *you*. Surely you're not involved in *the plan*?'

'Aye. I am.' He replied as simply as he knew how.

She pulled away again, staring at him, wide-eyed. 'No, I can't believe that. You're too smart for that.' She closed her eyes and then opened them. 'Tell me you're lying.'

He couldn't look at her. 'I'm not. It's God's truth.'

She kept her eyes on him. '*The plan*? That same old plan I've been hearing about ever since I was born? That plan the old folks are always mumbling about? All that foolishness? And now you, yourself, are telling me you too are *involved* in it?'

'Aye. That's what I'm telling you.'

'And that's why . . .' Her voice trailed off. 'That's why our own marriage plans are always being delayed? Because of that stupid old *plan*? Malcolm, they've been sitting around talking about their old *plan* for almost forty years! It's never happened! It won't ever happen! And you and I are delaying our lives until *the plan* finally works?' She tugged her coat collar closer around her neck. 'Oh, Malcolm, that's terrible! It's worse than terrible. It's stupid! Stupid *and* terrible! I can't believe it. Not from you. I simply can't believe that you would let yourself get messed up in such a thing. Such a stupid and dangerous thing!'

'I'm a nephew,' was all he said.

In shock she put both hands to her mouth, stared at him for an instant, then closed her eyes and turned her head back to the window.

'It'll be over soon,' he said softly. 'Things are moving very quickly now. Everything is falling exactly into place. You'll see. It'll work this time.'

Fiona didn't reply. She wondered why there were no tears.

'It'll be over soon,' he repeated. 'I promise you. As soon as we get Lois in there, it'll be over. But you mustn't tell anyone I told you. I gave them my word I wouldn't tell you. Do you understand what I'm saying? Please don't tell anyone.' She refused to speak. He touched the strands of blonde hair that peeked out between her coat collar and her hat. 'As soon as it's over, as soon as we are certain *the plan* has been set into motion, then you and I will be married. Trust me, Fiona, I truly promise you that.'

But Fiona didn't say another word to him all the rest of the journey.

*   *   *

The next afternoon Fiona busied herself between the pub and the kitchen, tidying up little tasks that should have been done the day before. She was watering the large fiscus tree near the window in the lobby when she looked out and saw them getting out of the taxi. Oh God, she thought to herself. They really did come back. I was so hoping they wouldn't.

'Hi Fiona!' Lois was the first to greet her when they came into the hotel.

'Fiona,' Midge said and smiled.

'Well, here we are again,' Bob said. 'You can't get rid of a bad penny, or whatever the expression is. I hope you have a couple of rooms for us. We didn't make reservations we just assumed the hotel wouldn't be full.'

She put a brave smile on her face. 'Of course! There's always room for friends. Lois, how do you feel? Better, I hope.'

Lois nodded. 'Oh yes. I really don't know what came over me. It was the *strangest* sensation. You know, I don't remember any of it. I remember sitting there feeling like I was about to faint and the next thing I know I'm on the floor with my arms around poor Mrs Scully. Weird!'

Midge volunteered more information. 'The medium lady said that can happen, where sometimes the sitters get taken over instead of the psychic. She says she's seen it a couple of times herself, but Lois was the first one to ever do it during one of her sessions.'

Lois grinned sheepishly. 'Leave it to me. I felt fine afterwards. I mean, there was no headache or wanting to faint or anything. My knee did get a little banged up, though, I hit one of those metal chairs as I fell. Mrs Scully got a bruise on her elbow. I feel bad about that.'

'Well, at least it's over and done with.' Fiona went behind the counter and took out three guest registration cards. As she handed them to the Americans she asked, 'How long will you be staying in Dumfries this time?'

'As long as it takes,' Bob answered flatly.

231

'As long as *what* takes?' Fiona replied.

'For my wife here to find the site of that house and get this idea out of her system.'

Fiona gave the Brunos the same room they had had before and she put Midge right beside them. After they had unpacked, they met, of course, in the hotel pub.

Fiona's father and mother were behind the bar and even though the early winter sun had only just started lowering the heavy winter night snugly into place, the bar was lined with customers. The Brunos were greeted by several of the regulars and Bob, being in an expansive mood for some reason, bought drinks for everyone in the place. With hard-drinking Scotsmen, this made the Yanks more popular than before.

'Where's Fiona?' Lois asked her mother. 'She and Malcolm have a date?'

'No,' the woman shook her head and smiled. 'She went to the films with some girlfriends. She and Malcolm aren't speaking. Again.'

'Why? What did Malcolm do?'

'D'know. She told me last night when they returned from Edinburgh that Malcolm was a stupid fool and she was thinking about calling off their engagement.' The woman smiled. ' 'Course she's only done that twice before already. But this time she sounds like she means it and just between us – ' She lowered her voice slightly – 'it wouldn't break my heart. Malcolm is a good boy, but he's got no job and doesn't seem to be looking for work. He gets his dole money and goes fishing with the boys and that's the most of it. A couple of times I've asked him what his plans for the future are and he's merely said they were all in the air. Fiona's a pretty lass, don't you agree?' Lois agreed. 'Then she can do better. I'm thinking of having her go over to the States in a while. I have a sister in Boston. She moved over there when her husband got a job taking care of a golf course at a country club. You Yanks come over here and hire our boys when it comes to golf courses, did you know that?' Lois said she didn't. 'Well, it pays very, very well and in the winter with the snows and all, they go to Miami where my sister has a flat right on the beach. Supplied rent free by the club in winter, would you believe?' Lois expressed her expected amazement. 'So I figure that with the people my sister knows and with the people Fiona can meet at that country club, my girl won't have to worry about catching a decent lad for a husband.' Lois agreed again.

Fiona's father took advantage of a break in pulling beer handles and arranged himself comfortably behind the bar, in front of the American visitors. 'Fiona tells me you went to a session with a medium in Edinburgh?' They murmured that indeed they had. 'I've never been to one of those things. We were taught not to believe in any of that stuff when I was a lad. But,' he grinned, 'I did have an aunt over near Moffat and she claimed that one day as she was coming out of the post office there was a troop of soldiers marching past. All in red coats and gold braid and carrying muskets. Two men on horseback were leading them. Well, my auntie pressed herself back against the post office wall in shock and then just as quickly they were gone. Vanished right before her eyes. Horses and all! 'Course my uncle accused her of stopping off on the way for a pint or two but we all knew auntie didn't touch alcohol. Except maybe for a wee bit of sherry at Christmas time.'

Before the visitors could comment, a young man farther down the bar, said 'Aye, I believe she saw them all right. Before I married my Helen she was living with her mum and dad up in Galashiels. She told me that one day as she looked out the front window she saw a carriage with four horses drive up very fast and stop directly across from her house. Then as she watched, she saw a man and two women get out of the coach, very fast they did, and the women were wearing big skirts and large hats with feathers in them and the man was in breeches and a waistcoat with buttons. My Helen said she *knew*, don't ask her how she knew but she says she just did, that they were running away from something and that they were going to be killed. Then she blinked her eyes and the whole bunch was gone, people, horses, carriage and all!' There had been a hush in the pub as he told the story. 'Never saw them again, she didn't. Never saw anything else like it, either. My Helen's not one to invent. You can vouch for that, right Sid?' The young man beside him nodded. 'Scared the bejesus out of her, but only afterwards. Only after she realized that she had been seeing ghosts.'

'Aye,' others chorused.

'Strange things happen, that's true,' said Fiona's father.

' 'Tis not right to talk about such things,' an old man at the end of the bar muttered.

Midge grinned and raised her glass to salute the young man whose wife's name was Helen. 'Thanks for telling that. I love those kind of stories.'

'If you like ghosts you'll love Maxwell Castle,' Sid said. 'Now, I haven't witnessed it personally myself, but they say on certain hot summer nights you can see a lady dressed all in white walking along carrying a candle. People have seen her and the candle. But there isn't any floor there any more, they've all fallen in, but this lady walks in a straight line where the floor used to be. Walks just as straight as if the boards were still there.'

'Aye,' again came the murmur after this tale, followed by 'my father claims he saw the apparition' and 'wouldn't go near the place myself' and 'shouldn't fool with things like that.'

Midge raised her glass again. 'I'll drink to that one too.'

'Say,' Lois said. 'Have there been any local stories about Aleister Crowley? You know, that black magician who lived in Corra?'

A sudden silence descended over every single person at the bar.

'That picture that I was talking about?' Lois turned to Fiona's parents. 'The house I tried to find in Corra? Well on a tourist map in Edinburgh I saw the same house and it said that it used to belong to Aleister Crowley.' She turned to the men at the bar, all of whom were listening to her. 'You know who I mean of course. He was very famous in the 30s and 40s for his Black Mass and his group of followers.'

There was absolutely no response from any of them.

Lois searched the row of faces. There was no flicker of recognition. 'But I saw it on a map in Edinburgh,' she insisted, 'and so it must be a tourist place. I mean, you must have heard about it, living here all this time.'

Nothing.

'Come on, now. You've been telling us all these ghost stories. Fill me in on the one about Crowley's house in Corra.' At the still silent response she turned to Bob and Midge. 'Can you believe this? Well maybe,' she said to the line of unsmiling men, 'maybe it made more news when it was still standing. Somebody told me it was burnt down.'

'Aye,' the old man finally said. 'It did that. And then they tore the shell of it down, stone by stone. Nothing is left of it.'

'Aye.' The others nodded and murmured in agreement.

'Too bad,' Lois continued, 'I would have loved to have seen it. We're going there again tomorrow. If the house has been destroyed at least I can see where it used to stand. I can walk in the spot where it once stood.'

'You don't want to do that,' the old man toward the end of the bar said. 'Just leave it be. Visit the ruined churches, take pictures of the sheep in the fields, even go up to Loch Ness and look for the monster but forget about Corra and the house. Forget about that.'

'I just want to stand on the site where it used to be. You know, just to say I did it.'

The men began to move away from the bar, some adjusting their scarves into their coat collars, others putting on their woollen gloves. Helen's husband and his friend Sid took final swigs from their mugs and started towards the door. When they passed Lois, Sid said: 'It's not something you play the tourist with. That place is dangerous.'

'That place?' Lois' voice rose. 'I thought everybody said it didn't exist. How can it be dangerous?'

Neither of them answered her. They just buttoned up their coats and went out the door. Lois watched three others do the same. Then the old man at the end of the bar spoke up. He was one of the last to leave. 'Sid meant that even the bare spot on the ground, where that house once stood, is full of evil and death.'

'Because of Aleister Crowley?' Lois asked.

'Because of Satan himself!' The old man fumbled for his gloves, then started for the door and the blackness of the winter street. 'Because of the very devil himself!'

* * *

Fiona came into the hotel just before eleven that night.

'Did you enjoy the picture?' her mother asked.

She shrugged. 'I suppose so but I didn't scream as much in this one as I did in the other one. Kimberley yelled her head off every time the murderer lifted his axe, but it got tiresome after awhile. Did Malcolm ask for me?'

'I haven't seen him,' her mother replied.

'Oh? Good. I don't want him hanging around here.'

'Are you quite sure?'

'Yes. At least I think I am.' She sighed. 'Oh mum, I don't know. He makes me so angry sometimes.'

'What did he do this time? You haven't told me, you know.'

Fiona wished she could tell her mother about Lois and *the plan*, but she knew what the woman's reaction would be: horror and confusion. No, she'd have to wait and come up with *a plan* of her own. 'It's personal, if you don't mind mum.'

The woman smiled. 'I don't mind. Whatever you decide has got to be your choice anyhow. Now look . . . there's only old Doc Fulham in the pub, and with the way there seems to be a terrible storm heading this direction we probably won't have many more customers tonight. Why don't you settle the cash drawer and I'll look in on the kitchen. Maybe we'll close everything early tonight.'

'Good idea, because I'm going back to Kimberley's to sleep. I don't want to see Malcolm poking his nose around here tonight and not tomorrow morning either.'

Dr Fulham sat all alone at the bar, nursing a pint of lager. An old bachelor who had retired from medical practice in Glasgow years before, he usually closed the Waverley pub before going on down the street and closing the other pubs in the town. 'Evening, Miss Fiona,' he said as she came behind the bar.

'Evening,' Fiona replied and looked at his glass. 'Are you all right?'

'Fine,' he nodded. 'This is my last one. Got to be going. Understand there's a storm brewing.'

'Aye,' the girl replied. 'Feels like it the way the wind has shifted.' She went over to the street door and threw the latch, then turned the sign so the side that said 'closed' was visible to any last-minute boozer. She went back to the cash register behind the bar, rang no sale and started counting the bills and the coins.

'Did you have a good time in Edinburgh yesterday?' Dr Fulham wanted to talk.

'Aye,' was all she replied.

'Was the American lady pleased to have her brooch returned?'

She stopped counting the bills. 'How did you know about the brooch?'

'Common knowledge,' he said. 'Are the Americans going to stay around for a while?'

'I don't know. For a few days, perhaps.' She stacked the small green one-pound notes next to the larger blue five-pound ones.

'I heard the woman say they are going to Corra tomorrow. They're looking for that place.'

Fiona didn't turn around.

'They're determined this time, it seems. I wish them luck. I wish us *all* luck.'

Now Fiona did turn. 'What do you mean by that?'

He shook his head. 'Nothing. I don't mean nothing.'

'You know something, don't you?' She put the uncounted ten-pound notes back in the cash drawer and came over to where he was sitting. 'What do you know?'

He smiled: 'I trust I know a good many things at my age.'

'About the American woman, I mean.' Fiona stared at him, her eyes trying to dig past that old fool smile.

'I know nothing about her.'

'You know what they've got planned for her, don't you?'

The old man's eyes narrowed. 'I don't know what you're talking about.'

Fiona kept staring at him. 'I think you do.' She leant over him. 'Are you part of it as well?'

'Part? Part of what?'

'*The plan.*' She surprised herself by saying those words aloud. 'Are you also in on *the plan*? You know what they're going to do with the American woman, don't you?'

'I don't know where you are leading me with this kind of talk, Miss Fiona. I have no plans.' He grinned. 'Not at my age.'

Fiona didn't smile. 'They're going to do something terrible to Lois,' she said never once taking her gaze from his face. 'I want you to tell me. Malcolm wouldn't tell me what it was, but he said they've got it all figured out. They've used Malcolm in this but now he's finished. He's not going to have anything more to do with them.'

'Them?' Dr Fulham slid off the bar stool. He shook his head. 'Whatever Malcolm told you, I know nothing about.'

'That woman is frail, you know. She's not in the best of

237

health. I just pray that whatever they've got in store for her isn't going to be too much for her. Lord, whatever it is, might even *kill* her.'

Dr Fulham began his shuffle towards the door, buttoning up his overcoat as he went. 'Miss Fiona, it sounds like you've been sampling some of the stock from behind your father's bar. For a big girl who wants to get married, you're not making a lot of sense.'

'I think I am,' she said in a lower voice. 'I think I'm making a whole lot of sense. I'm going to tell them in the morning.'

He stopped. 'Tell who? Tell them what?'

'I'm going to tell the Americans that they're in danger, that Lois could be in mortal peril. I'm going to tell them not to go to Corra, not to get mixed up with Malcolm and his damnable *plan*. I will,' she closed the cash drawer with a slam and closed the subject of what she had to do in her mind, 'as soon as they have their breakfast. I'll warn them.'

The old man reached the door and undid the latch by himself. 'Suit yourself, child. Follow your feelings about . . . whatever it is you're talking about.' He opened the door then touched the brim of his cap to her. 'See you tomorrow evening, as usual. Then you can tell me how this all comes out. Good night to you.'

'Good night,' Fiona replied.

Dr Fulham went slowly down the five cement steps to the sidewalk. He looked into the blackness for signs of the storm that was heading his way. He stood for a moment to put on his gloves, then he turned left and started across the quiet street. Every other night he turned to his right, to where the other pubs were waiting, but not tonight. Tonight he shuffled through a deserted car park and then down a short incline to the railway station. It was still open, he could see a light in the waiting room. He pushed open the heavy wooden door and made his way across the stone floor to a group of pay telephones. He took off his right hand glove, unbuttoned the last three buttons of his overcoat and fumbled in his trouser pockets. He came up with a ten-pence coin and lifted the receiver. He dropped in his coin and waited for the dial tone.

'It's Fiona,' he said when someone on the other end

answered. 'Malcolm's Fiona. At the Waverley. She knows.'
He listened. 'I don't know how much he's told her, but
she knows enough and she knows the American woman is
going to be involved. She knows about *the plan*.' He listened.
'Aye, that's what I said, Malcolm told her.' He paused. 'I
know we told him to be silent. I was there when we told him.
More than once, too. But he went ahead and did it anyway.'
Another pause. 'Tomorrow. She said she'd tell the Americans
about it tomorrow. After they've had their breakfast.' He
stopped to listen again. 'Look, I don't like giving you this
information any better than you like getting it. I'm just
doing my duty. It's your decision now.' He hung up.

* * *

Fiona jumped as the first clap of thunder detonated above
her. Then as if someone had turned a garden hose on the
pub windows, the rain came crashing. She went to the
door and threw the latch shut again, then walked into
the small lobby and made sure the front windows were
closed and locked against the rain. Her mother appeared
on the staircase.

'You still going to Kimberley's in this weather?'

'Aye. It's not that far. I've got my boots and brolly.'

'Well go if you must, but be sure and turn off all the lights
before you do.' Fiona nodded. 'Good night, luv.' The woman
went back up the stairs.

Fiona double-checked to see that all the registered guests
had taken their keys up to their rooms and then she locked
the front door, throwing a switch that plunged everything
but the one night light into darkness. Next she visited the
kitchen, making sure all the gas burners had been shut off
and the refrigerator door closed. She flicked a switch near
the doorway and all the lights in the kitchen went out. She
started up the dimly lit back stairs on her way to her room.
She needed to get her night things and put on her rain
things before leaving for Kimberley's. She was glad Malcolm
hadn't tried to talk to her tonight. She didn't have anything
to say to him. Not yet. Not tonight. Tomorrow it would be
different. Tomorrow she would tell him about warning the
Americans. Tomorrow he would know that his crazy old
plan hadn't worked. Tomorrow he would have to give her a

239

wedding date. With *the plan* consigned to the dustbin there could be no more excuses.

A man came out of the shadows on the first floor landing. Fiona stopped, startled.

He came down two steps, towards her.

She wanted to call out to her parents but no sound came from her voice. Quickly she turned to start down the stairs.

There was another man at the bottom of the staircase and he was coming up towards her.

She could hear the first man behind her. Then she felt the tugging against her neck. It was cold and thin. The man behind her began to tighten the length of piano wire. She put her hands up to her throat, tried to claw away this terrible pressure. She tried to scream but the wire was digging into her throat muscles, clamping down across her jugular vein, cutting off any minute intake of air. The man twisted the wire. She felt the blood boiling under her face. She tried again to pull away that thin line that was overwhelming her, that thin line that gave her such pain, that thin line that was ending her life. The man gave the wire one last twist and Fiona slumped into the waiting arms of the man in front of her.

In the darkness and in all that rain nobody in Dumfries saw the two men emerge from the side door of the hotel and dump the girl's body into the back seat of the car. Because of the noise of the rain nobody inside the hotel heard the motor start up or heard the car pull away. Because of the storm, there wasn't one other vehicle moving along the side road the car took to get to Corra, and that village, dozens of times smaller than Dumfries, was closed down and as deserted as an old movie set. When the car came up the long driveway there were several faces peering out of the windows of the huge house. Out of the house Lois Bruno called *my* house. The car went to the rear of the house and stopped. The two men got out quickly. Then three others, two men and a woman, joined them. The stinging raindrops poured over their hooded rubber coats as they slid Fiona's body from the back seat and carried it down the back lawn over to a round object made of stone. One of the men lifted the wooden cover that sat on the stone walls. The others lifted the body and let it slither over the walls and fall to the bottom of the long-dry well. The woman took a flashlight out of her raincoat pocket and pointed the beam inside the well. Fiona's eyes were open. Her face had already started turning black. Her yellow hair was fanned out around her in stark contrast to the greys and blacks and browns of the other pieces of rotting flesh already down there.

CHAPTER EIGHTEEN

The hotel waitress showed them a table near the window. 'I warn you, Midge,' Lois smiled, 'if you order the full Scottish breakfast be prepared to ask for a doggie bag. They serve you a lot of food!'

'That's something neither my waistline nor my hipline needs to hear. I'll just have toast and coffee,' she told the girl.

'No eggs?' the young waitress asked. 'No cereal? No sausages?'

'Look, if I was as young as you are and had your figure, I'd take it all, but – ' Midge patted her hips. 'I've reached a certain age in life where one plate of eggs and sausage takes two weeks of dieting to get rid of. Just coffee and toast please, darlin'.'

Bob laughed. 'You're not that overweight.'

'It's this dress,' she said. 'The man who designed it also designs for Audrey Hepburn. One size fits all.'

As they were relaxing over their second cup of coffee (Midge did relent and have a scone with jam and cream 'just to see what one tasted like'), Malcolm came into the dining room and over to their table.

'Morning,' he said. All three, including Bob, smiled at him. 'Lovely day, isn't it?'

'Beautiful,' Lois said. 'That storm last night must have chased away every cloud in the sky. It's a pale blue everywhere up there now. Just lovely.'

'Going to Corra, are you?' he asked, then quickly added: 'Mind if I go with you?'

The women looked at Bob. 'It's my husband's decision,' Lois said. 'He's the driver.'

'I could drive you there,' Malcolm said. 'I know the way. You could just sit back and relax, Mr Bruno.'

'Well – ' Bob looked to Lois for some sort of signal and not getting one said, 'Sure. Why not? You drive and I'll relax. I've never been that keen on driving on the wrong side of the highway.'

'Grand,' Malcolm beamed. 'I'll let you finish your coffee. I'll be in the lobby.'

'Well that's a switch,' Lois said. 'The day before yesterday you never wanted to see that kid again, and now you're letting him drive the car.'

He sipped his coffee. 'Well, I've been thinking. Maybe I was too harsh with him after the seance. I blamed him for something I didn't have any idea about. I was upset. So, if I can make it up to him by letting him play chauffeur, then I'll feel a little less guilty.'

'Makes sense,' Midge said. 'Malcolm's not a bad guy. Cute, too.'

'Midge,' Lois shook her finger at her friend, 'let me remind you that the cute guy is spoken for.'

'Yeah,' Bob said, 'where is Fiona? She's usually on the front desk in the morning.'

'She's a sweetheart too,' Midge conceded. 'Bright and pretty. They make a nice couple. And,' she added, pushing herself away from the table and standing up, 'if I reach for that last scone that's lonesomely sitting all alone on that plate, I'll make a nice couple all by myself. Come on, let's get the show on the road.'

They put the engraving, wrapped in its plastic and brown paper, into the trunk of the car. Malcolm got in, on the right side, behind the wheel and Bob sat beside him. In the back seat, Midge was behind Malcolm and Lois behind Bob. Malcolm shifted gears and the car pulled quietly away from the kerb. The young man made all the right turns and soon they were out of town, heading down the asphalted roadway to Corra.

Midge looked out the side window. 'Everything is so fresh here,' she said. 'Even though it's winter things look so much better than they do back in New York. God, can you imagine the slush and dirty piles of snow everybody's tramping through over there?'

No one replied. Bob was watching how Malcolm handled the rental car and Lois was looking ahead, around Bob's shoulder, waiting anxiously to arrive in Corra. This had to be it, she told herself. This is the third and last try. All I get are three times up at bat and if I strike out, it means returning to New York without ever knowing the truth. If there *is* a truth. Damn, it's too bad the house had been destroyed but if I can just stand on the site of where it used to be, maybe I can get some kind of impression about Tony. There's no doubt in my mind now that this is all being done by 'them' up there. The spirits are leading me to Tony. I know that what happened at Mrs Scully's confirmed it.

She shifted her gaze and stared at the back of Bob's head. And he's been so sweet through it all, she said to herself. Any other husband would have had sixteen fits by now but he's suffered through it all with me. He knows, too. He knows I have to discover what this is all about. When it's over then the three of us can go home. She looked at Midge. No, the four of us: me, Bob, Midge and Tony.

'Look out!' Bob was the first one to see the two men in the middle of the road and his reflex was to reach out and grab the wheel. Malcolm saw the men a split second later and quickly applied the brake. The car skidded slightly, veered to the right and stopped.

One of the men, large and bulky and wearing a tweed cap and a dark overcoat, came over to the driver's side. He was carrying a rifle. Malcolm rolled down the window.

'What's the trouble?' Malcolm asked.

'The road has been washed out around the bend,' the man replied.

'Washed out?' Lois exclaimed.

'Aye. Last night's storm. Created a landslide and broke up the road when it came down the hill, I'm afraid you can't pass.'

'But we've got to get to Corra,' Lois insisted.

'Sorry, missus, but nobody's going to get past that pile of rocks until the highway people remove it.'

'So what are we supposed to do?' she asked anxiously.

'Turn around and come back when you can get through.' He didn't smile. 'That's all I can tell you.'

'Are you sure about this?' Malcolm asked. 'The road is impassable?'

'Aye. That's what I just got through telling you.'

'Malcolm – ' Lois tapped him on the shoulder. 'There must be another road down to Corra, isn't there?'

'Not from here, Mrs Bruno,' he said. 'Only if we go back to Dumfries and then take the coast road south and swing back up below Corra by going through Barnbarroch and then Dalbeattie. It's an awful long detour. It'd take us a couple of hours at least. Maybe more if the storm damaged the coast road as well.'

'Why don't you just turn around and wait until the road is open?' the gruff man with the rifle suggested.

Bob spoke for the first time. 'I don't understand. Why are you carrying a gun? Is there some danger?'

'Looters,' was the man's reply.

'Looters? What the hell is there to loot out here in the middle of nowhere?'

'Look,' the man said to Malcolm, 'just turn around and take your group of Yanks back to wherever you found them. We have to keep the road clear for the workmen when they arrive.'

Malcolm looked at Bob and then around at Lois to get her reaction. 'I suppose we have to go back,' Lois said slowly. 'I'm disappointed as hell, but we can always wait and do this when they've cleaned up the mess.'

Midge reached out and squeezed Lois' knee, then winked at her. 'Huh-uh,' she said. 'I've got an idea. Don't ask any questions. Just go with it.' Before Lois could reply, Midge had opened the car door and was standing beside the man with the rifle. 'Would you do me just one little favour?' she said, using her Scarlett O'Hara voice. 'I mean, just a bitty one – or as you folks over here say "a wee one?" Just for me?' She put one fluttery hand to her breast.

The man stepped back a couple of paces. 'What is it?'

'Because we only have today here, and we just *can't* come back tomorrow or whenever ya'll get those awful old rocks cleaned right away, and I won't be able to ever see this little old valley never again, probably not evah in ma life.' Lois winced as Miss Scarlett began to sound like Hattie McDaniel. 'Ah wondered, suh, if'en y'all wouldn't mind posin' for a snapshot? You and the other gennleman ovah theah? With the artillery in his hands?'

'A photograph?' The man backed off another two steps.

244

'Well, I don't know . . .'

'Oh, I wouldn't be a bit of bother! I have ma Polaroid right heah in ma handbag.' She reached into her purse and took out the instant camera. 'Just one little old picture! The two of y'all with those mag-nif-i-cent mountains in the background.'

The man turned to stare at the short, nobbly hills behind him. 'Well . . .'

'Oh, thank ya so kindly! Aren't you just the sweetest thing? Come on, come on, y'all.' She motioned to those in the car. 'This gennelman has agreed to let me take just one little picture of him and that uther handsome gennelman over theah. Come, come, come. Don't dawdle, y'all. The gennelman have uther things to occupy theah time.'

Bob turned to Lois. 'What is this?'

'I don't know. She said to go along with it. So,' Lois started to get out of the car, 'let's go along with it.'

Midge played scene director with as much command as Scarlett positioning her gentleman-callers at a cotillion. 'Lois y'll stand by that gennelman theah and Bob you get a tiny bit closer to the other distinguished gennelman with the rifle and then you two most gracious gennelmen, you stand closer together. Malcolm, y'all hunch down between our two new friends.' She stepped back far enough to get them all in the picture. 'Lois, sweetie, will y'all put your hand on the gennelman's shoulder? Yes, that's fine. Bob darlin', will y'all put your hand on the gennelman's shooting weapon? Just to touch it. That's fine. Now let me see if I'm capturing those magnificent mountains behind y'all. Oh, I am!' She lowered the camera. 'Isn't this thrilling?' Back the camera came to her eye. 'Don't y'all move now. Not a smidgen.' Her finger hit the button, there was a whirring sound and the photograph, already starting to develop, slid out of the end of the camera. 'Thank you evah so kindly, gennelmen. This will be a cherished memento to show ma grandchillun some day. Okay, everybody, let's get back in the car. Let's turn the car around and see what next excitin' adventure awaits our little party.' She walked quickly to the car, opened all four doors and motioned them back inside. 'Hurry up,' she said, her Miss Scarlett voice gone, 'get inside the goddamned thing and shut the doors.'

The doors slammed and Malcolm twisted the key in the ignition. 'Turn this fucking thing around and head back the way we came,' Midge ordered. 'Do it quickly. I don't want those goons to see this picture.'

Malcolm did as he was ordered and gravel spun out behind his rear wheels. Lois looked out the back window. The men were still in the middle of the highway, standing watching.

'Midge, what in the hell was all that about? You reminded me of a New Orleans drag queen,' Bob said.

'Thanks for the compliment. Malcolm, get some distance from those bastards.'

The car went for another minute, then rounded a curve. 'Okay,' Midge said, 'they can't see us now. Stop the car.' Malcolm did as he was told, pulling over onto the roadway shoulder. 'Just as I thought.' Midge looked at the fully developed print and then passed it to Bob. 'Those goons aren't real. See? They don't appear in the picture.'

Bob looked at the photo. 'We do,' he said in amazement, 'but you're right, *they* don't.'

Lois peered at the picture over the front seat. 'I'm there and I've got my hand floating in the air. It should be touching the guy's sleeve but there's just a space where he was. You too, Bob, you had your hand on the other guy's rifle but all that came out is you with your hand cupped in the air. Malcolm, you're kneeling between the two of us. Those guys just *aren't* behind you.'

All three now looked at Midge. 'It was just a hunch,' she said. 'Somehow I knew those guys weren't really there. The whole thing didn't look kosher, didn't fit together. I mean, all of a sudden there is a landslide and we can't get to Corra? No,' she shook her head, 'those guys were a set-up and now we've got to call their bluff.'

'A set-up?' Malcolm asked.

'Yeah,' Bob replied, 'it's what I accused you of the other night. I'm sorry.'

'That's okay,' the young man answered. 'But if they were not in the picture, if they were not *real*, who were they?'

'Or *what* were they?' Lois added.

'They were very clever thought transferences,' Midge said. 'Somebody or a whole lot of somebodies went to a great deal of trouble and energy to protect those guys in front of us. They did a really super job. Those goons were almost believable. Even the *rifles*. Now that takes *real* energy. They almost had it down pat but what made me suspicious was that when the guy first stopped us and started for the car he didn't have a rifle in his hand. But by the time he got to us, it had materialized. It takes a helluva lot of concentrated energy to get something as heavy as a rifle to materialize when you want it.'

Lois stared at her friend, seeing her in a different light. 'How do you know so much about this stuff?'

Midge grinned. 'There's a lot about me you don't know, darlin'. Someday when we have some time, I'll fill you in.'

'But we're talking about powers far beyond what Mrs Scully was demonstrating,' Lois said. 'How come you spotted it and why haven't you ever told me about your knowledge of this stuff?'

'Later,' she smiled again at Lois. 'I promise. Right now we've got to go back there, get past that roadblock and get to Corra.'

'I agree,' Lois replied.

'Malcolm,' Midge ordered, 'turn this mother around and put your foot on the accelerator and go like hell. Plough straight through those guys!'

'But they've got guns – '

'Those aren't real guns,' Midge said, 'and those goons aren't real either. Come on, turn this thing around and charge through them as fast as you can.'

The young man hesitated. 'I don't know . . .'

'You don't know what?' she asked.

'If I want to do this or not . . .'

'Malcolm's right,' Bob said. 'We can't ask him to do this. This is our problem and we have to handle it ourselves.' He opened his door and came around to the driver's side. 'Come on, kid, slide over. I'll drive from now on.' Malcolm willingly slid from under the steering wheel onto the passenger side. He looked around at the two women and grinned sheepishly. Bob turned on the ignition, shifted gears, then swung the car onto the other side of the empty roadway. He shifted gears again and pressed his foot on the accelerator. All the way to the floor. The car shot around the bend and aimed itself at the two men who were still standing in the centre of the road.

'Be careful!' Lois screamed.

'Don't worry, I will be,' he replied through his teeth.

'Run right through the bastards!' Midge yelled.

The car sped towards the two men. They saw it coming and raised their rifles.

'Oh God!' Malcolm moaned and shrank down in his seat.

The car was yards away, then feet away. Lois closed her eyes. Malcolm already had his closed. The rifles were pointing right at them. Bob yelled something and pressed his foot as hard as he could and the two tons of metal shot straight into the men, then kept on going down the highway.

Lois opened her eyes and looked out the back window. 'They're still standing there,' she said in awe. 'We hadn't run them over. They're watching us go. I don't believe this!'

Midge laughed and relaxed. 'With everything else that's happened to you since you got that damned engraving and you don't believe *this*? Darlin', this was peanuts compared to what has already taken place.'

Lois glanced at her. 'Somebody for some reason,' she said softly, 'doesn't want me to get to Corra.'

'Oh,' Midge laughed, 'understatement of the fucking year!'

When the car finally passed the small sign that said 'Corra', Lois shuddered. She didn't know if it was from the cold or whether it was a reaction from some dreaded thing deep inside her. She wanted to get out and run the other way. Yet, she encouraged herself, this is what they were here for. This is where it would all be tied together. This was her last chance.

'Is that pub open?' Midge pointed to the place called the 'Bonnie Prince'. 'Let's go in, have a beer and plan our next move.'

'Oh, God, *that* place,' Lois grimaced. 'We've been in there. It's run by Dracula's sister.'

'It's not the friendliest place in town,' Bob said.

'It's the only pub here,' Malcolm volunteered.

Bob shrugged. 'Okay with you, hon?' Lois murmured an okay. He turned the wheel and brought the car to a stop in front of the pub. 'Are you going to take the engraving?' he asked Lois. 'Maybe somebody in there will help us now.' He unlocked the trunk and handed the package to her.

The four of them entered the pub and, to Lois' relief, the rude woman who had been behind the bar was nowhere to be seen. Instead, there was a short burly man with a pot belly and a dark stubble for a beard. Two men were standing at the bar and, at a table near the window, a man and a woman were nursing glasses of beer. Midge chose a table and, when Bob and Malcolm returned with the drinks, Midge raised her glass mug and saluted them all. 'To success,' she said.

Lois put on a brave smile. 'Yes, let's hope so.'

'You're Americans aren't you?' the woman at the other table called over to them. 'What on earth are you doing in this dump?'

'Looking for a house,' Midge called back, 'and yes, we're Americans.'

'A house?' the man frowned. 'We're from Miami. You're buying real estate here?'

'No,' Bob replied with a smile, 'just trying to find a place. A place we want to see.'

'London is the place to buy, if you're buying,' the man said. 'Go south if you wanna buy.' He gestured in a direction that might have been south and the diamond in his gold pinkie ring glittered.

'Morris wouldn't buy up here,' the woman with him said. 'No investment value.'

'In London it's been going up twenty-seven per cent a year! Can you imagine. A one-bedroom apartment in an average neighbourhood goes for hundred twenty, hundred eighty thousand dollars. In the States you get a whole house with a goddamned lawn and garage for that.'

'Morris is thinking of going into real estate,' the woman said. 'He's in shoes now but like I always tell him, when things get bad you can't live in a shoe. I sure am no Mother Hubbard. A house is an investment for life. Isn't that what I always tell you, Morris?'

He nodded. 'So what kind of a place are you looking to buy?'

'We're not looking to buy anything,' Bob repeated.

'It's me, I'm the curious one,' Lois offered. 'I'm trying to find this place,' and she motioned to the brown wrapped package leaning against her chair leg. 'It's an engraving of an old house that used to be here. We're trying to find where it was.'

'An engraving?' Morris' wife asked. 'You mean like an antique?'

'Sort of,' Midge replied. 'Probably a couple hundred years old. At least.'

The woman got up and came over to their table. 'Mind if

249

I have a look? Sometimes people have told me I should be in the decorating business. They say I have the eye.' She watched closely as Lois undid the string, then the paper and finally the two layers of plastic bubble-wrap. 'Oh yeah,' she took it into her hands which had three diamond rings on them, one was at least ten carats. 'It's of an old house. And look, it says "Corra" down here. That's the name of *this* place!'

'Uh-huh,' Midge said drily, 'that's why we came *here* to look for it.'

'Look, Morris, isn't this a lovely old antique picture?' She carried it over to their table.

He stared at it. 'You people don't intend to stay in this rat trap do you? Most unfriendly bunch of Scots we've met on the whole trip.'

'Oh yeah,' his wife looked at the picture again, 'that's the place where they were so rude to us.'

'Rude to you?' Lois rose halfway up out of her chair.

'Yeah,' Morris said, 'I told them if you don't want to run a goddamned hotel, then don't put a goddamned sign out front that says hotel.'

'That's exactly what he told them,' his wife said.

'They've got some old bitch on the front desk who practically chased us out of the place before we could get across the lobby. She yelled that they didn't take people without reservations. I hope you folks got reservations.'

Lois went over to his table. 'Are you sure? I mean, are you positive the place you tried to get into and this house in the picture are the same place?'

'Positive,' he said. 'We drove up a driveway that's just off to the right of this picture and the house was sitting there. Same place, same little balcony off the second floor, same everything.'

'But we were told it had been burnt down, destroyed years ago.' Lois insisted.

'Well they sure as hell rebuilt it in a hurry,' Morris replied, 'because we walked into this very place last night. Hell, all we wanted was a clean room and a shower.'

'It's the same house.' Morris' wife agreed. 'I remember looking at it all the way up the drive. My decorating eye, you know. Then when they were so rude it stuck out more in my memory, if you know what I mean.'

Lois sat down at the table. 'Can you take us there?'

Morris shook his head. 'We're going up to Glasgow. I've got a fella coming for drinks about two.'

'It's no big deal to get there,' the wife answered. 'You can find it yourselves. Here. Let me draw you a map.' She turned over the round paper coaster that had been placed under her beer mug and Morris handed her a ballpoint pen. She drew quickly – after all, she had 'the eye' – and handed the coaster to Lois. 'Here's where we are now – ' She indicated the pub with her pen. 'You go down this street, to your right then make the next left and you keep going till you pass a small stone bridge. Then in a bit you'll come to a grove of trees on your left. There's a driveway right there. It has a sign, "Hotel Thelema". You can't miss it.'

Lois looked at the table where Bob and the others were sitting silently. 'Didn't we go that way before?' He shrugged. She turned back to Morris and his wife. 'That's all we have to do? Just turn right, then left and keep going past that little bridge and it'll be on our left. With a sign?'

'Right on the road. In plain sight. That's what made Morris and me so angry. I mean, if you're going to advertise yourself as a hotel, then be a hotel, for God's sake.'

Morris glanced at his watch. 'Look, babe, if we're going to be in Glasgow by two, we'd better start making tracks.' They quickly got into their coats. Lois noticed hers was trimmed in mink. 'Lots of luck with that place,' Morris continued as he went towards the door, 'but don't buy it. Keep your money. Buy in London. Now *that's* where the action is. Twenty-seven per cent a year! Can't beat those odds.' They both waved, the door opened and they were gone.

'Isn't that something?' Lois was in a mild state of shock. 'After all the trouble we've gone through to find this place and it took a couple of obnoxious Americans to show us the way.' She moved back to their table and stared at the map on the coaster. 'All this time it was just down the goddamned road a piece.'

The man from behind the bar came over to them. 'You wrap that thing up,' he said, motioning to the engraving. Before anyone could reply, he said: 'Wrap it up and get it out of here. I don't want it in my pub.'

'Wait a minute,' Bob said. 'We'll leave in our own good time!'

'Not if you keep that thing in here with you,' the man said.

251

'Now get it out of here!' He grabbed the engraving and Lois jumped up and grabbed it back.

'What the hell do you think you're doing?' Bob demanded.

'Throwing you and that devil picture out of my place!' the man answered angrily. 'Take it out now and you people go with it!'

'If not?' asked Midge.

'Lady, there is no "if not". I run this pub and I say you get the bloody hell out of here.'

They got up from the table, Lois clutching the engraving close to her. Midge picked up her ale mug and drained it, then she and Lois walked towards the door. Bob and Malcolm, acting as rear guards, followed behind them.

Lois wheeled around. 'Why didn't your wife, or whoever she is, tell us where the house was when we were first here? Why all the secrecy?'

'My wife did right,' the man said. 'You have no business there and we have no wish to talk about that house. It's a place of evil! If you are going there then you must be evil as well!' He held the door open wide. 'I want no evil in my place. I want no dealings with the devil!'

The door slammed behind them when they stepped onto the sidewalk.

'I see what you mean,' Midge said, 'it really is your friendly neighbourhood pub.'

Lois walked quickly to the car. 'Let's go. Come on everybody, get in. Let's get this over with.'

They pulled away from the pub and turned right. Lois sat up front with Bob, acting as navigator. They went straight down the main street, then Bob turned at the next left. Soon they found themselves out in farmland. After another mile and a half they came to a small stone bridge and then crossed it. Lois held her breath. On their left fences went by, then trees and only more trees.

'There!' Lois yelled. 'Right there!'

Bob slowed the car to a crawl. All four of them looked in the direction she was pointing.

It was a new sign, painted in red and white. It was in the shape of a shield. Its careful lettering distinctly said: 'Hotel Thelema'.

CHAPTER NINETEEN

Bob turned the car off the main road and passed through the opening in the trees. He started up the gravel driveway but Lois put out her hand and stopped him.

'Please,' she said. 'I just want to look at it.'

There it was. Her house. Her Corra.

'It's exactly like the engraving,' she said in a soft, awestruck tone, 'exactly.'

'Well,' Midge couldn't resist adding, 'there are a few more trees on both sides of it and the grass could use a good lawnmower.'

'But it hasn't *changed*,' Lois was so pleased. 'It's just the way it was when the artist drew it. Look, there's the little balcony on the second floor and the heavy wooden door right under it on the first. And the windows! They're all there, four on each side of the door on both floors . . . The one by the door, there.' She pointed and Bob and Midge knew which window she meant. 'It's closed. In the engraving, it's still opened.'

'No, hon,' Midge said. 'It's been closed now. I noticed it when you showed those people in the pub.'

'Oh.' She turned to Bob. 'What do you think that means? Is that terrible little man still in there or has he already gone? Has he taken the child yet?'

'I really don't know. How could I know?'

'There's only one way to find out, hon,' Midge offered.

'Yeah.' Lois took a deep breath. 'Okay, Bob, let's get inside.'

He engaged the gear and the car crunched heavily over the gravel until he brought it to a stop just a few feet away from the front door. The driveway ended there. The way between the end of the drive and the front door was paved with large squares of white marble. They all got out of the car and as they passed the window, shut now, Lois looked at it and shivered. What had gone in there? she wondered. And, even

253

more frightening, what could come out of it? At the door, Bob reached up and banged the brass knocker which was in the shape of a full moon, complete with smiling face.

The door opened almost immediately.

'Yes? Hello! Please do come in!' The woman was grey-haired and rather bosomy.

Lois spoke first. 'We were wondering if you had accommodation for us. We don't have a reservation.'

'Please, please!' The woman shooed them inside and shut the door behind them. 'We were expecting you. Yes, of course there is plenty of room.'

'Expecting us?' Lois' eyes had been scanning the large entrance hall and she brought them quickly back onto the woman. 'What do you mean?'

'I'm Mrs Loveday,' she said, not answering Lois' question. 'I'm delighted you could all make it.' She looked around. 'Where are your things? Your luggage?'

'Back at the hotel,' Bob replied. 'The hotel in Dumfries. We really didn't expect to be staying here tonight. We didn't have any definite plans.'

'But you'll need your things,' the woman said quickly. 'Vitamin pills and dressing gowns and the like.' She turned to Malcolm. 'Young man, why don't you be a good lad and go fetch their baggage from the hotel?'

Bob shot a glance at Lois. 'You want to stay here?'

'Of course!' her reply was immediate. 'After all we've been through?'

'Yes,' Mrs Loveday beamed. 'Of course you'll stay. I'm glad we have that settled. Now, let me show you to your rooms. I have a lovely double-bedded suite for the two of you, with private bath and shower. I know how Americans miss their shower when they come to Scotland! And for you – ' She nodded at Midge – 'there is an equally lovely single apartment right across the corridor. Private bath and shower there too, of course.'

'I'm not staying,' said Malcolm.

'No, you're not,' Mrs Loveday said sharply.

'Where do you want us to register?' Lois asked.

'Oh that won't be necessary. Not at the moment.' She continued when she saw the expression of surprise on Lois' face. 'We can always do that later. Send the forms up to your rooms. It's more homely that way.' She looked at

254

Malcolm. 'I thought you were going to get their luggage.'

'I think I should go with him,' Bob said. 'We have to check out and pay the bill over there.'

'Make that trip, both ways, again today? Nonsense. You give this lad the details and he can handle all that for you.' She stuck out her hand and Bob fumbled in his wallet for some money. 'Now you go and get their things,' she ordered. 'Come back with them quickly. They'll need them.'

'I haven't packed . . .' Lois' voice trailed off.

'He can get somebody at the hotel to help him, I'm sure.' Mrs Loveday walked rapidly to the door, opened it, waited for Malcolm to obediently go through it, then closed it again. 'Now,' she smiled, 'let me show you to your accommodations.'

They walked across the huge entrance foyer. Lois felt guilty stepping on the beautiful oriental rugs that were carefully scattered across the green marble floor. If she had a rug like this in New York, she'd hang it on the wall, she told herself. Her gaze went up to a large oil painting. It was of Scots highlanders in full battle dress running after some ragged English soldiers. Bodies, none of them Scots, littered the ground. The gilded frame was as busy as the painting itself. There were other paintings on the walls, smaller ones, mostly of landscapes with mountains, waterfalls and grazing sheep. The walls themselves were covered in a dark green moire silk fabric and it shimmered and glistened as the light through the sheer curtained windows danced across its surface. There was little furniture in the foyer, but what was there was massive. A dark wooden table with crouching wild animals for legs. A carved sideboard with gilded handles and pulls. A leather sofa with matching leather highback armchairs. The lighting was all hanging from the high wood-beamed ceiling: three identical crystal chandeliers, fitted with small electric bulbs, that could be raised or lowered on chains fastened to the wall.

'This is quite a place,' Lois commented.

Mrs Loveday beamed and led them up a large curving staircase that was near a pair of massive carved wooden doors. The doors were closed. 'That's the dining room,' she said without being asked. 'That's where you'll have your meals today.' At the top of the stairs, they turned left and walked until they came to the end of the Persian-carpeted corridor. The several doors along the way, all shut, were painted a soft eggshell white and each had a large brass handle and hinges. Lois noticed there were no numbers on the doors. A hotel usually had room numbers, she thought. Mrs Loveday came to the last door on the right. 'This will be your room,' she said, pushing open the door.

Lois went in first, followed by Bob and Midge. She just stood there, gawking like a tourist at the rugs, the leather, the damask drapes, the lace tablecloths, the prints and paintings on the wall, the crystal decanters of whisky on the tigers-eye antique sideboard, the carved marble fireplace mantel, the reading shelf with books bound in leather and their titles in gilt. 'It's lovely!' were the only words she could find to say.

'Now I'll show you the bedroom,' Mrs Loveday walked across the wide sitting room to another closed door.

'I thought this *was* the bedroom,' Lois laughed. 'I thought that sofa converted into a bed.' She glanced at the others, embarrassed.

'No,' Mrs Loveday smiled, 'this is just the salon. The bed is in here.'

And indeed it was. An enormous almost king-size poster bed covered in shimmering blue silk. The canopy over it was in cream silk with tassels and fringes of the same blue. The bed sat up on a platform of carved and polished dark wood and there were two steps, on either side, that had to be used to climb into it.

'Now out here,' Mrs Loveday went to one of the windows and pulled back the blue velvet drapes and then the sheer white lace curtains, 'you have the side view of the grounds.' They all looked out. Lois recognized the grove of trees that was on the left side of her picture. 'And because this apartment – ' She gave it the French pronunciation – 'is on the corner of the house, you also have this view.' She walked to the other wall and pulled back the window dressings. Again they looked out.

'It's the back of the house,' Lois said. 'I often wondered what it looked like. I didn't think there would be a pond, though.'

'It's not a pond,' Mrs Loveday said. 'It's part of the lake. There is a lake two miles over in that direction and when the house was built they channelled the waters to fill in a deep ravine. Like most places in Scotland,' she laughed, 'you have a flat space for a while, then you either have a high place or a low place. This house was built on the edge of a ravine. The lake waters did an excellent job of backyard landscaping.'

'Would that have been the Earl of Corra, Roger Grenville, who built the house?' asked Lois.

'You've done your homework about this area, I see.'

'Not really about the area, just about this house. You see, I have an antique engraving of it. I got it in New York.'

'I gave it to her,' Midge said. 'Bought it at an auction in New Jersey.'

'New Jersey?' Mrs Loveday wrinkled up her nose as if Midge had just said 'toilet bowl'.

'I have it in the car,' Lois continued. 'I'll bring it in when Malcolm gets back.'

'Please do,' Mrs Loveday said. 'There have been many artistic renderings of this old house. I'd enjoy seeing yours.' She let the curtains fall back across the window. 'Your bath is in there,' she motioned to another closed door. 'There's toothpaste and shampoo and a hair dryer. The towels are on a heated rack. It's a great comfort on a cold Scottish morning.' She started out of the room. 'Now, miss, if you'll come this way, I'll show you your room.'

All three went with her. Midge's room was directly across the corridor from theirs. When Mrs Loveday opened the door they saw that, while it was smaller and set up for just one person, it was as elegantly and luxuriously furnished as their suite. 'Whoever does your decoration,' Midge said, 'does one helluva job!'

'Thank you.' Mrs Loveday smiled at the compliment. 'I'm the decorator. Of course, so many of the lovely items in the suites have been here for generations. I didn't buy them, just cleaned them up a bit and moved them around. It's not that difficult to make rooms look nice when you have such superb objects to work with.'

'All the rooms are done this way?' Lois was very impressed.

'Oh, yes, all of them. Most of the house, too. You'll see when you come down to lunch. Which reminds me,' she said, and started for the door. 'I'd better look in on cook. She doesn't know there'll be three extra guests. You will excuse me?' She went out of the room and her footsteps down the corridor were muffled by the long single piece oriental carpet.

Midge threw herself onto the large silk-covered bed. 'Now this,' she laughed, 'I could get used to!'

* * *

Lois surprised herself by just sitting in the elaborate salon of their suite and staring at the ceiling. 'It feels so *good* here,' she told Bob. 'I mean, just look at this room! It could be on the cover of *Palace Beautiful* or some such magazine. I've never lived in a place like this and yet it feels *right*. It feels like *home*.'

Bob sat beside her on the brocaded sofa. 'I've been to West Virginia, I've seen your home. And this ain't nothing like it.'

She reached out and took his hand. 'No, God no. Not West Virginia home but *home*. Does that make sense to you?'

'No, but then nothing connected with this house makes sense to me. It hasn't from the very beginning. Maybe,' he suggested, 'you had a past life here. Maybe you are remembering how the house felt when you were Lady Whatever-her-name-was.'

'Now you know you don't believe in that stuff! No, it's not that. It's a feeling of *belonging*.' She gazed around the room, contentedly. 'I can't explain it.'

'Don't try.' He squeezed her hand. 'Just enjoy.'

She had her eyes closed. 'Speaking of enjoying, how much is this place costing us? I would enjoy it a lot more if I knew we didn't have to hock our cars to pay the bill.'

He shrugged. 'I don't know. Mrs Loveday didn't say and I didn't ask. Can't be too much, though, two-hundred, two-hundred-fifty dollars a night. We can afford that.'

She smiled, her eyes still closed. 'I'm glad I married a man as impractical as you.'

There was a knock at the door. When Bob opened it an elderly man with white hair stood there, the bags from the Waverley Hotel in Dumfries at his feet. 'I've brought up your luggage,' he said. He turned and walked away, down the carpeted corridor.

Bob took the bags into the bedroom and while Lois unpacked and hung things up, he took a nip from the Scotch in the cut-glass decanter and stared out the back window. 'Can you imagine? They had a ravine, so they brought in a lake! Think of the work involved. Digging that channel, making sure it didn't flood, lining the banks. You know, every time I see an old building I can't help but admire the workers and the engineers who did it all. No scientific instruments, no gasoline engines, no hydraulic lifts. Just horses, wagons, shovels, and an amazing amount of muscle power. Try getting a contractor in the States to put up even a garage without all that expensive equipment and see what howling he does. Or see what a mess he makes of it, if he does build it.'

'So you feel it too?'

'Feel what?'

'The sense of accomplishment here, the sense of stability and survival and continuation. I think *that's* what I mean when I said I feel at "home". My folks were like that and so were the neighbours around us when I was growing up. They got out of bed in the morning and they had jobs and they knew what they had to do and they went and did them. Not like today. Not with the welfare cheques and the unemployment benefits and the free food centres. I think that's what I feel about this place. I think that's what I miss. It's the atmosphere here, not the plushness, that makes me feel at "home". She looked at him. He was watching her. 'You understand what I mean, don't you?'

He came to her and held her in his arms. 'Yes, my darling,' he said. 'I understand and I love you for it.'

She could feel the roughness of his cheek against hers. 'We're together,' she whispered in his ear.

'Yes,' he replied softly, 'and it'll always be that way.'

There was another knock at the door. When Bob opened it Mrs Loveday said: 'Luncheon will be served in five minutes. Please come down for it. You'll tell Miss Morrison as well, won't you?' Then she smiled, turned, and was gone.

The double wooden doors at the foot of the staircase were open and as the Americans entered the dining room, all three caught their breath. The room was enormous, high ceilings and more crystal chandeliers, carpets, a roaring fire in a massive fireplace at the end of the room and a huge polished mahogany table stretched out with enough seating space for about twenty people. It was the sheer size of the room which

259

made them gasp, for it took in the entire wing of the house. There were four windows on each wing and this room had all four of them to itself.

Lois glanced at the first window, the one nearest the wall. It was covered like the others in thick purple drapes. No daylight managed to get through. That's the window, she said to herself, that's the window in the picture. So the little man came into the dining room. Interesting. Then where did he go? Out into the lobby? Up the stairs to the second floor? Or down the hallway, in the other direction, away from the dining room and to wherever that way leads?

Only the near end of the table was set for lunch and two men who were already seated rose when they came into the room. Mrs Loveday made the introductions. 'These are the Brunos, Lois and Bob,' she said, 'and this is Midge Morrison.' The men smiled and nodded. 'This gentleman is Mr Frank Cornell – ' The white-haired man reached out and shook Bob's hand.

'You brought us up our luggage,' Bob said. 'Thank you again for it.'

'And this is Mr Jason Stockler.' He was much younger than Mr Cornell and quite handsome. He shook Bob's hand, then smiled at Lois and Midge. 'Pleased to meet you.'

'And you,' Lois said, thinking to herself, God, what a good-looking man!

Midge, of course, was all smiles at him.

'There are so few of us for lunch,' Mrs Loveday said, 'I thought we'd all sit close together. Makes this big old room less imposing.'

Bob sat across from Mr Cornell and Lois was across from the attractive Mr Stockler. She figured he was in his late thirties or early forties. He could easily have been a movie star: a cross between Robert Redford and all those men who had played James Bond. Midge sat on the other side of Bob, facing Mrs Loveday.

'Are you planning on staying long?' Mr Cornell asked Bob.

'I don't know,' he replied. 'Frankly, we didn't even know we'd be here today.'

'It's a lovely part of Scotland, this,' the white-haired man said.

'I agree,' Bob answered. 'We've found most of Scotland to be wonderful.'

'And you, Mrs Bruno,' Mr Cornell continued, 'do you like Scotland?'

'Oh yes! In fact,' she grinned, 'sometimes I get a little too enthusiastic about it and then Bob has to calm me down. It really is fantastic. My grandparents and my folks used to tell me about it when I was a little girl, but no amount of words can prepare you for it when you finally see it in person.'

'Your ancestry is Scottish?' This from Mr Stockler. His deep green eyes under his shock of flaming red hair sparkled as if a theatrical spotlight had suddenly been turned on them.

She blushed, not from the question, but from the pinpoints of emotion she felt as she looked at him. 'Yes,' she managed to reply, 'both sets of grandparents came from Scotland. My mother was born over here, in a small weaving settlement in the Highlands. Thanks to modern machinery, the group doesn't exist anymore. My father was born in the United States, but his parents came from near Aberdeen.'

'So your mother and father met in the States?' Jason continued with the polite questioning.

'In West Virginia. My grandparents, on both sides, went there to work in the coal mines. Not very pretty work.'

'So that makes you a double-Scotch but with no ice,' Midge said and then laughed at her own joke.

'I guess so,' Lois said. 'We don't think about it that way in America, of course. If you're born in the States you automatically consider yourself an American. Where your parents came from is not really that important. America is such a mixture of people that after a generation nobody really stops to wonder where you came from.'

'So the child of a Chinaman born in America, would not be Chinese?' asked Mr Cornell. 'He'd be an American?'

'That's right.' Lois nodded. 'He'd be an American first and a Chinese second.'

'Strange way of perceiving things.' Mr Cornell shook his head of white hair. 'If a British couple has a baby in, let's say Calcutta, that baby is never considered an Indian. Oh, perhaps the Indian government may consider him one, but as far as the parents and even he himself is concerned, he is British. First and foremost.'

'Even up here,' Jason added, 'if a child is born in Scotland

261

to Scottish parents, he considers himself a Scotsman, never English. If he goes down to live in England, as I have done, he considers himself *British* second but Scottish first. A Scotsman will never identify himself as English.'

'Yet you, as a Scotswoman,' Mr Cornell said, 'consider yourself as an American.'

'Yes,' Lois said firmly, 'and very proud to be one, too.'

The cook came in pushing an ornate, three-tiered teak-wood cart whose wheels rode smoothly over the plush carpeting. She silently placed a large covered soup tureen in front of Mrs Loveday, then a round wicker basket of bread and rolls. She left just as quietly. Mrs Loveday ladled the soup into the bowls that had been stacked beside her and passed them around the table. They ate in silence for several minutes, enjoying the cock-a-leekie soup, which everyone agreed was quite delicious. Lois noticed that her spoon was hallmarked silver and she was sure the dishes were either Wedgwood or Spode. When she dabbed the napkin against her lips she was not surprised to discover it was pure linen.

'Are your ancestors from Scotland, sir?' Mr Cornell asked.

'No,' Bob said, taking the last spoonful of his soup. 'from Italy. Down near Sicily. We're Sicilianos. Lois grew up on mutton and potatoes, I grew up on chicken and pasta. That's American for you.' He pushed his empty bowl slightly away. 'Two kids from the opposite side of the tracks, they meet, they fall in love, they get married.'

'The classic Hollywood theme,' Jason laughed.

'And children?' Mr Cornell asked. 'Have you any children?'

Bob glanced quickly at Lois beside him. She spoke first. 'We had a son,' she said in a firm voice, 'but he is no longer with us.'

'Oh?' Jason raised an eyebrow.

'No,' she continued in the same even voice, 'he was kidnapped last year. In September. He was only six years old.'

Mrs Loveday put one hand to her ample chest. 'Oh my dear, I'm so sorry for you!'

Both men muttered their regrets.

'It was quite a shock for us,' Bob took over from his wife, 'he was our only child and we are still having a terrible time reconciling ourselves to what has happened.' They were all staring at Lois, who kept her gaze on her empty soup bowl. 'But life must continue, we both understand that, so we've jumped back into the world of the living. This trip over here, for example, is one way we chose to get the shock out of our systems.'

'I started it all,' Midge said, 'I came across an old engraving of this house at an auction and I got it for practically nothing and because I didn't want it, I let Bob and Lois have it and that gave them the idea to find the place and visit it personally. I thought that while it was rather expensive, it sure was great therapy.'

Lois raised her eyes, examining the faces of the three strangers that sat across the table from her. Who were these 'friendly' characters? What did they know about Tony? Did they know where he was?

The next course was a huge slice of beef and kidney pie, hot and steaming in its mouth-melting crust. With it was served creamy mashed potatoes and richly buttered brussels sprouts. During this part of the meal, the conversation – all of it deliberate small talk – was about the U.S. president, about a photo that had appeared in the newspapers of Princess Diana in a rather daring gown and the merits of British soccer versus American football. Tony was not mentioned again.

Then came a soft cake and custard pudding piled into a high glass. Midge laughed when they told her it was called 'a trifle'. This was accompanied by large cups of black coffee. 'American style,' Mrs Loveday said happily, 'in your honour.'

It was all they could do to push themselves away from the table. Mrs Loveday remained in command. 'Jason, why don't you show our guests around the grounds? Give them some fresh air after this special luncheon.'

'Would you like that?' he asked all of them, but he was looking at Lois.

'Yes,' she said, 'that would be lovely. I'm dying to see what the rest of the house looks like.'

'If you don't mind,' Midge said, 'count me out. I'm kind of pooped. My stomach isn't accustomed to lunches like that. It was delicious, though. Gotta admit that.'

'And me,' Bob said, 'I thought I'd stay inside and maybe have a cognac. Would you care to join me, Mr Cornell?'

'Delighted,' replied the older man. 'A capital idea. Do you

play chess, Mr Bruno?' Bob shook his head. 'Pity. I like the game. Keeps you awake while your insides digest.'

'I guess that leaves just us,' Lois said to Jason. He gave her a dazzling smile.

They walked through the entrance hall and Lois marvelled, again, at how beautifully and richly it was furnished.

'Most of these things have been here for years,' Jason said. 'I used to play here when I was very young. Then my mother moved down to York and that's where I spent most of my childhood. I live in London now.'

Lois was about to ask him if his parents were related to the family who gave all those parties, the one Miss Partridge remembered, but she didn't. How could she believe anything that old woman had told her? Didn't she say this house had been destroyed? Burnt down years ago. She wondered if she should ask Jason about that, then decided to wait and see what information was forthcoming from him first.

Jason pointed to several banners hanging from the ceiling just at the entrance to the left wing of the first floor. 'Those flags up there were here when I was a child. I remember being fascinated by their colours.'

'Well, that one there, I can identify,' Lois laughed. 'that's the Stars and Stripes, but it looks like it only has forty eight stars. We've got two more stars now. That one there is French,' she said, 'and that, of course, is the British Union Jack. Now that one I'm not sure about.'

'It stumped me for a long time too,' Jason said. 'It's Tunisia, from the 1920s. Know what that one is?' He pointed to the last one. She shook her head. 'Italy. That's Mussolini's fascist flag. And that one, on the other end is the German Republic. Pre-Hitler.'

'What a strange collection to be hanging in a Scottish manor house. Whose idea was it?'

'They've always been there,' was his only comment. 'Look in here.' He opened a door on the right side of the corridor – the left was completely taken up with the four huge windows – and she peered into a room that was lined with books. 'The library,' he said. There were more oriental rugs scattered on the floor, a leather sofa and three armchairs in a far corner. The one dominant piece of furniture was a mahogany desk. It was at least six foot square and had a silver inkstand with a jade penholder in it. There were several photographs in silver frames.

'Lovely,' Lois said. She wished she could go in and see who were in the photographs. She'd leave it for another day. 'Is this room open to any hotel guest who wants to use it?'

She could see his reaction: she had taken him off guard. 'Ah, well, that I'm not sure of. I think it's rather a private place but,' he said, squirming off the hook of her question, 'I'm sure if you'd enquire of Mrs Loveday, she'd tell you.'

'You don't use the library when you stay here?'

'Oh no.' He shut the door quickly, then tried a laugh. 'When I come up here from London, the last thing I want to do is relax with a book. I see enough of them at my office.'

'What do you do? If you don't mind my asking.'

'I'm sorry, I didn't really introduce myself, did I? I'm a literary agent. Actually more of a literary executor than agent. The firm I'm with started out with new authors, living authors, but now most of the business seems to be taken up with the sale and management of authors who are dead.'

She smiled. 'How many best sellers can a dead author write?'

'It's not that, it's handling the royalties and the screen rights and foreign language translations for authors' families, their estates, if you will.'

'There's money to be made in that?'

'Oh yes, some books keep on selling for years after the death of the author. Often the original publishers don't want to be bothered with a dead writer, and the wife or children or even grandchildren will come to us and ask us to get the rights away, and sell the work to another. It works out very well, most of the time.' He grinned. 'One of the *real* advantages is that I don't have to deal with the temperamental artists themselves.'

'I'm impressed,' she said, 'but your company must spend a fortune in legal fees.'

'Not really. I'm a lawyer as well. My degree is from Oxford.'

'Now I *am* impressed,' she said. 'I've never met anyone with a degree from Oxford.'

'Do you want to shake hands again?' He smiled, reached out and took her willing hand in his. 'Pleased to meet you, I'm from Oxford.'

'Same here. I'm from New York.'

'Is that bigger than Oxford?' he asked in mock-seriousness.

'Yes, but in America bigger does not mean better.'

She linked her arm in his as they continued down the hallway. There was another door that led to a music room, complete with curtained stage, a piano and a concert-size harp. Another door, at the end of the corridor, was locked. 'What's in there?' she asked.

He shrugged. 'Don't know. I've never been able to get in there.'

'Some secret torture chamber?' she laughed.

'I doubt that. If they had one I should think it'd be in the cellar.'

'Maybe a room where the crazy first wife is kept locked up, away from view, like in *Jane Eyre*.'

'I doubt that too. That would almost have been in the tower. But there isn't a tower.'

'Look, I just noticed something. This door is painted black. All the others are an off-white. Come on,' she grinned, 'what evil lurks behind this sinister and forbidding door?'

'I have no idea. For all I know it could be the junk room, where everything they don't want is tossed inside and the door kept locked.'

'Interesting though,' she said. 'I like mysteries.'

'Somehow a pile of junk is not all that mysterious,' he said, 'not to me.'

'That's because you've got a lawyer's mind,' she laughed, 'you guys look at everything in black and white. We creative types see little mysteries everywhere.'

'Good heavens, what a woman! My condolences to your husband!'

'Now that I'll agree with you!' she said. 'And mine to your wife.'

'I'm not married,' he said simply.

'Oh?' She felt the blood rush to her face. 'Have I just made a fool of myself or what?'

'Or what.' He pressed her arm, still in his, a little tighter. 'Now I want to show you something else,' he said. 'This was always my favourite thing in the house when I was a child.' He walked to the end of the corridor and stood in front of the wall that went from the bank of windows to the far side of the corridor. The wall looked like all the other walls on the first floor except that in the centre of this one there was a radiant sun, about six inches round with stylized arms curving out in all directions from it. It looked as if it was made of plaster and painted the same colour as the wall. 'Watch,' he said. He pressed the very tip of the ray that went north, then quickly the one that went east. He did the same thing to the end of the ray that went south and finally to the one that pointed west. Immediately there was a rumbling and clanking sound and the entire panel slipped sideways to the right and into the wall. Suddenly Lois was standing at the edge of a five-foot drop. She could see the grass and trees outside. She stepped back from the opening.

'Wonderful, isn't it?' he was pleased with himself. 'A secret doorway, just like in those old horror films of the 1940s. When my mother first showed me this, I must have made it go back and forth twenty times. Finally, I got a whack on my bottom and I stopped doing it, but I've always loved this gadget.'

'The Victorians were amazing,' Lois agreed. 'The things they came up with.'

'The Victorians had nothing to do with this,' he said. 'It wasn't installed until 1935. Very clever, don't you think?' He pressed a small plaster rosette on the wall and the door slid back into place. 'Even from outside you can't see where it joins the solid wall. I'll show you when we get around there.'

They walked back the way they had come and Jason opened the front door. They stepped out into the crisp afternoon air. Lois stood on the marble terrace just outside the door and her eyes swept across the huge front lawn. It was exactly as in her engraving, except now she was seeing it from the opposite angle.

'It needs mowing,' he said. 'Difficult to do in wet weather like they've been having.'

She looked to her left. Their rental car was parked there, where Malcolm had left it when he brought the luggage. Her gaze shifted to the right and the grove of dense trees. 'It's exactly like my engraving of this place,' she told Jason, 'everything looks the same as it did back then except that those trees over there have grown taller and are much more dense.'

He took her arm again and they started walking along the

front of the house, to the right. 'Nobody ever goes in there,' he said. 'They just let it get wild. Keeps out the neighbours, I would imagine.'

Lois wanted to say that she knew someone who went in there, a small, round man with a cloak and a floppy hat and he was carrying a child. 'Looks spooky,' was all she said aloud.

They came to the corner of the house and turned right again, walking along the side wall. He asked her if she was cold and she shook her head. When they came to the section where the secret door was, he pointed out that not even a seam could be seen from the outside. The stone used in building the walls masked the slightest hint of the sliding door. They continued along the side of the house and came to the corner and their first view of the water.

'Did they really channel this in from another lake? Was there really a ravine back here?' She shivered. A wind was ruffling the surface of the water, making tiny white caps.

He nodded. 'A couple of hundred years ago, I think it was,' he replied. 'They needed to fill up the ravine and they needed water for the house, so it was a practical application of man and nature. Then, too, don't forget, in those days the Scots were always fighting someone. If it wasn't with the English it was among themselves. By flooding this area with water they effectively prevented any enemy surprising them by sneaking in from the rear. Clever huh?'

She shivered and got closer to him. 'Certainly added to the value of the property. In the States we dig a swimming pool in the backyard and think we've done something wonderful.'

'I don't think you want to go swimming in this pool,' he replied. 'There's about a seventy-five-metre drop-off right at the very edge. It gets deeper the farther out you get.'

She shivered again. 'The rest of the grounds are pretty clean,' she said. 'I thought there would be barns, a walled garden and caretakers' cottages and all that. There's only that round thing there. What is it?'

'A well,' he said simply.

'For water? I thought you said they got their water from the lake.'

'They do. That well's no good. All dried up. They never use it anymore.'

'Interesting,' she said and stared again at the only structure

268

visible from the back of the house. 'You'd think there'd be more things out here like picnic tables, a patio, maybe a barbecue pit or a gazebo. You'd think the hotel would put those things in for their guests.' She watched the expression on his face.

'Nobody ever goes out here, I suppose. Anyway,' he changed the subject, 'I don't know what we are doing out here either. Let's get back inside. You're starting to turn blue.' He took off his jacket and placed it around her shoulders. 'Of course, blue is my favourite colour.'

Back in the suite, Lois expected Bob to be there. He wasn't. She looked out of both the side window and the rear window, saw the trees and the lake, but no sign of him. She went across the hallway and knocked on Midge's door. When the woman opened it, Lois said: 'I've lost my husband.'

'No you haven't, he's in here. We've been talking. Come on in. How was your guided tour with Mr Wonderful?'

'Interesting,' she replied.

'The estate or the guide?' Midge asked mischievously.

'If Bob wasn't sitting here, I'd give you a different answer. But since he is, only the estate.'

'He is a good-looking devil,' Bob admitted. 'I'll bet he keeps his wife waiting nervously at home.'

'He isn't married.' And as she said it she realized she was starting to blush again.

'Oh?' Bob came over to her and grabbed her wrists. 'Quick Midge, I must protect my property! Where's the lock and chains?'

'I've got 'em,' Midge retorted, 'but you can't have them yet. I'm saving them to hogtie Jason and drag him into my lair. You can have them after I'm finished. Or,' she laughed, 'after he's finished.'

Bob shook his head. 'I'm surrounded by horny women! Is there anything worse?'

'Some men would be overjoyed by the prospect,' Lois said and linked her arm in his. 'Anyway, you've still got me. I'm not trading you for any wealthy literary agent lawyer who looks like he should be modelling for Calvin Klein.'

'Aha!' Bob replied. 'So you did notice!'

'Little difficult not to, Bob darlin',' Midge said. 'I mean, I'd have that guy's babies any day. Or, if not babies, I'd certainly enjoy the process of trying to make a few.'

Bob made a face at her, then he smiled. 'If I may change the subject for a minute, from sex to architecture. Lois, what do you think of this place?'

'Incredible,' she replied. 'I've never been in a house as large and as magnificent as this. And it feels so good. I can't keep that thought from my mind, how good it *feels*. Staying here just might even be worth all the crap we went through to get here.'

'Even the lady on the train who tried to steal the picture?' he asked.

'Yes, and even all those rude people who kept telling us the house didn't exist. I don't blame them. If I had a treasure like this in my home town I don't think I'd want strangers poking around in it. Especially awful American tourists. We're the worst, you know.'

'And . . .' He paused, took a deep breath, then continued . . . 'and Tony? Even thinking you saw Tony? Is this place worth even that?'

'I'm sorry about that,' she said softly, 'you know I am. My imagination was working overtime. My nerves were frayed.' She kissed him lightly and he pulled her closer to him. She felt his warmth next to her and she thought: I'm not going to screw this up. I'm not going to tell you or Midge that I think my baby boy is still alive. If he's here, I'll find him. I haven't seen him outside the house, nor in the rooms I've already inspected. But if they've got him here, I'll get to him. I won't go away without him.

*   *   *

'Should I dress up?'

Lois looked at him. 'Well, it is the evening meal. In a place like this I imagine they expect gentlemen to wear jackets and ties. Wear your blue blazer and that tartan tie you bought in Edinburgh.'

'I'm not going to wear that tartan here,' he said. 'I'm not Scottish. I don't have a clan tartan. I'm Italian.'

'Then wear a couple strands of spaghetti around your neck and fasten them with a meatball.'

'Very clever,' he said.

'I thought so.' She was wearing a deep green knit dress with a matching long-sleeve jacket. It had simple lines and had cost her a bundle at Saks Fifth Avenue. She liked wearing green. It showed off her red hair, which was combed straight tonight and almost touching her shoulders. She put on classic pearl earrings and a matching double stranded pearl necklace. The pearls weren't real, but she'd paid enough for them to fool anyone but an expert. Her shoes were smooth, unadorned dark brown leather. 'How do I look?' she asked.

He gave her the once over and then a low whistle. 'Do you want to lie down on the bed and talk about it?'

She turned back to the dressing table mirror, giving her hair a few more quick strokes with the brush. She watched her reflection. Interesting, she told the attractive woman looking back at her, that's the first time since we've been to Scotland that Bob has mentioned, even jokingly, having sex. Granted, I've been bananas ever since we got here and nobody wants to screw a crazy lady, but even in New York we hadn't been getting it on. She brushed a little faster. When was the last time? Have we made love in the past month? Probably not. I had my period a couple of days before we flew over here and it ended the last day we were in Edinburgh. Thank God I don't bleed gallons and have those terrible cramps like some women do. Maybe I'll make it up to him tonight. After dinner. I'll bet it's fun having sex in that big four poster bed.

'Can I take a rain check until tonight?' she asked.

He grinned, came over to her, pushed aside her smooth red hair and kissed her on the back of her neck. 'Do I take that as being a "yes"?' she said smiling at the handsome young couple in the mirror.

The dining room already held several people when the Brunos and Midge made their entrance. Mrs Loveday hurried over to meet them. 'Goodness, don't you look lovely?' she said. 'Such a becoming colour and with that red hair! . . . Everybody! Everybody!' She clapped her hands briskly and the conversations that had been going on ceased. There were seven others in the room, five men and two women. They had been standing, with drinks in their hands, and talking in small groups. Now they turned their attention on the newcomers. 'Friends and fellow guests,' Mrs Loveday said in a formal voice, 'I'd like you to meet Mr and Mrs Robert Bruno and their friend Miss Midge Morrison. They are from

America.' There was a murmur and everyone smiled. 'Mrs Bruno's first name is Lois. Now, over here – ' She took Lois' elbow, steering her to three men. Lois failed to notice that she wasn't bringing Bob or Midge with them. 'This is Dr Edward Fulham.' A short man with receding grey hair smiled and took her hand. 'And this is Signor Carlo Luchessi. He's from Italy,' she explained. 'And this gentleman is Mr Manar Halmfazzi, from Tunisia.'

'Syria,' he corrected her.

'Well, you were born in Tunisia,' she said. He nodded and smiled and put Lois' hand in his large copper one. 'Over here – ' Mrs Loveday kept Lois moving to the next group. 'We have Madame Marie-Anne Dupré, this lady is Frau Helga Baumgartner and this gentleman is Mr Andrew Mountolive.' Lois shook all their hands and said how pleased she was to meet them. 'And here is Malcolm. You already know him.'

'Malcolm! What a pleasant surprise. How nice to see you again!'

'Evening, mum,' Malcolm smiled.

Lois looked around the room. 'Is Fiona with you?'

'No, I haven't seen her today. She's probably busy at the hotel. 'I think she's angry with me.'

'She'll get over it,' Lois flashed him a warm smile, 'staying angry is about the only weapon we women have.' She turned to the others. 'You're going to have to excuse me if I don't remember all your names. I'm terrible with names!'

'Don't worry about it,' Madame Dupré said in a broad French accent, 'here we like to think of ourselves as one big family.'

'An international family,' Lois said. 'I feel like I'm at a cocktail party at the UN building. Are you all guests here?'

'Most of the time. We do some travelling, but we keep coming back. We like it here.'

Lois nodded. 'I can see why.'

'And you.' The man identified as Mr Mountolive asked in an accent that was a mixture of old school English and something else. 'Are you enjoying your stay here at Thelema? Terribly impressive house, don't you agree?'

'I do indeed. I was just saying to my husband before we came down for dinner – ' She looked around for Bob and saw he was several feet away from her, alone, watching her. 'I said to him how happy this house made me *feel*. I really couldn't put my finger on what it was.' She looked at him again, hoping he would join in the conversation. He didn't. 'I'm a designer back in New York,' she struggled to explain, 'and I just love being with beautiful things.' She smiled at them again as she realized every eye was on her. 'And being with charming people like yourselves, as well.'

At that they all beamed.

'Have you been to Italy?' Signor Luchessi asked. His string tie bobbed over his thin neck and very apparent Adam's apple. His shoulders were thin but his belly was fat and Lois could only think of him as pear shaped. 'Italy has some beautiful houses, also.'

Lois shook her head. 'I'm afraid I've not been. Bob and I have talked about it, of course. He's Italian, you know.' Signor Luchessi bowed slightly in Bob's direction. 'I mean, his family come from Italy. He was born in the United States.'

'And your family?' Mr Halmfazzi, from Tunisia but now from Syria and wearing a dark loosely fitted suit, asked.

'From Scotland,' she said with pleasure. 'Both sets of grandparents. My mother was born over here and went to the States when she was quite young and my father was born over here.' She laughed. 'I mean, over *there*. I was born in the State of West Virginia. Have you ever heard of it?'

They all said, yes, they knew about it.

At that moment Jason came into the room. He walked straight over to Lois, picked up her right hand and kissed the back of it. 'Hello again,' he said.

Lois shot a quick glance at Bob. 'Hello. Thanks again for the guided tour.'

'Anytime. What would you like to see next?'

'I think,' Mrs Loveday interrupted, 'that she would like to see some dinner on the table, and so would I. Why don't we be seated and I'll ring for cook and tell her we're all here.'

They went to the large polished table which was now completely covered with an enormous white linen cloth. Even though the table was several feet long, there was so much material in the cloth that it almost touched the floor at both ends and both sides. Lois wondered who had to iron it. The fine chinaware was in white with borders of thick gold braid. There was a gold letter 'T' in the centre of each

273

piece. Underneath each soup bowl and saucer, there was a large plate, made of metal and plated in gold. The hall-marked silver was there again, two knives, two forks, two spoons, all with the letter 'T' on their handles. There were three crystal goblets at the head of each setting: one for white wine, one for red wine and one for water. Each was also engraved with 'T'.

'It's for "Thelema",' Jason said as if reading her mind. As at lunch, he was directly across from her. Everyone sat down and the cook came immediately into the room with the soup tureen and three large silver woven baskets of bread and rolls.

As Lois looked around the table, watching the others spoon their soup, she noticed that one place setting remained empty, untouched.

Again Jason read her mind. 'That's the fourteenth setting,' he said. 'There are thirteen of us tonight and thirteen is not a lucky number, so one more was laid. You'll find this is a rather superstitious bunch.'

'It's also tradition,' added the white-haired Mr Cornell, who was seated to her right. 'It's put there in honour of the founder of the hotel.'

Lois looked at him. 'Oh?'

'He was a noble,' Signor Luchessi said from the other side of the table. 'You know how the British are about nobility!'

Before she could ask the noble's name, Midge said, rather loudly, 'God! Do you people always eat this way?' She had just seen the cook bringing in the rack of lamb. 'I thought lunch was something to write home about, but this spread is incredible. Lois, hon, I'm going to have to take out the seams of every one of my dresses when I get back to New York.'

'I may have to let mine out before we leave,' Lois laughed, 'but then it's not a bad way to go. I could adapt to this lifestyle very easily.'

Jason, about to take some lamb from the serving tray the cook was holding, raised his eyes to hers. 'Do you mean that?'

'What?' she asked. 'Do I mean what?'

'About adapting to this lifestyle, to this place.'

'Yes, a good question,' Madame Dupré's accented voice came quickly. 'You think perhaps, you could live here?'

Lois grinned and prepared to take a slice of the meat. 'Sure I *could*, but there are a lot of ifs involved.'

'Ifs?' Mr Halmfazzi looked at the others. 'What "ifs"?'

'Well,' Lois said, 'I could live here very nicely *if* I didn't have a job in New York and *if* my husband wasn't the manager of his father's company in the States and *if* I didn't have any bills to worry about. There's a lot of *ifs* in that statement. Sure,' she said, smiling around the table, 'it's wonderful here but even talking about living here is only dreaming out loud. You can't pay for rice and beans at the supermarket with dreams.'

There was a silence, then Jason said softly, looking at her, 'Suppose it was all arranged?'

'Suppose what was arranged?' she smiled.

'Everything.' He returned the smile.

'Yes,' put in Madame Dupré, 'suppose every one of your objections were overcome?'

'Overcome?' Lois repeated.

'Yes,' Mr Mountolive with the British/Whatever accent said, 'suppose that you didn't have to worry about a career, or money or paying bills ever again. Would you live here?'

'I have a job,' she protested cheerfully, 'and so does Bob. Why, he runs his family's business. I love games like this,' she said suddenly. 'We used to do it when I was a kid. We used to sit around and imagine what we would do if we had a million dollars. It was a lot of fun. We used to invent the most outlandish things to spend it on. Buy our own aeroplane. Eat all the chocolate ice cream in town. Buy the school building and then tear it down. Get all our teachers one-way tickets to China. Take trips around the world. But, none of us ever made that million. Very few of us ever made it out of the coal fields of West Virginia.'

Mr Cornell put his hand atop hers. 'Getting out of your world *now* could be your destiny. The answer to your childhood dreams.'

'I don't think so,' Lois laughed.

'You don't believe in destiny?' Jason said, still staring at her.

She blushed and looked down at her plate. 'I suppose I do,' she replied slowly, 'but this . . . all this . . .' And her hand gestured broadly as her gaze swept the elegant room. 'All this luxury sure isn't part of my destiny. *That* I know.'

'It could be,' Jason hadn't taken his eyes from her. 'Think about it.'

* * *

Lois sat in the foyer by the warm fireplace, in a conversational grouping of leather settees and oriental rugs, talking with Madame Dupré and Frau Baumgartner while Bob and the other men, and Midge as well, had cigars and brandy in the dining room. The women talked of children (all moved away now) and husbands (both dead now) and of travel (such a chore now) and of the weather (very cold again now). Lois listened politely, added a few comments of her own, told them about her work in New York and tried to describe what it was like living in West Virginia. Both women were interested in her parents. What did they do? Were they retired? Were they in good health? Were they happy?

Finally Lois caught herself fighting a yawn. 'Goodness,' she said, 'what must the time be?' As if on cue, the tall grandfather clock in the corner struck twelve. 'I don't believe it,' she said and rose from her comfortable place on the settee. 'No wonder I'm tired. You ladies will excuse me?' They remained seated but extended their hands. She shook them. 'Suddenly I feel as if someone had pulled the plug,' she said. 'All my energy has gone down the drain.'

'We understand,' Madame Dupré replied. 'I'm sure it has been a very long day for you.'

'I'll see you in the morning, at breakfast,' Lois said.

Both women shook their heads. 'No,' Frau Baumgartner spoke quickly, 'we hardly ever take breakfast. If we do it's coffee and some toast in our rooms.'

'That's right,' the Frenchwoman confirmed. 'For us breakfast is not so important.'

Lois laughed. 'In Scotland? Where they load your plate with eggs and sausages and potatoes and sweet rolls and where the coffee cups are enormous?'

'If I ate that every morning,' the German woman said, 'then I would be just even more enormous.'

'I enjoyed meeting you.' Lois bent and gave each of them a kiss on the cheek. 'I really did. It was interesting talking with you. Good night.'

The women bid her good night. Before Lois started up the

staircase, she looked into the dining room. Bob was still there, still talking, still with a drink in one hand and a cigar in the other. Not overly surprised, she saw that Midge also had a drink and a cigar. She went up to her room. Bob hates cigars, she thought. He's really putting up a front with those old men. Yes, they were old. All of them older than she was. With the exception of Malcolm, of course. Jason was probably closer to her in age, but he was still older than she was, he had to be somewhere in his early forties. She made a mental note to figure out some sly way to find out exactly how old he was. Or maybe, she grinned to herself, by now Midge had asked him, asking him that and any number of other personal things, in her rough but well meaning way. She liked Midge. The woman was a little loud, a little vulgar, a little overweight and a little pushy, but she had been a true friend whenever she needed her. You didn't find very many like that anymore.

In the suite, she undressed, took a warm shower and sprayed her naked body with a soft gardenia scent that she knew Bob loved. He had given her a bottle of it after their first date, asking her to wear it on the next one. The next time, he silently undressed her, sniffing her warm skin for his favourite scent. Each spot where he thought he found it, he licked slowly and sensuously. When he finally entered her she had never been so aroused. It would do the trick tonight, of that she was sure.

She put on a new nightgown, a bright peach filmy thing that she had bought one summer. It was too sheer for a winter night in Scotland, but she didn't expect to have it on very long once Bob got into bed. Fortunately there was a warm fire in their bedroom. She brushed her hair and pulled it back with a matching peach ribbon. She arranged the pillows against the headboard, so she would be sitting up when he came into the room, then she turned off all the lights – the glow from the fire would be enough – and got into bed. She folded her hands in her lap and waited.

She awoke with a start. Something was not right. She realized she had fallen asleep and glanced quickly at the bed. Bob was in it, the covers pulled up almost to the tip of his nose. There was a crick in her neck, where she had slept with her head twisted sideways. She rubbed it and glanced again at Bob. So much for gardenias and romance, she thought.

Her shoulders were cold. The fire had burned down to glowing embers, giving off neither light nor heat. She had to go to the bathroom and she had to get out of that frothy peach thing and into a nice sensible warm nightgown. She slipped from the bed and walked lightly across the chilly carpets in her bare feet. Even the toilet seat was cold, so she sat on it only as long as was absolutely necessary. She wondered how people put up with cold toilet seats in byegone days and then remembered they didn't have toilets in their houses, let alone seats for them.

As she came out of the bathroom she noticed that the drapes over the window to the rear of the house were pulled open. No wonder this place was like an ice box! The drapes helped keep out the cold. Bob must have pulled them back when he came to bed. She hurried, still in her bare feet, across to the tall window and stretched both hands to grasp the material, to pull the left hand side and the right hand side together at the same time.

That was when she saw Tony.

He was standing in the lake. No, he was standing on the lake. On the water about six feet from the shore.

Her entire body went icy. Not just her feet and shoulders.

He walked slowly, looking down at the water around his toes, and taking it one step at a time.

She didn't know whether to scream, call Bob or pull the curtains shut. So she did nothing. She just stood there, arms stretched to the drapes, centred in the window like a figure crucified.

Tony reached the edge of the lake, then stepped from the surface of the water onto the grass. He looked around him and then up at her. Looked up at the window. Looked up directly into his mother's face.

Lois clutched the drapes. If she had not she would have fallen to the floor.

The child, wearing the grey trousers and the blue jacket, waved at her. His little hand went back and forth several times. His mouth opened and in the strange moonlight she saw his lips move. If she could have heard it, she would have heard 'Mommy!'

She whirled around, letting go of the drapes and ran to the bed. 'Bob!' She thought she was yelling, but her voice had almost no sound.'Bob! Wake up! It's Tony, Bob. It's Tony!'

Bob shook his head, waved one hand at her to get away, and pulled the blanket up over his face.

She yanked it down frantically. 'Wake up!' Her voice had regained a little of its strength. 'Wake up! It's our baby! Tony's outside. By the lake!' She shook him again.

He didn't open his eyes. 'Ah c'mon hon, f'Christ sake . . .'

'You're drunk!' She stepped back, disgusted. She ran back to the window again. He was still there. Still looking up at the window, still with an occasional wave.

She dashed from the bedroom and into the elegant connecting salon. She fumbled with the chain at the door. Damned thing, Bob must have hooked it. She managed to free it and opened the door. She stopped and looked at Midge's closed door. Should she call her? No. There wasn't time to stop and wake Midge up and she would want to know what was the matter and then she would have to get dressed and . . . all of this raced through her mind in a flash of an instant, so she turned and ran down the carpeted hallway. There were the stairs, dark now and curving into the blackness of the ground floor. She almost flew down them. Her bare feet touched the cold green marble of the foyer, then warmed slightly as she hurried across the oriental carpets to the front door. She grabbed the knob and yanked. It didn't budge. She twisted the knob. It still didn't open. 'Damn!' she said aloud and then wondered why the door handle was undulating. She realized it was because she was looking at it through her tears. She had started to cry and hadn't noticed.

She stared blindly around the darkened foyer. Where was the key to the front door? Which room did Mrs Loveday sleep in? She would have the key. Then she remembered.

She turned and ran down the corridor, away from the hallway and dining room. She passed the library and the music room and the room with the dark-painted door.

The sun was there, sculpted with its symbolic rays spreading flat against the end wall of the corridor. Quickly she pressed the tips. North. East. South. West. The clanking began, the whirring of hidden machinery and the panel slid sideways into the wall.

A blast of cold early-morning air hit her suddenly and she gasped in surprise. There was almost a five-foot drop from the level of the hall to the ground. She had remembered that.

She gathered her flimsy nightdress around her hips and jumped out into the blackness. She felt her feet hit the grass, then she slipped, tipped to one side and fell on her back. She pushed with the palms of her hands, righted herself and started to run along the side of the house. Its shadow put that stretch of lawn in complete blackness.

She came to the edge of the house and ran down across the wide lawn, down through the ice cold grass, down toward the edge of the water where her little boy stood waiting for her.

'Tony!' she yelled.

'Mommy!' The child started toward her, running on his short little legs to meet her. He slipped, got up, mud and grass clung to his fingers, and kept running in her direction.

She could feel the pressure building up in her lungs, feel the catch in her side from the running, feel the cold against the soles of her feet, against her back and shoulders.

Then suddenly they met. She held out her arms and he hurried into them.

'Mommy!' he sobbed.

'Oh, Tony! Oh, my God, my baby! My baby!'

He clung to her, little hands around her neck, making crying noises that came from deep within himself.

She hugged him, felt his hot tears on her face, felt his chilly hands on her body. She could feel his heart, beating rapidly like a frightened animal's, against her breast. 'Oh my God!' She was crying so that she could hardly form the words. 'Mommy's found you, darling. Your mommy's here. Oh thank you Jesus, Mommy's here!'

CHAPTER TWENTY

It was Mr Mountolive who found her. He was up at dawn, as usual, for his 'morning constitutional'. Hadn't missed a morning walk in thirty-five years. He had been pacing briskly across the lawn, watching the steam rise in vanishing spirals from the surface of the lake, when he saw the mound of peach-coloured cloth on the grass. He broke the cadence

of his measured footsteps and hurried to her. When he saw
who it was and realized he didn't have the strength to lift
her himself, he ran back into the house and summoned
Mr Cornell. Together they managed to get her off the frosty
ground and up the stairs into her suite. Bob was still groggy
from the previous night's booze.

By the time they had put her in bed, Mrs Loveday had
heard the commotion and was in the room. So was Midge.

'She must have been out there all night,' Mrs Loveday said,
fussing over Lois, washing her hands and feet clean of dirt and
grass stains and sponging her tear-streaked face with warm
water. 'She'd better get out of this thing, too.' She started
removing the filmy peach nightdress from around Lois'
unconscious body. Midge gave her a hand and the men looked
discreetly away. They found a warmer nightdress hanging
on a peg behind the bathroom door and the two women
slipped it over Lois' head as if they were dressing a doll.

'What time did you hear her go out?' Mr Cornell shouted
at Bob.

Bob shook his head, still not quite certain what was
happening.

'He asked you, you ass,' Mrs Loveday screamed in his face,
'what time she went out there?'

Bob muttered something about Lois being asleep when he
came to bed.

'You're worthless!' Mrs Loveday yelled at him. 'Worthless!'

'Now wait a Goddamned minute,' Midge said angrily.

Mrs Loveday whirled around. 'You stay out of this! You're
not here to meddle, you know.'

'I just don't think that Bob should . . .'

'And you're not here to *think* either!' Mrs Loveday shot
back. 'Your part's done, so just stay out.'

'I doubt if raising our voices is going to solve anything,'
Mr Mountolive said mildly. 'The important thing is that this
woman doesn't catch pneumonia or whatever and die on us.
Not after all the care we've taken. We can't afford to have
her die on us.'

'What was she doing out there?' Mr Cornell looked at
Lois, unconscious, her head on a pillow, her red hair fanned
out around her face like those pictures of Esther Williams
descending into her swimming pool. He frowned at Bob.
'You were supposed to be watching her.'

'I was asleep. Hell, it's not my fault that you guys gave me too much to drink last night.' He looked at his wife, so innocent and vulnerable. 'Maybe she was sleepwalking.'

'Have you ever known her to sleepwalk before?' Mr Mountolive asked.

'No,' Bob admitted, 'never.'

'Humph!' Mrs Loveday snorted. 'She wasn't drunk, this I know for a fact. Both Anne-Marie and Helga told me so before they went home last night. They said she only had two Scotches.'

'Maybe she just decided to go for a walk,' Midge suggested. 'You know, in the moonlight and all that.'

'A walk?' Mr Cornell raised his white eyebrows. 'In the cold and wearing only that flimsy thing and no shoes? Hardly.'

'It was an idea,' Midge said.

'And I told you – ' Mrs Loveday came closer to Midge and spoke almost without moving her lips – 'that you were not supposed to *think*. So stay out of things!'

Mr Cornell raised his hand like a policeman directing traffic. 'Ladies, please, all this bickering isn't going to solve anything. We must decide what we're going to do. Obviously, Lois has to be watched. Someone must stay here and keep an eye on her and then find out exactly what she was doing down by the lake. We must sit by the bedside and when she awakens interrogate her. In a pleasant manner, of course.'

'I'll do it,' Bob volunteered. 'After all, I am her husband.'

'You can't be trusted to do *anything*,' Mrs Loveday said icily. 'You can't be counted on to do a simple thing like keep your own wife in bed.'

'I told you, I had too much to drink.'

'And you know where you can shove your bottles!' the woman retorted angrily.

'Please!' Mr Cornell held up his hand again. 'Please, dear sister, this animosity is not getting us anywhere.'

'What would father have done?' said Mr Mountolive.

Mrs Loveday pointed at Bob. 'He would have thrown this fool out long ago!'

'No,' Mr Cornell said. 'He would have been clever enough never to have included him in *the plan* in the first place. Mr Bruno can be listed as one of our mistakes.'

'How else would we have got her here?' Mr Mountolive demanded.

'There would have been other ways. We just chose the easiest and most obvious.'

'And the most expensive.' Mrs Loveday glared at Bob again.

'But I did it,' Bob said, 'and now you owe me.'

'And you shall be paid. This family keeps its word,' replied Mr Cornell.

Mrs Loveday took control again. It annoyed her that she had lost it for a moment. 'I want everybody out of here. I'll stay with Lois and I'll get the answers when she awakens. The rest of you get out, go about your business. If I'm not down by lunchtime, you'll all eat in the kitchen today. No use putting on the show if our star isn't able to attend the performance.'

The two men, Mr Cornell in his dressing gown and slippers and Mr Mountolive in a jacket and a pair of green trousers that hugged his knees like a First World War army uniform, marched briskly out of the suite at Mrs Loveday's command. Bob, who had struggled into a dressing gown, and Midge, already in one, left the suite and went into her room across the hall.

Midge closed the door, then put out her arms. Bob came into them, willingly. He held her head against his shoulder. 'Damn her,' was all she said.

Bob held her tightly. 'Why did she do it? I mean go outside? With almost nothing on?'

'If she gets sick, that's going to fuck up all our plans.'

'As if I hadn't thought of that,' he said.

'It's going to work out okay, my darlin',' Midge whispered soothingly. 'Don't worry, my love. It's going to work.'

* * *

The meeting in the church-like room had come to order. The chairs in the semicircle were occupied by white-robed members who had hastily been called to the emergency meeting. Candles burned at the altar and the large bleeding Jesus looked uncomfortable amidst the flames.

'They showed her the child last night,' the leader of the group said.

'They *what*?' a woman almost screamed.

283

'The child. *Her* child,' the hooded leader said. 'They let it come out of the hiding place and they let her see it.'

A murmur of shock rippled around the semicircle. 'Can you believe they would *dare*?' another woman asked.

A man's voice spoke up: 'You mean they gave him back to her? Just like that?'

'No,' the leader seemed to have all the information, 'they let her get to him, let her hug him.'

'She actually held him in her arms?' said another female voice.

The leader nodded, the tall peak of his white hood shimmered in colours from the candle flames. 'She hugged him and he hugged her. For at least five minutes.' He paused.

'Then what?' a man asked.

'Fortunately one of our members saw them. He stopped it.'

'Thank sweet Jesus we have sentries in their back wood.'

'Aye.'

'Blessed Jesus.'

'Thank you Lord.'

'He put a chloroform rag to her nose. She never heard him behind her.'

'Praise Jesus,' said a woman, 'that we thought to equip our sentries with such a thing.'

'Our Lord will protect us without them,' a masculine voice reminded them harshly.

'Aye,' this from a female, 'but our Lord always appreciates a little help now and then.'

'And the child?' a woman asked.

'Aye,' a man questioned, 'what about the wee one himself?'

'Our sentry left him alone. Didn't touch him,' the leader replied.

'That's only right. It's the woman who is guilty, after all.'

'The sentry watched from the grove of trees and after a while they came back up and took the child down with them again. They must have watched the whole operation with their periscope. The lad was well wrapped against the cold,' the leader continued. 'She wasn't. The mother was wearing almost nothing.'

'Shameless!' a woman said quickly. 'Naked in front of her own wee child!'

'What did our man do about the woman?' another voice asked. 'Did he leave her to lie there? He should have, shameless harlot of Babylon that she is.'

284

The leader shook his head under his hood. 'As he was observing and wondering what to do, he saw one of them approaching down the lawn. So he held back.'

'One of the family?'

'Aye,' the leader replied. 'One of those descendants of Satan himself. When the old man discovered the woman he ran for help. Another of that demonic tribe came soon out and carried the woman into their lair. Thusly was it all observed and reported to me.'

There was a silence in the room marred only by a sputtering candle.

'So now she knows he's still alive,' someone said.

'Exactly,' the leader replied, 'and that should make it easier for them to convince her to stay with them.'

'She could inform the police, you know,' someone said.

'I'm surprised they didn't think of that. It's a risk they'll be taking.'

'This is turning into an impossible situation,' a woman said, 'it ruins everything for us.'

'Not exactly,' replied the leader.

'Of course it does,' the same woman continued, 'she's going to stay with them now. She'll never leave as long as her child is there. We counted on her seeing through them but now she won't leave unless she takes her child with her.'

'Aye,' spoke up a man, 'and you know they are not about to let him go. Not with all the effort they've already put in to get him here.'

'Why did they do it?' a man's voice rose. 'Why show her the child? Why now?'

'No, no,' said the previous woman, 'this is the end. This ruins everything.'

'Not necessarily.' The man in the leader's robes stood up. 'There is one more thing we can do.'

After a long pause, they lowered their heads and made the sign of the Cross. The candles flickered around their Lord's ghastly crucified feet.

'There is one more thing,' the leader repeated. 'The part we were saving for last. The part we hoped we would never have to put into action.'

Another long silence followed, then a man said softly through his white hood: 'We have never killed before.'

'Our sweet Lord Jesus is against killing,' a woman added.

'But they must be driven out,' a man insisted. 'They must be driven out in His name! The purge must be made, but we can accomplish it with His compassion.'

'Aye.' The leader was still standing, still towering over them. 'There are times when heretics and sinners threaten our Lord and at those times desperate measures must be taken. We are not talking about Christian lives here. We're not talking about many lives. Just a few. Theirs and the American woman. Her child too, of course. He's also carrying the accursed blood. A few sinful lives snuffed out in the name of Jesus will stop their *plan* and put an end to their infamous cult.'

'You are right,' a man agreed. 'I don't like harming the child but why should we permit those few rotten fish to spoil all the others in His net? Why worry over a few, if their removal benefits all mankind?'

'In the name of Lord Jesus,' said the leader and crossed himself.

'Amen,' they all responded and again made the sign of the Cross.

'Blessed be His name.'

'Amen.'

* * *

She opened her eyes for the first time around two that afternoon. Mrs Loveday was dozing in an easy chair next to the bed. She lay there for a few moments, studying the ceiling, trying to get her mind to establish where she was. She shook her head, trying to knock away the webs invisible spiders had strung across her brain. Then she remembered.

She sat up, wild eyes looked frantically around the room. 'Where is he?' she screamed.

Mrs Loveday became alert, as if someone had shot a gun off near her ear. She got up and came up the steps to the bed. Her hand went out and stroked Lois' forehead. 'Now, now,' she soothed. 'It's all right. It's all right now.'

Lois pushed the woman's hand away. 'Where is he?' Her voice was shrill, her eyes still searching.

'He's downstairs with the others,' Mrs Loveday kept on soothing, 'they're in the library. Talking.'

'In the library?' Lois made an attempt to get out of the bed, but the older woman held her down firmly.

'I'll get him as soon as you've calmed down,' she said.

Lois looked at her, puzzled. God, how her head ached. 'In the library? He's talking . . . with others?'

'Yes, and I'll get your Bob up here as quick as you like.'

Lois fell back onto the pillow. 'Oh Bob. Yes. I didn't mean . . .' She stopped. Everything came flooding back into that achingly empty space between her eyes and her hairline. She pictured Tony, felt his little arms around her again, heard his sobbing voice calling her 'Mommy'. She closed her eyes and sighed deeply, because what immediately followed in her memory was the distrust she had for the people in that house. Tony was somewhere on the grounds and they were keeping her from him. Why? Tony was still alive. She had *always* known he was. For some reason these people had him. For some reason they had managed to get her over there. Get her into the house. For some reason they had let her see her baby. Why? What did they have to gain from all this? She opened her eyes and stared at Mrs Loveday. That wasn't a sweet and caring dumpy lady in front of her. It was a schemer, a plotter, a kidnapper and Lois told herself she had to be wary of her. Wary of them all. She was all alone in this, there was nobody she could turn to. Bob and Midge knew *why* she had wanted to get inside the house but neither of them believed that Tony was in here. In here, alive. She had to play it calmly. She'd have to be real cool. It was the only way to find her baby and get them out of there.

'You don't have to disturb Bob,' she said to Mrs Loveday. 'I'll be all right. I'll get up and get dressed.'

'What happened, dear?' The woman had a Kleenex in her hand and she dabbed at Lois' face with it. 'We were all so worried.'

'You needn't have been,' Lois said, playing her own game with her. 'I just overslept. That's all. But my head does hurt a bit. It must have been the drinks last night. I was very tired and they must have packed a hidden wallop.'

'They said you only had two,' Mrs Loveday continued to fuss around her.

'My head feels like I had two hundred.'

'But what were you doing out there?' Mrs Loveday took her hand in both of hers, cupping them as if she had entrapped a butterfly. 'Out on the lawn and in that freezing cold?'

Lois shut her eyes as if trying to remember, though actually, she was stalling for time. 'On the *lawn*? What are you talking about?'

'Why, that's where we found you, or rather Mr Mountolive found you, early this morning. You were only wearing a light nightie. What on earth possessed you?'

'On the lawn?' Lois repeated, averting her eyes from the woman.

'Yes, the lawn. When we found you, you were completely unconscious and you've slept all the morning away and part of the afternoon. What were you doing out there?' Her tone was calm but Lois could sense the hardness beneath it.

'I was on the lawn? You brought me back inside?' She widened her eyes at the woman. 'Oh, Mrs Loveday, you must be mistaken. I had a couple of drinks and went to bed.' She tried a smile. 'But you're joking, aren't you? This is some kind of a Scottish jest?'

Mrs Loveday pulled herself to her feet. 'I assure you, young woman, that I am *not* jesting. You were found this morning unconscious on the lawn down by the edge of the lake and I want to know why.'

You old bitch, Lois thought and continued to smile at the woman. 'I really don't know what you're talking about. *If* I went out there last night, I don't remember it. All I remember is coming to bed and just now waking up. With a terrific headache.'

Mrs Loveday put her hands on her hips. 'You don't remember?' Her voice was harsh. 'You really don't remember?'

I remember everything, you bloody cow, Lois thought. She liked that expression 'bloody cow'. She had heard it in London and from the reaction of the woman who got called it, it must be a wonderful insult. 'I don't remember,' Lois said. 'If you'd call my husband, I'd appreciate it. I'd like to get up and get dressed now.'

The woman stared at her, hard blue eyes under her streaky dark hair, then her gaze softened. Deliberately. 'Shall I bring you up a nice cup of tea?'

'I don't think so, thanks. Just ask Bob to come. Okay?'

The woman nodded, turned and marched out of the room. Lois heard the door close in the salon.

She slid out of the bed and stood up. Her head spun. She grasped the bedpost and hung on. After a few deep breaths the spinning was less noticeable. Whatever it was they used on me, she thought, sure did the trick. I must have gone out like a light. Damned old bitch, she thought again of Mrs Loveday. She went unsteadily to the window and pulled open the drapes. There was the lawn and the lake but no sign of Tony. She didn't expect to see him standing there. Still, it would have been wonderful. She went into the bathroom and looked at her face in the mirror. No make-up, hair all over her face . . . Then she noticed the nightdress she was wearing. How did I get into this? What the hell did they do? They undressed me! What a fucking nerve! She looked around the bathroom. What did they do with her peach outfit? The one she had put on for Bob last night? Oh, there it was. She could see an edge of it peeking out of the dirty clothes hamper in the far corner. She went over to it, took it out and stopped suddenly.

'There!' she said aloud. 'I've got them now. I've got them all!' She studied the nightgown, delighted that it was soiled. Delighted that there were several dirty handprints on the material, handprints made by a small child who had fallen in the wet grass and who had been crying. Tony's handprints. Tony was alive and he was somewhere on these grounds and now she had the proof. It wasn't just the ravings of a distraught mother now, it was proof positive in a very material way. She hugged the nightdress for a moment, then hurried it over to the bed and worked it under the mattress.

She was in the bathroom when Bob arrived.

'Are you okay, hon?' he asked. His ears were still ringing from the orders he had received from Mrs Loveday and the others. Lois didn't remember going outside. Lois didn't say what she was doing out there! You go up there and you find out the truth! Find out what she knows! 'Hon,' he called again, 'you all right in there?'

'Fine,' she called back. 'I'll just be a minute.' She finished washing her face, and then ran a comb several times through her hair. She did not look good. Oh well, Bob had seen her looking worse than this. She opened the bathroom door and he was right there, waiting for her.

'Mrs Loveday said it was okay to come up now,' he said.

'Since when do you need permission to come into my bedroom?' she asked.

He grinned. 'You know what I mean.'

She gave him a light peck on the cheek, then went into the salon and threw the bolt on the door. She came back into

289

the bedroom and shut the connecting door with the salon behind her. Then she came over to Bob, motioned that she wanted him to go with her over to the far wall. He looked puzzled, but followed her. When they were in the corner of the room, Lois hugged him unexpectedly. Then she pulled back and smiled. 'Bob! I have the most wonderful news!' she said in a whisper. 'Tony is here! He's somewhere on the grounds of this house and he's alive!'

'What are you talking about?' he said loudly.

She put her finger to his lips. 'Ssh. Don't tell a soul. Not even Midge. She blabs everything she knows. Last night, after you came in and fell asleep, I woke up. I don't know why I did, probably because I was sleeping in an uncomfortable position. Well, I got up to go to the bathroom and I looked out the window over there,' she pointed at the rear window across the bedroom, 'and there was Tony. He looked like he was walking on top of the water. Of course, that couldn't be true but he did stop and look up and see me. He saw me and he waved at me and I waved back.'

'You saw Tony?' His voice was thick. 'Are you sure?'

'Positive! So then I ran out to get him . . . And I did. I held him and I hugged him and he hugged me – and oh Bob . . .' She started crying, both from happiness and frustration.

'I don't see how . . .' he began, trying to find words.

'But I did!' She was laughing now through the tears. 'I did and he seems to be healthy and well fed. And then, just as I was about to pick him up and bring him back inside the house, someone came from behind me and put something to my nose. That's all I remember.' She searched his face. 'Isn't it wonderful? Tony's still alive and he's here! Bob, I was right from the very beginning. From the very first time that I had those feelings to come over to Corra and look for Tony. You remember how they were? How strong those feelings were? Well, I was right! I'm *always* right when I listen to my hunches! Now all we have to do is find him and get the hell out of here.'

'Find him?' He was still trying to sort out the sudden complexities of it all.

'Yes. Find him. Get him out of here and get to the police and have these people arrested. Kidnapping *is* a crime in Scotland, isn't it?'

'Uh, yeah, yeah I think so.'

'Okay, now listen, here's what I'm going to do. I'm going

to play it real cool, see? I'm not going to go to those people and start screaming and threatening and carrying on. I'm going to watch and see how they play their hand.' She walked away from him and then whirled around toward him, excited with her new plan, pleased she was one up on the other side. 'I'll ask a few questions, I'll listen very carefully, and if I can, I'll do a little snooping around when they're not looking. I don't know why these awful people took him and right now that's not important. The important thing is for us to get Tony and then get out of here. The police can discover why these bastards are doing what they're doing. After I get my baby, I don't give a damn what their reasons were.' She clutched his arm for reassurance. 'You do know what I'm saying, don't you? You've got such a funny expression on your face.'

He pulled away from her grasp. 'Sure, I hear what you're saying. It all seems so . . . so improbable. Tony here? Kidnapped by these old folks? Shit, Lois, that's one helluva accusation you're making against these people. Kidnapping? That's a serious charge.' He watched the excitement of the situation fade from her eyes. He was sure he had calmed her down. 'You can't go around accusing people of kidnapping. You've gotta have proof. Where's your proof?'

'You want proof?' she said loudly. 'I'll give you proof!' She walked to the bed, reached under the mattress and pulled out the peach nightdress. 'Look at these. See these smears? These are Tony's handprints. Look, you can actually see the marks of his little fingers where he held me. I'm sure any fingerprint expert could make a case for us out of this.'

He took the nightdress and examined it. He could see the prints, quite clearly. Small and muddy and obviously that of hands and fingers. Why hadn't any of them noticed that in all the confusion this morning? 'I see what you mean,' he said.

'So now I want you to play it cool as well. Don't ask any leading questions. Just ask little ones that can build on each other. Then you and I will compare notes. These people are too smart to give us outright answers, but if they don't know we're wise to them, they won't be aware that we're putting together a jigsaw puzzle with their replies.' She took the nightdress and started putting it back under the mattress.

'I don't think that's a good place for it,' he said.

'Why? I can't leave it hanging in the bathroom.'

'No, but someone's bound to find it when they come in

to change the sheets. You'd better let me hide it.'

'Where?'

'I'll put it in the trunk of the car and lock it. Nobody will find it there.'

'Wonderful idea!' She handed him the garment. 'Be careful. Don't let them see you with it. Stick it under your sweater until you get it to the car.' He nodded and she watched in satisfaction as he shoved the thin peach nightgown under his heavy knit sweater. She walked with him to the connecting door and opened it, then she pulled back the bolt on the hallway door. She kissed him on the mouth. 'Isn't it great?' she whispered. 'Tony's alive and we have proof!'

'Great!' he put on a false smile. 'See you downstairs in a little while.' He walked down the corridor and she shut the door, deciding to take her own sweet time about getting dressed and making an appearance for that bunch.

Bob went into the kitchen where Mrs Loveday was helping the cook prepare the evening meal.

'How is she?' the woman asked. 'What did you find out?'

'She saw Tony,' he said simply.

'She *what*?' the woman's voice rose and the cook looked startled. 'Impossible! There's no way that child could have got out. She's lying.'

'I don't think so,' Bob said. 'Somebody down there goofed. Look.' He reached under his sweater and pulled out the nightgown. 'See these? They're Tony's handprints. From when he hugged her. His hands were wet and dirty. No, she saw him all right.' He watched her reaction to this news warily. Lois had brought their plans close to disaster.

The woman looked at the nightdress. 'They do look like a child's hands,' she admitted.

'Exactly. She's going to use this, to show the police.'

'Like hell she is,' the woman said. She marched over to the large kitchen sink, threw the nightdress into it and turned on the hot water tap full force. 'Like hell she is!'

* * *

'Did you see him?' Bob asked.

Midge was pouring them large doses of gin. 'Yeah. He looks real good.' She added some tonic water and a slice of lemon to each glass and wished people in England knew what ice cubes were. They were sitting at a long pine table in what was called the servants' pantry. The few chairs around the table were as mismatched as most things in the kitchen that adjoined it. Mrs Loveday had given both of them orders that they were not to use the dining room or dirty up the entrance hall. Midge shoved the glass across the table at him. 'He didn't see me, of course. They've got it fixed up with a one-way mirror thing. You can see in, but he can't see you by looking out. It's a pretty neat set up they've got down there. That bald bastard knew how to do things. You have to row out about twenty feet from the edge of the lake and even then you can't see the entrance until you're right on top of it. Then they clamp on some metal thing with four walls and a pump sucks up all the water inside the walls. It works fast.' She took a large gulp from the glass. 'Aah, that's hit the spot . . . Anyway, then there's a metal ring that you pull on and it lifts up a metal door. I think the door has some kind of rubber around the underneath to seal out the water, you know, like those rubber things on the edges of refrigerator doors?' He nodded and took a drink from his own glass. 'And the stairs are right there,' she continued. 'You step out of the boat and go down the stairs, dry stairs, and you're in a series of rooms. And there's Tony with all the comforts of home.'

'What about air?'

'Mr Cornell showed me the exhaust system that they put in about seventy years ago. It's amazing. Fans bring in fresh air and other fans take out the stale air. The outlets are in the wood, hidden by trees and vines and stuff. You have to know they are there to find them. It's really the perfect hiding place, under the lake and all. That Crowley was a sneaky son of a bitch.'

'He must have been,' Bob agreed, 'to have put together all this.' He paused, looking at her over the rim of his glass. 'So you saw Tony. You think he's okay?'

'Why don't you see for yourself? You're his father.'

'No. We've already discussed this. I don't want to see him. I've washed him out of my thoughts. At least, as much as I can.'

'Don't tell me you're starting to have a heart,' she grinned.

'No, he doesn't exist for me any longer. He's dead for me.'

'But not for Lois.'

He shrugged. 'Well, wasn't that the way it was supposed

293

to be? I don't want to see him. I just want to get out of here.'

'And get your money,' she said.

'Of course.' He took another pull from the glass. 'I've earned it. After everything I've done, I'm not about to walk away from here without what's coming to me.'

'Half a million dollars?' Her smile had turned into a grin. 'That's a helluva lot for snatching your own kid.'

'And getting Lois over here,' he replied, 'don't forget about that. It hasn't been easy playing the game all the time, trying to convince her *not* to come when I was really dying for her to be exactly where she is right now. Which is upstairs in this house wondering if she's going bananas or not. Imagine her reaction if I had just come out and said let's go to Scotland? In January? Hell, we've discussed this, you and I. Her doing it all on her own puts me in the clear. Her acting like a nutcase all over New York and London and Edinburgh and Dumfries? There isn't a jury in the world that would believe her if my ass was ever hauled into court on a kidnapping charge.'

'It came close with those damned handprints on her nightgown, I'll tell you. I'm glad she showed them to me before she showed them to the police. Anyway, when this whole organization falls apart, if it ever does, she won't be able to come yelling that I forced her into it. If something goes wrong and she gets away from here and brings in the police, I've got all my tracks covered. I've made damn sure I've built up a defence against anything she could throw at me. I've taken this thing step by step. All the evidence I've been building up so far puts me in the clear. I'm the unhappy husband who had to finally give in to his wife's crazy ideas. *I* wasn't the one that wanted to come to Scotland. *I* had to cancel the tickets for Jamaica. Lost money on the deal, too. *I* didn't want to come to this God-forsaken house. It was her idea. *I* had reservations to return to New York directly from Edinburgh. It was because of her craziness that I had to cancel them at the last minute. It'll cost me too, but it's all in some airline's computer system if she ever starts yelling for the police.' He took the bottle and poured himself another large dose of gin. 'She won't be able to tell a judge and jury that her husband made her do it. *She* wanted to find this house. *She* wanted to find her child. *She'll* be the one who'll make the decision to stay here with all these loonies. Not me. She won't be able to blame me. I'll be off spending my half million.'

'With me.' Midge raised her glass to him.

'With you,' he said.

'And no regrets?' she asked him. 'No regrets about your own son?'

'With half a million dollars filling my pocket, there's no room for regrets.'

* * *

Lois went to the salon door as soon as she heard the knock.

'Can I come in and tidy up, mum?' The elderly woman she recognized as the cook was standing there with a vacuum cleaner and a wheeled cart with freshly ironed linen and freshly washed towels. 'I hope you're feelin' better.'

'Yes, thank you,' Lois stepped back and the woman pushed the cart into the salon.

'I'll just do the bathroom and run the sweeper and change things, if you don't mind, mum. Do you know if your friend is in her room or not?' She motioned across the hall.

'I really don't know,' Lois replied. 'I haven't seen anyone so far today except Mrs Loveday and my husband.'

'Aye, I heard about it this morning. Walking in your sleep, was you? I had a nephew that used to do that. Finally they tied his foot to the bedpost so he couldn't roam too far. One night there was a fire and the poor lad went up the chimney as smoke because he couldn't get hisself untied. Tragic, it was. Is it true that if somebody awoke you while you were walkin' like that, that you'd drop dead from the fright of it?'

'I don't know,' Lois replied, 'I don't walk in my sleep. Never did.'

'My sister should have bought a bell.' The woman picked up a bunch of keys that were on a metal ring.

'Bought a bell?' Lois asked.

'Aye. Instead of tying poor Bertie to the bedpost, she should have tied a bell to his leg. That way he would let folks know when he was walkin' in his sleep. I told my sister that and she said it was a wee bit late for me to have come up with that idea and why didn't I tell her sooner? Well, I told my sister, Bertie's problem was your problem, now wasn't it? I'm not about to stick my nose into other people's problems. Don't you consider I was right, mum?'

'Absolutely.' Lois tried not to smile.

'I always thought I was too.' She took the keys and went across the hall and after knocking on Midge's door, she took one of the keys and unlocked it, swinging the door open. Then she came bustling back into the bedroom suite. 'Your friend's not in. Give the place a bit of an airing, I will. Cigarette smoke and all, you know. In old houses like this one, it lingers for ever so long.'

'I would imagine.' Lois kept her eyes on that bunch of keys. 'I'll start in the bathroom if you don't mind.' The woman took a wooden box crammed with detergents, scouring pads and brushes. 'Won't be but a minute.'

'That's all right,' Lois said lightly. 'Take your time. I was just going downstairs anyway.'

'I'm not inconveniencing you, am I, mum?' The woman stopped halfway across the bedroom and looked at her.

'No, not at all,' Lois assured her. 'Take your time. Don't hurry on my account.'

When she heard the water taps start running in the bathroom, Lois grabbed the collection of keys and hurried out into the hallway. She went to the door just down from the one to her suite. She fumbled with several keys until one of them turned easily in the lock. Quickly she pushed open the door.

The room was almost bare. There was a cheap metal bed with nothing on it but a sagging mattress. Faded drapes were unable to keep out the afternoon sunlight. The floor boards were dull and bare. There were nails on the wall and lighter squares in the wallpaper where pictures had once hung. The room smelt of mildew and disuse.

She closed the door, locking it rapidly. Then down to the next door. She was surprised when the same key worked in its lock. She figured it must be the master pass key. This room was almost bare as well. A few broken chairs against one wall. A wooden clothes closet with its double doors sagging open like a grin trying to hide a bad tooth. The window was completely bare and the sunlight caught the motes of dust that her entrance stirred up from the grimy wood floor. She came out and locked the door.

She ran down the hall, wondering which of the doors to try next. She couldn't take too long. The cook would be missing her keys soon. There was a door just to the right of the staircase. She tried the key and again it worked smoothly. She stopped momentarily before going in. Someone slept in this room, because the grimy sheets were still rumpled on the cheap department store bed. There was a ragged scatter rug near the bed and a small table, painted yellow, that looked as if it came from a garage sale. There was a table lamp, one of those modern uglies with a long metal neck and a shade that looked like the Martians had landed. A wardrobe closet was open and she could see it held men's clothing. One of the jackets looked familiar. Then she remembered. Mr Cornell had worn it to dinner the night before. There were some books piled on a desk. She glanced at one, then opened the cover. Mr Cornell had put his signature inside it. 'So this is *his* room,' she commented aloud. 'Mrs Loveday said all the rooms were furnished like ours yet he lives in this squalor while right down the hall we are living like the Duke and Duchess of Windsor. What the hell is all this?'

She was about to shut the door when she noticed a small silver frame with a photograph in it. It was atop a cluttered dresser. She picked up the frame and then almost dropped it in shock. There, staring straight at her with his large dark eyes and his bald and shining head, was the little man in her engraving! The same son of a bitch who had snuck up the lawn and had vanished into the house. She recognised him immediately. She couldn't forget *that* face. Even though this was a photograph and the little man was only a drawing, the resemblance was uncanny. She took the frame closer to the window, to get a better look at it in the daylight. She knew that face. She was sure she had seen it somewhere else. A photograph that had stuck in the back of her mind. Not just from the engraving, but from a book or magazine years ago.

Then the memory flooded back. It knocked her physically off balance. 'Oh shit!' she said aloud and hastily put the frame back on the dresser, wiping her hands on her skirt. 'Oh, mother! That's Aleister Crowley. That heartless son of a bitch is Aleister Crowley! Jesus, Lois, what have you gotten yourself into?'

* * *

Malcolm knew it was no use trying to hide, not from that family. That was why he returned on his own volition that morning, parked his car around by the side and went in through the kitchen door.

'Oh dear,' said the cook when she saw him. 'You look a fright. Haven't you been sleeping?'

He frowned. 'I had things to do,' he said simply.

'Did you hear about the goings-on here this morning?' she asked as she wiped down the counter top. 'The American woman went walking in her sleep last night and she saw her little boy. Can you beat that? The lad somehow got out from under and came on dry land and she saw him. Told Loveday she didn't, when Loveday asked her. But her husband said she did. Her husband told Loveday she admitted she saw him. Saw him and hugged him. Cheeky, ain't she? I mean, lying that way to Loveday and all.'

'Ah!' Mrs Loveday came into the kitchen and stopped short when she saw Malcolm. 'There you are. I wondered what had become of you.'

'I came back,' he said calmly. 'I came back to tell you I'm sorry.' He didn't want to rock the boat, not with these people.

'You're sorry? Sorry, is it? Oh, I figured it had to be you! The nurse confirmed it. Why? Why did you do it, Malcolm? Whatever got into you to do it?'

'I d'know.' He didn't look at her.

'You don't know? You had better know, young man, and you had better have a very good reason for doing what you did. A very good reason!' She turned around and started out of the door, then stopped. 'You wait there. Right there. Don't you go wandering. You have some explainin' to do to us all.'

The cook stared at him. 'What did you do? What's she so hot and bothered about?'

Malcolm looked her straight in the eye. 'It was me that did it. I brought up the little boy. I let him see his mother.'

The cook put her dishcloth to her mouth. 'Oh Malcolm! May the saints take mercy on you, lad!'

In a few minutes Mrs Loveday was back and with her was Mr Cornell, Dr Fulham and Frau Baumgartner with Madame Dupré. Mrs Loveday pulled a chair away from the table and motioned for Malcolm to sit on it. He sat. The others formed a circle around him.

'Now lad,' Mr Cornell said as evenly as the anger inside him would allow. 'Tell us all why you did it. Tell us all why you let the American woman see her child.'

'I was upset with you,' he replied. 'Upset with all of you.'

'Upset?' Frau Baumgartner repeated the word.

'Yes,' the young man said, 'upset. I did all that you asked me to do with the Americans. I guided them to Corra but I didn't show them how to get to the house. You had told me not to. It had to seem as if she found it by herself. That's what you told me. Let her find the place on her own. That way nobody could be accused of leading her into this place.'

'It was part of the agreement with her husband,' Dr Fulham reminded him. 'That's the way he wanted it.'

'It would have been so much easier just to bring them here straight away,' Malcolm said.

'The husband wanted it done that way,' Mrs Loveday said in an annoyed tone. 'You know that. It was part of the bargain.'

'That still doesn't explain why you let the lad be seen,' Dr Fulham said.

Malcolm didn't look at any of them, just stared at his hands resting in his lap. 'I stole that brooch from the hotel,' he said calmly, 'and then I took it up to Edinburgh and I even got her to attend the seance of Mrs Scully. I mean I did all that for you . . .'

'For us,' Dr Fulham said. 'Don't forget you are one of us.'

'Forget? How can I forget?'

There was a pause. 'So?' Madame Dupré broke the silence. 'Continue to explain.'

'Then Fiona started.'

'Fiona, is it? Hah!' Mr Cornell's anger rose to the surface. 'I thought so. I thought she was behind it all.'

'What did Fiona have to do with it?' Frau Baumgartner wanted to know.

Malcolm sighed. Deeply. 'She is getting restless,' he said. 'She wants to set a date for our marriage. So do I.' He looked up at them now. 'So do I! I want to set a date and I want to get married and I want to forget I ever got messed up in any of this! In your old *plan*!'

'I don't see the need to rush into a marriage,' Mrs Loveday smiled and looked at the others standing around the young man. 'I think Fiona will wait. Don't you, Fulham? Don't you think she'll wait, Baumgartner?'

'Oh yes,' Frau Baumgartner smiled at Mrs Loveday. 'She's not going anywhere. She'll wait.'

'Wait for eternity, if necessary,' added Madame Dupré.

Malcolm didn't see the looks they were exchanging. 'Well, I got tired of waiting. I am tired of waiting and I'm tired of all this stuff and bother about the Americans and the *plan*. I thought I could hurry things up, you know, show her the child and make her decide to stay.'

'Just like that?' asked Mr Cornell.

Malcolm shrugged. 'Yeah. Just like that.' He looked up at the white-haired man. 'And why not? What did I do that was so wrong?'

Dr Fulham put his hand on the young man's shoulder. 'Did it ever occur to you that possibly if she saw her child before she had agreed to stay on with us she just might go to the police?'

Malcolm frowned. 'The police? Why would she do that?'

'Why would she do that?' Mrs Loveday almost slapped his face. 'Why *wouldn't* she do that?'

'She'd tell the authorities in a minute if she could!' Mr Cornell's face was red under his white hair. 'Now we don't dare let her out of the house! Now we have to watch her every move! Thanks to you.'

'No thanks to you, he means,' added Dr Fulham.

'She goes to the police,' Malcolm said, 'so what?' But as he asked he already knew the answer.

'The police come here and they search the grounds, that's what,' Frau Baumgartner said.

'And the American woman gets hysterical and demands they arrest us and they *do*, God forbid,' Mr Cornell was getting angrier by the second, 'and they go into every room and look under every bed and finally they discover the underwater room. *Then* what?'

Malcolm shook his head. 'How could they discover it? Not if anybody doesn't tell them.'

'Many people know about that room,' Dr Fulham said. 'Many people in the village have heard about it. Do you think the villagers wouldn't tell the police? Do you think the villagers wouldn't be overjoyed to have the authorities come in here and destroy everything? Do you think . . .' his voice trailed off. 'No, of course you don't think. If you had thought you wouldn't have done what you did.'

'Her child being here was our trump card,' Madame Dupré scowled at Malcolm. 'It was the final move in this long involved game we have been playing with the American woman. If we saw we were losing her . . . if we saw she was refusing to stay with us . . . then we were going to use that card. Either she stays or her little boy dies. That card would

300

have cinched it for us and you threw that card on the table long before we were ready to reveal it. You!' She spat in his face. 'You! You don't deserve to be one of us!'

He wiped his cheek and looked at her spittle on his fingertips. It was yellowish and sticky. 'I'm sorry,' was all he could say.

Madame Dupré mimicked him: 'I'm sorry!' Her tone changed. 'You'd damned better be sorry!'

He kept staring at the spittle on his fingers. 'I won't do it again. I promise.'

'Do it *again*?' Mrs Loveday laughed. 'Again? There's to be no *again*, Malcolm. Not for you. Oh no.'

He looked up at her, his eyes squinting in doubt. 'I don't understand . . .'

'I think you do,' she said.

'I said I was sorry!' His voice rose in protest.

'It doesn't matter what you said,' Mr Cornell shook his head. 'does it, my boy? The deed has been done. Saying you are sorry won't undo your foolish act.'

'I'll go get it.' Mrs Loveday left the circle and walked quickly out of the kitchen.

'Get what?' Malcolm's eyes were wide.

'I think you know,' Dr Fulham said. 'I think you know.'

No one spoke until Mrs Loveday reappeared beside them. In her hand she held an axe.

'No!' Malcolm screamed and the others held him down.

'Surely you must have expected this, Malcolm,' Frau Baumgartner said.

'You knew the consequences,' Mr Cornell added.

'Father's axe,' Mrs Loveday lightly caressed the sharp edge.

'Made especially for him in Tunisia,' Madame Dupré admired the family heirloom.

'It's never gone dull,' Mrs Loveday's finger rode lightly over the blade.

'I remember when I saw him use it in Munich,' Frau Baumgartner smiled at the double-headed weapon, made of gleaming steel and inscribed with dozens of small symbols and hieroglyphics. 'That awful Nazi woman. You know, the one with the Hitler Youth Brigade? Right into her chest it went. There was blood all over her clothes. I was only a child but I remember ripping her swastika badge from her blouse just before the others bundled her away. Threw her in the river, they did. Of course,' she shrugged, 'there were always bodies floating in the river in those days.'

'No! Please!' Malcolm struggled under the gripping hands.

'He used to keep the blade shiny by rubbing it with the rendered fat from Indian sacred cows,' Mr Cornell recalled. 'There was a friend of his outside Bombay who would secretly kill one of those cows and then send the fat in tin containers to father. Father claimed it put new energy into the blade.'

'I'm sure it did,' Dr Fulham declared, 'being sacred and all.'

'Now you just get to your feet, Malcolm,' Mr Cornell said, 'and walk over to the sink.'

Malcolm started to moan. 'Please don't.'

'Over to the sink,' Mr Cornell repeated. 'That's right. One foot in front of the other. That's a good lad.'

'Didn't he used to make candles out of some of that sacred cow fat?' Madame Dupré asked. 'I thought I heard something about that.'

Dr Fulham shook his head. 'He tried, but they didn't burn. What he did use to do with it was smear it into the vaginas of some of his Scarlet Women. Just before penetration.' He grinned. 'Father claimed it put new energy into his magick wand.'

'I'm sure it did,' Dr Fulham repeated, 'being sacred and all.'

Malcolm had been steered over to the sink. 'That's right, lad,' said Mr Cornell. 'Now put your hand here. On this.' He slid the cook's chopping board to the edge of the sink.

'No,' Malcolm whimpered, 'please dear God, no!'

'Hand on the board, please,' Mr Cornell repeated.

'Please don't do this,' Malcolm begged. 'Please God, don't.'

'Hand on the board.'

'I said I was sorry . . .'

'Put your hand on the board, Malcolm!' Mrs Loveday commanded.

'I don't deserve this . . . I only . . .'

Frau Baumgartner grabbed his wrist and slammed his hand down onto the chopping board.

'Loveday,' said Mr Cornell, 'I believe he is ready. Will you do the honours?'

Malcolm's legs began to tremble and Madame Dupré grabbed his trouser belt and hoisted him with it.

'In the name of all those most high,' Mrs Loveday intoned as she raised the axe, 'in the name of all those most low,' the blade caught the glimmer of the afternoon sun streaming

302

through the kitchen window, 'we offer this sacrifice for the good of one and all.'

'No!' Malcolm screamed.

The blade fell swiftly. It hit Malcolm's arm with a crunching thud. The metal shattered his wrist bones as it sliced through the muscles and nerves. His blood shot across the kitchen counter, splattering the wall behind the sink.

Mr Cornell pushed Malcolm's arm into the basin. He looked at the moving fingers, twitching like fat spider legs drenched in blood. He frowned. 'You didn't get it all, Loveday.' He grabbed Malcolm's arm and brought what had once been Malcolm's wrist back onto the chopping board with a plop. The hand lay at an angle, pointing back at the young man. 'It's still attached,' he said. 'Give it another whack.'

Mrs Loveday raised the axe, stared at the spot she was aiming for and swung the blade again. This time the hand moved, by itself, and fell into the sink. 'That's better,' he said.

Malcolm stared in disbelief at his fingers, still moving in all that blood.

'Now the other one,' Mr Cornell said.

'What . . .'

'He doesn't feel a thing yet,' put in Dr Fulham. 'Get the other one off before the shock hits him.'

'I said the other one!' Mr Cornell reached across for Malcolm's left arm but Madame Dupré had already pushed it across the sink. It fell dumbly onto the red, glistening chopping block. Mr Cornell positioned it. Then he stepped back. 'Again, if you please, Loveday.'

The buxom woman raised the dripping axe above her greying head. 'Another gift for you, dear spirits,' she intoned. 'Another proof of our great love for you.'

Malcolm stared at his wrist. Then didn't even blink as the blade came down upon it, cutting neatly behind the wrist bone, slicing through flesh and blood vessels and muscles and nerves. He watched as his hand flipped over, by itself, and his fingers curved upward as if to catch a falling raindrop. Then the fingers curled tightly inward, his nails digging into his unfeeling palms.

Mr Cornell shoved the two bleeding stumps into the sink. Madame Dupré stood behind Malcolm, pressing his body against the counter, making sure he didn't get away.

Mr Cornell turned on both taps and Malcolm watched as

the clear liquid began to mingle with his red blood. It pushed little streams into the red and made little rivers that trickled and twisted and backed up and broke free. He still didn't feel the pain. He didn't wonder why. His brain had switched off. It was too stunned to relay the information of what had happened at the ends of his arms. The water and blood moved up, slowly, along the sides of the sink. There was no longer a definite clear river and a definite red river. There was now only a vague scarlet swamp, flecked occasionally with small floating dark clots. Malcolm kept staring at the liquid, his severed wrists and hands hidden now by the colour. He wanted to turn and say something to his aunts and uncles who were still so close to him, but there was no energy. No energy at all. It would have taken too much energy to look at them, too much effort to open his mouth. There was no point in it. No point in much of anything now. No point at all. His body gave one violent spasm and then slumped forward.

They took his arms out of the water and Dr Fulham wrapped each stump in a tea towel. Then they carried him out of the kitchen and out to the side of the house. The three women supported his body as the two men undid the lid on the well. His trousers snagged and then ripped as he was slid over the edge, but aside from that there was no trouble in getting rid of his body.

In the kitchen the cook, who had been standing in a corner and watching, had started wiping away at the bloodstained walls and counter top. 'Better get this mess cleaned up,' she said aloud. 'Haven't even started supper yet and me with three extra guests to feed.'

CHAPTER TWENTY-ONE

In the suite, and alone, Lois stared out the back window, looking at the lawn and the waters of the lake but not really seeing them. Her unguided and unauthorized tour of the other rooms on that floor had sent a jumble of mixed signals to the front of her conscious mind. Seeing that photograph of Aleister Crowley. Seeing how poorly the other rooms were furnished. Holding Tony. Waking up back in the bedroom. Bob's continuing reluctance to believe that Tony was alive and somewhere on the grounds.

That last one was the puzzler. Bob. Her husband. His attitude then. His attitude now. He changed their travel plans and let her come back to find the house, yet he was distant and doubtful of her now. Again.

'Is he trying to drive me crazy?' she said aloud. 'Am I in the middle of an old Ingrid Bergman movie?'

Was he trying to do that? Was he, for some reason, out to prove that she was going insane? Why can't he believe me about Tony? Damn, I held Tony last night. He came into my arms and he was warm and alive and his heartbeat echoed through me. I *know* he did. I *know* what's real. Yet Bob refuses to listen, refuses to comfort me. Why?

She stopped and thought of the other little boy, the dead child Bob had identified. She had often thought of him and of his mother and wished she knew who the child had been. Then she could get to the woman and hold her and stroke her hair and tell her her terrible ordeal of waiting is over. Is that why Bob refuses to admit Tony is still alive? Because it would also mean admitting he had made a mistake? That he'd identified the wrong body and caused hardship and suffering to complete strangers?

'He patronizes me.' She spoke aloud. 'That's the word for him: patronizing.' He's not listening to anything I say. He doesn't *care* about anything I say. Oh, he'll give me a peck on the cheek and call me "hon" but he continues to do whatever he set out to do from the beginning. And sex? She laughed to herself. What's that? We haven't had sex for a month. It's been downhill in the bedroom department ever since Midge brought that damned engraving into our lives.

She stopped her train of thought, and changed tracks. 'Midge,' she said slowly. There's another one. How come she fits so easily into all this? She takes it all for granted. She knows what turmoil I'm going through in this place, yet she acts as if she's doing nothing more than enjoying herself on a two-week holiday. Midge knows more about me than most people. It's my fault. I needed her and dumped my troubles on her and now she's become part of my life. She's managed to insinuate herself into what's happening all around me. She says she's my friend. She acts like my friend but now there's this nagging in the back of my mind that possibly Midge isn't everything she seems.

Lois went over to the wardrobe closet and took out the outfit she had saved for special evening occasions. Tonight would be a very special occasion. She was determined to turn it into one. She slipped into the mustard-yellow wool skirt. It was pleated like a Scotsman's kilt and had a fine blue line running down the edge of each pleat. The blouse was of white silk, neatly tailored, almost boyish except for the frill of white lace that cascaded down the front covering the buttons. She slid into the jacket, a tightly knit confection of deep blue wool with buttons the colour of the mustard skirt. Her shoes were shining blue leather, with stiletto spike heels. She looked at the overall effect in the mirror, then fluffed her red hair one last time. She stared at the attractive woman who stared back at her. 'What are they trying to do to you?' she asked the woman in the mirror. 'You don't have any money. They have nothing to gain. You're just an average American working girl whose parents were West Virginia coal miners. Why is everyone lying to you? What do the people in this house want with you and Tony?' She stared at the reflection but it didn't give her any of the answers. 'You wanna find out, darlin'?' she asked the image. 'So do I and tonight's the night! No more bullshit for us and that means for Bob and Midge as well.' She adjusted the collar of her jacket and gave the woman in the mirror a big smile. 'Lookin' good, kid. Now let's go get 'em.' On the way out she grabbed the keys to the rental car and put them in her skirt pocket. 'Just in case,' she said aloud.

Lois made an entrance. Deliberately. She stood framed by the massive double wooden doors of the dining room, the silk of her blouse shimmering in the light of the candles on the table.

'Well, there you are, my dear,' Madame Dupré said. 'We were starting to be worried.'

'Yeah, hon,' Bob said. 'I was just coming up to see if you were all right.'

'Me?' Lois gave a little laugh. 'Of course I'm all right. It just took me a little longer to get ready than I had thought. That's all.'

Midge, a drink in one hand and a cigarette in the other, smiled at her. 'Well, you did a good job of it. You look great!'

Everyone else in the room quickly agreed.

Jason crossed the room to be at her side. 'I hear you had a bad turn this morning. I'm sorry.' His large blue-green eyes never left hers.

Again, she laughed. 'That's what they tell me, but I really don't remember anything about it. Can't imagine what it was but,' she was looking around her, 'I don't sleep walk. I never have.'

'There's always a first time for everything, my dear,' Mrs Loveday bubbled. 'Never say never.'

'Right,' said the short paunchy Englishman named Dr Fulham. 'Never is a word we never use around here.' Then he laughed and the others joined politely in.

Mr Halmfazzi took her right hand and kissed it lightly. 'But you are all right now? No desire to run out onto the lawn instead of sitting down to dinner?'

'No desire to do that at all,' she said to him. 'As a matter of fact I haven't had anything to eat all day.'

'Well then,' Mrs Loveday took charge, 'why don't we all sit down and I'll inform cook she can begin serving.'

They took virtually the same seats as they had the night before. Lois had Bob on her left and the white-haired Mr Cornell on her right. She recognized the dinner jacket. It was the same one that had hung in that dismal cluttered bedroom. Midge sat on the other side of Bob and as Lois raised her gaze she saw that she was sitting directly across from Jason. Her pulse raced for a few seconds, then she said: 'Where's Malcolm? Isn't he joining us tonight?'

'Ah . . .' Mr Cornell began. 'He . . . ah . . . won't be with us.'

'He doesn't live here, you know,' said Frau Baumgartner.

'He has his own life,' Mr Mountolive said and then looked embarrassed. 'What I mean is, he has other things to do.'

Lois smiled. 'You mean like Fiona?'

There was a heavy pause around the table. Finally Mr Cornell said: 'Yes, you could say that. He and Fiona are together tonight.'

'Rather than with us.' Mr Mountolive added, 'He is my nephew, you know.'

'Your nephew?' Lois' voice rose slightly. 'And he knew you were living here?'

'Of course,' the old man replied. 'We've been very close.'

The question why, if Malcolm had been coming to see his uncle here, that he didn't mention it when Lois had shown the engraving to the American couple in the pub in Corra was on the tip of her tongue. She picked up her crystal water glass and washed the question back down her throat. She'd see what other cards were dealt. It was too early to start playing her hand.

The cook came in with the soup tureen. Conversation, when there was any, dealt with the weather, the Dumfries soccer game that afternoon and the news of old Mrs Treater's cow that had wandered into her kitchen and how the volunteer fire brigade had been summoned to get it out.

Soup dishes were collected and the cook wheeled in two large birds, roasted and crisp on silver platters. 'Goose,' Mrs Loveday explained. 'They're not always so plump this time of year.' She carved the rich meat and placed generous slices of it on the fine chinaware. Spoonfuls of grated turnip, buttered carrots and braised celery were added, then three small roast potatoes. All this was covered with a rich pale brown gravy. The cook filled their wine glasses with a crisp dry white wine from Portugal. 'We think it's the best with goose,' Mr Cornell explained. Lois tasted it and thought it was delicious. Midge had already emptied her glass and the cook gave her more as she passed back that way.

'I recall a rice dish that father used to love when he was in Tunisia,' Mr Halmfazzi said suddenly, waving his silver fork in his brown hand. 'There's a taste of it in this celery.' He licked his lips lightly. 'A herb of some kind in here makes me remember.'

'Your father?' Lois looked at him.

'Yes. He loved food. Loved to eat. He was a big man, you know. Very hearty appetite.'

'I recall him one day in a restaurant in Paris,' Madame Dupré laughed, 'when he ordered *escargot d'or* and they had brought him *escargot florentine*. What a scene he caused! He stood up, held the plate aloft and everybody in the direct line from where he was standing to the kitchen door ducked under their tables.'

'Did he throw it?' Midge asked.

'He was just about to when some of the sauce dribbled onto his fingers and he licked those fingers and thought it was surprisingly good, so he sat down and proceeded to calmly eat the florentine as if it had been what he'd ordered all along. He could be so funny!' She laughed. 'So unexpected.'

Lois looked from the Tunisian man to the Frenchwoman. 'This was Mr Halmfazzi's father, you're talking about?'

'Yes.' Madame Dupré speared a bite of potato and raised it to her lips. 'And also mine.'

There was another long pause around the table. Lois didn't have to look around to know that all eyes were on her. She knew instantly that the man from Tunisia didn't just happen to remember that long-ago taste. It was part of their programme for her tonight.

Finally Lois said: 'Your father and your father? You both had the same father?' They nodded, smiling at each other as they did so. 'But your last name is Dupré and yours is Halmea . . .'

'Halmfazzi,' the dark-skinned man corrected.

'Then why do you have different last names?'

Dr Fulham spoke up. 'Wasn't it Shakespeare who said "What's in a name?" '

'So you two are brother and sister?' They nodded. 'Same mother?' she asked.

'Oh good lord, no,' Madame Dupré laughed. 'My mother was the daughter of a Paris socialite. Manar's mother was an Arabian girl who worked in a restaurant.'

'Her parents owned the restaurant,' Mr Halmfazzi said icily. 'She wasn't merely some pick-up girl as you intimate.'

'So,' said Lois slowly as if she had been working it out on paper, 'you two are half-brother and half-sister.'

'Splendid,' Mr Cornell said. 'And so am I as well. I too am a half-brother.'

She stared at him. 'To Madame Dupré and Mr Halmfazzi?'

'To all of us,' Frau Baumgartner said brightly. 'We are all brothers and sisters, one unto the other.'

Lois wanted to get it right. 'Different mothers?'

'Correct.' This from Mr Mountolive.

'But the same father.' Lois watched them closely.

'Again correct,' Mr Mountolive replied. 'To quote Professor Higgins in *My Fair Lady*, I think she's got it!'

Lois looked quickly at Bob, to get his reaction, but he was sipping his wine, staring at her over the rim of the glass.

'Let me take a wild guess,' she said in a level voice. 'That place at the end of the table, the one always set and waiting for the man who founded this hotel, as you call it, that man was your father.'

'Very good indeed!' chimed in Mr Mountolive.

309

'Now let me go even farther and guess even wilder: your father was Aleister Crowley.' Now it was her turn to stare at them, as they glanced at their uneaten food or at each other. 'Well, am I right?'

'You're very good,' Jason said, and gave her one of his dazzling smiles. 'We didn't expect you to get it on the first try. We thought it would take longer.'

She wasn't smiling. 'Americans aren't always as dumb as they appear.'

'We never doubted,' said Mrs Loveday, as if that would take care of everything.

She looked at Jason. 'How could you be Crowley's son? Didn't he die in the mid-forties?'

'I was born the year before he died,' Jason explained. 'Father was sixty-nine years old when I was conceived. My mother was an American, a WAC. You know, the Women's Army Corps. She was stationed over here during the war. I was born in the States. I never saw my father and my mother never saw him again after she went home.'

'Sixty-nine years old and a young female soldier?' Midge lifted her wine glass. 'I'll drink to that. He must have been quite a man!'

Pieces began falling into place in Lois' mind. 'So this isn't a hotel? You are not all just passing through?' They grinned and someone said: 'Hotel? Not bloody likely.'

'So that's why you treated that American couple the way you did? Almost throwing them off the property when they came in asking for a room.'

'Well, they were so inconvenient and pushy,' Mrs Loveday recalled. 'Here we had no sooner put up the sign than in they drove, honking their horn and demanding I give them a place to stay. We didn't want them here. We only wanted *you*. Surely you must understand that by now.'

'And surely,' replied Lois shaking her head, 'I don't understand *anything* by now. Would somebody please like to start from the beginning? Is there anybody willing to fill in the blank spaces?'

'I suppose I could,' said Mr Cornell.

Lois glanced at Bob. 'And how about you, dear?'

'Me?'

'Yeah. How many gaps can *you* fill in?'

'I think I should be the one,' Mr Cornell continued. 'Being

310

the eldest member of the family, that must be my primo-genital responsibility at this point.' He picked up his empty wine glass. 'Loveday, dear, will you fill this for me?' He waited until the glass was full, then he began to speak. 'To start at the beginning, I must start with father. He was a most extraordinary man. Most extraordinary.

'He was English, you know. Born in the medieval town of Leamington Spa in Warwickshire. Very famous place, you know. Wonderful castle there with paintings by Reubens and that sort. Stratford-upon-Avon is just down the road a bit. Shakespeare lived there, you know.'

'He was born on October the twelfth, 1875,' Mr Mountolive interrupted. 'That makes him a Libran.'

'The very best possible sign, of course,' Madame Dupré said quickly.

'Oh yes,' agreed Frau Baumgartner. 'Librans are wonderful people. So creative!'

Mr Cornell gave them both a disapproving look. 'His father, our grandfather, was a prosperous brewer. "Crowley's Ales", the labels on the bottles said. We have a few of them in the house,' he smiled at Lois, 'empty now of course. So father didn't have to worry about money, but he did have to worry about religion. You see, grandfather was a Christian fanatic. He belonged to some group calling itself the Plymouth Brotherhood and he even preached from its pulpit at times.'

'A preacher owning a brewery?' Lois asked calmly.

'Exactly. You can see how that created confusion in father's young mind. Anyway, father could not abide all the sanctimonious claptrap and the rituals and negativeness of Christianity. He detested sitting hour after hour in church on Sundays and Wednesday evenings and hated having to listen to Bible stories the rest of the week. He also hated his parents' friends who would come to dinner and thank Jesus for every mouthful of peas they ate.'

'So he rebelled,' volunteered Signor Luchessi in his Italian accent. 'He became intolerant of his papa's feelings and of the mama's as well. He would do and say terrible things just to shock them. One time grandmama was so angry that she screamed at him – ' And Signor Luchessi switched quickly to a falsetto voice: ' "You are the Great Beast that Revelations prophesied. You are the evil one! You are the Beast 666!" And you know what? Papa didn't consider

311

that an insult. He *liked* it!'

'So they sent him away to school,' Mr Cornell continued, 'and when he was old enough he went to Trinity College in Cambridge. It's a most prestigious place of learning, in case you Americans have never heard of it.' Lois nodded. 'He studied very well, he was a brilliant student, but in his free time he would read books about magic and the occult and secret mystical societies. He even experimented with Buddhism for a while but it was too tame. He wanted to try everything, he felt there was so much more to be experienced.'

'When he was twenty-two,' Mr Mountolive interrupted Mr Cornell again, 'he read a book that told about the secret brotherhood that was living in hidden caves high in the mountains of India. These men, or these spirits, whatever you want to call them, were in control of the whole world. They could do anything, change anything, simply by willing it so.'

'And he went to India to try and find them, right?' Lois asked.

'No, not immediately,' Madame Dupré offered the information. 'He started the search for a connection with the Great White Brotherhood in London. He knew about a group of wise men who called themselves the Order of the Golden Dawn. Their leader claimed to have regular communication with the Brotherhood in India.'

'But he didn't agree with the leader on many points and finally he left the membership. So angry was he that he published all their secret rituals and blew a hole into the Golden Dawn that never sealed over.' Mr Cornell shook his head of snow-white hair. 'Father got into a great deal of hot water over that one.'

'Then he went to India,' said Madame Dupré. 'He was determined to find the real sources of power, to get right into the White Brotherhood. He'd already formed his own secret organization and called it the Order of the Secret Star, or *Argenteum Astrum*. He went all over India and down into Ceylon – it's called Sri Lanka today – and he delved into yoga and all sorts of things.'

'He probably would have done a lot more, if he hadn't had that woman with him,' Mrs Loveday snorted from her position near the serving plates. 'Never could understand what he saw in her.'

'She just wasn't his class,' Mr Cornell continued. 'Her name was Rose Kelly and she was born in Scotland, very near to

312

where we are now. Father always loved this part of the world the best.'

'He was almost thirty when he married her.' Mrs Loveday still had that sour expression on her face. 'As clever as he was, you'd have thought he'd have known better.'

'But she was important to him, you'll have to grant her that,' resumed Mr Cornell, 'because – ' He turned his attention back to Lois. 'Because when he was on his honeymoon in Cairo, Rose suddenly started doing automatic writing. You know, getting information from the spirit world by holding a pencil and letting your hand be taken over.' Lois had heard of it, even tried it a couple of times. 'Now Rose Kelly was the farthest thing from being a psychic or a spirit medium that father had ever seen, and so when she started these occult manifestations he scoffed at them. Then she told him the spirits said they were going to dictate through her a great truth. A revelation that the world was waiting to hear and that he, our father, was to be the human teaching instrument to bring this knowledge to the world. So, naturally,' Mr Cornell grinned, 'father paid a little more attention. What came out of it was a published volume called *The Book of the Law*. It was a short book. A spirit called Aiwass worked through Rose for three days on it.'

'Aiwass?' Lois let one eyebrow rise.

'Yes. Father said that Aiwass is not only a spirit but also a source of energy. He called it a magical current of solar-phallic energy. I hope, my dear, I don't offend you by using the word "phallic".'

'No,' she said, 'I've seen a couple of them in my life.'

Mr Cornell went on: 'Now this Aiwass spirit also claimed that he had been worshipped by the ancient Sumerians. They called him "Shaitan, the devil-god". In ancient Egypt, they called this energy the great god Set. According to father, this spirit was the originator of all mankind. He created the earth, put Adam and Eve in it and then appeared to them as a serpent to see how much they had learned. But the Christians deliberately refused this spirit, and twisted his name from Shaitan and Set into Satan.'

'So your father worshipped Satan?' Lois watched the expression on the old man's face.

'No,' he said rather loudly, 'he was guided by Shaitan. Not Satan. He never *worshipped* anybody or anything. That's a

313

false story that has been circulating for years. Father was a good man and a very clever manipulator of natural energies.'

'He was also over-sexed.' Jason said this looking directly at Lois. 'He'd go to bed with anything that was warm.'

'Now that's not quite true,' said Dr Fulham. 'He had his fair share of female lovers . . .'

'As well as male lovers,' Jason reminded the older man.

'And male, yes. Why not? He was dealing with human energy, human sexual energy and the energy he was after was neither masculine or feminine, it just *was*. Like water power *is*. Like wind power *is*.'

'So the old boy was bisexual?' Midge said.

Mrs Loveday scowled at her. 'He was nothing of the kind! He preferred having sex with women but he liked to experiment with men from time to time as well.'

'And that's not being bisexual?' Lois asked her.

'It is not!' the woman snapped. 'It is being a releaser of human energies!'

'If I may continue,' said Mr Cornell. 'Father tried to give the world the message about the Law of Thelema. That's where this house gets its name,' he smiled at Lois. 'Hotel Thelema? Rather clever, I thought. The Law of Thelema was very simple. It stated: "Do what thou wilt shall be the whole of the Law." Now, that doesn't mean "do as you please," but rather "do only what you have to do and nothing else". That became, I'm afraid, something of a problem for father in his later years because he still wanted to do it *all*, still wanted to experience everything. But in society those days, and even in today's more permissive society, he found out he couldn't do it *all*. People began to point fingers at him, ridicule him, chase him out of wherever he was living and inflicted upon him general harassment. He went to the United States for three years during the Great War and while he was there he was initiated into the highest rank of his Order by Egyptian gods who appeared to him disguised as beautiful women. The temples of worship were their bodies and if he was to enter the temple he had to enter the body.' He suddenly stopped. 'Am I confusing you?' he asked Lois.

'No, but you'll have to admit you had one strange daddy!'

Mr Cornell ignored that. 'Now this new discovery of his also tied in with his mother calling him "The Beast" when he was young. For in Revelations, Chapter Seventeen, it tells of the

"Scarlet Woman" who rides on the back of the Beast. The two symbols of energy united and rushing forward together.'

'But where do all of you come into all of this?' Lois interrupted him and motioned for Mrs Loveday to fill her wine glass.

'He's just getting to that part,' said Frau Baumgartner.

'Yes, I'm just getting to that. You see, once father realized he actually *was* the prophesied Beast then he understood that to be complete he needed to have a Scarlet Woman with him. So he searched for her. Wherever he went he would meet women and they would fall for his charms and go to bed with him.'

'Just like that?' Lois asked. 'It was that easy?'

'For father it was. He was a man of intense personal magnetism. After he left your country, he came to Sicily and founded his Abbey of Thelema. It was a wondrous stone house, sitting on a steep cliff overlooking the sea, and every morning and every evening the group around him would give thanks to the sun. He began to polish some of his rituals and eliminate others that didn't produce the desired results. He became a true master of the occult. There was almost nothing he couldn't do once he set his mind on it.'

Madame Dupré spoke now. 'He was absolute authority in the abbey. His word was law. His devotees had to do what he wanted. His Scarlet Women had to do what he demanded. There was much energy fornication on that hilltop, I can tell you.'

Lois didn't know whether the Frenchwoman was joking or not. 'What happened to the abbey? Is it still there?'

'No,' Mrs Loveday answered, 'it was disbanded. The Italian police made them get out.'

'Why? They didn't approve of a black magician in their town?'

'Not only that,' the woman said, 'but some stupid follower of father's got himself killed. We're all sure father had nothing to do with it.'

The others nodded in agreement.

'That was in 1924,' Mr Cornell said, 'and for the next nine years he was in and out of various countries trying and ultimately failing to set up another abbey, trying to maintain his devoted members in a closed community. He went to Tunisia, to France and even to Germany, but it was 1933 and he and Hitler didn't like each other. So he came back to Great Britain. He wrote some books, he did some lectures and he tried to keep his ideas in front of the public. One of his Scarlet Women wrote her life story, and when the British

315

public read all the things father had supposedly done they referred to him as The "Wickedest Man in the World". I think father liked the title.' Mr Cornell smiled.

'So he came here, to Corra, and retired and died here? Is that right? Do I have the ending of your story?' Lois asked, sipping her wine.

'Alas, no,' Mr Halmfazzi said. 'Father came back to England without a penny. He was also addicted to heroin. That took most of his money. He died in a little cottage, a dirty little place, down in Sussex, near the sea. They carried out his wishes and had his body cremated. Then the ashes were sent, airmail, to several of his still devoted followers in America.'

'And that,' Jason concluded, 'is father in a nutshell.'

'Or in an airmail envelope,' Lois said.

The cook came back into the dining room to clear away the plates and Lois realized that she had eaten almost nothing. She'd been listening while the others ate.

She wanted to keep them talking. 'Something I don't understand,' she said, and they all looked at her, 'is if your father died broke and a dope addict, where did he get the money to maintain this place? I mean this is a mansion. Paupers don't own palaces.'

'I can reply to that quite easily,' Mrs Loveday said. 'It is my home. I was born here. I inherited it from my mother, who passed away at an early age.'

A light came slowly into Lois' eyes. 'And your mother was one of Crowley's . . .'

'Scarlet Women.' Mrs Loveday finished the sentence for her.

Lois turned to Mr Cornell. 'And your mother was also?' He nodded. She pointed at Madame Dupré. 'Yours too?' The woman nodded. 'Mr Halmfazzi, your mother as well?'

'Yes, my dear, my mother was privileged to become impregnated by Aleister Crowley. Every one of us here in this room have had mothers who were chosen to bear his magical child. And we are, you understand, we are all magical for we have been conceived from the sperm of the highest master the earth has ever known. We have been conceived in the midst of his most sacred energy ritual. We have been carried in the womb of she who was chosen expressly by the master. That is why we are important to the world and that is why we must survive.'

Lois looked at them all. 'You're serious, aren't you?' she said, her voice low.

'Quite serious,' Dr Fulham replied. 'We are children with a mission and that mission must be carried out.'

'When I was growing up,' Mrs Loveday started putting slices of lemon cream pie on dessert plates, 'and I found out who my real father was, I rejoiced. My mother had always told me that my father had been killed in the First World War. One day she took one of father's books, one of Crowley's books, and showed me his picture in it. She was a little tipsy and feeling depressed that day and I suppose that's why she did it. I didn't have any brothers and sisters, that I was aware of at the time – ' She beamed at the others around the table. 'And both my mother's parents had died early. So it was just Mummy and me. I read the book and I was so proud! That great master, that internationally known spiritual leader, that magnetic man, was my father! Mummy didn't know where in the world he had gone. She had told him about my birth, by letter, but he never replied. She said he was busy doing other things, creating more magical children to carry on his work. Mummy was sure that when the children grew older he would bring us all together and we would form the most powerful organization in the universe. I mean, how could we lose? Look who our father was! We had his blood. With indoctrination, we could one day do all the miracles he performed.'

'Did you ever meet him?' Lois asked.

'Oh yes, several times. After Mummy died and I inherited this place I read in the newspaper that he was in Munich. I went over there and stayed for two months.'

'She was visiting father when I was born there,' Frau Baumgartner said, 'in 1933.'

'Yes.' Mrs Loveday beamed with pleasure. 'Can you imagine how wonderful it was to have a sister delivered almost while you watched? I had been so lonely, but suddenly I had a family. It was wonderful!'

'We have all spent some time with father,' Mr Cornell said. 'Some longer than others, but none of us ever lived with him. You know, like ordinary children live with their father. He didn't want us around. He said it took from his energy.'

'And besides,' spoke up Signor Luchessi, 'he had already discharged that energy that took to make us.' He turned bright red. 'If you'll pardon the word "discharge."'

'When I was with him,' Mrs Loveday said, 'I asked him if he was ever going to bring us all together. Unite us under one roof and teach us everything he knew. He said that had been part of his plan but events over the years had weakened him and discouraged him. Many of his closest followers had deserted and published terrible untruths about him. When he came back to England in 1934 I wanted him to stay up here in Corra with me. I told him I would take care of him. But he refused. He said he had very little time left and he didn't want to be stuck away in the country. I sent him some money from time to time. I didn't have an income, just what I was able to salvage from selling the furniture and paintings in the house. The year before he died I went down to the coast to see him. Both of us knew it was the last time. He looked so thin and frail. It was a crime because he had been a vigorous healthy man.'

'That's what heroin can do.' Lois found herself being sympathetic to the woman.

'I don't think it was the heroin,' Jason spoke up. 'I think he was just tired of living and tired of seeing everything he had planned go wrong. It's just a guess because, as I said, I was the last of his magical children and I never met the man.'

'While I was down there for that last visit,' Mrs Loveday continued, 'I asked him again about reuniting all the magical children. He said it would be a good idea and it would be the one way his work could outlive him. Not surprisingly, for father was a meticulous man, he gave me a list of the Scarlet Women and in what city they had performed the sexual magic ritual. The list was several pages long. I counted almost two hundred and sixty women in six countries over a thirty-year period. He left many magical children in the United States when he was there during the First World War and a few dozen when he was in Italy in the early twenties.'

Signor Luchessi smiled and gave Lois a courtly nod of his head.

'Then came Tunisia and France and then Germany, and finally the women in England again. I discovered I had dozens of older brothers and sisters and many that were younger as well. The problem was how to locate them. He had no addresses or telephone numbers. Just their maiden names and if they produced a son or a daughter. When I read in the paper that he had died – it was a terrible shock even though I knew it was coming – I decided to put the plan into operation. I decided to try and locate as many of my brothers and sisters

318

as I could and by bringing them together form the most powerful group on the face of the earth.'

'I was one of the first to come over,' Frau Baumgartner said. 'Loveday and I had stayed in contact all those years. You know, birthday cards and that sort of thing.'

'I managed to find twenty-eight of father's children who were still alive. Doubtless there are at least as many more out there but we cannot locate them. Several of those twenty-eight came to stay here, or at least to visit here. Alas, some of them have already passed away. Some who were older than I, some who were ill. We have the preserved bodies of eight of them in the catacombs under the waters of the lake.'

'Under the waters?' Lois looked puzzled. 'Was this something else your father suggested?'

'Oh no,' the woman laughed. 'My mother's father had it built. He had a great deal of money and, he thought, a lot of time left and he was a bit of an inventor. He rigged up a suite of rooms in the lake with circulating air fans and oxygen tanks. Later I added electricity and bathrooms. Grandfather was sure the world was going to come to an end and it would be by another great flood. Worse than Noah's. So he had living quarters built under the lake. When the flood did come, he and his family would be safe.'

'You said you have bodies down there?'

'We do. Our brothers and sisters who have lived here and passed away have been preserved in vats of chemicals and waxes. We couldn't bury them, not around here. The local population would have desecrated their tombs. The local people don't like us, I'm afraid. They know how powerful we can be. They've seen some of the things we can do when we channel our energies.'

Mr Cornell coughed lightly. 'I don't think we want to go into that. Not just now. Just suffice to say that we have been able to alter the weather at times and to be able to make some crops flourish while making other crops fail. The locals are very suspicious of us.'

'And with all good reason,' Lois said. 'They think it's witchcraft. It sounds like witchcraft.'

Mr Cornell shrugged. 'That's the trouble with the world today: they lump everything together and the average person doesn't stop to differentiate between one system and another. We use the natural energies, the same ones that are used in witchcraft, but we manipulate them differently. We have a firmer command over them. Father taught us that. All the magical children have special powers. It's in the blood. In the birthright, if you will.'

'It would have been much easier for us,' Lois said, 'if the locals hadn't lied about not knowing where this house was. They told us it had been torn down, that it had gone up in flames, that there was nothing here but an empty field. Why didn't they just tell us where it was and warn us to stay away?'

'It's part of their superstition, part of their fear,' Madame Dupré explained. 'Even before Loveday inherited this house, the rumour was out that her mother was working with the devil and that Satan himself had spawned Loveday. That was why she was so lonely. Nobody in the area wanted anything to do with her or her mother.'

'She's right,' Mrs Loveday confirmed. 'And when, after the Second World War, my brothers and sisters started coming here and we started practising and perfecting father's rituals and spells, then they really became unnerved. They threw stones at the windows and burned crosses on the lawn. We even had a car full of Catholic priests who started sprinkling holy water around the walls. We used one of our spells and turned the water into fire. Suddenly eight black-robed priests were rolling over and over, trying to put out the fires in their cassocks, most of them too dumb to throw away their buckets of flaming holy water and burning sprinklers. It was so funny to watch them howl.'

'I was here when that happened,' said Jason. 'We all laughed, but the townsfolk didn't. The police came and investigated us but they couldn't charge us with anything because there was no proof we'd done anything. It looked as if the good Fathers had done it to themselves. Which, in a way, they did.'

'All we do is use nature's own energies,' Mr Cornell repeated, 'and it has nothing to do with the devil.'

'Or Christianity,' said Dr Fulham.

'Heaven forbid!' said Frau Baumgartner. 'Father always hated Christianity and so do we.' Her tone softened. 'Do you go to church in America?'

'No,' Lois admitted, 'I don't. I was a Protestant before I got married and Bob was a Catholic. We couldn't work it out, so we opted for no religion at all. But I still believe in Jesus,' she added quickly.

'We believe in Jesus as well,' Mr Mountolive replied, 'but we don't believe in all the man-made claptrap of religion that has distorted Jesus' teachings. Throw out the statues and the crosses and the hymn books. Shut down the church buildings. We don't approve of them and if Jesus came back tomorrow I'm sure he wouldn't approve of what they have done in his name either.'

Lois took a deep breath and decided it was time she asked the first of her big questions. The second one had to do with Tony. The first one was only about herself. She didn't know what pose to adopt when she asked it. Should she play Bette Davis and pace the room with a cigarette in her hand? Should she be June Allyson and sit there staring at them with her big blue eyes? She chose Joan Crawford playing the role of company executive. She pushed out her chair, got to her feet, then walked around the chair and stood behind it, both hands on its back. 'All of this stuff about your father and how all of you are illegitimate bastards is very interesting,' she said, her voice calm and even, 'but what you haven't told me yet is why *me*? Why have you brought me here? What do you want from *me*?'

'Why, my dear,' Madame Dupré chirped, 'that should be obvious. We want you to come home. After all, you are also a Crowley!'

She felt the floor move beneath her feet, as if the San Andreas Fault was just under the house, and she was glad she had braced herself on the chair back. 'I'm a *what*?'

'A Crowley,' Madame Dupré repeated.

'Yes my dear,' said Mr Cornell, 'you are our father's purest great-grandchild. In this generation, you have more of his blood in you than any other person on earth.'

She started to mutter something and then realised that her Joan Crawford was about to become Lucille Ball if she didn't get back in control. Her gaze went around the table, stopping at each face. She was stalling for time, stalling until she could organize her racing mind. Finally, she chose the simple way out. 'I don't understand.'

'Of course you don't.' Mrs Loveday smiled at her. 'We all knew the information would be a shock.'

Lois shook her head. Nothing was forming into reality inside her brain. 'I can't be a Crowley. My last name isn't Crowley. My maiden name was Duncan.'

'Of course it was dear,' Mrs Loveday continued, 'we know

that. And we also know your mother's maiden name was Burns.'

Lois nodded, numbly. 'Well then, I fail to see how I could be . . .'

'Why don't you sit back down?' Mr Cornell rose and took her arm, helping her back onto the chair. She reached a shaky hand for her wine glass and drained what was in it. 'You recall our explaining father's Scarlet Women?' She nodded. 'Well, your grandparents were both children of Aleister Crowley. They were both conceived by father. Their mothers were Scarlet Women.'

'That's ridiculous!' were the only words she could summon to protest.

'Your grandmother, after your mother was born, married a Scotsman named Burns.' Lois nodded. 'He too, Trevor MacNeel Burns, was the son born from the sacred ritual between Crowley and another Scarlet Woman.'

'Are you saying my grandparents were brother and sister?'

'Half-brother and half-sister. Same father but two different mothers. The mothers were both chosen for their excellence of breeding and their great affinity with the world of spirit. That made your mother, by blood tie, still half a Crowley. Like we all are. We are all half of our father's blood and seed.'

'I never heard of any of this when I was growing up. Then what happened?'

'Then your mother married your father.'

'Okay,' she said.

'Your father was chosen especially for her. He *too* was a direct son of father's. His mother was a Scarlet Woman and by him marrying your mother, you were awarded with another half of father's blood.'

'You see,' spoke up Jason, 'your father was a son of Aleister Crowley and your mother was a granddaughter. And before you ask why wasn't there a bigger difference in their ages, let me remind you that father started siring children in 1916 and didn't stop until 1945.'

A picture of her mother and father back in West Virginia projected onto the movie screen behind her forehead. Two decent people of humble origins yet seemingly happy with each other. 'Did they know?' she asked. 'Did they know about having the Crowley blood and all that?'

'Oh yes,' Jason answered. 'They knew about it from an early

322

age and they knew it was part of *the plan* to eventually marry and have children. A very happy coincidence was that when they met for the first time they fell in love. It has been a good marriage.'

Lois nodded. 'Yes, it has.'

'But,' Mr Cornell continued, 'your mother had a very difficult time giving birth to you and at delivery the doctor in the hospital in that small town managed to scar her womb. A year or so after you were born she had to undergo a complete hysterectomy. The possibility of the two Crowley descendants having any more children was doomed. But fortunately, you were healthy and survived. You've also proven you can bear children.'

She was amazed at how calm she felt. The news was a shock, yet at the same time it really didn't surprise her. Genealogy had never been attempted by her folks, not even in the days when *Roots* caused everyone to start searching for theirs. When she would ask about great-grandparents she got vague stories of unknown weavers in long-deserted and forgotten hillside villages. Too poor to own a box Kodak was the reason she was given that there wasn't a family album going back farther than herself lying on a pink blanket with her pink behind in the air. Those books on Crowley . . . had she really found them or was she *meant* to find them? Hearing this about her parents should have upset her, should have made her angry and doubtful of their love for her, but yet they had been the most wonderful two people in her world. They had loved each other and, in turn, had loved her. That their love had all been arranged, that their marriage was part of *the plan* wasn't important. And it really had nothing to do with her, because she was born long after *the plan* had been put to work. She looked at the faces around the table again. 'So you are all my uncle and aunts or great-uncles and great-aunts.' It wasn't a question that needed answering. 'That's why I'm here. This is to be a *family* reunion.'

'It wasn't easy getting you here, believe me,' spoke up Mr Halmfazzi. 'The things we had to do!'

Lois nodded. 'Like the man in the picture. The little bastard under the glass.'

'Now, now,' Mrs Loveday chided, 'don't refer to your great-grandfather in that way.'

Lois looked at Bob, trying to discern what his emotions

323

were during all this. He only stared at the tablecloth. 'How did you do it?' she asked them. 'How did you make him move? A magnet? A microchip? You know we took the picture to an expert and he took it apart and inspected everything and he couldn't find anything wrong.'

'That was quite simple.' Dr Fulham beamed with pride. 'It was the application of one of father's energy rituals. One of his more elementary ones, actually. It took some collective effort on our part but I'm glad to hear that the results were as we intended. Jolly good show, everyone. Jolly good.' He was still beaming.

'So there was no kidnapping?' She heard her words and stopped herself from mentioning Tony just yet. 'That little man in the cape was not going to eventually appear at that window,' she pointed at the first window near the wall, 'that window, and carry out a small child? It was all rigged.'

'If it had been necessary,' Mr Mountolive said in his strange accent, 'then we would have had him running toward the trees, but we were hoping you'd arrive here before that.'

'So the man in the cape is not here? He's not hiding somewhere in the house?'

'No, no,' Mrs Loveday smiled. 'He only exists on paper.'

Mr Mountolive raised his wine glass. 'I think we all owe ourselves a toast. The mental image we created under the glass fooled her. And fooled the experts. Jolly good show, indeed!' The others lifted their glasses and toasted one another with murmurings of a job well done.

'Did they know about this? About the engraving?' Lois asked when the glasses had all been put on the table.

'They?' Mr Cornell asked.

'My mother and father. Did they know about the little man under the glass?'

'Oh no,' he replied quickly. 'We told them nothing. We haven't been much in communication with them. It's better that way, us here and them way over there. They would be difficult to control, don't you see? No, they knew that one day you would come to Corra but when and how, that was our secret.'

Lois frowned then turned to Midge. 'How did you get that engraving? I mean really get it? You didn't find it at an auction in New Jersey.' Midge remained silent. 'Did you?' Lois almost shouted.

'She didn't,' Mrs Loveday replied. 'We sent it to her from over here.'

'You sent it? You people have been in correspondence with *Midge*? She knew about all this in advance?'

'I did, hon,' Midge admitted. 'I've known about this group for years. My own grandmother was one of Crowley's Scarlet Women but she married an Irish truck driver and their child, my mother, married a Baptist farmer in Kansas, so that kind of puts me way down on the Crowley totem pole.' She smiled and hunched her shoulders. 'Sorry.'

'Sorry!' Lois blurted. 'You've been in on this all along and now you're sorry?'

'What can I tell you?' Midge tried to keep smiling.

'You could have tried the truth!' Lois was red with anger. 'I thought you were my friend!'

Mr Mountolive interrupted: 'Appearances are always deceiving where this family is concerned.'

'But Midge could have told me!' Lois insisted.

'And then you wouldn't have come,' Frau Baumgartner said. 'It's as simple as that.'

'So the book with the ghost story,' Lois continued, 'you didn't find it on a Madison Avenue bus.'

'We sent it to her along with the engraving,' Mr Cornell explained. 'She was to give you the picture first and then if that didn't get you over here, she was to show you the book. I trust you brought the book back here with you? It was from father's library, you know.'

'I don't know what I did with it,' Lois said. 'I brought over the engraving, though. You're welcome to that thing back.'

'Good,' Mrs Loveday said. 'It used to hang in the music room. I'll be glad to put it where it belongs.'

'And the other things?' she said quickly. She knew she was getting awfully close to asking them about Tony but she had to get all the other questions cleared away first. 'Let's start with the man in customs at Heathrow Airport. He didn't want me to bring the picture into the country. How did you work that?'

They looked at each other. Obviously, they didn't know what she was talking about.

'A man in customs?' Mr Cornell looked around the room as if the man might be hiding somewhere in there.

To Lois' surprise Bob spoke up for the first time. 'I won't go into all the details but when we went through customs in

London there was an official who didn't want us to bring that picture in. I had to take him outside and talk with him. As it is, I have a paper glued in my passport that says I have to take that damned thing back out with me.'

'Who could it possibly be?'

'Do you know anything about that, Dr Fulham?' Mr Mountolive asked.

The pudgy doctor shook his head. 'It wasn't one of us,' he answered slowly.

'And the old woman on the train?' Lois hit them a second time.

'On the train?' Signor Luchessi looked startled. 'What train?'

'From London to Carlisle. She sat with us for a ways, then grabbed the engraving and started to run with it. Bob chased her for at least two miles until she tossed the picture into the ocean. You don't know anything about her, either?'

'Upon my word,' muttered Dr Fulham, 'this is most strange.'

'Anything else?' Mr Cornell asked.

Bob said, 'How about the two guys who claimed they were from the CIA and told us to go back home?'

'The CIA?' Signor Luchessi made a face and then almost made the sign of the Cross. 'Good heavens, man, that is the *last* organization we wish to be involved with! Can you believe it? The CIA?' He looked at Mrs Loveday. 'I think you should tell cook we need more wine. Oh dear, the CIA.'

There was a silence around the table. It was as if each of the Crowley children had forgotten it was necessary to breathe.

'You know,' said Mr Mountolive, 'what this sounds like.'

'Yes, I do,' replied Mr Cornell.

'The Brethren,' sighed Frau Baumgartner.

'Exactly!' Jason said. 'It sounds the sort of thing they would do. Somehow they found out about Lois coming over here and wanted to stop her.'

'The Brethren?' Lois asked.

'They are Christian troublemakers, my dear.' Mrs Loveday's tone was rather sharp. 'They wear long white robes and babble on about Jesus. They've attacked the house several times and once they accosted Mr Mountolive on the street and he almost died. They're terrible people! Not nice at all.'

'Of course,' Madame Dupré agreed. 'It could only be them.'

'They don't want you here,' Mr Mountolive said. 'They

know you are part of *the plan* and they have vowed to defeat *the plan* every way they can. They are an ignorant bunch. Secret meetings and hooded robes and a bleeding Christ that looks like he's been hit by the 11.05 to Edinburgh. Damned bunch of hypocrites, they are. Always have been. They want us dead.'

'Wonderful!' said Midge. 'Wouldn't you know I'd get stuck in the middle of some of that shit?'

Lois turned on her. 'Midge, shut up!'

'Please!' Bob reached for Lois' hand but she pulled away. 'You don't have to talk to Midge like that.'

'Don't tell me what I have to do, Bob Bruno,' Lois said after an intake of breath. 'I'm saving you. I'm saving your part for last.'

'Look, hon . . .'

'Don't "hon" me!' she snapped. 'Don't ever call me that again!'

Midge sighed. 'You're over-reacting to all this.'

'Look.' Lois glared at Midge. 'Didn't you understand me when I told you to shut up? What more do you need? How about that goddamned picture shoved down your lying throat?'

Mr Cornell touched her arm. 'I, too, think you are possibly over-reacting.'

'Don't you understand? They tried to drive me crazy? They gave me the picture, they pretended nothing was wrong with it, they acted as if I was going bananas. They *wanted* me to go bananas! Isn't that true?' She was looking at Bob. 'And who were the creeps who broke into my apartment and took a syringe full of my blood? Was that more of the Brethren's doing?'

'No,' said Mr Cornell. 'We set that up. Malcolm was the one who took your blood. He went to New York and met another Crowley cousin and they did that job. I'm sorry they messed up your flat, but it was to make the police think they were just ordinary burglars. Nicely done too, as I understand it.'

'Malcolm?' Lois got up, automatically doing the Bette Davis role without realizing it. 'Malcolm? Fiona's boyfriend?' She stared at the ornate plaster ceiling for a full minute. 'Why? Why was it necessary for you to have my blood?'

'To make perfectly sure you were really a direct line from father,' explained Dr Fulham. 'Do you know what DNA is?'

'Not completely,' Lois admitted angrily, 'something to do with blood types.'

'Exactly,' said the medical man, 'we had your blood compared with the sample of blood we have of father's and it was exact. Yours is identical to his. It was just one more precaution that we had to take before we could be sure you were the one. Everything about you proved positive. It was all quite encouraging, really.'

Lois paced the room now, aware that every eye was on her – every eye except her husband's. He continued to observe the pattern of the white linen tablecloth. Why wasn't he defending her? Why wasn't he getting indignant when he heard about the Brethren? Why didn't he show any emotion when it was discovered Malcolm had made the trip to New York just to steal her blood? 'Bob,' she said, 'are you all right?'

He nodded, still not looking at her. 'Fine. No problem.'

'Well, I have a problem,' she said to the seated group. 'My problem is *why* do you want me here? Even if I *am* a Crowley – and I prefer to doubt it rather than believe it – why me?'

'You're the last of the line,' Mr Cornell said simply. 'You're the purest of all the descendants. You are our one hope.'

'Hope?'

'Of continuing the family line,' he said.

'Of bringing the Crowley blood and the Crowley magic into the next century,' added Mr Mountolive.

'By assuring us that what father and the family stood for will not perish but endure in its battle against the Christians and the world.' This from Signor Luchessi.

Lois leaned against the dining room wall. She felt secure in its strength. 'And I accomplish all this *how*?'

Mrs Loveday smiled. 'By having Jason's baby, of course.'

Thank God that wall was there! 'Having Jason's baby? Are you kidding?'

Jason was staring at her now. 'I don't think it's such a bad idea,' he said. 'You and me, together on some mattress, screwing for posterity.'

'I think that could be put slightly more delicately,' Madame Dupré looked pained.

'How?' Lois demanded. 'Like maybe a play by Oscar Wilde? What shall we call it? *Ass for Aleister? Copulating For Crowley? You* give it a title!'

Jason laughed the loudest, some of them didn't smile at all.

'Look,' he said, 'you're among family now. You don't have to try and shock us. Very little does anymore. The whole idea is that since I am the youngest of father's direct children and you're the youngest and purest of all the other descendants, we should have a baby together. Maybe two or three. I'm only in my early forties. I can still make babies.'

'And you could live right here while you were carrying the child,' Mrs Loveday said. 'And of course you'd want to stay a few years longer and watch the child grow up.'

'Then if you had another one,' Frau Baumgartner added, 'you'd be here even longer. We would have time to teach you all of father's magic rituals. You would soon be doing all the things we can do and you could teach them to your children.'

'All his books and magic paraphernalia and even his robes are here in the house,' Jason said. 'We've got his spells and the formulas to his potions and incense. It's all been carefully saved. Waiting for you. Right on this floor. Right behind the door that's painted black.'

'I thought,' said Lois, 'that you didn't know *what* was behind that door.'

'I lied,' he said and smiled at her.

'You lied about a lot of things,' she said.

'You could become the matriarch, if not of a Perfect Race at least that of a Perfect Family.' Mr Mountolive put one hand to his breast. 'In you resides the blood of the future's most creative children. All you have to do is bear them. We will do the rest.'

Bob still wasn't looking at his wife.

Lois reached behind her, touching the security of the wall with both palms. 'There's just one small fly in your ointment,' she said. 'I'm not free to marry Jason or have his children. I'm a married woman. That *lump*, who hasn't come to my aid once this evening, is the man I'm married to. It would be difficult to have a baby with Jason and not destroy my marriage.'

'Lois,' Midge said suddenly, 'it's already destroyed. Wake up girl, you and Bob are a thing of the past.'

'Oh?' she said. 'That's news to me.' She felt she was in command. 'Bob, what do you say about that? Are we through? Washed up?'

He raised his glance now and stared her straight in the eyes. 'Yes. We are. When I leave here, I'm leaving with Midge.' He looked away from her, not able to watch the terrible expression that distorted her face.

She wanted to slide down, slide onto the floor and just sit there and cry. What was happening to her world? Jesus Christ, was this *reality*? Was there any reality anywhere inside these four walls?'

'Bob and I are in love,' Midge said evenly. 'We were afraid you'd find out too early, before we could get you over here.'

'Who's this we?' Lois demanded.

'Me and Bob, of course. He gets you over here, he gets paid and we split.' Midge took another sip from her wine glass. 'We had to play it real cool, hon, but it worked.'

Lois just stared at the two of them, unable to open her mouth and create any words that would express her surprise and her anger. 'I . . . I think I'd like to sit down,' she said. Mr Cornell took a chair over to her and she sank gratefully on it. 'So I don't have a marriage and I don't have a best friend and I don't have a way out of here. Damn it!' She was too angry to cry. 'This must be what it's like when the doctor tells you that you have terminal cancer! It must be like this! It leaves you numb and unable to think. I should be furious at you, Bob, but all I can do is wonder when I'm going to wake up and find out this is all a dream, a nightmare.'

Bob glanced over at her. 'It was an opportunity,' he said softly. 'Our marriage wasn't going anywhere. We argued more than we talked. You were more interested in your career than the apartment and being a housewife.'

'So when he got a chance to earn all that money,' Frau Baumgartner spoke up, 'he jumped at it.'

'It only took us a couple of visits to convince him,' Mr Halmfazzi said. 'Our other brother in New York was very persuasive.'

'Ah! The half a million dollars was what was persuasive,' replied Frau Baumgartner.

'Half a million dollars?' Lois got up from her chair and walked over to Bob. 'You sold me to these people for half a fucking million dollars?'

'He did,' Midge said.

'You stay out of this, bitch!' Lois would have struck her had she been closer. 'I asked him. I asked my husband, or don't you have the testicles to reply?'

'A half a million,' he admitted. 'More money than I've ever had before. That's what they promised me if I got you over

330

here and you agreed to stay and produce a baby.' He looked up at her now. 'Come on, hon, admit it. Our marriage was on the rocks. It would have ended anyway, so why shouldn't I make something on the deal? After all, I am a businessman.'

'You're a businessman second,' she replied, 'first, you're a son of a bitch.'

He shrugged. 'That may be your opinion now but after you're here with your family for a while, you'll forget about me. I know how your mind works.'

'I thought I knew how yours worked,' she said, 'but obviously I didn't.' She walked away from him, back to the chair against the wall, then stopped and with a puzzled expression turned back to face him. 'Why? Why didn't you just buy me a ticket and send me over here? You knew where this house was all along. So did Midge. Yet we went around and around and got more and more involved when it would have been so much simpler to just come here directly. Without all the neurotic bullshit.'

'It was part of Bob's plan,' Midge answered. 'Bob and I figured that if anything went wrong, if you decided not to stay, if you decided to call the police about Tony or if you accused him of deliberately identifying the wrong dead body in the morgue, then he could end up in jail.'

'Identifying the wrong body . . .' Lois had a look of vindication in her expression. 'So I was right. Tony isn't dead! I held him last night and I spoke with him and he loves me!'

'You are quite correct, my dear. Your son Tony is very much alive. He's here on the estate.' Mrs Loveday decided it was time for the last piece of the puzzle to be set upon the table. 'Your husband arranged everything with the brother in New York, even down to details on how to catch your son and bring him over here.'

'That's kidnapping!' Lois said loudly.

'Right,' Bob agreed, 'and a federal offence in the States. If you wanted to you could have my ass in jail for the rest of my life.'

'And I just may,' she replied quickly.

'And I can prove that you are not of sound mind and body, that you are in fact off your rocker. I've got witnesses of that Thanksgiving Day when you saw Tony at the glass door. Anthony and Anne will testify how irrational you were.'

'But Tony *was* there,' Lois insisted.

331

'Of course he was,' Bob replied. 'It had all been set up with the guy that grabbed him. But no court will believe that. They'll believe me, the poor harassed husband. Don't forget: I told my friend the psychiatrist about your craziness and the appraiser we took the engraving to thought you were bananas.'

'And the police and that doctor in Edinburgh,' Midge was glad to add, 'they all think you're a mental patient. If you try to make trouble for Bob and me, we've got all the witnesses in the world to say you are making it up, that you are crazy.'

'And all of you knew about this?' she said to the Crowleys around the table. 'All of you agreed to it and approved it?'

'Yes, dear,' Mr Cornell said. 'It was all part of *the plan*.'

'You know, Bob,' she got up from the chair and walked over to him. 'I should hate you, but I can't. I can't bring that emotion up right now. Oh, I'm shocked and deeply hurt but there's no hate. I probably will hate you later, *despise* is probably a better word, but not right now. It's strange but I think I know why.'

'Why?' Now he couldn't look at her.

'Because you brought me back together with my baby. You took me to where Tony is. I don't really need you in my life but I *do* need my child, my Tony. I knew he wasn't dead. I knew that wasn't his body in that coffin. I knew that was Tony in the department store in London and in the back of that car in Edinburgh. I knew it!'

'If I may make a slight correction,' Dr Fulham said, 'that was your son in the shop and in the car but afterwards, when you found him on the hillside and he turned into that awful creature, that wasn't Tony. That was us, back here in Corra working the magic energies. We told you we were good at what we do.'

'You can learn to do it as well, my dear,' said Signor Luchessi. 'What we do is so easy that we are often afraid the common people will figure it out and turn it on us.' His bow tie bobbed on his Adam's apple. 'The masses are so stupid. It's Christianity. It's held them down and kept them in fear. The masses are actually *afraid* to do what we do. Their priests tell them it's a sin and the work of the devil.' The tie bobbed again. 'All the better for us.'

Mrs Loveday came over to Lois with a glass of wine. 'Here, dear, you need this.'

Lois sipped and thought, then said: 'So if I agree to stay here and become one of this happy family, I can have Tony back? Is that right?'

'You weren't supposed to see Tony last night,' Dr Fulham said. 'We were saving him for our final card. If you refused we were going to tell you the child was here. Unfortunately, you saw him too early. Malcolm brought him up to the surface of the lake. Malcolm was angry with us, angry about what we did to his blonde girlfriend.'

'To Fiona?' Lois' voice rose. 'What did you do to her? She's such a sweet girl.'

'It's not important,' said Mr Mountolive, brushing the air as if he was waving away a troublesome fly, 'but Malcolm was angry when he found out about it and as a revenge he let you see Tony. Malcolm has been chastised for his actions.'

'It looked like Tony was walking on water,' Lois remembered. 'How did you do that trick?'

'No trick,' said Mrs Loveday, 'there's a clear plexiglass walkway from the entrance of the catacombs under the water to the edge of the lawn. We had it installed a couple of years ago in case anyone needed to get out there and didn't have a boat. A kind of emergency run, you might say. It does look like you're walking on water,' she chuckled, 'just like Jesus. I never thought of it that way.' She chuckled again.

The wine helped steady her. 'So if I agree to stay, I get Tony back. Right?'

'I can't see why you wouldn't agree,' Mrs Loveday replied, 'you don't have anything to go back to. No marriage, anyway.'

'You're not answering my question,' Lois insisted. 'You kidnapped my child and have been holding him prisoner here. If I stay on and bear Jason a child, then I'll be reunited with Tony and both of us will be free to leave.' Her gaze went around the table. 'Is that right? Is that the deal?'

'But you probably will want to stay,' Madame Dupré answered.

'Is that or is that not the deal?'

'We could never accept Tony as being one of us,' Dr Fulham said. 'His father has no Crowley blood at all.'

'I'm sure Tony won't be too upset over that,' Lois said drily. 'Is that the deal? Then Bob gets his half million and he and Midge walk into the sunset holding hands. That the deal? Well?'

'We were hoping that you would be happy to rejoin your true family,' Mr Cornell said softly, 'and that you wouldn't think of it as a *deal*, but yes, those are the conditions we have put forth. A deal, if you so choose to call it.'

She went over to Mrs Loveday. 'Let me have some more of that wine. I need it. Thanks. You all understand, dear uncles and aunts, that in any business deal both parties have to agree. One side makes an offer and the other side either accepts or refuses.' They nodded. 'Well, you've made your offer and now here's my response.' She held her breath and watched their faces. 'I'm not buying it.'

Midge was the first to exclaim. 'What? You're out of your mind!'

Bob was next, obviously startled by her refusal. 'There's really nothing you can do. You've *got* to take the deal. You're in a corner.'

'No.' She whirled on him. 'I'm not in any corner. You're in the corner and you've put yourself there. You and your two-faced girlfriend. I'm in no corner because I have all these doors and all these windows and I can get out of any one of them and go to the police and tell them what has happened to Tony. I've got the car keys right here in my pocket! Oh yes!' Her pleated skirt swirled around as she headed towards the huge wooden dining room doors. 'The police will listen to me. The local cops know what a bunch of loonies you all are. They'll listen when they hear about the kidnapping and so will the cops back in the States! They'll listen especially well!'

'Please Lois,' Jason called to her. 'You'd only make things worse!'

'Worse than what they are? Sorry Jason, nothing personal, but I just don't want to be fucked by you! Or by any of the rest of you!' She turned and ran towards the door.

'Stop her!' Mrs Loveday commanded.

Lois grabbed one of the large brass handles and pulled the door open. She turned around for one last look at Bob and then the tears came. It was with blurred vision that she bumped into the round little woman they called the cook.

The woman was knocked slightly to one side by the collision, but she ignored it and ignored Lois as she rushed into the dining room.

'Come quick all of you!' She shouted. 'They're dead! Them down in the catacombs. Dead!'

CHAPTER TWENTY-TWO

They rushed from the dining room and down a small corridor that led to the kitchen. No one said a word, they were all too stunned by the news. Lois had stopped in her tracks, when she heard what the cook had said, wondering what to do, where to go. Bob ran to her, and took her by the elbow. She shook him off.

'I don't want you to ever touch me again!' she said.

She ran with the others now, her idea of getting to the police set aside by the fact that her son might be hurt. They reached the rear door, someone yanked it open and they crowded through it, then outside, suddenly, on the icy wet grass in the frost wet blackness of a Scottish winter night.

Mr Cornell and Mr Halmfazzi raced across the underwater plexiglass ramp, uncaring or even unthinking, that their shoes and trouser cuffs were getting wet. Lois could see a glow arising from about twenty feet from shore. She didn't have to be told, she just knew it was an electric light from the passageway into the catacombs. That's where Tony was, she told herself. My baby's down there. She started for the edge of the waters and a strong hand held her back.

'Don't go.' It was Jason. 'Maybe you'd better not see.'

'My Tony's in there!' she screamed at him. 'He needs me!'

'My brothers will bring him out. Don't worry. He'll be all right.' She tried to break away from him but he only held her tighter. 'There's nothing you can do.'

They stood and watched as the two figures that were Cornell and Halmfazzi disappeared down the shaft of light. In a minute or so one of the figures emerged carrying a bundle, hanging limply, in his arms. He started walking back to shore when Lois screamed.

'Tony! Oh my God, my baby!'

Jason held her as Mr Halmfazzi reached the edge of the grass. He placed his burden carefully on the icy lawn. Mrs Loveday shone a flashlight on the boy's face.

Yes, it was Tony. Yes, he was dead.

Jason let her go then, and she ran to the unmoving little figure, his eyes open, his mouth twisted, his hands curled into tight balls and his knees raised and pressed together. She fell on him, smothering his rapidly cooling face with her kisses and cradled him in her arms. She didn't say anything, she only repeated some age-old cry of a mother in distress. Jason stood beside her, watching, unable to help.

Then Mr Cornell and Mr Halmfazzi came back to the surface of the lake, this time carrying the body of a woman dressed in a white nurse's outfit. As they placed her on the lawn the Crowley women clucked around her lifeless form. Then they picked her up and started toward the still open rear door of the house.

Mr Cornell came over to Lois and put his hand lightly on her shoulder. 'I'm sorry, my dear.' She nodded, like a dumb animal. 'It was some kind of poison fumes. The air down below reeks of it. They must have put it in the intake fan. Even the little dog we bought for him is dead.'

'You think it was the Brethren?' Jason asked.

The white-haired man nodded, wearily. 'Who else?'

'But *why*?' Lois heard her voice moan. 'Why my baby?'

Jason knelt down beside her. 'To get at you,' he replied simply. 'To drive you away from here. To stop you from continuing the Crowley line. To make you hate us.'

'But Tony isn't a Crowley. His last name is Bruno!'

'But you are a Crowley and they will stop at nothing to destroy one of us.'

She tried to get to her feet but the weight of the dead body threw her off balance. Jason picked Tony up, then gave Lois his hand. When she was steady on her feet he handed the child to her. She cuddled him in her arms, brushing at a speck of dirt on his cheek. 'He was so little for his age,' she said softly. 'Look at those little hands. He was so precious!' Tears streamed down her face.

'It's for reasons exactly like this one,' Mr Cornell said to her, 'that the Crowley line *must* continue. We must fight to survive and give the world our message. Can't you see it's more important than ever now?'

She lashed out at him. 'I don't want to hear it! My baby is dead and you stand there talking about carrying on a line! This is *twice* he has died for me! Do you know how terrible it is for a mother to lose her child? To lose him twice?'

Jason put his arm around her shoulders and turned her in the direction of the house. 'Come,' he said gently, 'let's go back inside.'

She didn't resist and started walking slowly up the lawn with Jason's warm protectiveness giving her strength. They passed in front of Bob and Midge. Bob glanced at the body of his son and then away. Midge stared at Tony curiously, then reached for Bob's hand. Lois didn't even realize she had been near them.

Bob walked over to Mrs Loveday, who had come back outside after carrying the nurse into the kitchen. 'I think we'll take our money and get out of here now,' he told the woman. 'I don't see any sense in us staying longer. We've done what we promised we'd do.'

'Yeah,' Midge said. 'You don't need us any more. Lois will stay. I know she will.'

'What makes you so sure?'

'Well,' Midge replied, 'she's seen that she doesn't have a marriage any more and now she sees that Tony is really dead. I mean, she can't fool herself *this* time. The kid is dead. The marriage is kaput. So she'll stay. What else has she got?'

'She'll stay,' Bob confirmed. 'You people are her family now. What's she got back in the States? Nothing.'

Mrs Loveday looked at him. 'So?'

'So I want my money,' Bob said. 'Now. Tonight. We'll take it and clear out.'

'I don't think so,' the elderly woman replied.

'What do you mean you don't think so?'

'I don't think we are so foolish here at Thelema that we would give you a fortune and then have you leave and shoot off your mouth to newspaper or television people. We can't afford the notoriety. We don't want that kind of publicity.'

'Wait a minute,' Bob's voice rose. 'I did what you asked to be done. I delivered my wife and my son to you. Now I want my money! For Christ's sake, why should I go and blab about what's happened here tonight? I'm in this as deep as the rest of you, but I'm not a Crowley.'

'I don't think so,' Mrs Loveday said again.

Bob grabbed her arm and twisted it roughly. 'Don't pull that bullshit on *me*, old lady! I want what's mine!'

Mrs Loveday managed a smile. 'I'll be most happy to give

337

you what you deserve . . . Mr Mountolive? Dr Fulham?'

The two men, who had been standing directly behind Bob and Midge, moved quickly. Midge was the first to crumple to the ground as the piano wire dug deeply into her throat. Bob's first reaction was to try and tear the terrible pain away with his hands and then to try and turn to punch whoever was doing this to him, but the breath in his lungs wouldn't move. He could not inhale or exhale. The thin line around his neck was destroying him.

Mrs Loveday looked primly away as Bob's eyes began to bulge and blood ran swiftly from the engorged sockets. When she looked back again, he was lifeless upon the grass.

As the two men dragged the bodies across the lawn and over to the covered well Mrs Loveday sighed. 'Where did he think we would get half a million dollars? It's all we can do to keep this house in shape. Strange how Americans seem to think everyone living in a mansion must be wealthy.'

Mr Mountolive pried off the lid. Mrs Loveday shone her flashlight down into the well. There was Fiona, her skin blackening, yet the yellow of her hair was as bright as ever. Atop her, his long arms across her legs, his red hair hard against the stone wall, was Malcolm. 'Such a pity!' the woman said. 'What's the world coming to when one can't trust one's own nephew?'

Midge went first, landing with a thud on the two other bodies, her plump hands still twitching.

They threw Bob in and heard his head bump along the wall until he too thudded onto the bodies at the bottom.

Mrs Loveday flashed her light one more time. The two men peered in.

'Well, that's done,' said Dr Fulham. 'I thought it would be more difficult.'

'The weak ones always go quickly. Father said they had no backbone, just a tongue with strong muscles to impress others. Father would not have approved of either of them.'

'Put the lid back in place, Mountolive,' Mrs Loveday said. 'We'd better get into the house.'

Jason supported her as she carried Tony's body into the dining room. To her it seemed the warmest room in the house, and she wanted the warmth for her darling child. With her right hand (the left one still clutching the body to her breast) she swept dishes and crystal and napkins and

338

silverware off onto the floor. Jason didn't try and stop her. She stretched her son out on the white tablecloth and took the flowers from an arrangement in the centre of the table and laid them neatly around him. She made a border of grief from the bright blossoms and green leaves. She had stretched out his legs so that his little ankles touched. She had crossed his tiny hands over his chest. She had tried to smooth down his unruly red hair and she had dabbed at some mud that was on his cheekbone. She looked up. The members of the family were huddled together in the doorway, watching her.

'I'm so terribly sorry, my dear,' Madame Dupré said. 'Is there anything we can do to help?'

Lois wiped the tears that brimmed in her eyelids with the back of her hand. 'You want to do something? Don't you think you've already done enough? My baby is *dead*! Do any of you care about that? Do any of you care about *him*?'

'We all care about that. And care about you as well.' This from Mr Mountolive.

'Then use your magic!' she screamed, and her voice echoed off the crystal chandeliers as well as the crystal shards on the floor. 'Use your magic!'

'Our magic?' Mr Cornell walked over to her. 'I don't understand. You are obviously upset and we appreciate that but . . .'

'Bring my Tony back to life!' Her voice was high and shrill. 'If you are all so smart, so full of your Goddamned father's magic, then do some of it for my son! Bring my son back to life! Or can't you do that?' She went to the doorway, hardly seeing their faces for the tears that ran down her own. 'Is your damned magic only good to frighten people and make cartoon characters run around under glass? Is there any compassion in what you do? Is it all evil? *All* of it?'

She was now sobbing hysterically and Frau Baumgartner reached out and took her in her arms. The German woman cradled her and made little shushing sounds. 'Hush now. You're family. We are all family here. Of course we care, and of course we will try to help. What is family for if not to help one another?'

Lois pulled away from the woman's shoulder, looking wildly around. 'Where's Bob? I need my husband,' she moaned. 'He should be here with me. With Tony.'

'He's gone, dear.' Mrs Loveday said.

'Gone? Bob is gone?'

'I'm so sorry,' the woman said softly, 'but he and that Midge person took their money and they left.'

'Bob and Midge . . . gone?'

Mrs Loveday stroked Lois' hair. 'Pulled out. Deserted you, my child. Abandoned you even as your dear little Tony was being stretched out on the table.'

'I want my husband!'

'The man is no good, dear,' Mrs Loveday said, continuing to stroke her hair. 'He is worthless. He isn't a Crowley.'

'Oh my God,' Lois whined from some hidden place deep inside her. 'Oh my God!'

Frau Baumgartner led her over to one of the dining chairs and sat her carefully in it. Lois closed her eyes, and thought of Bob and Tony and Midge and the emptiness that her life had fallen into so suddenly.

She didn't watch the others as they started bringing things into the dining room. Mr Halmfazzi came in with three bronze incense burners and, placing them one at Tony's head and two at his feet, he lit the tapered sticks and the odour of jasmine wafted slowly up in dark smoke. Madame Dupré came in with a silver crucifix and set it on the table. The figure of Christ, however, hung upside down, his feet stretched across the top bar, his arms hanging, hands loosely below his head. Signor Luchessi came in with several bouquets of paper flowers, black blossoms on black stems, which he scattered over the tiny corpse on the table. Dr Fulham was busy setting up two dozen silver candlesticks and once they were positioned exactly he lit each taper. Someone turned off the overhead candelabra and the room was illuminated solely by these twenty-four candles. Black candles.

Lois looked up in time to see Mr Cornell come into the room. He was dressed in a long black robe of some shiny material that covered his entire body down to his feet. The robe had huge sleeves and a cross, with thick arms about ten inches long, which seemed to float over his heart. Around his forehead he wore a wide band of gold, twisted and sculptured in the form of intertwining snakes. He marched solemnly over to the table and stood there, close to Tony's head.

Then Lois saw Jason come into the room. He was wearing a similar robe, except that it was in brilliant red. Across the chest were embroidered triangles, circles and flowing lines

340

like water rushing downhill. He didn't glance at Lois but took his place at the foot of the table.

The others found places between the two men, standing almost shoulder to shoulder. They reached out and held hands. Madame Dupré on one side of the table and Signor Luchessi on the other stretched their arms across the white linen tablecloth.

Then they began to chant. It sounded like English, yet, to Lois, the words were impossible to decipher. Someone rang a small silver bell as the inverted crucifix was lifted and passed to each one, who, in turn, raised it to his lips and passed it on.

Madame Dupré began to sing. It was high and nasal and obviously in French, but again Lois didn't understand the words. Then she switched to English and the same tune spoke of angels and death and resurrection. As she sang, the others swayed.

She finished and after a hushed silence, Mr Cornell picked up a small golden bowl that Lois hadn't noticed. He dipped his fingers into it and they came out sparkling with some thick liquid. He reached out and lightly made the sign of the Cross on Tony's smooth forehead. Then he daubed some of the liquid on the child's hands and finally let it dribble down his body, from the boy's collarbone to the soles of his shoes.

The chanting changed tempo. The women began to raise their voices, the men to lower theirs. They seemed to be calling to someone, calling across a void of blackness and eternity. They reached out, touched Tony, kissed their fingers, then reached and touched him again.

Lois got slowly to her feet and came closer to the table. She kept her eyes on her child, kept watching for the first signs of his returning to life. Then she felt a hand on her arm. It was Jason's. He smiled at her and silently steered her down to the end of the table, where he resumed his position. The others made way so she could enter the circle.

The chanting changed tempo again. This time it was only the men, and Mr Halmfazzi's voice could be heard above them all. It reminded Lois of travel films she had seen of Morocco and minarets and men on rugs bowing toward Mecca.

Jason's hand slid down and took hers in his. She looked up at him. 'It'll be all right,' he whispered. 'It'll be over soon.'

Mr Cornell dipped his fingers once more into the bowl and

came over to Lois. He touched her forehead with the sticky substance then smeared some across her lips. She felt his prying finger at her mouth and when he smiled so kindly at her, she opened her mouth and he dabbed her tongue with the mixture that was in the bowl. It tasted like honey but she knew there were other things in it as well.

She felt Jason's hand squeeze hers and this time when she looked at him, she managed a smile. His hand was warm and reassuring. She thought that his solid masculine touch promised her peace and protection and solace.

Abruptly the chanting changed yet again. Now it became a singsong of up and down notes, up and down slides of tone. The chanters swayed with the rhythm. Lois found herself swaying as well. She felt her body move almost automatically with the bodies of the family – her family – around the table. She could feel Jason's strong hand holding hers. She closed her eyes and let the incense fill her lungs. It had become beautiful. Beautiful and restful. The singing in her ears, the sweetness in her mouth, the incense in her head, the comfort of being with people who cared.

Jason put his other hand on her forehead. It was warm and so very understanding. She smiled at him again. The singing was now a steady humming in her brain, the chanting seemed to mellow, giving her images of country lanes, smooth footpaths, gleaming playground sliding boards. She closed her eyes to get a better feel of the smoothness of the sliding board. It was made of polished metal and looked as safe and familiar as the sliding board they had in the playground of her elementary school back in West Virginia. She felt herself sliding down it, sliding freely and willingly down into another level of her mind. Down into another dimension where the pain had gone, where she was free of the sorrow of Tony's death. Where she was alone with Jason. Where nobody or anything mattered but the fact that she was there with Jason and he was holding her, caressing her, lifting her skirt as he gently laid her down on the incredibly soft green grass.

The chanting swelled as she heard Jason murmuring in her ear. She kept her eyes closed and smiled as she felt the warmth of his breath on her face. Then his hands, those understanding and tender hands, started moving up her legs. They stopped and lightly massaged that tender area between her legs. She groaned in pleasure and acceptance.

She felt the hands remove the flimsy material of her panties.

And Jason sank into her. Sank into her with so much love and devotion, that there was no surprise, no pain, just the ecstasy that this wonderful man should have found her, should have wanted her.

She could smell the jasmine. She could hear the faraway voices and somewhere a surf washed lazily upon a sandy beach. She felt Jason moving inside her. She moved with his rhythm, waiting for the sense of joy that was about to pour from his body into hers. She waited for it, longed for it, and when it did come, rushing with an explosion of lights and colour and music, she let her own joy explode back toward him, over and over and over again.

Then in an instant everything was destroyed. The first window near the wall shattered into a thousand fragments, and into the room came glass and noise and smoke from torches carried by figures in white robes.

CHAPTER TWENTY-THREE

Mrs Loveday screamed as four men clambered through the window and onto her dining room floor. 'It's them!' she yelled. 'My God, it's the Brethren!'

Madame Dupré and Frau Baumgartner made a dash for the door as did Mr Mountolive and Signor Luchessi. Mr Cornell, his black robes shivering with indignation, charged the leader of the pack and began beating him over the head with a silver candlestick. The man staggered backward but not before his flaming torch set Mr Cornell's outfit on fire. He kept swinging at the invader, unaware or uncaring that he was ablaze.

Dr Fulham grabbed two candlesticks from the table, one in each hand, and in spite of his girth and his age, went at the white-robed intruders like a wildcat in a gunny sack. The four Brethren turned back towards the broken window and dived out of it, landing on each other on the lawn. Dr Fulham began tearing at Mr Cornell's blazing robes. He yanked the drapes from the window and, with the help of Mr Halmfazzi, managed to beat out the flames. The two men picked up the white-haired old man and rushed him from the room.

Jason, still on top of Lois, got up as quickly as he could, adjusting his long red robe. He looked from the broken window to the woman on the floor wondering which had preference for his time, then he got down on his knees and dragged Lois under the table. She was out of sight, the tablecloth went almost to the carpet. Jason started blowing out all the candles around Tony's body, plunging the room in darkness. Then he too, ran from the room, and started up the stairs.

Lois opened her eyes. It took her a second to understand where she was. She tried to get up but her ankles seemed to be tied. She reached down and in both shock and surprise felt her own panties at her shoe tops. She yanked them off and rolled out from under the table. There was a wetness on her thighs, something warm and sticky. She stood up, and took Tony in her arms. 'It hasn't worked yet,' she said aloud, 'but it will. He will get better.'

There was shouting and the sound of many footsteps as she neared the door to the hallway. She could smell smoke and a shudder of fear ran through her. What should she do? Where could she run? How could she protect her child from whatever was happening?

She heard an explosion, then a woman scream and then a thumping sound. Lois peered around the door. Mrs Loveday was on the carpet in the hall, her eyes closed, a pool of blood rising from a hole in her chest.

Lois pulled back into the room, her stomach churning, then she looked down at Tony and realized she had to be strong for his sake. She could hear something happening in the kitchen, hear the yells and the curses. Then she saw black smoke billow out from the open kitchen door down the hall.

With her dead child still in her arms she ran across the hallway and hid behind a large leather armchair. Just as she ducked down three more of the white robes came running out of the dining room. She knew they must have come in through that window. She held her breath and put her finger to Tony's lips, crooning softly to him not to make a sound.

Jason and Mr Mountolive ran past her, headed down the hallway. Each had a pistol in his hand. Lois watched as they rushed into the room that was the library and then heard the shots they fired and the screams of pain their shots produced.

There was more shouting and more shooting and when Jason came running from the room he was alone. Lois idly wondered what had happened to Mr Mountolive.

The mob came out of the kitchen and poured into the hallway. Their torches were still burning. Many of their robes were smeared with ashes, some were smeared with blood. They saw Jason and they came for him. Aleister Crowley's youngest son headed towards the chair where Lois was hiding. He stopped suddenly. He could see the edge of her skirt. He knew she was there. Quickly, he turned and ran right into the group, firing his pistol as he cursed them. Two fell to the floor, their torches igniting their robes and spreading the fire across the large oriental carpet. Jason dashed up the staircase, the pack of Brethren following him. When he got to the top landing, he looked down and could clearly see Lois watching him. He pointed to the left, frantically trying to send her a signal. Then the men were on him, beating him, kicking him in the name of Jesus.

Lois knew what the signal meant. That hidden door at the end of the hall. The one with the sun emblazoned on it. She slipped out from behind the chair and started running down the corridor. The smell of smoke was everywhere. Surprisingly, it was no effort to carry her little boy. When she passed the library, she saw bodies on the floor. One of them was Mr Mountolive. The drapes over the large windows were a mass of fire. It hurt her eyes to look at it.

She got to the end of the corridor. There was the sun. Shifting Tony's weight in her arms, she pressed the north arm, then the east, the south and finally the west arm. There was a clicking sound and a whirring as the secret exit door slid into the wall. She stood there for a second, trying to judge how she should jump so as not to injure her baby, when her face was brightly illuminated by glaring torches.

'It's the American!' one of the white-robed figures on the outside cried. 'Stop her!'

Lois whirled around and began running back the way she had come. She got to the front door and stopped to yank on the handle. Oh, God, she thought, let it be unlocked. It wasn't. She heard their voices and saw three of them hoist themselves up from the lawn, through the secret door and into the house. They stopped just long enough for others outside to hand them their torches.

Lois bolted for the darkness of the dining room. Back where she had started, the only part of the house that now seemed to be in silence. If she could get under the table again, pull the cloth over herself and Tony, maybe they wouldn't see her. Maybe they would go away and leave her alone. She ran into the room, and with one free hand managed to pull the double doors closed. She dropped to the floor, scooted under the wide wooden table and held her hand over Tony's mouth so he wouldn't cry.

'You!' a woman's voice screamed from out of nowhere and a white-robed arm reached under the cloth and found Tony's ankle. The arm yanked viciously and Lois saw Tony slide from her lap out onto the floor.

'No!' Lois screamed and hurtled herself out from under the table. The white-robed woman was waiting for her. She had a knife in her hand made from the same metal as the crucifix around her neck. She lunged at Lois, and Lois sidestepped it. The woman tried again but Lois managed to duck as the swinging blade came for her face. The woman paused. 'It's time you got yours, you American whore!' She lunged again, but Lois was ready and she clawed at the white hood over the woman's head, twisting it to one side, effectively blinding the woman for a moment. Then Lois landed a body punch that had the woman grasping her abdomen as she sank in pain onto the floor.

Lois kicked the knife across the room and quickly hoisted Tony into her arms. She ran across the darkened room towards the broken window. She looked out. The lawn was empty. Only the car they had rented in Dumfries was there. 'And I've got the key,' she said and patted her jacket pocket with satisfaction.

She raised herself up onto the sill and, still holding Tony tightly in her arms, jumped out onto the lawn. She headed for the car wishing now she'd not worn the shoes with the stiletto heels. She paused, kicked them off, and kept going. She fumbled for the keys, found them and tried to unlock the front door. Damn, it was the other key! Why is it always the other key? She could feel the lock move, then she turned the handle and the door opened.

Then they were running in her direction, four white-robed figures from around the far corner of the house. Coming her way, towards her on the other side of the car. She turned and started running in the opposite direction, running across the lawn, running for the safety of the grove of trees that she had seen from her window. She paused to catch her breath and looked back. For some reason the hooded men had stopped and were searching the car. They hadn't seen her.

She took a deep breath and kept running, and as she did she recalled another figure who had taken a small child in his arms and jumped out of that same window and run across that same lawn and headed towards that same group of trees.

'Oh God!' she moaned. 'It's not the little man who's doing it! It's me! *I'm* doing it!'

The trees with their solid trunks overgrown with thick bushes swallowed her up instantly. She crawled on her knees for several feet, shielding Tony's face from the branches and twigs. Then, feeling like a rabbit hiding from a hunter, she sat and watched the house go up in flames. There was fire at every window. There was smoke coming through the roof. There were a few screams and an occasional gun shot, then she stopped watching or listening. She had to tend to her baby. She had her baby in her arms and he needed her.

'Don't worry,' she whispered in his small, cold ear, 'Mommy's here. Mommy's here.'

CHAPTER TWENTY-FOUR

She twisted the apartment door key with one hand, and turned the knob with the other. Then with one foot she swung the door open and carried the two paper bags full of groceries into the kitchen. She went back and shut the door, throwing the bolt and slipping on the chain. She went into her bedroom and took off her lightweight spring coat. June had finally arrived in New York and she was grateful for any of the warmish rays that the sun managed to send her way. Yet even with the heat turned full up, sometimes, she could feel the cold of Scotland, feel the dampness of the wooded grove through her clothes.

She went into the kitchen and started putting her purchases away. Canned goods in the cupboard, meat, fish and milk in the fridge, dishwasher liquid under the sink. She still didn't do a lot of cooking, still preferred to eat out, but now that there was only herself to cook for, she regarded it as a kind of test, a challenge to see what she could make that was delicious, different and only one portion.

The office had been a madhouse that day. A fast food restaurant had been unhappy with the way their menus looked and demanded they be done over. A poster for a summer theatre in New Hampshire had to be reworked because two of the stars scheduled to appear had cancelled. And Midge's sister had been in the office that day. She showed up with a detective, trying to find out what had happened to Midge. Lois had taken time out to explain it all again. First she had told the US Consulate in Edinburgh and then she had tried to explain it to Midge's mother: she didn't know where Midge and Bob had gone. She had been a little short-tempered with the sister because, after all, Midge *had* taken her husband from her. What did she expect? To get all emotional that the fat bitch was sunning herself on a tropical island somewhere?

Bob's parents had asked the same questions and she had told them the same thing: she didn't know. They insisted something must have happened to their son over in Scotland. He wouldn't just abandon the business his father had worked so hard to create. Their Bob was a good boy. Their Bob loved them. Where did Lois really think Bob was? As she sat in the living room, listening, his parents went through the apartment taking everything they thought had belonged to their son. They had come with cardboard boxes and large plastic bags. They loaded the back seat of their car and drove away. Lois didn't ask them what they took. It didn't matter and, quite frankly, she didn't miss anything of importance after they left. It was good not to see his ties in the closet and his shaving stuff in the medicine chest.

She didn't really expect to hear from Bob or Midge ever again. She didn't want to. What had happened to them was no more a concern of hers than characters in a television show who the viewer gets disgusted with and turns off before the final scene. Some people in the office suggested she file for divorce. She had replied 'what for?' and knew she didn't want to get married again. Not go through all that again. So why get a divorce?

She had spent two months in that hospital in Edinburgh.

She had come wandering out of the woods, still carrying Tony, when she saw the firetrucks about to pull away from the burnt-out house. The firemen had taken her to a local doctor and he had rushed her up to Edinburgh. The doctors there were worried about her exposure to the cold and worried about her mind wandering in and out of reality. In between doctors' visits she had been interviewed by the police. Scottish as well as American. All she could tell them was that she had been a guest at the Hotel Thelema and that there had been a fire and she had managed to escape with her son. That's all she would tell them. She was not going to tell them about the Crowley family. She was not going to tell them about the kidnapping in New York nor the magic that was worked for her dead baby. The police knew about the Crowleys. They also knew about the Brethren. Charred remains of both groups had been sifted from the ashes. And your husband? What happened to him? Why didn't he take the car if he went off with Midge Morrison? She would shrug and wish the nurses would come in and ask the officers to leave. She didn't know. She didn't want to know.

Then about a month after she arrived back home (she was issued a temporary passport and American Express gave her a new credit card) she woke up in the middle of the night feeling ill. She went into the bathroom and gulped down three aspirins but the sensation didn't go away. It was just as bad the next night, and the next. One morning after she brushed her teeth she started throwing up. Her stomach was empty, nothing spattered the inside of the bathroom sink but green bile.

That afternoon she went to her regular doctor. He examined her and then told her, quite pleasantly as if it was happy news, that he thought she was pregnant. She had protested and he suggested some tests. Three days later his secretary telephoned her in the middle of a business meeting and confirmed it. 'Yes, Mrs Bruno,' the woman had said brightly. 'It's positive. You're going to have a baby. Congratulations.'

The feeling of something alive inside her came again, as if it responded even by her thinking about it. She knew what it was. After all, she had already had one child. She recognized how her body acted when she was pregnant. One child. Little Tony. Poor little Tony. The medical people in Edinburgh had taken him away from her when she arrived at the hospital. They had embalmed him and then, later, when she fully understood he was dead, she told them to bury him. Where they did it, she didn't care, as long as it wasn't in a religious cemetery. She didn't want any Christians or any occult freaks alongside her little boy. She never visited his grave after coming out of the hospital. She had mourned him twice, what was the point of continuing the vigil?

She spent three weeks thinking about the child in her womb, wondering what to finally do about it. She couldn't keep it, of course. She no longer had a husband and this baby was *not* her husband's. That she was positive of. She and Bob had not had sex (she refused to call it making *love*) for at least a month before they went to Scotland. She had had a period in London. No, this child was not Bob's. When she gave it a great deal of thought there was a distant nagging in her mind of something that had happened in Corra. It was connected with candles and singing and a sweet honey taste. Jason was somehow connected with it, too. If only she could get that night sorted out in her memory. She recalled some bits of it. She remembered hiding behind the chair and Jason leading the white-robed men in the opposite direction. She remembered seeing poor Mr Mountolive dead on the library floor. She recalled the library drapes aflame. There was a knife, too, and a woman's scream as Lois somehow got the best of her.

What she did remember clearly, though, was the running from the window, across the lawn, into the trees and carrying her baby. Her dead baby. She remembered it because she had seen it before in the engraving, had read it before in that book of ghost stories.

The night of the fire, around the table, there had been something about her and Jason together. Damn – she wished she could recall what it was. Once the thought came to her that possibly Jason was the father, but she had shaken the idea free. No, not Jason. He had been too good and too loyal to her. He had saved her life. Besides, they had never been to bed together. Not that she could remember.

She didn't want this baby. She was alone and she would have to provide for it. She'd have to alter her lifestyle again, as she did when Tony was born. It was different this time. There was no Bob to bring home the money. She was young and had so many things she still wanted to do. A child would only get in her way.

She had to make a decision. Today at work had been

impossible. How could she continue to produce her best while she got fatter and sicker carrying this child? She was an adult. She was alone. She had to make the choice.

She went over to the telephone and dialled a number. A female voice came out of a recorder. 'Dr Gittleman's office is closed, but if you'll leave your name and number and a brief message, someone in the office will get back to you as soon as possible.'

She took a deep breath. 'This is Mrs Lois Bruno,' she said to the machine. 'I saw the doctor two weeks ago and spoke with him about the possibility of terminating my pregnancy.' She hated the word 'abortion'. 'The doctor knows the facts behind the case. Would you have him set up a definite date, please? Will you call me at work? I've decided to go through with it. Thank you.' She hung up.

She felt as if someone had just removed a ton of weight from her shoulders. She actually smiled at her reflection when she went into the bathroom. In the kitchen she put a potato in the oven and breaded a fresh fish fillet. She'd fry it just as the potato was done.

She wiped her hands on the dish towel, walked out of the kitchen and looked idly into what had once been Tony's room. It was almost empty now. She had removed the small bed and had given away all his clothes. There were a few boxes, sealed with shiny tape, that contained his toys. She would give them, one day, to the Salvation Army. How lonely and silent the room looked. She had enjoyed having Tony as part of her life. He was small and bright and sparkled like sunlight on water. She had thought he would grow up, that they would grow up together. Now he was gone. Bob was gone. She was alone.

She didn't want to be alone. She didn't want to grow old all by herself. She knew several career women in New York who were pushing middle-age without a husband or a family and it wasn't a pretty sight. Most of them smoked and drank too much and talked too loudly and went home every night to cuddle a poodle or a yorkie. No, she didn't want to be alone.

She poured herself a bourbon, waiting for the potato to bake. She didn't drink Scotch anymore. No more Scotch after Scotland! She detested the taste of the stuff. She stared out of the window, watching the cars parked under the thin trees that had started to sneak into summer with delicate white flowers. Across the street a couple walked hand in hand. An old lady, bent in a worn winter coat, walked lamely home with a cloth bag of groceries. A young woman got out of a parked car and waited while someone inside it handed her a baby. She held the child, fussing with it, until a young man got out and locked the car. Then they disappeared around the corner.

The new life inside her moved again. *Could* it be Jason's? When would everything that happened return to her? Was there a time when she and Jason made love? Was that possible to do and then block it out forever? With Jason? She smiled at the thought. 'Good-looking bastard,' she said aloud. 'If he is the father, you can bet the kid will be gorgeous as hell.'

She came back to the sofa and sat slowly so as not to upset the life that was growing in there. But what kind of a life will it have? What kind of a life will it *be*? Suppose it *is* something the Crowleys did to me, some witchcraft or hoodoo-voodoo, then what will it *be*? A demon? An angel? What did they call themselves? Magical children. Right. Maybe this child will be a magical child.

She drained her glass and got up. No, those aunts and uncles of mine seemed so normal but look what they did to Tony. Look how filled with hate they were. Look how they ended up. 'I will have you removed,' she said, and rubbed her belly. 'I'll have you cut out, discarded, thrown into the garbage and then I'll laugh! I'll sit back and laugh and laugh and laugh.'

She went for some more bourbon. Sipping it slowly she stood and gazed into Tony's empty room. Again. God, how many times have I done that? How many? She walked back into the living room. The new life shifted inside her.

She went over to the telephone and dialled the number. She waited until the answering machine stopped its message.

'Hi, this is Lois Bruno again. Look, tell Dr Gittleman that . . . uh . . . that I haven't *really* made up my mind yet about this termination stuff. I'll call him when it's . . . uh . . . when it's . . . when I'm definite.'

She hung up the phone and walked back to the window, one of the millions of lonely windows in Manhattan. 'I've got to do the right thing,' she said to three teenage girls laughing on the sidewalk below. 'I'll do the right thing. I'll know what to do . . . I think . . . when the time is right.' She took another sip of bourbon. 'I'll know . . .'

THE END